Sarmatian

Peter Darman

Copyright © 2019 Peter Darman

All rights are reserved. No part of this book may be reproduced or transmitted in any form or by any means without written permission of the author.

Formatted by Jo Harrison

Paperback Edition License Notes

This book is licensed for your personal enjoyment only. This book may not be re-sold or given away to other people. If you would like to share this book with another person, please purchase an additional copy for each person you share it with. If you're reading this book and did not purchase it, or it was not purchased for your use only, then you should return to Smashwords.com and purchase your own copy. Thank you for respecting the hard work of this author.

This book is a work of fiction. The names, characters, places, and incidents are products of the writer's imagination or have been used fictiously and are not to be construed as real. Any resemblance to persons, living or dead, actual events, locales or organizations is entirely coincidental.

Contents

List of characters 5

Chapter 1 7

Chapter 2 44

Chapter 3 59

Chapter 4 96

Chapter 5 123

Chapter 6 135

Chapter 7 156

Chapter 8 183

Chapter 9 227

Chapter 10 242

Chapter 11 261

Chapter 12 291

Chapter 13 309

Chapter 14 336

Chapter 15 348

Chapter 16 368

Chapter 17 389

Chapter 18 406

Chapter 19 433

Chapter 20 454

Epilogue 479

List of characters

Those marked with an asterisk * are Companions – individuals who fought with Spartacus in Italy and who travelled back to Parthia with Pacorus.
Those marked with a dagger † are known to history.

The Kingdom of Dura
*Alcaeus: Greek, chief physician in Dura's army, now retired
Almas: deputy-governor of Dura Europos
Bullus: centurion in the army of Dura
Chrestus: commander of Dura's army
Claudia: daughter of Pacorus and Gallia, princess of Dura, Scythian Sister, now adviser to King of Kings Phraates at Ctesiphon
*Gallia: Gaul, Queen of Dura Europos
Kewab: Egyptian, former Satrap of Aria, senior officer in the army of Dura
Lucius Varsas: Roman, quartermaster general of Dura's army
*Pacorus: Parthian, King of Dura Europos
Minu: commander of the Amazons
Rsan: governor of Dura Europos
Talib: Agraci, chief scout in Dura's army

Other Parthians
Akmon: King of Media
Anush: wife of Klietas
Castus: King of Gordyene
Haytham: prince of Gordyene
Klietas: native of Media, former squire to King Pacorus of Dura
Pacorus: prince of Hatra
†Phraates: King of Kings of the Parthian Empire
Rodak: governor of Assur in the Kingdom of Hatra
Shamshir: commander of Gordyene's King's Guard

Non-Parthians
Gaius Arrianus: Roman ambassador to the court of King Polemon of Pontus
Lusin: Armenian, Queen of Media
Menwi: Egyptian, wife of Kewab
†Marcus Vipsanius Agrippa: Roman, deputy of Augustus Caesar
Spadines: Sarmatian, ally of King Castus, chief of the Aorsi tribe
†Tasius: Sarmatian, leader of the Roxolani tribe
Titus Tullus: Roman, commander of King Polemon's Royal Bodyguard
Yesim: tribeswoman of Pontus, Queen of Gordyene

Chapter 1

Success is infectious. Dura's army had taken no part in the great victory won outside the town of Melitene in Cappadocia the previous summer. But everyone in the kingdom knew it was Dura's triumph. It had been Dura's chief scout and the commander of the Amazons who had alerted High King Phraates of the great enemy coalition that was preparing to invade Gordyene. It was Dura which sent its genius commander, Kewab, to assist King Castus in defeating that enemy alliance. And it was Kewab's plan that had won a great victory, perhaps the greatest victory achieved by a Parthian army. And Dura basked in the glory won by its favourite son. When Kewab and his soldiers returned to the city, he and they were greeted by cheering crowds, thousands chanting 'pharaoh', 'pharaoh', in recognition of his ancestry and his military skills. His soldiers were decorated with garlands, young women kissed the hand of the returning hero and pregnant women declared their intention to name their infants after him, even if they gave birth to females.

The whole army was paraded for the benefit of the returning heroes. The Durans and Exiles were arrayed in their cohorts, the dragon of cataphracts stood in full armour on their horses similarly attired, and the horse archers lined up in their companies before the Palmyrene Gate, the white tunics of Dura deploying next to the red uniforms of the exiles of Mesene, now resident in the reincarnated city of Mari. Dura's lords, their families and retainers also came to pay their respects to Kewab, their indiscipline and flowing black and brown robes in stark contrast to the well-dressed ranks of Dura's soldiers.

King Malik and Queen Jamal came from Palmyra with two hundred black-clad Agraci warriors to salute the man who had helped their grandson, the King of Gordyene, become the most feared warlord in northern Parthia. Castus was the young king who had cowered the allies of Rome and sent a clear message to Rome itself that Gordyene was to be meddled with at its peril.

In recognition of his services to Parthia and his talents, Kewab was asked to join Dura's royal council, though whether he liked listening to Almas discussing irrigation systems, rebuilding work at Mari or Ira's mind-numbingly boring lectures on Dura's finances, he did not say. Though to his credit he did manage to stay awake during council meetings, which is more than can be said of the aged Aaron and Rsan, governor and treasurer respectively, who often dozed off during proceedings.

When the dust of exhilaration had settled and life at Dura returned to normal, no one noticed seven weathered figures dressed in black robes riding from the north and entering the city without fanfare to journey to the Citadel. There was nothing to mark them out as being unusual or particularly conspicuous, which had been the point. They disappeared into the Citadel without notice. Treated as greater heroes than Kewab by the queen, they were all sworn to secrecy concerning the mission they had just completed, though each of them was rewarded by Gallia personally. They then slipped back into their former lives; all save one.

Klietas had left Dura in the aftermath of the assassins' return, and as he left another returned to the kingdom. Alcaeus, Companion, physician, austere Greek and former head of the army's medical corps, had been away for over a year. He had travelled to Syria and then taken ship to Greece, having been desirous to see Athens, the 'cradle of civilisation' as he termed it, before he died.

I had first met him in Italy, a sinewy Greek with a mop of thick black hair treating injured soldiers, who like him had been former slaves before finding refuge with the Thracian gladiator Spartacus. It was my great fortune that Alcaeus not only survived the crushing of the slave revolt but accompanied me back to Parthia. Now his hair and beard were grey, though still thick, his step was shorter, and he had taken to having a nap most afternoons. But his mind was as sharp as ever and his tongue as keen as the edge of a freshly sharpened *gladius*.

In the weeks after his return I had made regular visits to his home, a rather austere two-storey mud-brick house a short walk from the Citadel. He could have had a mansion like Byrd but, true to his Greek roots, preferred to live in modest circumstances. There were aspects to the house to indicate its owner was a man of substance, however, such as a stone floor instead of mud, a bathing room and servants to attend to his needs. But the furniture was functional rather than opulent, though the couches we reclined on were plump with cushions, and the wine we were served was not diluted according to the Greek custom but was rather a fine vintage from Susiana.

'General Kewab is the talk of the Roman world, or at least the bits I travelled through,' he told me.

'He is a rare talent,' I agreed. 'We are lucky to have him, though I worry we will not be able to hold on to him.'

He raised a grey eyebrow. 'Oh? I thought he was an officer in Dura's army.'

I ran a finger around the rim of my cup. 'That was years ago. He is now a satrap, was once deputy lord high general of the empire and Lord Melitene. By rights, he should be living in a grand mansion at Ctesiphon and attending the high king.'

'Then why isn't he?'

'Loyalty to Dura, I suppose.'

'Loyalty to its king, more like,' he said.

'I like to think so, but I fear Dura is now too small for a man of his reputation and talents.'

'Perhaps young Castus will start another war in which Kewab can fill the world with his radiance once more.'

'Parthia's western frontier is not a problem, or at least it should not be. The real threat lies in the east, and when the Kushans have finished fighting the Satavanhanas, they will turn their attention to Parthia's eastern kingdoms, notwithstanding the perpetual peace that supposedly exists between the Kushan Empire and Parthia.'

'How is your friend Kujula?' he grinned mischievously.

'Recovered and returned to full health, I am informed, which is bad news for Parthia.'

He looked thoughtful. 'Perhaps Gallia should send assassins to kill him.'

I had told him all about Gallia's band she had despatched to the north to do her dirty work, about how they learned of the alliance of enemy kings intent on attacking Gordyene, of how Tiridates had been killed in the Battle of Melitene, how her assassins had killed Prince Atrax, Laodice and Glaphyra, and how they had fallen foul of King Castus and taken offence at the actions of King Akmon. And how Titus Tullus had died in the hills of Pontus. Gallia had also reported with glee that King Amyntas of Galatia had also been killed, slaughtered in some internal quarrel. She had been delighted and relished in the vengeance she had served on her enemies. Her saw my glum expression.

'What did you expect, Pacorus, that Gallia would mellow with age and take to gardening to see out her autumn years? She is a Gaul and we all know the attributes of that particular race, not that I am one to generalise about tribes and peoples. Nevertheless…'

'All Gauls appear to have similar traits,' I interrupted.

'In her defence, her actions appear to have made Parthia stronger in the eyes of her potential enemies.'

'Has she, my friend? She has strengthened the hold of Augustus Caesar over Cappadocia, Pontus and Galatia, the latter having been reduced to a province under a Roman governor.'

Alcaeus shrugged. 'At the very least, Phraates must be delighted both Tiridates and Atrax are dead.'

I took a large gulp of wine. 'Phraates? As long as others are bleeding on his behalf, he is happy to play the god-king. It is an outrage he has not rewarded Kewab with a kingdom of his own to rule. If I were high king…'

He rose from his couch, picked up the wine jug and walked over to top up my cup.

'Ah, now we return to the age-old question. Why was not Pacorus of Dura created high king?'

'Because he did not want the position,' I shot back.

He retook his couch. 'I often wonder if you made the right decision, and whether Parthia, and Dura, would have been saved the spilling of an ocean of blood if you had seized the high crown after the death of Orodes.'

He smiled. 'It is irrelevant now. But at the very least, neither Tiridates nor Atrax will be fomenting any more trouble on Parthia's borders. You have Gallia to thank for that.'

I took a swig of wine. 'The fomenting now occurs within my kingdom, in that wretched Sanctuary.'

He chuckled. 'A former brothel, I believe. There is a certain amount of irony in Gallia's choice of headquarters for the Amazons.'

'There is only one headquarters in Dura,' I said irritably, 'and that is in the Citadel.'

At that moment, I spilt wine on my tunic.

'In the name of the gods,' I cursed.

He clapped to bring the head servant into the *andron*, the room reserved for entertaining that was the preserve of men only, a Greek custom Gallia found infuriating. The manservant saw my stained white tunic, disappeared and a couple of minutes later reappeared with a young girl carrying a sponge and a bowl of water.

'You should remove your tunic, majesty,' said the manservant, 'otherwise the stain will be permanent.'

'Fetch the king a new garment,' ordered Alcaeus.

The manservant bellowed a command to bring a new tunic, making us both jump and causing me to spill more wine down my tunic. Moments later a new garment was brought. I unbuckled my sword belt and removed the stained article, the servants lowering their heads to avoid gazing upon the body of the king. I put on the clean tunic, which felt abrasive against my skin. Alcaeus smiled. I did not.

'This feels like sackcloth,' I complained.

'It will make you more virtuous,' said Alcaeus.

I pondered for a moment. 'You mean wearing uncomfortable garb means a person will not have immoral thoughts because his mind is focused on his whole torso itching?'

He rolled his eyes. 'I assume you have heard of Plato?'

'A Greek, a thinker, I seem to recall,' I answered.

Another roll of the eyes, this time accompanied by a sigh.

'Plato was a Greek philosopher, Pacorus, which is more than a thinker, whatever that may be. To cut to the quick, he believed the well-being of society rested on the four pillars of wisdom, courage, justice and temperance.

'The first three are self-explanatory, but the fourth is sadly neglected, which is a pity because it is most important.'

I scratched my chest. 'So, in Greece, wearing uncomfortable clothes makes people better citizens.'

'Temperance is crucial in regulating the pleasures and basic desires of citizens,' he said very slowly. 'Self-control in all things prevents individuals becoming decadent and immoral.'

He stood and began pacing. 'For example, how did an army of around seven thousand Greeks hold off tens of thousands of Persians at the Battle of Thermopylae?'

'Better tactics, a very favourable position and a brilliant commander,' I answered. 'Plus, the help of the gods.'

He shook his head. 'Obedience, endurance, courage and self-control, the characteristics of Spartan society, held the pass at Thermopylae in the face of overwhelming odds, Pacorus, against a Persian foe riddled with decadence, depravity and corruption.'

'The Persians still won,' I said.

He pointed at me. 'Only through the base treachery of a Greek who showed the Persians a way through the mountains to allow them to get behind the Greek position.'

He retook his couch. 'Let me ask you a question. You find Ctesiphon distasteful?'

'I do.'

'Why?'

'Because it is full of scheming courtiers and their wives, who live in gilded cages, and over-ambitious priests who serve themselves instead of the gods.'

'No. It is because the immorality and decadence of Ctesiphon offends you, Pacorus. Because in your heart you are a moral individual who practises temperance. Why do you not wear the garments purchased for you in celebration of your sixtieth birthday? You remember them?'

I smiled when I remembered a white silk robe upon which were stitched red griffins, and a red silk sash that acted as a belt, a birthday gift from Byrd.

'They are in a chest in the palace somewhere,' I said. 'They were made by the Governor of Syria's tailor.' I wracked my brains. 'Cinna, that was his name.'

'And why do you not wear them on a daily basis?'

'I am not a Babylonian peacock,' I told him.

'I rest my case. You are at heart a simple, straightforward man, Pacorus, which is why you have achieved so much for so long. Kewab is cast in a similar mould, actually, which accounts for his many achievements.'

'I'm sure there is a compliment in there somewhere,' I said, scratching my shoulder.

'So, you have really retired?' he asked me, changing the subject.

'I have, unless Dura is attacked, of course. But there will be no more tramping around the empire for me. I'm too old to spend weeks on end sleeping in a tent and sitting all day on a horse.'

'Quite right,' he agreed. 'You and Gallia should organise a trip, a holiday.'

I laughed. 'Holiday?'

'Why not? Perhaps you could take her to Italy and then Gaul.'

I nearly choked on my wine.

'There is probably still an arrest warrant that has my name on it in circulation in Italy, Alcaeus.'

He wagged a finger at me. 'That is ancient history, my friend. If my experience in Greece is anything to go by, you and Gallia would be feted by all and sundry. The Romans love to be associated with living legends and individuals who have links to the past. You and Gallia fought Crassus and Mark Antony, and both have passed into Roman folklore.'

'You mean we are both ancient relics.'

He laughed. 'Naturally. But even me, a lowly physician in the slave army of Spartacus, was treated with respect and awe by the wealthy and influential of Athens.'

I grinned at him. 'No wonder you were away for so long if the fine ladies of Athens were making their couches available to you.'

'The spirit may have been willing, my friend, but the body manifested a serious dereliction of its duties in that department.'

'No regrets about leaving Athens?'

He looked reflective. 'The city I knew in my youth is no more. The buildings are the same, of course. And, loathe as I am to admit it, are in a better condition now than in previous years. The Romans are very clever. They rule Greece with a light touch, which has allowed the indigenous élite and wealthy to flourish. And Greek is an official language of the Roman world alongside Latin. In this way, Rome steadily and stealthily increases its grip over Greece and the Greeks. For example, that Roman ambassador who was killed in Pontus last year, along with our friend Titus Tullus.'

'I read the reports but cannot remember his name.'

'Well, did you know he was a Greek?'

'I did not.'

'A friend of Augustus himself, by all accounts. So, you see, every office is open to Greeks of good standing and access to wealth. That is how you conquer a people, Pacorus, by seducing them with opportunities and the prospect of a better life.'

He sighed. 'Perhaps one day there will be a Greek leader of the Roman world.'

'Then he can set Greece free,' I said naively, the effects of too much wine clouding my thoughts.

'People do not want to be free, my friend, they want easy lives with no responsibilities. And if Rome can give them that, they will see no reason to change their rulers.'

I usually stayed with Alcaeus all afternoon, but our musings and reminiscences were interrupted by Almas arriving at my Greek friend's home. The former commander of a dragon of horse archers had taken on more and more of Rsan's responsibilities as governor as my old friend's health failed and he became frailer with every passing year. Almas' military career ended abruptly when he lost his left hand during the Phraaspa campaign, turning his hand to commerce when he purchased an area of barren land in the western half of the kingdom that turned out to be rich in antimony. Ground down and made into a powder, it was exported to Egypt where rich women used it as face makeup, and throughout Parthia men and women applied it around the eyes as a defence against the glare of the sun.

The subsequent mining operation made Almas rich and allowed him to purchase a large house in Dura next to Rsan's. The pair became acquaintances and then friends, which would result in Almas becoming a servant of the crown once more, albeit in a civilian capacity.

Everything about Almas was business-like, from his neatly trimmed beard and well-groomed brown hair, to the simple leather cover over the stump on his left arm. Despite his wealth he had not allowed himself to run to fat, retaining the tall, lean physique that characterised so many of Dura's horse archers. He had a keen, eager mind that made him a bundle of energy, making it difficult for him to keep still.

I found him pacing up and down in the shade of Alcaeus' modest courtyard, stopping and bowing his head when he spotted me.

'You looked troubled, Almas.'

He extended his right hand, in which was a papyrus scroll.

'This has just arrived at the Citadel, majesty. I thought you would want to see it straight away.'

I took the scroll and saw the seal of the Governor of Syria pressed into the bitumen. The dark grey eyes of Almas never left the document as I unrolled it and read the Greek words. Relations between Dura and Syria were most amicable, the border between the province and kingdom being only loosely patrolled. Most commercial traffic went west to Palmyra and on to Damascus and the coast, or through Judea to Egypt. Direct communications between myself and the Roman authorities in Syria was rare, which was why Almas' face registered concern.

'It is not from the governor,' I told them. 'It is from someone called Marcus Vipsanius Agrippa, who requests an audience with me, though he does not say what about.'

'Odd,' said Alcaeus.

I handed the letter back to Almas.

'Find out who this Agrippa is. He must have some influence if he is using the seal of the Governor of Syria.'

The next day, Almas rode to Palmyra to discuss the matter with Byrd, whose business empire covered western Parthia, Syria, Judea, and parts of Egypt, Cilicia and Cappadocia. My old chief scout rarely visited the offices of his extensive transport network, delegating the day-to-day running to trusted subordinates. But he insisted on his head offices producing regular reports that were sent to Palmyra, and also sent his personal aides to carry out spot-checks on said offices. When Almas returned a week later, Byrd had informed him all about the Roman requesting to see me.

I sat with Gallia and the deputy-governor on the palace terrace, Gallia's expression changing from one of indifference to a frown and finally a scowl as Almas read from the notes he had written in Byrd's company.

'Marcus Vipsanius Agrippa is forty years old and a lifelong friend of Augustus Caesar. By all accounts he is somewhat of a protégé, having become a *praetor urbanus* at the age of twenty-four.'

'What is that?' asked Gallia, her blue eyes boring into the parchment Almas was reading from. Perhaps she hoped it would burst into flames and save her from hearing any more about this important Roman.

'The official responsible for the administration of justice in Rome, majesty,' Almas answered.

'Is there any justice in the Roman world?' she sneered.

I nodded to Almas he should continue.

'Well, after that position Agrippa became governor of Gaul.'

Gallia pressed her lips together and her eyebrows lowered.

'Oppressor of Gaul, you mean,' she hissed.

I shook my head at her. 'Not now, Gallia. Did Agrippa remain governor for long?'

'A year, by all accounts, majesty,' replied Almas, 'after which he became consul, a position of great power in the Roman world.'

'The post is akin to being a king,' said Gallia through gritted teeth, 'though Roman vanity would never admit to such a thing.'

'He and Augustus shared power,' continued Almas, perusing his notes, 'before Agrippa was appointed to the position of *aedile*, a magistrate responsible for public buildings in Rome. In this role, he supervised a substantial urban renewal programme in the city, building three new aqueducts, restoring the sewers and paving the streets.'

'Dura needs more paved streets,' I said. 'I have neglected my city for too long.'

They both looked at me with surprise.

'You have been busy saving the empire from internal and external enemies,' said Gallia. 'Besides, we have paved streets in Dura.'

'Not enough,' I lamented. 'The main thoroughfares are paved, but many of the side streets are in the same condition now as when we first arrived in Dura.'

'You have wisely concentrated on maintaining a strong army and ensuring the defences of the city are strong, majesty,' Almas told me, 'rather than waste funds on aesthetics.'

'Well said,' agreed Gallia.

But a morose mood came over me.

'I went there once, to Rome, I mean. It is a magnificent city, full of grand government buildings, ornate temples and luxurious mansions. It deserves to be maintained.'

Gallia rolled her eyes and Almas nodded politely.

'Perhaps the most interesting thing about Agrippa, majesty,' said Almas, 'was that he won the victory at Actium.'

I was surprised. 'I thought it was Octavian's victory?'

'Octavian, now Augustus, was the commander, majesty, yes, but devolved authority to his friend. Agrippa is a veteran general of some twenty years' experience.'

I picked up an almond pastry and took a bite.

'It begs the question: why is such a powerful Roman desirous to visit Dura?'

Gallia also picked up a pastry. 'Not out of courtesy, I can guarantee that. The Romans do nothing out of the goodness of their hearts. This Agrippa is after something.'

I finished my pastry. 'But what?'

Gallia picked up the small silver dish holding the cakes and offered it to Almas, who smiled and took a pastry.

'The only way we will discover what he wants is to meet with him,' I said. 'Convey my compliments to the governor of Syria, Almas, and inform him Dura's king, and queen, will be delighted to extend the hand of friendship to Marcus Vipsanius Agrippa.'

He stood, bowed his head to us both and marched from the terrace. I began to use the fingers on my right hand to count down the seconds.

'You should not welcome high-ranking Romans here, Pacorus.'

'Ten', I said, halting my count. 'You are getting mellow in your old age.'

'What? Don't be childish. Nothing good will come from you allowing this Roman to visit Dura.'

I leaned back in my chair, wincing when a sharp pain shot down my left leg. Gallia gave me a kindly look.

'Are you in discomfort?'

'Nothing I am not used to. Some days are better than others. I could do with a dip in that magical pool that Claudia used to cure Adapa of his leprosy.'

She smiled. 'I remember. I'm sure Claudia could arrange it.'

'The thought is tempting, especially on days like this.'

I glanced at her.

'I will invite Agrippa to stay in the palace during his sojourn in Dura.'

'What?'

'I would appreciate it if your assassins did not murder the second-most important man in the Roman world while he is a guest under my roof.'

'Under *our* roof,' she hissed.

'How do you know he is not planning to kill *us*?' she asked smugly.

'As far as I am aware, assassins do not send word ahead to the victims of their intentions, though I am not an expert in the field. Unlike you.'

She raised her eyes to the sky. 'Not all this again. What is done is done, Pacorus. There is no point raking over old ground.'

She was right, not that I approved of her actions, far from it. But I had neither the will nor the stamina to engage in what would become a drawn-out argument about the rights and wrongs of assassination.

'Has Haya said anything about Klietas?' I asked.

'I have not spoken to Haya since she returned from the north,' she said tersely.

When I discovered Klietas had left Dura I was disappointed, especially as he did not come to the palace to inform me in person. I spoke to Almas, who enquired of the man he had placed with Klietas concerning where my former squire had departed to. But the vague answer of 'Media' made me none the wiser and then my time had been absorbed in the rebuilding of Mari, the former ruins of a great city some forty miles south of Dura, which was being restored to accommodate the soldiers that had accompanied Kewab from the east, plus the exiles from Mesene. It was an undertaking that was absorbing a large amount of time and money, and the subject of Klietas was pushed into the background. Gallia told me it was his decision to leave Dura, that she respected it and so should I.

'I suppose you want me to be on my best behaviour when the Roman arrives?' she said, changing the subject.

'It would be appreciated, my sweet.'

'But I will be posting extra guards in the Citadel.'

'I would expect nothing less.'

With Agrippa given clearance to visit the King of Dura, the friend of the ruler of the Roman world was escorted from the border with Syria by Azad, the commander of Dura's cataphracts, and a company of his men in full war gear. Almas was also at the border to welcome Agrippa, and though I had not made it compulsory, all the members of the royal council, Chrestus, the commander of the army, Sporaces, commander of horse archers, Lucius Varsas, quartermaster general, Sophus, chief medical officer, and all their senior officers, gathered in the Citadel's courtyard the afternoon the Roman dignitary arrived in the city.

Gallia looked beautiful that day, her hair shining in the sunlight, her blue eyes sparkling and her armour shimmering with an otherworldly glow. The cuirass that was a gift from the gods, that no mortal hand had fashioned, accentuated her still shapely figure and made her stand out among all the mail armour, scale armour, burnished helmets and whetted javelin points glinting in the sun. She stood beside me and below us a hundred Amazons sat on their horses in the courtyard, their faces enclosed by the large cheek guards of their helmets, their white saddlecloths decorated with red griffins in the corners.

A century of Durans stood to attention in the courtyard and a fanfare of trumpets reverberated around the square when Azad led his company on to the cobblestones. Beside him rode a tall, imposing man attired in a magnificent bronze muscled cuirass, a large, expensive red cloak draped around his broad shoulders. On his other side was Almas. Immediately behind them was a score of Roman horsemen in mail armour carrying lances, and behind them a company of Dura's cataphracts, their faces hidden by full-face helmets.

I stood at the top of the steps leading to the palace flanked by Rsan, Aaron, and Chrestus. Ashk, the palace steward, pointed at waiting stable hands who rushed forward to take the reins of the mounts of the three men sliding from their saddles. Azad saluted the Roman and Almas invited Agrippa to ascend the steps to greet his waiting hosts. Marcus Vipsanius smiled, nodded and took a look around the occupants of the courtyard before doing so, wearing a slightly perplexed expression when his eyes settled on the century of soldiers that must have looked familiar and yet unfamiliar. Their weapons and armour would not look out of place on a Roman parade square, but their white tunics and white-faced shields sporting red griffin wings marked them out as belonging to a foreign power.

Agrippa walked up the steps briskly to stand in front of me, raising his right arm in salute and bowing his head.

'Hail Pacorus, King of Dura, former Lord High General of Parthia, victor of Surkh, Susa, Carrhae, Phraaspa, conqueror of the Kushans, Armenia, Cappadocia, Galatia and Pontus. Rome salutes you.'

I had been determined to remain stony faced when I met the friend of Augustus, to give the impression I was hard, unyielding, just like the soldiers of my army. But a smile crept over my face. I already liked this Roman who had obviously done his research. No one had mentioned the Battle of Surkh in an age. It was where I had acquired the scar on my right cheek.

'Welcome Marcus Vipsanius Agrippa,' I replied, 'victor of Munda, Philippi and Actium.'

I too had done my homework. 'Dura welcomes you and salutes your martial achievements.'

I extended an arm to Gallia. 'This is my wife, Queen Gallia.'

Agrippa turned his head and bowed it to Gallia, my wife responding with a dazzling smile. So far, so good.

'It is a great honour to meet you lady,' said Agrippa, 'long have I desired to cast my eyes on the most famous woman in the world, whose prowess on the battlefield is matched only by her grace and beauty off it.'

Gallia probably wanted to sneer, but this tall, broad-shouldered Roman with thin lips, a square jaw and strong brow was both handsome and a charmer. And when he smiled at Gallia she laughed back, delighted to be complimented by the second-most important man in the Roman world.

Like everyone who first saw Gallia's magical cuirass, Agrippa was bedazzled by the armour that clung to my wife's body like a second skin.

'Magnificent,' he muttered, his eyes staring directly at Gallia's chest.

It could have been an awkward moment, but Gallia stepped forward to link her arm in Agrippa's.

'It was a gift,' she said softly, the two of them walking into the palace's reception porch after I had introduced the members of the royal council to the Roman.

Gallia chatted to him about nothing in particular: the weather, was his trip comfortable and did he miss his wife? He in turn asked about the Amazons, whether she missed Gaul and how did her fair skin fare in the heat of Mesopotamia. They gave the appearance of old friends as they wandered through the porch into the throne room, the doors of which were open. Rays of sunlight flooded through the windows positioned high in the walls, the light illuminating the griffin banner hanging behind the two empty thrones sitting on the stone dais at the far end of the chamber. Only when he was within feet of the flag did Agrippa halt to admire my standard.

'This is the same standard gifted to you by the seer Dobbai, majesty?' he asked me.

His eyes examined the white silk, on which had been stitched a red griffin on either side, the whole banner edged with gold.

'It is,' I told him.

Gallia was impressed by his knowledge. 'It was presented to my husband when Dobbai was the personal sorceress of King of Kings Sinatruces. We were living in Hatra at the time and about to make our journey to Dura.'

'How long ago was that, majesty?' he enquired.

'Over forty years ago,' she replied.

He moved closer to the banner, one of the guards deployed around the dais moving to bar his way.

'Only a chosen few are allowed to lay their hands on Dura's banner,' I said.

Agrippa backed away. 'Of course. It appears freshly made. Extraordinary.'

He looked at me. 'I am glad to be viewing it in a quiet chamber as opposed to across a battlefield, majesty.'

'Me, too, Marcus,' I said. 'You may be interested to know that the armour I am wearing is older than my standard. Me and it have grown old together.'

It may have angered the gods, but I had given my celestial cuirass to Kewab, reasoning that since I had retired from military campaigning, it would be of more use to him than me. His victories in Cappadocia had elevated him to the position of demi-god in the empire, so he might as well look the part. In truth, I had found it too ostentatious and preferred the armour that had been another gift, albeit one from a gruff German rather than an immortal.

'It must have graced many battlefields, majesty,' said Agrippa.

I stroked the black leather cuirass, which was muscled like Agrippa's and was embossed with a golden sun motif on the upper chest, with two golden winged lions immediately beneath. It had fringed strips of black leather that covered the thighs and shoulders, which were decorated with golden bees. Most of the strips were not original, having been replaced over the years when the armour had been repaired, usually after a campaign.

We left the throne room to walk on to the palace terrace where couches had been arranged under the awning to make Agrippa feel at home, or at least put him at ease. Chrestus, Aaron, Ira, Rsan and Almas took their leave, leaving myself and Gallia alone with the Roman. Chrestus had placed guards around the terrace's stone balustrade to ensure Agrippa did not assassinate us both, an entirely unnecessary precaution. I had learned long ago that whatever the Romans were, they placed great store by rules and regulations, which extended to diplomacy between themselves and foreign powers. Rome expected her envoys to be treated with civility and respect and accorded foreign diplomats the same courtesy. That is why Agrippa would never attempt anything clandestine, and I in turn would never harm a hair on his head. It was also why I disliked the idea of assassins so much, for their base actions chipped away at the very edifice of civilisation.

Ashk took the Roman's cloak before he seated himself and enquired if he wanted to retire to his bedchamber to rest. Agrippa told him he was not in need of sleep. I noticed the gold brooch on the red cloak, which was decorated with a scarab motif.

I pointed at it. 'An Egyptian design, I believe.'

'You have a keen eye, majesty' said Agrippa, accepting a silver rhyton of wine from a female servant. 'It was a gift from Augustus after the successful conclusion of the Egyptian campaign against Mark Antony and Cleopatra.'

'Did you ever meet her?' asked Gallia.

Agrippa smiled when he tasted the quality of the wine.

'Cleopatra? A few times, majesty.'

Gallia was intrigued. 'What was she like?'

'Devious, untrustworthy and a corrupter of men,' he replied bluntly. 'Because of her, Rome was wracked by civil strife for years.'

Gallia caught my eye. Rome's internal strife had been to Parthia's gain, and we both wondered what new challenges a united Roman world would pose to the empire. Gallia grabbed the bull by the horns.

'Parthia wonders if a united Rome will once again seek to expand its eastern frontier at the expense of Parthia.'

'Caesar Augustus has stated that the Euphrates is the permanent boundary between Rome and Parthia, majesty,' said

Agrippa, 'and does not wish to jeopardise the peace that now exists between the two.'

'If you have come to Dura to hasten the return of the eagles lost at Carrhae and Lake Urmia, you should know that Dura, or its king, has withdrawn from the politics of the empire,' I told him.

'I am not here concerning the eagles, majesty,' he replied.

'Then what?'

'Satrap Kewab, majesty.'

Gallia's mask of civility slipped.

'Kewab is under Dura's protection and is not answerable to Rome's laws.'

'You misunderstand me, majesty,' said Agrippa in haste. 'I am not here for justice against Satrap Kewab but am authorised to offer him the post of governor of Egypt on behalf of Augustus Caesar.'

I nearly spilt my wine and Gallia's jaw dropped in astonishment.

'I believe that the satrap is currently without an official position,' added Agrippa, 'having been relieved of his duties by King of Kings Phraates.'

I should have been annoyed at this Roman who had dared to step into my kingdom to try to steal one of its jewels. But I had to admit it made perfect sense. For years Parthia had been watching and studying Rome and its leaders as a way of preparing for any threats that might appear on its western frontier. And Rome had been studying us. Alcaeus had remarked that Kewab had become the talk of the eastern Roman world, and word of his military prowess had obviously reached Rome itself. The Romans must have known Kewab had been dismissed from his position as lord high general in the east and Satrap of Aria, that kingdom now ruled by King Altan, much to my regret. And whereas Phraates had created Kewab deputy lord high general during the recent campaign against the enemies of Gordyene, it was only because the incumbent lord high general, King Ali of Atropaiene, had been unable to take the field on account of his broken ankle. I gave Agrippa a knowing look. He knew, as did I, that Kewab was a man without a real position, a satrap without a land to rule and lord of a town that was in a foreign land.

'Kewab fled Egypt to seek sanctuary in Parthia,' said Gallia. 'Why would he want to return to a land where there is a price on his head?'

'You are alluding to a time when Egypt was devoid of law and order, majesty,' smiled Agrippa, 'when civil strife between Cleopatra and her brother Ptolemy over who would be pharaoh resulted in much bloodshed. Fortunately, both are dead, and Egypt is under the firm rule of Rome.'

'That being the case, why would Rome wish a Parthian general to be placed in charge of its province?' asked Gallia.

'Augustus believes an Egyptian in charge of Egypt would facilitate a peaceful and prosperous province,' said Agrippa. 'Moreover, a man with Kewab's reputation would act as a deterrence to those thinking of inciting rebellion.'

'Kewab has explained to me how his father was murdered on the orders of the younger sister of Cleopatra, whose name escapes me,' I said.

'Arsinoe,' offered Agrippa.

'Yes, that's her,' I nodded. 'At the time of his murder, Kewab's father was besieging the palace in Alexandria where Cleopatra and Julius Caesar were in residence.'

Agrippa nodded. 'Yes, majesty.'

'And if I am not mistaken,' I continued, 'was not Julius Caesar the great-uncle of your master, Augustus Caesar?'

'Yes, majesty.'

I took a sip of wine. 'And Augustus Caesar would have no objection to an enemy of his uncle ruling Egypt in his name?'

'Caesar wishes to draw a line under the past, majesty, to put in place measures that will secure the future rather than rake over what has passed.'

'Very noble,' said Gallia. 'But why have you yourself bothered to journey here, when a simple letter to Kewab would have sufficed?'

'Not that we are not happy to see you, Marcus,' I quickly added. 'It cheers me that Romans and Parthians can enjoy each other's company.'

Agrippa smiled at Gallia. 'Out of courtesy and respect for the rulers of Dura. Caesar, and I concurred, was adamant that all dealings with regard to Satrap Kewab should be conducted openly and honestly, in the spirit of the healthy relations that now exist between Rome and Parthia.'

I raised my rhyton to him. 'And Dura both appreciates and respects the forthrightness Augustus Caesar has displayed in this matter.'

Agrippa was the consummate diplomat, never once mentioning the fact both I and Gallia had once been slaves in Italy, never referring to our participation in the Spartacus uprising, or the Servile War as the Romans termed it. He was at all times polite and made great efforts to be a considerate guest, his charm and good manners winning over Gallia, which was no small feat in itself. I sent a courier to Mari to bring Kewab back to the city. He had taken an interest in the rebuilding works, which allowed him to be near the troops he had brought with him from the east. Because Dura did not have an army of slaves to call upon, the laborious task of producing mud-bricks had to be undertaken by Kewab's troops and the exiles from Mesene. But as they were making what would be the bricks for their own homes, there was a general dearth of grumbling. The huge building project also kept thousands of men fully occupied and was a way of integrating them smoothly into the kingdom.

The process of making mud-bricks was simple enough, though messy and time-consuming. Soil and water were mixed to produce a thick mud, to which was added chopped straw. The composite mixture was then kneaded by feet for up to four days, after which it was left alone for another four days. The mixture was then poured into moulds and left for a while before being deposited on a drying floor sprinkled with sand and straw to prevent them sticking. After a week of drying, they were ready to be used as bricks for building or repairs.

While we waited for Kewab's return, I showed Agrippa around Dura. For a man used to living in Rome, Alexandria and Athens, my city must have been a disappointment. But if it was, he never let it show. He was clearly impressed by the size of the caravan park immediately north of the city, which was always full of camel caravans travelling east and west. We rode to the park the day after Agrippa had arrived and before he was due to meet Kewab that afternoon. As well as the guards employed by the caravan bosses themselves, the area was patrolled by Chrestus' legionaries to maintain law and order.

It was like a small city beside the larger one of stone and mud-bricks where I lived, a sprawl of tents, camels, horses, bored and irritable guards and equally flustered camel drivers. Swarming around them and their animals was a small army of traders offering food, clothes and tickets to the city brothels, government officials charging fees, and squads of soldiers patrolling the chaos.

'It is a curious thing,' said Agrippa, looking around the caravan park. 'All I see is camels, tents, people and horses, majesty, and yet within this park is the great wealth that has made your kingdom rich.'

I nodded. 'It is ironic the commodity for which there is an insatiable demand in Egypt, Parthia and the Roman world is light, compact and ideally suited to long-distance transportation.'

I pointed at the tents. 'The silk is stored in the living quarters whilst in the park and carried on camels when on the move. The caravans also transport dyes, precious stones, spices and medicines, all items that are relatively easy to transport on the backs of camels.'

'Do you levy tariffs on each commodity, majesty?'

I shook my head. 'We do not interfere with or examine the goods transported by the caravans, and neither do the other kingdoms the caravans pass through.'

He looked perplexed. 'Then how does Dura make money?'

'It charges a fee for every animal quartered in the park, and all traders selling their wares in the park are required to purchase business licences from the city authorities beforehand.'

'Each stopping place charges similar fees?'

I nodded.

'It must cost a great deal to transport silk from China to the Mediterranean.'

'It does,' I said. 'But consider this. Each of my wife's bodyguards, the Amazons, wears a simple white sleeveless silk vest beneath her tunic. If she had to purchase the vest, it would cost her a year's wages. And that is for a very basic garment. Those worn by the fine ladies of Egypt and Rome, not to mention their husbands, can cost four or five times that amount. The caravan bosses do not starve.'

'May I ask why the queen's bodyguards wear silk, majesty?'

'As a defence against arrows,' I told him. 'If an arrowhead pierces their mail armour, the silk makes it easier to extract from the torso. An arrow spins in flight, you see, and the silk would not tear but rather wraps itself around the metal head, thus making it easier to extract it from any wound cleanly.'

He sat still in the saddle, pondering what I had told him, around us the bustle, noise and pungent aromas of Dura's caravan park. Our horse archer escort swatted away flies from their faces, their horses using their tails to flick away the winged irritants.

'There is another matter I wish to speak to you about, majesty,' he said at last, 'a rather delicate matter.'

'Go on.'

'Caesar is most troubled by the behaviour of Gordyene, majesty, specifically its king. Whereas no one blames King Castus for defending his kingdom against the aggression of Pontus, Cappadocia and Galatia, he is concerned King Castus will take advantage of the current weakness of those kingdoms and launch a fresh war against Rome's allies.'

I smiled. 'You need not have any worry on that account, Marcus,' I reassured him. 'King Castus will only send his soldiers beyond his borders if he is provoked.'

I told him the story of how Prince Haytham had become gravely ill after his father, King Spartacus, had annexed northern Media, and how Claudia had travelled to Gordyene and explained the legend of the lion called Gordis, and how she had cured Haytham.

Agrippa was fascinated. 'How did she cure him, majesty?'

'With pen and parchment, I believe.'

'I do not understand.'

'She persuaded Spartacus to write an order recalling all his soldiers from northern Media and got his pledge that he would never again try to expand Gordyene at the expense of that kingdom.'

'What happened?'

'The soldiers returned to Gordyene and Prince Haytham recovered,' I replied.

'I have heard your daughter is a powerful sorceress, majesty.'

'Please inform Caesar that he should not worry himself unduly about Gordyene,' I said, changing the subject. 'Castus will not seek to expand the frontiers of his kingdom. Besides, he has a wedding to look forward to.'

'A wedding?'

'I hear he is to marry the daughter of King Ali of Atropaiene, which should swell Gordyene's coffers. The princess will command a big dowry.'

Agrippa looked around the caravan park.

'King Castus must now be one of the wealthiest kings in Parthia, majesty. His recent campaign won him not only a great victory, but also twenty-five thousand talents of gold.'

I looked at him in amazement. 'That much?'

'The price of convincing him to retire from Melitene cost Cappadocia, Pontus and Galatia a combined total of twenty thousand talents, majesty, plus the five thousand talents King Artaxias of Armenia paid to Gordyene to keep the peace.'

Twenty-five talents of gold – equivalent to seven hundred and fifty tons of the precious metal – was a huge sum. I worried that a young king with a victorious army and a full treasury might be tempted into rashness. Perhaps wiser heads would prevail. I prayed to Shamash it would be so.

I began coughing when a gust of wind blew dust into our faces. I turned Horns.

'I think we should get back to the palace, Marcus, before we begin to reek of horse and camel dung.'

He wheeled his horse around and rode beside me as we trotted from the park.

'What is done, with all the dung, I mean?'

I laughed. 'Romans are a most practical people. It is collected and the horse dung is sold as fertilizer, the camel dung is left out in the sun to dry it before being used as a substitute for firewood.'

At the Palmyrene Gate there was the usual press of people, carts, donkeys, camels and horses either exiting or entering the city, the vine cane of a hot and humourless centurion directing traffic. The commander of our escort rode forward and began shouting.

'Make way for the king, make way for the king.'

But he had difficulty making himself heard above the cacophony of raised voices, camels bellowing, roaring and bleating, and the braying of donkeys.

'The sights and sounds of prosperity, Marcus,' I shouted. 'It was very different when I first arrived at Dura all those years ago.'

I pointed up at the walls. 'The first person I met upon arrival was the city governor, whose body was hanging from the walls. The gates were closed, and nothing stirred. Would you like to take a closer look?'

'Majesty?'

I pointed up at the stone statue above the gates.

'Very much so, majesty.'

We left the horses with the commander of the escort and made our way on foot through the slow-moving throng, the centurion spotting me and ordering half a dozen of his men to close around us. As soon as I was recognised, people tried to crowd round me, not with ill intent but to wish me well and savour the moment of being within touching distance of their king. Kings and queens were for the most part remote figures who rode on horses surrounded by guards and lived in walled palaces high above the general populace. The idea of being in close proximity of the common people filled them and their nobles with dread, not least because if they were unpopular, they risked being assassinated. There was also the chance of becoming infected with some sort of dreadful disease from those who did not have access to doctors, medicines, baths, clean clothes and fresh bedding. Having spent weeks as a stinking, barefoot slave and three years in the company of a slave army, being close to commoners never troubled me. The same could not be said of Agrippa, who looked genuinely alarmed at the wall of smiling, filthy, misshapen faces that surrounded us.

His calm demeanour returned once we had ascended the steps to take us above the gates where the stone griffin stood gazing to the west, keeping watch over the road that led to Palmyra, the highway that gave Dura its great wealth. Protected day and night by four guards standing at each corner of the stone plinth on which it rested, the griffin was the silent guardian of the city and kingdom.

Agrippa ran a hand over the stone.

'It is a curious thing. Before this statue was carved, it was just a block of stone. And now it is a sacred totem, a symbol of Dura's strength and prosperity.'

'We are all mere superstitious mortals, Marcus,' I said. I pointed to the dagger in a sheath at his hip, the only weapon he carried.

'May I look at your dagger?'

He pulled it from the sheath and handed it to me. It was a simple affair with a triangular-shaped blade, brass hilt, wooden grip and brass pommel.

'A parazonium dagger, as carried by the Goddess Virtus, I believe, who presides over bravery and military strength. A small, insignificant weapon but one with enormous symbolism.'

He was delighted. 'How knowledgeable you are, majesty.'

I handed it back to him. 'Those who carry it are associated with might and leadership,' I said, 'and hope to be blessed with the qualities of the goddess. We are all toys of the gods, Marcus.'

That afternoon Kewab returned to the city and Marcus met with him to discuss him becoming governor of Egypt. I was determined that Parthia would not lose such a valuable son but was equally determined to play a subtle game with regard to Agrippa and his master's offer. I might yet persuade Kewab to stay in Parthia, but I had reckoned without the influence of Menwi, his wife.

Chapter 2

I knew little about the heritage, culture and politics of Egypt, and seeing as it was a Roman province and far from Dura and Parthia, I saw little reason to study its history in depth. I was grateful its nobles craved silk and therefore indirectly supported Dura's economy, and I was happy that one of its more famous sons had sought sanctuary in Dura after the murder of his famous father. Had I taken the time and effort to learn more about Egyptian society, it would have prepared me for the verbal roasting I would receive from Kewab's wife.

When they had first fled Egypt, making their way through Judea and Syria to reach Dura, they were relieved to be still alive. Kewab had offered his services to the army and he and his wife had lived in a very modest house in the city, Menwi giving birth to a child, a boy, and being content to be a soldier's wife. Or so I thought. But that was twelve years ago and since then Kewab had risen in the world, becoming the man who had single-handedly held Parthia's eastern frontier against the Kushans. The great victories at Kayseri and Melitene had elevated his reputation still further, which was why Agrippa was in Dura.

For her part, Menwi had given Kewab a second son during his time in the east and had also become used to living in the royal palace in Farah, the capital of Aria. How bitter must have been her return to Dura to live in a simple house again, albeit a mansion complete with servants, horses, gardeners and stable hands. The latter relieved me of Horns when I had eased my way out of his saddle after reaching Kewab's home, which was surrounded by a high stone wall to keep out unwanted guests. The mansion itself had white-painted walls to reflect the sun's heat and a red-tiled roof supported by white stone columns. All the floors were tiled with white marble and the interior walls and ceilings were white throughout to give it a spacious and airy feel.

Kewab and Menwi stood in the reception hall and welcomed me to their home, the satrap dressed in a simple white tunic and tan leggings, the attire of a common horse archer. Menwi's attire and appearance were altogether more elaborate. Like many Egyptian noblewomen, she wore a black wig over her own hair of the same colour, with blue eyeshadow and antinomy to line her eyes and eyebrows. Now in her midthirties, her light olive skin was flawless, what I could see of it. Alcaeus had told me the length of the dress worn by Egyptian women was in direct proportion to their social status. The longer the dress, the more important the wearer. And Menwi's white dress reached all the way down to her expensive red leather shoes.

Her dark brown eyes followed me as I hobbled into the reception hall, the steward taking my sword after I had unbuckled the belt. My horse archer escort, which would wait outside the mansion, were served refreshments by other servants.

Kewab and Menwi bowed their heads.

'Welcome to our home, majesty,' he said.

'Thank you for inviting me,' I smiled.

I was introduced to his two sons, Ramesses, the oldest, and Seti, aged six. They bowed, avoiding my eyes, and were then ushered from our presence by a rather stern looking nanny. Kewab invited me into the dining room where burning oil lamps were suspended over a long table. I eased myself into a large wicker chair generously stuffed with cushions and picked up a silver rhyton after it had been filled with wine, raising it to my lips.

'We give thanks to Ra before we eat,' said a scowling Menwi.

I put down the rhyton.

'Apologies, majesty,' said Kewab.

Before I could tell him it was quite all right, Menwi's voice filled the dining room.

'Hail to thee, Amun-Ra, lord of the thrones of the earth, the oldest existence, ancient of heaven, support of all things; chief of the gods, lord of truth; father of the gods, maker of men, beasts and herbs; maker of all things above and below; deliverer of the sufferer and oppressed, judge of the poor; lord of wisdom, lord of mercy; most loving, opener of every eye, source of joy, in whose goodness the gods rejoice, thou whose name is hidden. Thou art the one, maker of all that is, the one; the only one; maker of gods and men; giving food to all. Hail to thee, thou one with many heads; sleepless when all others sleep. Adoration to thee. Hail to thee from all creatures from every land, from the height of heaven, from the depths of the sea. The spirits thou hast made extol thee, saying, welcome to thee, father of the fathers of the gods; we worship thy spirit which is in us.'

She then clapped her hands to signal the meal could begin.

It was a lavish affair, with honey-roasted gazelle, spit-roasted ducks, strips of fish in sauce, wild vegetables and onions. An endless procession of side dishes included bread, cheese, butter, raisins, figs and nuts.

'You have spoken to Marcus Vipsanius Agrippa?' I asked Kewab.

'I have, majesty.'

'A most charming man,' opined Menwi. 'He has offered my husband the governorship of Egypt.'

I picked up a raisin. 'I am aware of Rome's offer, lady.'

'Then you are also aware of Parthia's ingratitude shown to my husband for saving the eastern half of the empire,' she hissed back with barely concealed venom, 'to say nothing of the services rendered by him on Parthia's western border during the last two years.'

'Menwi, that is enough,' Kewab rebuked her.

I popped the raisin into my mouth. 'I understand your frustration, lady, but understand that the Romans do nothing out of the kindness of their hearts. They wish to steal your husband to weaken Parthia, and they dangle the prospect of governor of Egypt before him to lure him away.'

'My husband is not a child to be seduced by a trinket,' she shot back, much to the embarrassment of Kewab. 'He is Parthia's greatest general.'

Kewab's mouth dropped open. 'I must apologise again, majesty.'

I picked up another raisin. They were delicious and must have been soaked in honey before the meal.

'I agree, your husband *is* Parthia's greatest general, and I most strongly desire that he should remain so. In Parthia.'

This delighted Kewab but perplexed his viper of a wife.

'What is a Roman governor,' I asked, 'but a glorified tax collector?'

'The governor of Egypt commands an army of twenty-seven thousand troops and a fleet of Nile ships,' stated Menwi.

I ate a third raisin. 'They are not soldiers, lady, more a police force to impose Rome's laws and extract money from Egypt's population.'

I looked at Kewab. 'How long does a Roman governor hold his position?'

'Around five or six years, majesty,' he replied.

'And after that?' I asked.

'The full restoration of General Achillas' estates to my husband, and compensation to myself for the loss of my father's linen business when he and my mother were imprisoned and later executed by the whore Cleopatra,' Menwi answered.

'Agrippa showed us documents signed by Augustus himself confirming the return of our respective families' wealth and lands, majesty,' confirmed Kewab.

'I cannot see you running a linen business, Kewab,' I smiled.

'He will not,' said Menwi, 'I will be running the business.'

I laughed. 'You?'

Menwi was not laughing. 'Unlike in Parthia, in Egypt women can own and operate their own businesses, work at a trade, inherit property and train in medicine. In Egypt, we will be able to live in our own palace, to live in the lifestyle we have become accustomed to.'

Live like a queen is what she meant. She was dripping with gold, from her earrings, diamond-encrusted necklace, armlets and the gold rings adorning every one of her fingers. I looked at Kewab, whose loyalty to me, Dura and Parthia had never faltered despite being stripped of his position of lord high general in the east and Satrap of Aria. He had been recalled by Phraates in response to the great threat against Gordyene and had risen to the challenge, winning a victory that had made all my battlefield triumphs pale into insignificance. And his reward? To be dismissed a second time by an ungrateful king of kings. And yet the high king might yet be able to rescue the situation.

'Have you given Agrippa your answer to his offer?' I asked Kewab.

'No yet, majesty.'

'Then I ask you to delay your decision until I have spoken personally to King of Kings Phraates.'

Menwi rolled her eyes but Kewab froze her with a glare.

'I shall inform Agrippa he will have my decision when you have returned from Ctesiphon, majesty,' he said happily.

When I returned to the Citadel it was late, Agrippa having retired to his quarters, the palace quiet and filled with long shadows. I found Gallia in our bedroom, brushing her hair in front of a mirror of polished bronze. I flopped down on the bed and stared at the ceiling.

'Have you heard of the Nile crocodile?'

'Vaguely.'

'Five hundred pounds of teeth and a vicious man-eater. Well, tonight I met one.'

She turned to stare at me. 'Have you been drinking?'

'Not enough, unfortunately.'

'I thought you were dining with Kewab?'

'I was, although I got the distinct feeling I was on the menu. His wife is a fearsome creature.'

'In what way?'

'Very outspoken to the point of rudeness.'

'You mean she sticks up for herself.'

I propped myself up on an elbow. 'Menwi seems to forget that her position is entirely dependent on Kewab, and yet if you had been at the meal, you would have thought she was the great military leader who had been insulted.'

'That is because you know nothing of Egyptian society, Pacorus.'

'I know its women have tongues sharper than a sword blade.'

She ignored my barb. 'Egyptian society maintains a duality between the male and the female. Just as its people worship both the sun and the moon. The sun is associated with the divine male, the moon with the divine female. Female voices are not crushed in Egypt as they are in Rome and Parthia.'

'Yes, you look very crushed.'

'Women can become pharaohs in Egypt, and no one questions their authority. Is Kewab going to accept Agrippa's offer?'

'He will delay his decision until I have journeyed to Ctesiphon.'

She was surprised. 'To what end?'

'To persuade Phraates to offer Kewab a position commensurate to his status and talents in order to prevent him leaving Parthia. To appeal to his reason and common sense.'

'What use is appealing to things that do not exist?'

Kewab informed Agrippa of his decision to delay giving him an answer until I had returned from Ctesiphon. The next day, the Roman accepted the Egyptian's invitation to visit Palmyra and King Malik and Queen Jamal rather than linger in the palace. From there he would journey back to Syria and on to Cyprus and Italy. Aa a parting gift I gave him the lavish silk robes that had been made for my sixtieth birthday, and which had been stored away in a wooden chest. They made me look like a Persian eunuch and so, though they had been a gift from Byrd, I reasoned that he would not be upset if they were used to improve Romano-Parthian relations.

Agrippa was genuinely touched and thanked me profusely. On the day he departed in the company of Kewab, the robes in the chest strapped on the back of a spitting, ill-tempered camel, he stood beside me at the top of the palace steps. Kewab, Rsan, Aaron, Ira, Almas and Chrestus were also in attendance, the Amazons on parade and a century of Exiles standing to attention in the courtyard below. The day was overcast but warm, rivulets of sweat running down the cheeks of Agrippa's mail-clad Syrian horsemen.

Gallia stepped forward and kissed him on the cheek.

'Rome would like to see the Queen of Dura grace it with her presence, majesty.'

Gallia smiled. 'I will consider your kind offer, Marcus.'

Agrippa turned to me. 'And the senate would welcome you giving a speech to its august members, majesty.'

'I've never given a speech in my life,' I told him.

'Now that you have retired from military service, majesty, I am sure you could turn to oratory to impart your wisdom to the world. Perhaps this might help.'

He unfastened his dagger in its sheath and handed it to me. 'From one friend to another, majesty.'

'I will endeavour to wear it with honour, Marcus,' I said.

We watched the second-most powerful individual in the Roman world trot from the Citadel in the company of Kewab. The symbolism of his visit had been enormous, and I was glad to have lived long enough to see Parthian and Roman generals sit down to dine together as opposed to butchering each other on the battlefield. But I was determined that one Parthian general would not be wearing the uniform of Rome. I turned to Almas.

'You and I are going to pay a visit to that farmer friend of yours.'

We rode a few miles south of the city to a ramshackle building with stables attached and a well for water. The former office-cum-farmhouse was empty and so we trotted on. Around us dozens of labourers and farmers were working in ripened fields of wheat, which extended as far as the eye could see both south and west into what had formally been barren desert. I pulled up Horns to admire the sun-ripened crops.

'Your determination and vision have made this possible, Almas,' I told him in admiration. 'Of all the victories won by Dura, yours over what was once barren land stands tallest.'

'The peace you brokered with the Agraci all those years ago has allowed Dura to develop its agriculture, majesty. Without peace, there would be no crops or farmers to grow them.'

Our small self-admiration society meeting was interrupted by the appearance of what I first thought was a beggar: an old man dressed in a filthy tunic, frayed leggings and nothing on his feet. He was wearing a straw hat to shield his leering face from the sun, which had turned his sinewy arms almost black over the years.

'Deputy Governor Almas,' he grinned, revealing uneven, stained teeth. 'We don't often have the pleasure of your company.'

'This is Cambiz, majesty,' Almas said to me, 'the old rogue I placed with Klietas to assist him on his farm.'

Cambiz squinted at me, quickly removed his hat and bowed his head.

'Begging your pardon, majesty, I didn't recognise you.'

'I desire information about Klietas,' I said.

'He's gone, majesty,' Cambiz replied.

'I know that,' I said. 'I want to know where he went. Do you know the name of his village in Media?'

He concentrated for a moment before shaking his head.

'He told me once, but I've clean forgotten, majesty.'

'Think, man,' snapped Almas.

Cambiz shrugged. 'It never cropped up much in conversation, lord, not like that she-devil he was besotted with.'

'Haya,' I sighed.

'Met her once,' said Cambiz, 'just before Klietas left with her. When he came back, he was not the same. Perhaps she knows where he took himself off to, majesty.'

I had questioned Haya concerning the whereabouts of Klietas, and indeed all the others whom Gallia had sent north to do her dirty work, but neither she nor they could shine any light on the name of Klietas' village.

'Shame,' reflected Cambiz, looking around at the fields, 'he had a lucrative business going for him. Now he is probably starving somewhere, all because of a woman.'

'That's enough from you,' Almas cautioned the older man

Cambiz shrugged. 'He was not the first to be ruined by a tight behind, tidy breasts and a dazzling smile, and he won't be the last.'

'Cambiz!' Almas shouted in frustration.

I nodded. 'You speak the truth, however crude. Do you think Klietas will return?'

'No, majesty, not in this lifetime.'

'The farm prospers?'

'Yes, majesty.' Cambiz tilted his head at Almas. 'I work it for Lord Almas since Klietas is no longer with us.'

I tugged on Horns' reins to wheel him around.

'Work it for yourself. You own it now.'

Almas registered surprise and Cambiz beamed with delight. We trotted away.

'That was very generous, majesty,' said Almas. 'Cambiz knows a lot about farming but is a notorious womaniser and gambler. Whether he keeps hold of the farm is open to debate.'

'It was obviously the will of the gods that he rather than Klietas should tend to the farm,' I said.

And it was surely the intervention of the gods that placed me at that spot at that particular time, for I heard Cambiz shout and pulled up Horns.

'Aref, over here.'

I spun in the saddle to peer at a figure ambling towards Cambiz, a reed basket on his back, and turned Horns to direct him back towards the farmer. Why I did not know but something, an instinct, a sixth sense, told me the stranger was of value. Or perhaps it was Shamash himself whispering into my ear.

The newcomer was obviously wretchedly poor judging by his filthy, tatty clothing, though his condition did not appear to weigh heavily upon him judging by the happy-go-lucky expression on his face. Cambiz saw us return and waited for the newcomer to get close before speaking.

'Aref, this is the king.'

The man called Aref grinned to reveal a mouth with no teeth and bowed.

'The gods bless you, majesty.'

He took the basket off his back, placed it on the ground and reached into it to pull out a fish, a carp.

'Aref was a friend of Klietas, majesty, who has a farm near the river. Young Klietas let him use his oxen for free in exchange for a fish supper every night.'

Aref held out the fish to me. 'Caught earlier, majesty. You and the queen are welcome to have it for your meal tonight.'

'That is very generous of you, Aref,' I said, 'but I have enough fish to eat.'

Aref, disappointed, put the fish back in the basket.

'The king wishes to know where Klietas has gone,' said Cambiz.

Aref slung the basket on his back. 'The village of Vazneh, ten miles south of the great lake.'

I jumped down from Horns and confronted Aref, who stank of fish guts.

'Are you certain?'

'Vazneh, ten miles south of the great lake,' Aref repeated. He was clearly mentally deficient but, like many with such an affliction, had a memory that recorded minutiae that he could divulge with ease, like a clerk consulting itemised scrolls in a library.

'Make a note of the name,' I instructed Almas.

The deputy governor reached into a saddlebag to pull out a small wooden tablet with a wax surface, which could be written on using a metal stylus. After it was inscribed, the wax could later by warmed and smoothed over for fresh notes.

'How do you spell it?' asked Almas.

Aref gave him a dumbfounded look. He was obviously illiterate.

'Vazneh,' he repeated.

'Spell it as it sounds,' I told Almas, walking back to Horns and hauling myself into his saddle.

I too reached into a saddlebag and pulled out a small leather pouch filled with drachmas. I tossed it to Aref.

'For your help.'

He dropped the basket to catch the pouch, his eyes lighting up when he saw the contents.

'You lucky bastard,' said Cambiz.

'Not luck, fate,' I told him, turning Horns and digging my knees into his sides.

Now I had the information and could embark on my journey to kill two birds with one stone.

Chapter 3

The spring melt waters were now subsiding, but the current of the Euphrates was still strong and its level high. On the other side of the river, in Hatran territory, the land had been flooded. There were no farms on the other side of the river, the wealth of Hatra being the Silk Road that ran through the city, and the fertile lands to the north of the capital, specifically around the city of Nisibus. Happily, the waters had not breached the river defences built by Almas, but the dams and irrigation ditches that drew water off the Euphrates were working at peak efficiency, turning what once had been a desert into a thick belt of greenery stretching south from the city of Dura to a distance of nearly three hundred miles.

When both the king and queen left Dura, they were invariably escorted by a full complement of Amazons, the commander of whom carried my griffin banner. But as I was travelling alone and the trip would be short, the Ctesiphon leg, anyway, I decided to take an escort of horse archers instead.

'I will be away for three weeks at most,' I told Gallia as we relaxed on the palace terrace and watched the light drain from the world.

'It is a fool's errand, Pacorus. Even if Phraates was of a mind to keep Kewab in the empire, what could he offer him?'

'The throne of Mesene,' I replied.

'Sanabares rules Mesene, Pacorus, and he is one of Phraates' favourites.'

When Nergal and Praxima died their vision of a harmonious Mesene in which Parthians and the marsh people, the Ma'adan, lived peacefully side-by-side died with them. Sanabares was a rich noble from Susiana who believed marsh dwellers had no place within the Parthian Empire. He was by any standard totally unfit to rule one of the poorer kingdoms of the empire, which nevertheless had flourished under the rule of my friends. Those Mesenians who had no stomach to wage war against those who had become their friends and neighbours were now resident in my kingdom. Rather exile than fighting an unwinnable war in the marshlands of southern Mesene.

'It actually makes perfect sense,' I said. 'Sanabares can be made the satrap of Babylon, Kewab can be made king of Mesene and the exiles from that kingdom can return home.'

She gave me a sympathetic look. 'It makes sense to you, but to Phraates it would be seen as you questioning his authority and wisdom.'

'You know as well as I do that Sanabares will plunge Mesene into ruin, just as Chosroes did all those years ago.'

'It is amazing how history seems to repeat itself,' she agreed. 'Only this time we will not be marching to remove the incumbent King of Mesene.'

'Not unless he marches against us first,' I said.

'And what of young Klietas?' she asked.

'I want to convince him to return to Dura, to his farm, which by all accounts is prospering.'

'He made it quite plain he wished to leave the kingdom.'

I stood and walked over to the balustrade, peering at the mirror-like waters of the Euphrates below.

'And we all know why he wished to leave the kingdom.'

'Not all this again, Pacorus.'

Fishing boats were pushing off from the shore, lanterns hanging over the sides of their vessels to draw fish to the surface. There was no wind in the warm evening air, the sound of crickets filling the air and the moon shining like a huge silver ball in the night sky.

'You should not have used Haya to entice Klietas to join your band of assassins. It was a cruel deception.'

She was unmoved. 'The kingdom needed him.'

I turned to walk back to my chair, servants coming on to the terrace with lighted oil lamps to provide us with illumination, others bowing before taking away the nuts and figs we had been nibbling.

'You are a good man and a just king, Pacorus, but sometimes justice and fair play are not enough.'

'I disapprove of assassination.'

'I rest my case,' she smiled.

'You have set a dangerous precedent,' I cautioned.

'By removing Dura's enemies? I think not. Will Parthia lament the passing of Atrax or Tiridates, of Amyntas and Glaphyra? Of course, if you had handed Atrax over to Spartacus all those years ago, I would not have had to send assassins to kill him. And then perhaps Rasha would still be alive.'

She was toying with the stand of black hair hanging from her necklace, the same lock of hair she had cut from the dead body of Rasha after she had fallen on the Diyana Plain.

'I do not regret any action I have taken, Gallia.'

'In that we are the same,' she replied. 'Changing the subject, what will you do when you fail to persuade Klietas to return to Dura?'

'You seem very certain with regard to what Klietas will do.'

She gave me a knowing smile, which I found intensely annoying. The female complement of the assassins had closed ranks and divulged nothing about what occurred during their mission. A sullen Talib had returned to Palmyra to report to Byrd, though when I questioned my old friend about what Talib had revealed, he had told me his protégé was a remote, haunted man. With Klietas gone, there was only one individual who could perhaps shed any light on why my former squire had abandoned a golden future.

'Centurion Bullus, how are you?'

I had contacted Bullus' cohort commander to request he be allowed to leave his unit to accompany me on the journey to Ctesiphon. He stood before me in the throne room looking immaculate in his mail armour, burnished greaves and gleaming helmet decorated with a magnificent white transverse crest in the crook of his arm. The helmet was over-sized to accommodate his large, shaven head, adorned with battle scars, his mail armour also generous to accommodate his broad shoulders.

'Well, majesty,' he replied.

'Your commander has spoken to you?'

'Yes, majesty.'

'We will leave for Ctesiphon in the morning. And after we have visited the high king, I intend to go searching for Klietas.'

A trace of a smile creased his thin lips.

'Something amuses you, centurion?'

'It might be a long trip, majesty, seeing as no one knows where he has gone.'

I stood and stepped down from the dais.

'Allow me to bring you up to date, Bullus. I have the name and location of Klietas' village in northern Media.'

I jabbed a finger in his thick chest. 'I wish to know why he threw away the chance to make something of himself, to rise in the world to become a prosperous farmer and perhaps, one day, a lord of Dura. But perhaps you can tell me.'

He stared ahead, unblinking.

'I am just a simple soldier, majesty.'

'We will see. Until tomorrow, then.'

He saluted, about-faced and marched from the throne room.

The following morning, he presented himself in the Citadel's courtyard, along with twenty-five horse archers commanded by a young captain by the name of Navid, whose wispy beard was testament to his youth. Sporaces, commander of Dura's horse archers, had selected him specially, pointing out he was a rising star among the junior officers of his dragon.

'He looks about twelve,' I remarked to Sporaces beside me at the top of the palace steps. 'Then again, every soldier in the army looks like a fresh-faced youth to me these days.'

My left leg suddenly crumpled beneath me and I was in danger of falling. Bullus jumped down from his horse and sprinted up the steps to grab my arm, Sporaces holding the other one.

'Are you fit enough to ride, majesty?' he asked.

'Should I fetch a medic?' asked Bullus.

The pain in my leg subsided and I was able to stand on my own.

'I'm fine,' I told them.

I gingerly walked down the steps to a waiting Horns, who was flicking his tail in irritation, clearly wanting some morning exercise. I caught sight of Navid and his men, who all appeared to be teenagers, staring at me with concern. I must have appeared ancient with my greying hair and hobbling walk.

'Protect the king at all times,' Sporaces told Navid in a loud voice so the others would hear. 'Dura is depending on you.'

Navid and his men swelled with pride. The captain saluted.

'Yes, general, you have my word.'

He spun in the saddle and pointed at two of his men, who wheeled their horses around and trotted from the courtyard.

'Where are they going?' I asked.

'They will scout ahead, majesty, to give warning of any enemy,' replied Navid.

I looked at Sporaces, who was smiling with satisfaction.

Horse archers tended to be lithe, sinewy men riding swift horses, unencumbered by armour such as the cataphracts wore. Their defence was to stay beyond the range of hostile horsemen armed with lances and swords, using feints, speed and intricate battlefield manoeuvres to outwit, confuse and run rings around an enemy. The Scythian bow gave them the ability to engage targets up to a range of three hundred paces, though Dura's horse archers were trained to operate at much shorter ranges, working closely with the legions to move through formations of foot soldiers to deliver devastating volleys of arrows against both enemy horsemen and foot soldiers. But if horse archers were caught or cornered, they were easy meat for cataphracts or mounted spearmen.

Navid pushed his men hard and we covered at least twenty miles in the first two hours of our journey, crossing over the pontoon bridges near the city and hugging the eastern bank of the Euphrates south. The sun was soon quickly climbing into a cloudless sky to bake the earth and those travelling on it. At the rear of our column were six camels loaded with tents, fodder, food and other supplies, but they carried no extra arrows. We were visiting the residence of the high king, not embarking on a campaign.

Navid called a halt after two hours, leading his men and king into a stand of date palms, giving us the opportunity to dismount, rest and water the horses. He was clearly nervous concerning having the responsibility of protecting his king as he posted guards around the trees and sent scouts to reconnoitre ahead, behind and on the flank, an order I instantly countermanded.

'We don't need to send out riders in all directions,' I told him. 'Just post a couple of guards on foot at the edge of the trees. We don't want to tire the horses, or your men, unnecessarily.'

He stood rigidly before me. 'Yes, majesty. Apologies, majesty.'

'Stand easy, Navid. Relax. We are not fleeing for our lives.'

Out of the corner of my vision I spied Bullus stretched out on the ground with his back against the trunk of a date palm, running a sharpening stone along the edge of his *gladius*.

'You could do worse than follow the example of Centurion Bullus over there,' I said. 'He knows when to expend energy and when to save it.'

'Yes, majesty,' replied Navid, doing an excellent impersonation of a stone statue.

I wandered over to Bullus, indicating he should remain seated, flopping down beside him. We had shared many dangers together and though he was but one centurion among many, our adventure at Irbil had created a bond between us that made rank and social status irrelevant off the parade ground.

I pointed at Navid striding around the camp like a man weighed down with a mighty burden.

'What do think of our young captain?'

'He's in the wrong army,' he said casually.

'How so?'

'I'm sure he desperately wants to cover himself in glory before dying heroically. Shame for him Dura's army has now retired from war.'

'It stands ready to defend Dura and Parthia, Bullus, if required to do so.'

'Has he offered to clean your sword yet?' he grinned.

'Who?'

'Navid.'

'No, why?'

'He will, majesty. He won't be able to resist getting his hands on a magical weapon.'

That night, after we had ridden forty miles and made camp beside the river, Navid did indeed offer to clean my sword. An offer I refused. I did not bother taking my command tent on the short trip, though I did draw the line at sleeping in the small eight-man calfskin tents used by Dura's soldiers. Instead, I slept in a black goatskin Agraci tent pitched in the centre of our small camp. I invited Bullus to share my tent, knowing he would feel uncomfortable sleeping among horse archers, an invitation he gladly accepted.

On the third evening of our uneventful journey, sitting on stools outside the tent, staring into the flickering flames of the campfire, I began to probe Bullus on his excursion into Cappadocia. He was reticent at first, no doubt having been instructed by Gallia to keep his mouth shut. But a hearty meal of rice, meat from a gazelle brought down by Navid's bow, and liberal quantities of wine, loosened his tongue.

'Klietas was a lamb to the slaughter,' he reflected. 'He was ecstatic at first, he and Haya masquerading as a married couple.'

'A married couple?'

He drank some wine. 'All part of the ruse to allow us to move around Cappadocia more easily. They slept in the same tent and he got her pregnant, the idiot.'

I was confused. 'Haya was pregnant?'

'She got rid of it, some sort of potion concocted in that Sanctuary frequented by the Amazons. It broke Klietas' heart. That is why he left Dura, majesty. He's just a simple lad, at heart.'

He looked at me. 'He's not cut out to be a killer.'

'Not like you, Bullus, eh?'

He shrugged. 'We all have to make use of the skills the gods have blessed us with, majesty.'

We talked until the campfire was a pile of grey ash and the eastern sky turned red and purple as the dawn came to the world once more. He told me about the killing of Governor Cenk, which allowed Gallia to alert Ctesiphon of the enemy kings gathering at Melitene, of how they returned to Cappadocia where a bedraggled Atrax stumbled across their camp. Of how he was killed and his head and those of his companions were severed and put on stakes.

'That upset Klietas, seeing as they were Medians like him.'

I was appalled. 'I can imagine.'

'Talib remembered a story told to him by Lord Byrd,' said Bullus, 'of how you had done the same in Cappadocia many years ago when your commander had been killed in battle.'

I was taken back to a time when I was barely out of my teens, when Bozan had been killed by the Romans in a battle. We had cremated his body on a pyre surrounded by the severed heads of our enemies mounted on wooden stakes. It seemed right then. I thought it gratuitous now.

He told me about the flogging of Azar and their capture after the murder of Glaphyra.

'I have seen some gruesome things on the battlefield, majesty, but when the Amazons and their young versions pounced on that old woman, it sent a shiver down my spine.

'I can imagine,' I shuddered.

He stretched out his legs. 'But I firmly believe the gods were with us, just as they were at Irbil. We were captured and then rescued by King Castus' bodyguard and hauled off to Vanadzor. Then a strange woman with large breasts saved us.'

I put down his words to the copious amounts of wine he had consumed.

'Why did you need saving?'

'King Castus wanted us dead.'

He told me why the dreadful Shamshir had been sent to search for Haya, thinking she would become his queen. But Castus found out about Klietas getting her pregnant and all thoughts of Haya becoming the Queen of Gordyene evaporated. And when Bullus described the busty woman, her male accomplice with pale skin and white hair, and their seemingly miraculous escape from Vanadzor, I knew he was telling the truth. I touched the lock of Gallia's hair around my neck.

'He's an ungrateful little bastard,' said Bullus. 'Castus, I mean. We saved him and his kingdom from invasion and he tried to kill us all.'

'He won a great victory at Melitene, Bullus.'

'Kewab won that battle, majesty, those that were there told me so. He's some talent, that one.'

'That he is, Bullus. That he is.'

After four days we arrived at Seleucia, the great city on the west bank of the Tigris. Its population was around eighty thousand, and in the long years of peace enjoyed by the empire since the Roman defeat at Carrhae, and notwithstanding the hurricane that had swept through Parthia when Tiridates had attempted to seize the high crown six years ago, it had become a flourishing urban centre. Seleucia was also strategically important, being the gateway to the east of the empire. It had been founded over two hundred and fifty years before by Seleucus I, called Nicator – 'The Victor' – one of the successors of Alexander of Macedon who had conquered the world. Seleucus had gone on to establish the Seleucid Empire and the city named after him had walls that resembled the shape of an eagle with outstretched wings. Towers stood at regular intervals along their length. The main road through the city ran from the central gatehouse in the western wall directly east to the stone bridge spanning the Tigris, which was about four hundred yards wide at this point.

The city's businesses were doing a brisk trade, the streets were teeming with people and the air was filled with the aromas of spices and incense. Seleucia was a Babylonian city, its most important temple dedicated to Marduk, the deity who guarded the kingdom and the city of the same name. I had Navid report to the guard commander at the western entrance to the city, who sent a rider to Ctesiphon to announce the King of Dura was approaching. Normally, he would have reported to the city governor first, but since the treachery of Governor Dagan, who had defected to Tiridates, Phraates had abolished the post.

An unending procession of camel trains passed over the bridge spanning the Tigris, its waters below dark, and quickly moving. When spring had passed and the furnace of summer arrived, those waters would slow and change colour to a muddy brown, the level of the river would drop, and a stench would rise as the Tigris struggled to flush away the city sewage dumped in the river. Ctesiphon had no such problems. Water was brought from the Tigris upstream of the river and effluent disposed of by sewage channels maintained by a small army of slaves. There were no shops, market stalls or drinking establishments within the white-faced walls of Ctesiphon. All occupants were strictly vetted as to their suitability to breathe the same air as King of Kings Phraates. Even the slaves tended to be young and attractive. The exception were the fierce Scythian axe men who surrounded the high king at all times. Under the command of Commander Adapa, the former leper now chief of Phraates' bodyguard, they were specifically chosen for their size, fierceness and dexterity with a double-bladed battle axe.

It was Adapa who met us at the entrance to the palace complex, a magnificent replica of Babylon's Ishtar Gate that made a great impression on Navid and his young horse archers. It was the first time they had visited Ctesiphon and its magnificence was a world apart from the austere practicality of Dura's Citadel. The entrance was a huge double gate decorated with over five hundred figures of bulls and dragons. Huge banners of the bull of Babylon and the eagle clutching a snake of Susiana flew from its ornate battlements where purple-uniformed archers and spearmen patrolled the walls.

We trotted through the gatehouse to be momentarily surprised by a fanfare of trumpets sounded by a line of mounted signallers, all wearing shimmering dragon-skin armour of overlapping polished silver scales stitched on to a hide vest.

The mounted lancers behind them also wore dragon-skin armour and burnished helmets sporting purple plumes, their round shields faced with leather painted purple and sporting a white bull motif. The purple pennants on their lances carried an identical symbol.

Adapa brought his sword up and then lowered it slowly to salute me.

'Greetings, King Pacorus, welcome to Ctesiphon.'

He fell in beside me as I nudged Horns forward and we headed up the Processional Way, a road some eighty feet in breadth paved with white limestone and red braccia slabs. There was not a weed to be seen anywhere along its length and all the slabs appeared pristine, having been washed at the beginning of the day and indeed on every day.

'It is good to see you Adapa, you look well.'

He did, a strapping man magnificently attired on an equally fine equine specimen, a huge purple saddlecloth covering its back, in the corners of which had been stitched golden bulls. Adapa was bare headed, his thick black hair falling to his shoulders, his handsome face cracking a smile.

'Certainly better than the first time we met, majesty.'

'Indeed. I trust the high king is in good spirits.'

'Excellent spirits, majesty, as is your daughter.'

Like the rest of Ctesiphon, the palace was a place of beauty, bright light and sweet fragrances. An immense building of white marble, gold, silver and ivory, it was filled with richly attired nobles and their wives, white-clad priests and palace officials striding around in soft slippers so they moved silently around the home of the high king. Phraates had assembled his court to welcome me to his palace, nobles and their wives dressed in a dazzling display of red, blue, orange and purple robes – always purple – with gold, silver, ivory and diamonds decorating their ears, heads and clothes.

'Don't let me down now,' I whispered to my left leg as I slowly made my way from the gold-leaf-covered doors of the throne room towards the dais where a beaming Phraates sat.

Adapa walked beside me, courtiers breaking into applause as we approached the high king. Phraates was in his prime now. He was still pale, but then a light skin was a sign of nobility, for only soldiers, commoners and slaves toiled under the searing Mesopotamian sun. But he did not look sickly as he did when he had been a teenager; rather, he appeared healthy and confident. And he wore the heavy gold crown of his mother lightly on his head. As ever, he held a golden arrow in his right hand, which he pointed at me.

'Bow your heads to Parthia's saviour.'

Claudia beside him on the dais smiled and dutifully obeyed, as did everyone else in the chamber save me, Phraates and Adapa. I had to admit I was surprised and rather embarrassed. But I managed to make it to the dais without hobbling, bowing my head to Phraates.

'Hail, great king.'

'It is good to see you, King Pacorus,' smiled Phraates, 'come. Join me in my study.'

He walked down from the dais and waited for me to catch up to him before striding to a door at the rear of the cavernous chamber. Applause was ringing in our ears as two burly Scythian axe men fell in behind Adapa, Claudia by his side, and two more opened the door to allow us to enter a wide corridor. The walls of the corridor had been decorated with a mural that illustrated Tiridates' rebellion. I slowed my walk to admire the fine detail.

'Ah, of course, this is the first time you have seen it,' beamed Phraates.

It was a beautiful artwork and as far removed from reality as was possible without becoming comedic. A handsome, brave Phraates was depicted fighting on the battlements of Seleucia, an episode I had no memory of, before being persuaded by a pleading Claudia to flee the burning city, which in fact had been untouched during the rebellion. His flight to the Alborz Mountains was depicted as a royal grand tour, complete with musicians and scribes, rather than a desperate escape with a group of beggars, which was the reality. The mural also showed Phraates immersing himself in a magical pool – it had been rather Adapa and his fellow lepers – after which he emerged surrounded by an ethereal light, making him look like a demigod. Finally, Phraates was shown leading his army in the great victory outside the walls of Ctesiphon, crushing the enemy with lightning bolts thrown from his hand. In reality, Phraates had taken no part in the Battle of Ctesiphon where King Silaces had died saving our lives in what had been a closely fought contest.

'A most stirring work, majesty,' I lied, wanting to scoff at its absurdity. I pointed at the depiction of Claudia, who was shown as a beautiful young woman with a voluptuous figure, lustrous black hair and wearing glittering armour.

'The artist has captured Claudia to a fault.'

She looked daggers at me as we left the corridor to enter the high king's study. The room dripped with gold, from the gold statuettes of a bull and eagle with a snake in its talons that sat on his large mahogany desk, to the ornate chairs with gold feet positioned behind and in front of it. Even the female slaves who served us wine in jewel-encrusted rhytons were wearing gold earrings. Clearly, Ctesiphon was enjoying a golden age in every sense of the term. The Scythian axe men took up position behind Phraates, Claudia seating herself beside me and Adapa beside her, which seemed overly familiar.

'You wrote in your letter to me,' began Phraates, 'that you wanted to discuss a most urgent matter regarding Satrap Kewab. Is he ill?'

'No, highness,' I said. 'The Romans have offered him the governorship of Egypt and I do not wish him to take the post.'

Phraates' brow creased. 'He is in your army, is he not? Cannot you order him to stay?'

'Technically, highness,' I replied, 'he left Dura's army when you appointed him Lord High General in the East and Satrap of Aria. After he was dismissed from those positions, I offered him a home in Dura. But the fact is, he is a satrap without a kingdom to administer and a general without an army to command.'

Phraates looked at me expectantly.

'I fail to see what this has to do with me?'

Ingratitude had always been a flaw in Phraates, but to lightly wash his hands of a man who had saved the eastern half of his empire and more besides was breath-taking. I was too old to engage in verbal sparring so got straight to the point.

'Kewab deserves a kingdom to rule, highness.'

Phraates took a sip of wine, stood and walked over to the large map of the Parthian Empire painted on wooden boards on the wall of his office. It had hung there since before the reign of his grandfather, also called Phraates, but on closer inspection I noticed it had been updated. The capital city of each kingdom was written in gold leaf, as were the rivers, mountain ranges, seas and the names of each kingdom. Phraates examined the map and gave me an evil leer.

'I could make Kewab king of Elymais, but that would entail killing Queen Cia and her young son Silaces.'

I was appalled. 'That would be unacceptable, highness.'

He walked back to his chair. 'I jest, King Pacorus, but the reality is there is no vacant throne for Kewab.'

'There is Mesene, highness.'

He stopped smiling. 'Mesene? My close friend Sanabares sits on Uruk's throne.'

'With respect, highness,' I began.

'No!' he said forcefully. 'I will hear no criticism of Sanabares. The throne was vacant following the tragic deaths of King Nergal and Queen Praxima. I appointed Sanabares and he retains my full support. Any move against him will be interpreted as a move against me.'

So, there it was. Despite plunging Mesene into chaos, Sanabares would remain king of that kingdom.

'King Pacorus,' smiled Phraates. 'It is unfortunate that a man of Kewab's talents is now superfluous to requirements, but such is the fate of warlords when peace spreads across the land. Kewab is Egyptian, is he not?'

I nodded. 'Yes, highness.'

'Then this offer of the Romans could be construed as a sign from the gods, is that not the case, Claudia?'

'The Romans are a godless people, highness,' said my daughter, 'but Kewab's fate lies away from Dura, it is true.'

We looked at her.

'Would you care to elaborate?' Phraates asked her.

'No,' she replied bluntly. She turned on me.

'Your plan is nonsensical, father. Why would Kewab, a man who has spent the last few years fighting the Kushans and then Rome's allies, be content to rule a poor kingdom plagued by marsh people?'

'He would restore peace between Parthian and the Ma'adan,' I replied.

'A man with Kewab's talents would go mad ruling a backwater such as Mesene,' scoffed Claudia. 'Sanabares is perfectly suited to rule Mesene.'

'Thank you, Claudia,' smiled Phraates.

'Sanabares is unimaginative, dull and a sycophant,' opined Claudia. 'I doubt he has had a thought of his own in his whole life. I doubt he even realises Mesene is a wretched kingdom full of snakes, scorpions, marshland and desert. He has a crown, and like a small child with a new toy, will sit quietly playing with it.'

Phraates was not amused. 'Just because you do not like him, Claudia, does not make him ill-suited to being King of Mesene.'

'On the contrary, highness,' said Claudia. 'I think your choice of making Sanabares ruler of Mesene was inspired.'

Phraates, well used to my daughter's sharp barbs, did not rise to the bait.

'If Kewab wishes to desert the king who has done so much for him,' the high king said to me, 'then so be it. Then again, he is Egyptian, so I suppose a part of him always wished to return to his homeland.'

Claudia suddenly stood, bowed her head to Phraates, gave me a smile and marched from the study, telling us all as she departed,

'Kewab will not be going to Egypt.'

I was not amused and called her back, to no avail.

'She is wont to do things like that,' said Phraates apologetically. 'The Scythian Sisters are a law unto themselves. And now, King Pacorus, I have things to attend to. Perhaps you could meet me in the Hall of Victory tomorrow.'

The banquet given in my honour that night was a sumptuous affair, the nobles and their wives packing the feasting hall that had a grand vaulted ceiling covered in gold leaf. I invited Navid and Bullus along, as they had never eaten in such grandeur. Navid hardly ate at all as far I could tell, whenever I looked at him seated on a separate table from the high table where I sat, he was either staring up at the ceiling in wonder or gawping at beautiful noblewomen with sultry faces and expensive jewellery. Bullus beside him, meanwhile, was devouring everything within reach.

The fare was splendid, including chicken, fish and even ostrich, the animals being raised in Babylon's royal park. For those who liked their meat with a 'bite', there were sausages made from spiced meat stuffed into animal intestines. And for those who avoided meat altogether, platters were piled high with bread, butter, yoghurt, boiled eggs and cheese, with side dishes of dates, olives, grapes, seeds and nuts. The usual oceans of beer, wine and pomegranate juice – a favourite among noblewomen – accompanied the food.

Phraates was in a very convivial mood, seated beside me until duty called and he rose to visit other tables. He had turned into the consummate high king, all smiles and cheer to those who remained loyal to him, an untiring enemy to those who opposed him. He had to be ruthless: retaining the allegiance of eighteen separate, self-governing kingdoms was no small task. Kings could easily be offended, as I was about to find out.

Claudia was not in attendance at the banquet, Adapa informing me she had a headache but would see me the next day. He too departed the meal early, blaming a delicate stomach for his premature departure. I was thus left alone on the top table, until a short man in a white robe cleared his throat behind me.

'My name is Macarius, majesty, and I am King of Kings Phraates' chief treasurer. I wonder if I may speak with you?'

I drank some more wine. 'Be my guest.'

He sat himself in the chair Adapa had vacated and smiled obsequiously at me. He was a scrawny specimen with sharp features and a small pointed beard that he began stroking as a slave placed a gold rhyton before him and filled it with wine. His brown eyes never left mine as he picked up the vessel and took a sip.

'I wanted to offer my congratulations to you, majesty.'

'For what?'

'I have taken a keen interest in the economic affairs of Dura for some time, majesty, and have been eager to convey my admiration for turning a barren wasteland into a thriving kingdom.'

I drank some wine. 'In truth, Treasurer Macarius, it was the vision, talents and labours of others who are not here this evening that have transformed my kingdom.'

'My minions inform me that once the lands around the city of Dura were but desert,' said Macarius. 'But now date palms and fields adorn the land, the kingdom turned fertile by an irrigation system that is the envy of the empire, if not the world.'

'Your minions have been busy,' I sighed.

'And they also inform me Dura is now an exporter of wheat, rather than an importer.'

How I wished I was sitting next to Bullus getting drunk.

'I believe so,' I said politely.

'Last but not least, majesty, our records show that more people live outside the city of Dura than within its walls, many more. Massively more, in fact.'

Why don't you go back to your records and minions, you tedious little man?

'The population of the kingdom has increased substantially, yes.'

He began tapping the table top with a finger, which I found immensely irritating. Tap, tap, tap. Then he stopped. His eyes narrowed.

'And yet, majesty, my records show that the annual tribute paid by the Kingdom of Dura has remained the same ever since you became King of Dura, some four decades ago.'

'So?'

He sipped at his rhyton. 'I think you will agree that the integrity of the empire depends on kingdoms paying their fair share of the annual tribute. Though I do not have the precise figures, I believe Dura owes Ctesiphon's treasury a substantial amount of gold as arrears. If I may be so bold…'

I did not mean to grab him by the scruff of the neck, nor did I wish to make a scene at a banquet that had been given in my honour. But his pompous, condescending words were the final straw. Gallia's manipulation of Klietas had rankled me, Kewab seemed destined to leave Dura, and Parthia, and no one seemed to care, and now some nonentity of a clerk was attempting to extort money from me. I dragged him to his feet.

'Listen to me, you jackal. If you think I am going to be lectured to by a man who has never held a sword in his hand you are sadly mistaken. Unlike at Ctesiphon, Dura's wealth is spent on its army, an army that has paid a high price in blood in defence of the empire.'

His eyes were bulging in terror and he was having difficulty breathing, making pained gasping sounds as my fingers tightened around his neck.

'I would rather throw gold into the Euphrates than send it here, to be wasted on statues, paintings and clothing worthless court officials.'

'King Pacorus, put down my treasurer at once.'

In my anger I had clean forgotten about the dozens of other guests in the hall, who now sat in silence, staring in horror at the unbecoming spectacle unfolding at the top table. The babble of convivial conversation had died and an angry Phraates stormed over to where I held Macarius. I released the treasurer, who gasped for air and collapsed into his chair.

Phraates turned to face the guests.

'Everyone out.'

They did not delay in leaving, the hall filling with the scraping of chairs as the high king's courtiers scurried back to their grandiose homes. Scythian axe men ushered them on their way, closing the doors to the chamber after the last had departed.

Phraates glowered at me. 'I am waiting.'

I pointed at Macarius. 'This wretch attempted to extort gold from me, highness. I took exception to his tone.'

Phraates frowned and glared at Macarius. 'Well?'

'A misunderstanding, highness,' he babbled. 'I meant no offence.'

'Leave our presence,' ordered Phraates.

He bowed and hurried away, leaving me alone with the high king. Phraates walked slowly to the end of the table, around it and sauntered to his chair, slowly lowering himself into it. He clicked his fingers to indicate slaves should bring him wine. He pointed at my chair.

'Sit down, King Pacorus.'

I did so.

'Well, that was one way to bring the evening to a close. I told Macarius Dura's tribute would not be amended until after your reign had ended.'

'I will not be told by a book keeper what to do,' I protested.

He nodded. 'But is that not what you have fought for, King Pacorus, for Parthia to be governed by laws instead of men wielding swords, to be a place where commerce and peace have replaced war and bloodshed?'

He was right, and he knew he was right, which did nothing to sweeten my humour.

'I do not take kindly to being lectured to by a petty minded official, highness.'

'Macarius is very much like you, King Pacorus.'

'He is nothing like me,' I insisted.

Phraates smiled. He was enjoying himself.

'Oh, but he is, King Pacorus. Just as you believe individuals should be treated fairly and without prejudice, so Macarius believes the kingdoms of the empire should be accorded fair and equal treatment. He believes Dura paying less than it should with regard to its annual tribute is unfair to other kingdoms.'

'As I told him, highness, the wealth of Dura is spent on its army, which keeps Parthia safe. Whereas if it was sent here.'

I looked up at the gold ceiling.

'It would be spent according to the wishes of the high king,' he said forcefully, 'according to custom, which you have also fought for so long to preserve. We are all servants of Parthia, King Pacorus, its gods, laws, customs and history.'

He rose from his chair and sighed. 'Men should be free to go about their business in peace, should they not?'

'They should, highness.'

'If a great warlord can choke a man to death in public, just because he has taken offence at the truth spoken to him, what does this say of Parthia? It says it is a lawless place, an abode of barbarians and savagery. The old King Pacorus would have been appalled at such a notion.

'I will see you in the Hall of Victory tomorrow.'

Suitably chastened, I slunk away to my bedchamber. Phraates was right, I had behaved like a brute. But more than that, as I lay awake staring up at the ceiling that night, a flickering oil lamp beside my bed, I realised my time had passed. All my life I had fought for a Parthia that would be free and just and that notion had become a reality. It was a new age, but I was a relic of a past era: a more troubled, violent time where kings had fallen to my sword. I heard the mocking laughter of Porus, Chosroes, Narses and Mithridates. Had I really become everything I despised?

I received little sympathy the next morning when I met Claudia in the palace's private garden, though game park would have been a more accurate description. The well-watered lawns were bisected by well-tended paths, date palms, cypress trees and rose bushes. Large ponds filled with goldfish reflected the palace to symbolise the unity of heaven and earth, to tie the residence of the high king to the realm of the gods above. Fountains filled the garden with the pleasant and calming sound of running water. Magnificent peacocks wandered freely on the lawns; white-clad slaves equipped with silver dustpans waiting to scoop up their dung with small brushes.

Those privileged to walk in the high king's garden led cheetahs on silver leads, or at least their slaves did, walking a few paces behind their masters and mistresses to safeguard them should the beasts decide to exercise their jaws and claws. White gazebos provided shade and rest for guests, one of which I was directed to by the slave who had carried a message from my daughter to meet her in the garden. I found Claudia reclining on a couch with golden leonine feet, two strapping Scythian axe men standing guard outside the gazebo. I passed one, who bowed his head.

'Ah, Hercules himself,' smiled Claudia.

I sat on the couch opposite her. 'Hercules?'

'A figure from Greek mythology, father, who reportedly strangled two snakes sent by a goddess to kill him when an infant, though you had your hands around the neck of only one snake.'

I felt myself blushing. 'I regret doing so.'

'The court will be talking about it for weeks, how the normally moralistic King of Dura disgraced himself in the presence of the high king. I did not think you cared so much about Satrap Kewab.'

'It was nothing to do with Kewab,' I replied.

'Then what?'

'I take exception to anyone trying to extort money from me. Ctesiphon has enough gold.'

'I hope the rest of your mission is more successful, father.'

She gave me an evil smirk.

'Your young officer of horse archers was very forthcoming with information when I cornered him earlier. You shouldn't blame him. I threatened to turn his seed into poison if he lied to a Scythian Sister.'

'You can't help yourself, can you.'

'Why waste your time on a poor farmer who has turned his back on the chance of prosperity? He sounds like an imbecile.'

'He saved my life,' I told her.

'You feel you are in his debt; obligated to him?'

'I owe him a second chance.'

'Mother told me about her wraiths. How marvellous, and how beneficial to Parthia.'

'I do not approve of her assassins.'

'Naturally. You prefer to kill your enemies face-to-face, on the battlefield.'

'It is more honourable.'

She emitted a low cackle. 'Spoken like a true noble, who views war as a sport that is to be conducted according to strict rules and regulations. What's that?'

She pointed to the dagger given to me by Agrippa, which was fastened to my sword belt.

'A gift from a Roman guest we were entertaining at Dura, a very important Roman, I might add.'

She pulled out a necklace from under her black robe and pointed it at me.

'Are you going to turn my seed into poison as well?'

She raised an eyebrow at me. 'Your days of impregnating women are long gone father. This is a charm in the shape of a centaur, a human-headed horse. It is an ancient Scythian symbol representing power and invincibility. You should not bring the symbols of the enemy to Ctesiphon.'

'It is just a dagger.'

'No, father. It is a talisman and it will seek to draw whoever wears it to Rome and its centres of power.'

I rolled my eyes. 'You see conspiracies everywhere.'

She leaned forward. 'When you live at Ctesiphon, father, you learn to sleep with one eye open.'

'I thought you had the ear of Phraates himself.'

'He trusts no one, likes no one and takes advice and counsel when it suits him. These are the attributes of an excellent high king.'

'I am meeting him in the Hall of Victory later.'

'He wants your permission to return the Roman eagles to their former owners.'

I was surprised. 'He does not need my permission to do anything.'

'He is not devoid of diplomatic or political skills, and he does respect those who have served the empire well. Especially you, father.'

'Me?'

'You were the one who argued he should be high king following the death of Orodes, and who put him back on the throne when he lost it to Tiridates. And now that you have retired from military affairs, you are no longer the spectre in whose shadow Phraates had to linger.'

It was true I had lobbied hard on Phraates' behalf, partly because I believed he was the natural choice, being the son of Orodes, but mostly out of loyalty to my dead friend and his wife. Both Gallia and I had been immensely fond of Orodes and Axsen, and we were determined to keep their legacy alive. All in all, Phraates had not turned out to be a bad high king.

I stayed and chatted with Claudia for a while, about how Eszter and Dalir were faring, would Salar and Isabella have any more children, and when would Dura be seeing here again.

'I'm happy here,' she told me, 'in as much as anyone can be happy in this world.'

'Do you ever get lonely?'

'No,' she answered firmly.

I could not imagine her making friends with any of the over-painted noblewomen who competed with the royal peacocks for attention, nor their husbands. And being the adviser of Phraates would naturally lead to her being the rival of others who desired that position. But she did seem happy and remarkably untroubled. Perhaps she had the friendship of a high priest of one of the temples located with the palace complex. I hoped so.

The Hall of Victory was also a temple of sorts, one dedicated to that most elusive and fleeting of deities: military triumph. Later, after I had left Claudia, I made my way there after receiving a summons from Phraates. It was a modest-sized limestone building constructed on a stone plinth to the rear of the palace, surrounded by a beautifully dressed stone wall and accessed via a single wooden gate. The wall was high so no one could see into the hall's compound. It had been constructed to resemble a Greek temple. Rectangular in shape, it was flanked by rows of white marble columns and accessed by a vestibule. This led to the sanctuary where the eight captured Roman eagles resided, each one mounted on its own sandstone plinth. In the centre of the hall stood a bronze statue of the god Marduk, the deity of Babylon, and around the walls stood Babylonian guards in their purple leggings and tunics.

The collection had been laid out tastefully and took full advantage of the sun's rays flooding through the windows immediately below the roof of wooden beams and terracotta tiles. The stone plinths had been positioned so they were bathed in sunlight, the gold and silver eagles glinting and seemingly moving to give the impression of live birds as the sun traversed the sky.

Phraates was waiting for me at the entrance, two large Scythian axe men standing behind him. He was not much smaller than they, a testament to him growing into the role of high king in every way. He wore a lavish purple silk robe fastened at the waist by a gold belt, his golden arrow in his right hand and a luxurious pair of red leather boots on his feet. Decorated with silver bulls, they had soft leather uppers and were secured by wide straps which passed under the foot and crisscrossed up the lower leg.

The Babylonian guards at the entrance snapped their spears to their bodies as we passed them, entering the hall that was filled with the soothing aroma of *kyphi*, an incense containing frankincense, myrrh, saffron, cinnamon and cassia. The incense was burned in the hall every day to both cleanse the captured Roman standards of any evil and to make the interior pleasing to Marduk and hopefully garner his blessings. Few were allowed into the hall, Phraates restricting entry to all save himself and those who had had a hand in capturing the trophies on display.

We stood in silence for a few moments, staring at the standards. I smiled when I saw that the guards in the chamber were wearing soft shoes so as to make as little sound as possible when they took up station and were relieved. The Hall of Victory was certainly a place of quiet reflection, unlike the occasions on which they were captured.

'Twenty-nine years ago,' I said softly.

Phraates gave me a quizzical look.

'The Battle of Carrhae, highness,' I said, 'it was twenty-nine years ago. The eagles have not aged one bit. If only I could say the same about myself.'

'In Roman eyes, the eagle is associated with their chief god Jupiter,' he said, 'the God of Victory, so-called. And yet if he is so powerful, why is it that his emblems adorn this hall?'

'Crassus was vain and foolhardy, highness. The gods cannot help those who are blind to reason and common sense.'

He gave me a sideways glance. 'The negotiations with the Romans are going well, King Pacorus. Next year I should have my son back, and the Romans will have their eagles. I hope you do not mind?'

I was shocked by the question. Phraates had never been a considerate person, concerning himself only with his own ambitions. He had always been callous and aloof. Perhaps he was mellowing.

'Why should I mind, highness? If returning these totems ensures you get your son back and cements peace between Parthia and Rome, then it is a small price to pay.'

In truth, I seldom thought about the eagles, though memories of those who had helped me capture them often filled my mind. As I breathed in the incense, I remember Surena, the headstrong marsh boy who rose to win the hand of an Amazon in marriage and a kingdom, only for his wife and child to be taken from him in childbirth, and the subsequent bitterness that engulfed him costing him his life and his kingdom. I remembered Vagharsh, my standard bearer, being killed at Carrhae by Parthian arrows in a cruel accident; and Lucius Domitus, my friend and commander of Dura's army who fell before the walls of Hatra before we met Crassus at Carrhae. All long gone. All greatly missed. My head dropped.

'Are you ill?' asked Phraates with concern.

'No, highness,' I said, 'just weary.'

'Do you wish to sit?'

I smiled. 'The weariness I speak of will not be cured by sitting, highness. When you reach my age, you will understand.'

I was stunned when he laid a hand on my shoulder.

'I can see the long years of service to Parthia have taken a mental and physical toll on you, King Pacorus. If it is any consolation, you have the thanks and respect of its high king always.'

It was the first time he had spoken to me in such a manner ever and I was genuinely touched. I honestly believed Phraates had become a more rounded individual who seemed to have developed a conscience.

We walked from the hall into the sunlight as companions of a sort, two men linked by a common concern for the welfare of the empire and a bond of mutual respect. Phraates beckoned over a Scythian brute who was holding something in his right hand, which was dripping something on to the white stone slabs. The Scythian halted and held up what he was holding for Phraates to see. I screwed up my face in horror as I beheld the severed head of Macarius, eyes bulging from their sockets grotesquely. Phraates smiled at the hideous spectacle.

'The day has not yet arrived, King Pacorus, when, as you succinctly put it, a minion can hector the saviour of Parthia in my own palace. There are a hundred men who can be chief treasurer. There is only one King Pacorus of Dura.'

Phraates looked up at the sky.

'It is going to be a beautiful day.'

He frowned at the piece of offal.

'Take it away, it's disgusting.'

I left Ctesiphon the next day.

Chapter 4

When I was a boy, people spoke admiringly of the Kingdom of Hatra being the shield that guarded the western frontier of the Parthian Empire. But my father did not guard the empire alone. He had formed an alliance with other kingdoms to ensure Parthia's territorial integrity: Gordyene, Media and Atropaiene. I did not realise it at the time, but I walked among giants in my youth, men of iron and honour who ruled their kingdoms with justice and firmness. The peace they forged I took for granted, we all did, which left us unprepared for the darkness that descended on the empire when they departed the stage. They were all gone now: Varaz of Hatra, Balas of Gordyene, Aschek of Atropaiene and Farhad of Media.

Media. How that kingdom had suffered in the aftermath of Farad's death. The gods had blessed Media with an abundance of underground water and natural springs, plus streams that flowed from the Zagros Mountains to the east and the annual rains that soaked the ground. The result was fertile soil in which it was possible to grow a wide variety of crops: barley, wheat, flax, onions figs, grapes, turnips, oats, lentils, dates, pomegranates and olives. Media was a beautiful shade of green during the winter and spring, turning to bronze as the sun ripened crops in the fields in the summer and autumn. The multitude of villages clustered around springs and beside streams grew mostly barley, a valuable food source that could be ground down into flour to make bread, made into soups or fermented and turned into beer. They also kept sheep and goats, which fed on the stubble of the wheat and barley fields in late summer and autumn. Villages also possessed their own orchards, vineyards and small gardens. Media was so fertile that it was not only able to feed itself, but also exported food, wine and beer to other kingdoms, earning it the title of 'breadbasket of the empire'.

It was now the end of spring and as we rode through southern Media the landscape resembled a patchwork of different colours. There were squares of bare earth around some villages, well-tended fields full of wheat and barley around others. Some settlements were teeming with adults and children; others appeared empty. Some *were* empty, their mud-brick homes abandoned, their fields and orchards overgrown with weeds.

'I am surprised King Akmon allows such disrepair in his kingdom,' sniffed Navid when we passed by a ghost village.

He was riding on my right side, Bullus on my left, as we trotted at the head of our small column. Before I left Ctesiphon I had penned a short missive to Akmon informing him I would be paying him and Lusin a flying visit, though there was no guarantee he would be in residence. But I was sure Lusin would be and I was looking forward to seeing their young son, whom they had named Spartacus.

'How much do you know about Media?' I asked him.

'Its rulers are King Akmon and Queen Lusin, majesty, the king being the son of the late King Spartacus of Gordyene and

Queen Rasha, and the grandson of your brother, King Gafarn of Hatra.'

'Very good, Navid. But do you know anything about its recent history?'

His brow creased in concentration. 'I know you and the queen took part in the defence of Irbil three years ago, majesty, and your army marched to its relief and afterwards defeated the rebel army of Prince Atrax on the Diyana Plain. That was a glorious day.'

I thought of the body of Rasha laid out afterwards and the grief that engulfed me and Gallia at her loss.

'It was part of the tragedy that is modern Media, Navid,' I told him.

I made a sweeping movement with my arm.

'When I was your age, or thereabouts, this land was ruled by a great king named Farhad, who was a loyal servant of the empire. He was followed by another great king, a man I was proud to call friend by the name of Atrax.'

I heard Navid take a sharp intake of breath. 'Atrax, majesty?'

'Not the one we fought on the Diyana Plain,' said Bullus.

'King Atrax was his grandfather,' I said, 'who was sadly killed fighting the Armenians and Romans during the Phraaspa campaign over ten years ago.'

'Twelve years ago, majesty,' Bullus corrected me. 'I remember it well. Coldest campaign I ever fought in.'

'That campaign was a disaster for Media,' I said morosely, 'for after the death of Atrax his wife, my sister, eaten up with bitterness and resentment, manoeuvred Media into an alliance with the Roman general Mark Antony, which ultimately led to the near ruin of this kingdom.'

'Your sister ruled Media, majesty?' enquired Navid.

'Yes,' I answered, 'though through her son, King Darius, a weak individual who fathered Prince Atrax and two daughters, whose names escape me. But it all came down to my sister, Aliyeh, hating me and doing everything in her power to bring me down.'

'Why did she hate you, majesty?' asked Navid.

'That's none of your business, boy,' snapped Bullus.

'The truth is the business of everyone, Bullus,' I said. 'I will tell you why, Navid. Media is one of the oldest kingdoms in the empire, a place of tradition, ancient customs and strict protocol. That is why the marriage of a princess of Hatra and a prince of Media was such a good match.'

Navid was confused. 'But *you* were a prince of Hatra, majesty.'

'Ah, but I sullied my home and family name by allowing myself to become a Roman slave, you see. Worse, I had the temerity to return from slavery with a former slave who became my wife. In Aliyeh's eyes it went from bad to worse when I became king of the outlaw Kingdom of Dura. But what really aroused her loathing of me was allowing my friends Gafarn and

Diana to become King and Queen of Hatra, *the* most traditional kingdom in all Parthia.'

'The gods smile on those two kingdoms,' said Bullus. 'If you and the queen were not meant to rule Dura, majesty, then the kingdom would not have prospered as it has over the years. The same goes for Hatra, as well.'

'Which galled my sister even more,' I chuckled. 'But the alliance she forged with Mark Antony brought ruin on Media. The high king and the *triumvir* fought a battle outside Irbil, which would have been a Roman victory had it not have been for the arrival of King Spartacus and the army of Gordyene.'

'King Spartacus saved Media,' said Navid.

'King Spartacus raped Media,' I said bitterly. 'He killed thousands of Medians at the Battle of Mepsila eight years ago, afterwards seizing northern Media, and during Tiridates' rebellion he again invaded Media to besiege Irbil, killing more Medians in the process. He was a plague on this kingdom.'

Navid was shocked by my declaration but I was unrepentant. For all his talents, Spartacus had indeed raped Media. I halted Horns and pointed at the land.

'Villages and farms are deserted because their occupants are either dead or were captured and sold as slaves. That is the reality of war, Navid. It is a curse that infects mankind and I pray to Shamash that one day a cure will be found.'

He did not understand. How could he? He was young and enthused with the aura of invincibility, steeped in the military tradition of Dura, whose army had never lost a battle, whose battle honours stretched back over four decades. Every new legionary, horse archer and cataphract was shown the Staff of Victory and the silver discs decorating it, each one commemorating a victory won by the army they were joining. An army beloved of the gods, who had gifted its king a sacred banner that never aged and could not be damaged by mortal weapons. Or so Duran mythology would have it.

'It will take many years before Media recovers,' I added. 'If it ever does.'

Some ten miles from Irbil we were met by a detachment of cataphracts led by General Joro, the commander of Media's army. In his sixties, he had first served under Farhad and then Atrax, managing to keep his head as he served under Darius and then, for a brief while, Atrax. Joro was a traditionalist and a stickler for rules and regulations. He never asked me why I was travelling to Irbil, raised the subject of my sister or the dire events that had been inflicted on his kingdom. A huge black banner emblazoned with a silver dragon motif billowed behind him as he halted his horse and bowed his head to me. I saw his blue eyes searching for my own banner.

'I left it and the Amazons behind in Dura.'

'Majesty?'

'My banner. Ride with me, Joro.'

He enquired about Gallia and Dura as we trotted north, the fields either side of the dirt road full of ripening crops and tended by dozens of men and women as we neared the capital. Clearly the area around Irbil was prospering, even if the outlying districts were not. Joro stared directly ahead, speaking only when requested to do so, though his tone was both friendly and forthcoming.

'The king and queen are well?'

'Very well, majesty. The queen is pregnant.'

I was pleased. 'That is good news. Perhaps she will have a girl this time. How fares the kingdom?'

'Irbil prospers, majesty, but the kingdom still carries the scars of the conflicts that have plagued it these past few years. Some say it will take ten years for it to fully recover. Others say longer than that.'

The kingdom may have been suffering but Irbil was bustling. It had always been a major city stretching back to Assyrian times some two thousand years ago. Once the whole city had been surrounded by a wall, but until recently the hundreds of buildings circling the stone mound on which the citadel stood had been undefended. That had now changed, and all the city's buildings were now protected by a massive mud-brick wall that was as yet to be completed.

I felt my chest swell with pride when I saw the brown brick wall that rose above the deep, wide ditch in front of it – all the vision of Dura's quartermaster general, Lucius Varsas, who had been seconded to King Akmon in a desperate effort to strengthen his rule. That rule had been sorely tested when Irbil had been besieged by Prince Atrax, but he and the city had held and now it had arisen to become a great stronghold.

It took us a while to move from the city's southern gatehouse, a massive four-storey structure with arrow slits in each storey and topped with a fighting platform to hold more archers and also slingers and javelineers. The thick wooden gates were reinforced with metal braces and panels as a defence against battering rams. The walls either side of the gatehouse were high and thick, with square towers at regular intervals along their length. Most of the towers were still under construction, being encased in wooden scaffolding and worked on by a small army of labourers.

Inside the city, the streets were thronged with people, shops were doing a brisk trade and all the streets and buildings I saw as we moved slowly towards the citadel were clean and well maintained. The hubbub of the city contrasted sharply with the quiet and calm of the citadel, positioned atop a stone mound and reached via a long ramp cut into it on its southern side. A large dragon banner hung from the citadel's gatehouse, which gave access to a sanctuary of order, royalty and nobility. A quarter of a mile in diameter, only the king and queen, their most trusted nobles and their families, royal bodyguards, and the priests who served in its temples lived in the citadel. And slaves, of course, the human livestock that ensured the lives of the rich and privileged and the daily routines of the temples were able to function smoothly.

Akmon and an obviously pregnant Lusin greeted me in the palace courtyard, the queen looking radiant, her chestnut curls shining in the sunlight. She smiled at me after I had eased myself from the saddle, a slave rushing forward to take Horns' reins and lead him to the stables. Trumpeters standing in front of the palace guard – soldiers looking remarkably like Roman legionaries, though with grey leggings and blue tunics – sounded a fanfare as Akmon and his queen walked forward and tipped their heads to me. Lusin threaded an arm in mine.

'How is the leg, majesty?' she smiled.

'Like me, old and failing. Congratulations by the way, on being pregnant, I mean.'

She kissed me on the cheek. 'Nonsense, you have many years left in you. And thank you. Akmon wants another boy but I am hoping for a girl.'

'That is what I pray for.'

'Irbil welcomes you, lord,' said Akmon sternly.

'It is good to see you,' I told him.

The oldest son of Spartacus looked very kingly in his shining scale-armour cuirass, blue tunic and gold crown. He wore his dead father's sword at his hip, a beautiful weapon that had been forged in Hatra, its pommel in the shape of a horse's head providing a clue as to its provenance. Akmon looked past me when he spotted an old acquaintance.

'Centurion Bullus. Fate seems to keep bringing you back to Media. I am glad to see you after the drama of our last encounter.'

Bullus saluted the king. 'Good to see you, majesty.'

There was a potentially awkward moment when Vahan, brother to Lusin, made an appearance after we had entered the palace, the darkly handsome Armenian avoiding my eyes as he presented himself to me. He had been captured at the Araxes when Spartacus had deceived me and Gafarn into invading Armenia. I had sent him south to Irbil where I knew he would be out of the clutches of a vengeful Spartacus, which had probably saved his life. Tall like Akmon, he had broader shoulders and darker eyes. I slapped him on the arm.

'I am glad we are meeting again under happier circumstances.' I told him. 'How do you like being an uncle?'

Now he looked into my eyes. 'It is very agreeable, majesty. I try to visit Irbil when I can.'

'Then let's take a look at your cousin, then.'

Lusin plucked her son from his cot and handed him to me to hold, the infant giving me a curious look before bursting into tears. The great-grandson of the man I had followed in Italy looked much the same as all babies, but he had a powerful set of lungs, no malformed limbs and sparkling blue eyes. He also had no control over his bowel movements.

'I think he needs changing,' I said.

Lusin took him and handed him to a nurse, who hurried away to wash and change the young prince.

'So, lord,' said Akmon, 'what brings you to Irbil?'

Irbil's palace of necessity was more compact than the sprawling excess of Ctesiphon, perched as it was atop the mound that made it virtually impregnable. Fresh, cool water came from deep in the earth to supply it and the whole citadel, and its height meant the occupants were spared the noxious fumes produced by thousands of people and animals packed into the buildings and streets surrounding it below.

I recounted the tale of Klietas as I ate with Akmon, Lusin and Vahan in one of the king's private rooms to the rear of the banqueting hall, a pleasant, intimate affair where we sat in huge wicker chairs filled with cushions and rested our feet on padded footstools. Oil lamps hung from chandeliers and slaves attended to our every whim.

'I have to tell you, lord,' said Akmon glumly, 'I hold out little hope for your former squire. I am ashamed to say the north of my kingdom has become a wasteland, bereft of law and order, and indeed people.'

I sipped at my silver rhyton, the vessel shaped to resemble a crouching dragon.

'Roman, Parthian and Armenian armies have done much damage to your kingdom, Akmon. It will take time to heal the damage.'

'It is not only damage to the land, King Pacorus,' said Lusin. 'Media has lost too many sons in the recent wars. The land is empty because there is a shortage of people to work it, especially in the north.'

She looked at her husband. 'If your brother had paid you the gold he promised, then we could have used it to re-populate the north.'

'Gold?' I enquired.

Akmon rolled his grey eyes. 'As part of the negotiations that followed my brother's victory at Melitene, Cappadocia,

Pontus and Galatia agreed to pay a combined total of twenty thousand talents of gold to Gordyene.'

'Yes, I heard,' I said.

'Not only that,' continued Akmon, holding out his rhyton to be refilled. 'Armenia also agreed to pay reparations to Gordyene for taking part in the campaign.'

'King Artaxias paid the amount in full, I saw the wagons leave Artaxata,' said Vahan.

'Five thousand talents of gold,' Lusin told me, 'which was supposed to be paid to Media, which aided Gordyene in its war.'

'So where is it?' I asked naively.

Lusin's lush lips tightened. 'In Gordyene's vaults, I have no doubt. King Castus is greedy. That gold could have been used to rebuild Media, to attract farmers to the kingdom to work the land.'

'Have you asked your brother for the gold?' I probed Akmon.

Another roll of the royal eyes. 'My enquiries have met with a deafening silence, lord.'

One hundred and fifty tons of gold – five thousand talents – was a kingly sum and would act as a great incentive to lure farmers to Media. Akmon was staring into his rhyton and I could see Lusin was fuming, while Vahan appeared embarrassed.

'Have the Aorsi refrained from raiding your homeland?' I asked Lusin's brother.

'Yes, majesty, the border is, for the moment, quiet.'

'That is something,' I said.

'King Artaxias does not trust Gordyene,' he told me.

'With good reason,' I agreed.

'He is seeking an alliance with the Romans, lord,' said Vahan.

My ears pricked up. Armenia had once been a close ally of Rome, but Mark Antony seizing the family of Artaxias before sending them off to their deaths in Alexandria, plus his subsequent annexation of Armenia, had put paid to that. Artaxias had fled to Ctesiphon to seek sanctuary, after which he and Phraates had become allies.

Vahan had obviously had his rhyton refreshed a number of times, for the wine lubricated his tongue.

'King Artaxias feels King of Kings Phraates has done nothing to rein in the excesses of Gordyene, but rather has encouraged them. The Roman ambassador to Pontus convinced my king to join the coalition against Gordyene, unwisely it turned out.'

'Indeed,' I agreed.

Vahan emptied his rhyton. 'But Rome has extended the hand of friendship to Armenia, majesty, and my king is inclined to take it. Armenia has lost many sons of late.'

'If the Aorsi refrain from their cross-border raids, will Armenia respect Parthia's northern borders?' I enquired.

'Yes, majesty,' Vahan replied instantly. 'Armenia craves peace and stability.'

'As do we all, brother,' added Lusin.

Vahan clicked his fingers to attract the attention of a nearby slave holding a wine jug, watching the red liquid being poured into his rhyton.

'Pontus, Cappadocia and Galatia have been laid low by Parthia, and where there was once law and justice, anarchy and chaos rule.'

'Perhaps you should not drink any more, brother,' advised Lusin.

Vahan was not listening. 'The Roman ambassador himself, along with the commander of Polemon's palace guard, General Tullus, were butchered in the hills of Pontus last year. There is now rebellion in Pontus where there was once peace. And trouble has spread to Armenia like a pestilence. The Sarmatians have overrun large parts of the kingdom along the western shore of the Caspian Sea.'

He continued to drink until he fell into a semi-conscious state, after which slaves carried him to his bedchamber.

'I must apologise for my brother, lord,' said Lusin.

'We are all sick of war, Lusin,' I told her.

Akmon was shocked. 'A strange thing for Parthia's greatest general to say, lord. I have heard men say your presence on the battlefield is worth twenty thousand soldiers.'

I laughed fit to burst. 'Whoever told you that has never been on a battlefield. You yourself have seen the horror, the confusion, inhaled the stench of…'

I saw the delightful Lusin sitting in her chair and had no wish to upset her.

'My biggest regret is taking Dura's army into Armenia and then Pontus, where it had no business being. It was forged as an instrument of defence, not aggression, and I will have to account for the actions I took in a foreign war.'

'You are too hard on yourself, lord,' smiled Lusin.

'If, in some court of the immortals, you are ever judged, lord,' said Akmon, 'those called to your defence will be many, including the King and Queen of Media. Without you and Queen Gallia, Prince Atrax would have taken this city and executed us both.'

Lusin rose, walked over and embraced me. 'We love you and Queen Gallia.'

I felt my eyes moisten. 'That is very generous of you, Lusin.'

'I regret having one of the queen's women flogged, lord,' said Akmon, 'but I was placed in an impossible position…'

I held up a hand to him, Bullus having explained the incident of Azar being flogged.

'She got off lightly, and I would have done the same. The whole affair left a bad taste in my mouth.'

'I'm glad Atrax is dead,' said Lusin. 'I am envious of the Amazons, lord, and they and their queen will always be welcome in Media. Is that not so, Akmon?'

Her shining brown eyes bored into him.

'Yes, yes,' he mumbled unenthusiastically. 'But I think you go on a futile journey, lord. No news comes from the north of my kingdom. Even the post stations lie broken and abandoned. It is the abode of ghosts, and I fear Klietas might now be one.'

To convince me to abandon my search, the next day Akmon introduced me to his royal archivist, a diminutive individual with a wispy beard and long fingers, who smelt of musty old parchments. His aroma was appropriate for he inhabited a world of papyrus scrolls stacked in row upon row of pigeon holes in the palace library. His name was Dilshad, which meant 'happy heart', but he was curt to the point of rudeness. He was all smiles and deference when Akmon was explaining to him I was about to travel to the north of the kingdom and did I have any information on the village of Vazneh, but when the king left his demeanour changed like the weather on a windy day.

'Follow me,' he said curtly, scuttling away down a dimly lit corridor leading to a large room filled with rows of shelves holding papyrus scrolls.

'Don't touch anything,' he snapped, muttering under his breath, suddenly stopping at the end of a row of shelves and turning to me.

'Can your majesty inform me of the name of the lord who rules the land this village you are looking for is situated in?'

'I cannot,' I said, holding out a piece of papyrus on which the name of the village was written. 'But I know the name of the village.'

Dilshad huffed dismissively. 'Does your majesty know how many villages there are in the Kingdom of Media?'

'Not off the top of my head, no.'

A groan. 'Hundreds, which makes giving me its name meaningless.'

'It is ten miles south of the great lake,' I stressed, beginning to lose my patience.

A flicker of interest. 'Ah, that will narrow down the options. Please follow me.'

Off he scuttled again, disappearing down another row of shelves holding what looked like hundreds of papyrus scrolls. I followed, the end of my scabbard banging against a desk leg of a scholar-librarian writing on papyrus. He gave me a murderous look as ink spilled on the papyrus.

'Have a care,' hissed Dilshad.

The library was a strange place, a building with small windows cut high in the walls to allow some light to enter, though not enough to read without the aid of an oil lamp. The subdued lighting was to preserve the scrolls and make the room cooler than if it had been exposed to large amounts of sunlight. But oil lamps were dangerous in a hall containing wooden shelving and thousands of bone-dry papyrus scrolls, and so attendants patrolled the desks at which scholars and scribes worked, keeping a close eye out for any dangers.

'Bring me light,' Dilshad said to one such attendant, who rushed off to do his master's bidding.

'Here we are,' said the chief librarian, pulling a scroll from a shelf.

He walked to a nearby empty desk and sat at it, looking up at me when I casually went to pluck a scroll from its resting place.

'Do not touch anything,' he hissed.

The attendant returned with an oil lamp and placed it on the desk. Dilshad was still muttering to himself as he unrolled the scroll. Each scroll was identical, the papyrus being rolled around a winding boss, the text becoming visible to the reader as he wound the scroll from right to left, as Dilshad did now. The text was organised in columns, each scroll containing around fifteen hundred lines of handwritten text. For ease of reference, each scroll had a parchment ticket glued to its edge, which stuck out when the scroll was laid flat and which recorded what it contained.

'Yes, yes,' said Dilshad to himself, peering at a column of text. 'There, Vazneh.'

I moved closer to examine the text and saw Vazneh listed.

'The village belongs to Lord Nerseh, or used to.'

'Used to?' I queried.

Dilshad pointed to a black cross against the lord's name.

'He is dead, majesty, most probably killed in the Battle of Mepsila. I have a list of casualties if you wish to see it.'

'That will not be necessary. Is there a map of Lord Nerseh's lands?'

He carefully rolled up the scroll and looked up at me.

'There is, though you may not take it out of the library. I will have a copy made for you.'

He rose and stepped across to the shelf to replace the scroll.

'How long will that take?' I asked.

'As long as takes,' he answered testily, shaking his head as he walked away with the oil lamp.

I retraced my steps, absently glancing left and right at ancient and new scrolls, the history of the Kingdom of Media gathered in one place. Dura had the minutes of the weekly royal council meetings and the accounts of the kingdom, but nothing to compare to the records stored in this library. I shuddered when I thought of King Spartacus capturing such a place, and I was glad I, and Gafarn, had prevented him from capturing Irbil in the aftermath of the Battle of Mepsila.

'If someone had told me that one day I would find the King of Dura in Irbil's library, I would have scoffed at the idea. But here you are, a retired warlord seeking knowledge.'

I recognised the voice and saw a huddled figure sitting at a desk, poring over a scroll. A bony hand pointed to the desk adjacent to her own.

'Sit down, son of Hatra.'

I did so, smiling at the haggard face encased by a black hood, her visage cast in a dim yellow light by the oil lamp flickering on the desk. I pointed at the scroll.

'Are you researching the ingredients of a new poison?'

'Don't be facetious, it does not suit you. You are still angry with Gallia, I take it. That would account for your childish decision not to bring the Amazons with you on this current mission.'

'I have an escort that is quite sufficient.'

'So, you go to rescue the young farmer?'

The hairs on the back of my neck stood up in alarm.

'Rescue him from what?'

She rolled up the scroll and peered at me, her black eyes looking into my soul.

'I thought you had retired from military affairs?'

'I have.'

'I have to tell you, son of Hatra, if you go north you risk unravelling all that you have laboured to achieve.'

'I am just going to try to persuade Klietas to return with me to Dura, that is all.'

She sighed. 'Still concerning yourself with the welfare of waifs and strays after all these years. Have you learned nothing, son of Hatra? Some individuals cannot be saved.'

'I owe Klietas a great debt,' I insisted. 'He saved my life.'

'And was richly rewarded for it, too richly in my opinion.'

'He was wronged.'

'No mawkishness, please. I advise you not to go north, not that you ever took any notice of my advice. Men have a stubborn streak that can be infuriating.'

'What lies in the north that worries you?' I probed.

She ignored my question. 'How is Gallia?'

'As hard and unyielding as ever.'

'You object to her despatching assassins to kill Parthia's enemies?'

'Yes.'

'Why?'

'It is underhand.'

A low cackle. 'But more efficient.'

'Than what?'

'Two armies spending all day butchering each other. Do you ever think about the countless thousands who have died because of your orders?'

'I have never unsheathed my sword except in the defence of the empire.'

'That is not quite true, son of Hatra. What about when you marched into Persis to take revenge on Prince Alexander, who was responsible for raping Claudia?'

'Am I on trial?'

She changed the subject. 'Claudia has exceeded my expectations.'

I thought of my carefree young daughter who had turned into the aloof, calculating Scythian Sister at Phraates' right hand.

'It was not the life I wanted for her.'

A groan. 'You cannot control the whole world and all those who inhabit it, son of Hatra.'

'I grow tired of this world, and lament those I loved who have departed it.'

'The usual whine of the elderly. But I have some good news for you.'

'Oh?'

'As you are determined to ignore my advice, you will not have the time for morose thoughts, which should come as a relief to all those around you who have to endure your self-indulgent lamentations.'

'You are, as ever, a comfort.'

'Claudia was right, by the way.'

'About what?'

'That trinket of the enemy that dangles from your belt. It will draw you towards the servants of Rome.'

I looked at the parazonium dagger. 'It was a gift and it would be the height of bad manners to discard it.'

She shook her head. 'Ever the hopeless romantic. Well, if you will excuse me, I have work to do.'

I laughed. 'Work? What possible work could you have to do?'

'Hush, this is a place of study and quiet contemplation, not that I would expect you to understand such gentle virtues. Warlords tend to be like the weapons they wield: blunt and unsophisticated.'

She pointed a bony finger at the papyrus unrolled on the desk.

'I don't suppose you have heard of Homer?'

I wracked my brains. 'A Greek writer of antiquity.'

'Very good, son of Hatra. This is *The Iliad*.'

'The poem about the Trojan War,' I said. 'I read it when I was a boy. I rather enjoyed it.'

'Naturally. Boys and young men like war and bloodshed, and the ten-year Trojan War was certainly bloody.'

'I wanted to be Achilles,' I reminisced.

A belittling chuckle. 'A self-centred brute.'

'He fought to defend Greek honour.'

She emitted an unnerving cackle. 'Greek honour? Is there such a thing? The entire Trojan War was fought to protect the so-called honour of one Greek king, Menelaus of Sparta, whose wife Helen ran off with Prince Paris of Troy.'

'What was Menelaus expected to do?'

'Perhaps ponder on why he had been such a bad husband that his wife ran off with the first handsome young man to come along?'

She pointed at me. 'The point is, son of Hatra, countless lives were lost, and a great city was reduced to ashes to avenge a personal slight. Rejection and insult trigger anger. Remember that, in the coming time of trial.'

I grew alarmed. 'What trial?'

'Will you allow me to read in peace? You have a farmer to search for. Who would have thought it, the great King of Dura fretting over the fate of a meaningless farmer? But then, they say old age addles the mind. Farewell, son of Hatra.'

She turned back to the manuscript and refused to speak any more. As usual, her warnings were shrouded in mystery and cryptic comments. But I was determined to seek out Klietas and speak to him, if only to return to Dura having achieved something after my failure at Ctesiphon.

Dilshad's archivists produced a map that provided details on how to get from Irbil to Vazneh, being a roll of papyrus, upon which was drawn the road from the capital to the village. It included the villages we would pass, along with streams and rivers we would encounter during the journey. Dilshad also gave me a leather tubular case to hold the map when on the move.

'It is the best my cartographers could do in the short space of time, majesty.'

'It is excellent,' I told him, perusing the settlements along the way.

'Are all these villages occupied?' I asked, pointing at the various settlements either side of the road, stretching to the southern shore of Lake Urmia.

'The further one travels from the capital, the fewer occupied villages,' he told me. 'That is why I fear you will find no one living in Vazneh, majesty. Northern Media was devastated by Mark Antony and then King Spartacus. The refugees from the north never returned home.'

I rolled up the map and slipped it into the leather case.

'None?'

He shrugged. 'Perhaps a few, though there have been no tax revenues from the area in the past few years.'

Kingdoms did not despatch tax collectors to gather revenues. Outside the capital and royal estates, which were administered by the crown, the realm was ruled on behalf of the king by individual lords, who were given tracts of land to farm and administer as the king deemed fit. They were permitted to accrue personal wealth from their lands in return for military service when called upon, with a share of their wealth paid annually to the crown. Each king's accountants held a detailed record of every lord's estate, including the number of villages he held sway over, to determine the taxes he should pay to the crown. These annual taxes were paid in either gold, silver or, more usually, grain, which in the days when Media had been untroubled by war, was exported to neighbouring kingdoms.

'Thank you for the map,' I said.

The next day, a fresh breeze blowing through the citadel to invigorate the senses, Bullus, Navid and the rest of my escort sat on their horses in the palace courtyard, the camels grunting and spitting in disapproval at being kept waiting. Two ranks of palace guard stood to attention in the sunlight, their metal helmets glinting and the sun reflecting off whetted spear points. This unit of soldiers had once numbered five thousand men, and under the first King Atrax had been a formidable fighting force. Now, sadly, it was a shadow of its former self. Out of politeness I had refrained from enquiring as to its current strength. But I doubt it totalled more than two hundred.

Akmon and Lusin looked resplendent in their blue royal robes, the queen's curls tumbling to her shoulders. As before, pregnancy obviously suited her. The severe Joro stood behind the couple, a deep frown etched on his face. He kept glancing at me and then my escort, giving a slight shake of the head.

'We wish you a safe journey, King Pacorus,' smiled Lusin, stepping forward to kiss me on the cheek. 'And do not be a stranger.'

Joro cleared his throat loudly, prompting Akmon and his wife to turn to look at him.

'You have something to say, Lord Joro?' said Akmon.

'I think King Pacorus should be escorted by more men,' answered Joro.

'An excellent idea,' nodded Lusin.

'I go to search for one man in Media,' I said, 'rather than marching to war. I have sufficient soldiers.'

'There may be brigands in the area,' said Joro. 'I regret to say that parts of northern Media are currently not under the rule of law.'

'A situation that we are doing our utmost to rectify,' stated Akmon sternly. 'My father's depredations inflicted great sorrow on Media.'

'Castus should pay us reparations, in addition to the gold he already owes us,' reiterated Lusin.

'The queen speaks wisely, majesty,' added Joro.

Not wishing to be drawn into a quarrel, I tipped my head to Akmon and Lusin and walked to a waiting Horns, a stable hand bowing his head before handing me his reins. I slowly hauled myself into the saddle and took my helmet decorated with fresh goose feathers from Navid. A line of mounted trumpeters sounded a fanfare as I turned my horse and he trotted from the courtyard. I led the mounted column through a citadel whose streets and alleyways were pristine, passing immaculate brick houses and whitewashed stone temples. Sentries stood to attention when we rode through the gatehouse, the huge dragon banner of Media billowing in the wind above us. Below was the bustle of Irbil; beyond the verdant landscape of Media.

Chapter 5

Dilshad's map proved a great aid as we cantered north, following the road to Vanadzor before veering right to head northeast towards Lake Urmia. On the first day, we rode through villages filled with people, well-maintained mud-brick homes with thatched roofs and ringed by equally well-maintained orchards and vineyards. Children stopped their playing to wave at us, before concerned mothers ushered them out of sight. Men working in fields stopped their work to stare at us, unsure what to make of the column of white-uniformed soldiers with a man wearing black armour at their head. But we did not stop and when it became clear we were not a threat, the men resumed their work. The fields of wheat and barley cheered me, though Bullus succinctly summed up what we were all thinking when we left one village.

'We were about as welcome as a plague of locusts.'

'An apt analogy,' I said. 'Soldiers have inflicted great misery on Media these past few years. The common people have little reason to cheer when troops suddenly appear.'

'We meant them no harm,' stated Navid, innocently.

'They do not know that,' said Bullus. 'In any case, where there are more women than men, civilians are naturally suspicious of young, lusty soldiers.'

He gave me a mischievous grin.

'Why are there more women than men?' asked Navid.

'Because many of Media's menfolk are dead, boy,' Bullus told him bluntly. 'You must have killed a fair few yourself.'

Navid frowned at the veteran. 'Dura fought beside Media in the war against the rebel Atrax.'

'It gets confusing, Navid,' I said. 'Fighting alongside Atrax were many Median lords and their retinues. They are all dead now, to add to the thousands of slain when King Spartacus decided to torture Media. Gordyene has much to answer for.'

I was thinking of the deception of Spartacus when he had lured Dura and Hatra into Pontus, which ultimately had cost him his life. We would have all gone to the afterlife had it not been for the genius of Kewab, who had aided Gordyene again a year later to give Castus a victory that had elevated Gordyene to become a major power in northern Parthia. Reason enough to reward the Egyptian. But it appeared the Romans would now benefit from his talents.

The further we ventured from Irbil the less people we saw. I heard Dilshad's shrill voice in my head as we rode through abandoned villages, weeds growing among huts, animal pens deserted, passing unploughed fields and overgrown orchards.

The land changed, too. The flat verdant plains gave way to rolling, hilly country, bisected by many watercourses. In the distance were mountains but the terrain was still green and fertile, watered by babbling brooks, freshwater springs and rain. On the third day we were lashed by a heavy downpour, horses plodding on with heads down as they and their riders were buffeted by rain. We pulled our cloaks around us for protection. Yellow-brown in colour, they were a far cry from the white cloaks worn by Dura's cataphracts, which were thinner and used for display purposes. The standard-issue army cloak was a big, thick woollen affair that was undyed, and which retained it natural lanolin to make it water resistant. Boiled flax oil was applied at regular intervals to keep it waterproof. As a result, it became rather smelly but was vital for wet- and cold-weather campaigning.

Our tunics were white linen and short sleeved, our leggings baggy to provide ventilation in the Mesopotamian heat. In winter the army wore long-sleeved woollen tunics and thicker leggings. Dura rarely saw snow, but the winter months could be harsh and night-time temperatures fell to below freezing.

On the fourth day after leaving Irbil, we came across Vazneh, just as Dilshad's map predicted. It was located in a fertile plain surrounded by low-lying hills covered with trees, mostly alder and oak but also pine. The air was fresh and invigorating as we cantered towards the settlement, a collection of mud-brick huts with thatched roofs, ringed by apple, plum and pear trees. Before we reached the village we splashed through a wide stream that curved around the village before making its way north, towards Lake Urmia ten miles distant.

'Ten miles south of the great lake,' I said.

'Majesty?' queried Navid.

'Nothing.'

Like the hundreds of other villages in Media, fields ringed the settlement, most filled with crops still green, but others overgrown and full of weeds. Bullus drew his sword when he saw individuals with what looked like spears but were in fact hoes. Navid saw them, too.

'Ready,' he called to his men, prompting twenty-five bows being plucked from their cases.

More individuals came running from the fields into the village, perhaps a score or more, women among them. By the way they moved I could tell they were all in their prime. The horse archers formed into a line either side of their commander, arrows nocked in bowstrings, reins wrapped around their left wrists to allow them to shoot their bows unhindered, as well as pivot in the saddle without obstruction.

'Stand down,' I shouted, the fields and orchards now empty of individuals.

The village was around a hundred paces to our front and now looked deserted, the inhabitants having either taken shelter inside one or more of the huts or were waiting in some hidden location to spring a trap. I nudged Horns forward.

'You are with me, Bullus.'

'I would advise against that, majesty,' said a concerned Navid. 'They might have slingers or archers.'

'Klietas is an accomplished slinger,' I replied, 'though I am hopeful he will not knock me from the saddle without speaking to me first. Stay here until I return.'

I trotted forward, Bullus beside me, peering ahead to try to spot an archer or slinger.

'I hope this is the right village, majesty, because if it is not the inhabitants, who obviously have a dim view of soldiers, might indeed shoot you.'

'There is one way to find out,' I told him.

I pulled up Horns when we were around twenty paces from the first hut. I scanned the gaps between it and two adjacent dwellings, but another hut blocked my view of the centre of the village. It was deathly quiet. Bullus' martial instincts, honed by many campaigns and battles, made him uncomfortable.

'We should go,' he whispered, 'I can feel eyes on me.'

'I am King Pacorus of Dura,' I shouted, 'and seek one Klietas, who used to be a resident of this village before being forced to leave when war visited northern Media.'

Bullus was now holding his shield in front of him in a rather awkward position, gripping the central handgrip and resting the metal rim of the shield on the front of his saddle. He looked ridiculous.

'He's not here, majesty, we should go.'

'Wait,' I hissed.

'We mean you no harm,' I shouted.

'I bet they've heard that before,' quipped Bullus.

'Silence,' I snapped in irritation.

We sat there for what seemed like an age but was probably only a minute, the eyes of Bullus resembling those of a hawk as they flitted left and right, only he was searching for enemies, not prey. And then he appeared, looking fit and well, slightly stockier than I remembered but with his usual thick mop of dark brown hair tumbling to his shoulders. I eased myself from the saddle on to the ground. There was a time when I would have leapt from the saddle in joy at seeing him, but those days were long gone. Bullus shook his head when Klietas sprinted over and fell on one knee before me.

'Welcome to Vazneh, majesty.'

I grabbed his shoulders and lifted him up. 'It is good to see you, Klietas. How are you?'

Surprised at my familiarity, he was at first lost for words.

'Well, majesty,' he said at last, nodding at Bullus. 'Centurion.'

Bullus nodded back. 'Klietas.'

'Come and meet everyone, majesty,' beamed Klietas.

I pulled on Horns' reins. 'Tell Navid to keep his men outside the village,' I said to Bullus.

'You are going alone?' said the centurion.

'The king will be quite safe,' insisted Klietas.

I saw the sling tucked into his belt, along with a dagger and a quiver of arrows slung over his now broad shoulders.

'Where's your bow?' I asked.

'In good hands, majesty.'

The hands in question belonged to a rather plain-looking young woman with sparkling emerald eyes, who like the others prostrated themselves before me when I appeared in the centre of the village.

'Rise, rise all of you,' I commanded.

Klietas walked over to her, grabbed her hand and escorted her over to me, the other villagers, around thirty in total, all armed with a variety of makeshift weapons, including sickles, slings and clubs, eyeing me warily. To them I was just a man in armour armed with a sword, accompanied by other men on horses with swords and bows. Just like those who had once rampaged through northern Media, killing and looting its villages.

'I come in peace,' I said pathetically, though it was the only statement I thought might soothe their concerns.

'This is Anush, majesty, my wife,' beamed Klietas, oblivious to the cool reception directed towards me by the other villagers.

She fell to her knees, but I lifted her up. I saw her slightly enlarged belly and realised she was pregnant. I embraced her.

'I am pleased to meet the wife of the man who saved my life. When is your child due?'

'In the autumn, highborn.'

The other villagers now stood in a semi-circle around us, still clutching their weapons. I noticed two things about them: they were all young, being teenagers or young adults, and there were no children or old among them. Klietas suddenly became aware of them.

'Back to work,' he said.

Remarkably, they obeyed his command and shuffled away, several giving me sideways glances before departing back to the fields and orchards. I was impressed.

'You are headman here?'

He blushed with embarrassment but Anush had no such reticence.

'This village has arisen from the dead because of Klietas, highborn.'

I was intrigued. 'How did you do it?'

A village was in essence a unit for taxation and conscription, nothing more. It existed to produce food to feed its inhabitants and livestock and give the surplus to a lord who ruled it as tax. In times of war, the same lord would recruit the menfolk of the village to supplement his mounted retinue. In this way, the lords of the kingdom would fulfil their military obligation to their king. If the war went well, the village menfolk might return to their homes and families. If not, their bloated carcasses would provide meat for scavengers in some foreign land.

I had always liked Klietas, not least for saving my life when a bear had decided it wanted me for a meal, but as we strolled through the village and he told me his story, my admiration for him grew. He left Dura with a horse and a pouch full of gold, the profits accrued by his farm while he was beyond Parthia's borders seeking out the enemies of my wife. He used the gold to purchase a donkey, small cart, tools and seeds in Irbil, thence travelling north on his own back to his village. Once there, he rode around the countryside searching out any who still remained in the area, promising them a better life than the miserable existence they endured either living wild or working on farms mostly devoid of livestock and crops. His efforts resulted in Vazneh being re-populated with individuals who were young and hardy, two attributes vital to the task in hand.

'The first crop will feed us through the winter and the one after that will hopefully produce a surplus that I can sell in Irbil,' he told me.

We had reached the edge of the village, from where we could see orchards and fields, in the far distance the mountains that marked the border with Gordyene.

'You have done well, Klietas.'

I grabbed Anush's hand and squeezed it. 'You both have.'

Her hand was calloused and hard, a sign she had worked in the fields all her young life.

'Thank you, highborn.'

I knew then that he would never return to Dura and my journey had been in vain. But I was pleased he had, in the wasteland that was northern Media, planted the seeds of a new beginning, both figuratively and literally. As if reading my mind, he got straight to the point.

'Why did you come, majesty? Is it the horse? The queen said I could have it, but if you want it back…'

I stopped him in his tracks. 'The horse is yours, Klietas. I came to try to persuade you to return to Dura, but I can see you are building yourself a life here.'

I smiled at Anush. 'As well as creating life.'

I instructed Navid and his men to make camp outside the village, on the other side of the stream, so as not to unduly alarm the villagers. That night I ate with Klietas, Anush and two of his colleagues, a scrawny, feisty individual named Avedis and a giant of a man called Kevork. The former was a shepherd, the latter a blacksmith, but their stories were identical. Of how their families and villages had been destroyed first by the menfolk being conscripted to fight the enemies of Media, dying in a battle many miles away. I knew they were talking of the clash at Mepsila where thousands of Medians had been killed.

'Then the wild men on horses came,' said Avedis, bitterly. 'They killed all my sheep and tried to kill me.'

He pulled up his tunic to reveal a wicked scar on his belly.

'They left me for dead.'

'They ravaged this region,' agreed Kevork, shaking his huge head. 'They even killed the cats and dogs.'

For some reason this saddened me greatly. I had seen countless thousands slain on the battlefield but the thought of innocent animals being butchered needlessly plunged me into a sombre mood. I assumed they were speaking of the horsemen of Gordyene and an image of the loathsome Shamshir, the commander of King's Guard, filled my mind, though he and his men were always immaculately uniformed and never left the king's side. Still, murder and rapine were certainly his speciality.

'This land is now at peace,' I told them, 'you have nothing to fear.'

Outside the wind suddenly picked up, the wooden door of Klietas' hut rattled and the flame of the single candle illuminating its bare interior flickered.

'There is never peace, highborn,' said a melancholic Avedis.

At that moment, a god must have been whispering into his ear for his words were to prove prophetic. But the wind subsided and Klietas would hear no words of pessimism.

'Others will join our community and later in the year we will harvest wheat and barley, and pick apples, cherries, plums, peaches and strawberries. And next year we will have money to buy you some sheep.'

'If we had oxen we could plough more fields,' said Kevork, 'to grow more crops so you could sell the surplus this year. We have ploughs but no oxen.'

'There is only so much we can achieve with what we have, my friend,' said Klietas. 'Gula will protect us.'

I glanced at the clay statuette depicting a seated figure with a dog at its feet in an alcove cut in the wall. It represented the Goddess Gula, the 'great healer' who creates life in the land.

Ploughs pulled by animals allowed the land to be tilled more easily and faster, thus producing more food.

'We will soon be harvesting the barley,' said Kevork. 'The goddess has been kind to us this year.'

The next morning, men and women already in the fields and orchards just after the dawn broke, I sought out Klietas and found him rubbing down the horse he had been gifted by Gallia. He had moved into the headman's hut with Anush, it being larger than the others as befitting the status of the individual who occupied it. He stopped his activity when I appeared, bowing his head.

'You slept well, majesty?'

I stretched my back. 'As well as an old man full of aches and pains can in a draughty tent. Here.'

I tossed him a pouch full of drachmas. 'There is enough in there to purchase a pair of oxen.'

His eyes lit up when he looked into the pouch.

'You are too generous, majesty.'

'Nonsense. What use is having money if one cannot spend it on worthwhile causes.?'

An agitated Navid appeared at the entrance to the stable to interrupt our conversation.

'Horsemen approaching, majesty.'

Chapter 6

'How many?' I asked.

'My scouts report at least a hundred, majesty.'

'Uniforms?'

He shook his head. 'Too far away to identify, majesty. But they are heading this way.'

Klietas was alarmed. 'Why are horsemen coming here?'

'If they are Medians, they are probably just on patrol,' I told him. 'But they might be bandits. Word must have spread that the village of Vazneh is prospering.'

I looked at Navid. 'Get your men into the village, among the huts. If they are bandits and if they are heading here, I want to maximise the element of surprise. And tell Bullus to report to me.'

He saluted, returned to his horse, vaulted into the saddle and rode off. I laid a hand on Klietas' shoulder.

'Get your people out of the fields and into the village.'

I knew the riders approaching were not King Akmon's soldiers. He had told me his authority as yet did not extend to the north of his kingdom. That left two possibilities: the horsemen could be soldiers of Gordyene, or, most likely, they were renegades looking for loot and women and children to take as slaves. I had twenty-five horse archers, twenty-six including their commander, plus Centurion Bullus, who was the perfect foot soldier but who could not shoot a bow. In theory, if it came to violence and *if* my men achieved maximum surprise, they could easily cut down one hundred enemy horsemen.

In theory.

But battles are not theoretical affairs. They are confusing, nerve-shredding events in which the best-laid plans can turn to ashes in the blink of an eye. And the enemy would not be obligingly standing still, waiting to be killed. They would be fighting back, against horse archers wearing no helmets or armour. I clutched the lock of Gallia's hair at my neck and said a silent prayer to Shamash to aid us in our peril. A ludicrous thought passed through my mind: perhaps the horsemen were not heading towards us. Perhaps their target was elsewhere. My gut told me otherwise.

Navid mustered his men and deployed them in the village, which resembled two circles of over a score of houses around a central open space. Like most small settlements, it had grown haphazardly over the years, but always retaining a circular shape to facilitate defence against raiders.

Klietas and the others assembled in the open space, worried expressions etched on their faces, particularly the women. But everyone had a weapon of sorts, my former squire handing his sling to Anush, a quiver slung over his shoulder and his bow in hand. The villagers glanced at my horse archers positioning themselves next to houses in the inner circle of dwellings. Navid held the reins of Horns a few paces behind me.

I stood before the villagers. Bullus beside me, fully attired in war gear and gripping his shield, called for silence.

'My scouts have returned with news that a large party of horsemen is heading this way,' I announced. 'For what reason, I do not know. But I want to reassure you that we will do everything in our power to protect you.'

'It is the wild horsemen, highborn,' said Avedis. 'They have returned.'

'Keep inside your homes, out of sight,' I told them. 'Do not block my men's field of vision.'

'We prefer to fight,' growled the big Kevork, clutching a hammer in his big hand.

'If we are killed, you will get your wish,' said Bullus, bluntly. 'But until then, do as you are told.'

They exchanged glances and some mumbled to each other before shuffling away to their homes. Aside from Klietas' bow and a few slings, they had no proper weapons to speak of. Enemy horsemen would make short work of them.

'Wait here,' I called to Navid before pacing towards the edge of the village.

'I would advise against placing yourself in danger, majesty,' Navid replied.

'I am already in danger,' I retorted.

'He's full of advice, that one,' said Bullus, striding beside me.

'He's doing what he has been trained to do,' I replied. 'Sporaces informs me Navid is a rising star among his horse archers, destined for a high rank. A bit like you, Bullus.'

'Me, majesty? I'm just a simple soldier.'

'You could have had your own cohort by now.

'I like being a centurion, majesty.'

We reached the edge of the village, ahead of us a small orchard of apple trees and beyond that fields of barley. I scanned the low hills in the middle-distance but saw nothing save birds flying away from the village. Bullus began to tap the pommel of his *gladius*.

'It won't be long now,' he said, ominously. 'The air changes before a battle, or at least it does to me. It crackles with menace, just like now.'

'A soldier's instinct,' I agreed, 'born of long experience.'

I could feel my heart racing and knew he was right. I no longer saw any birds and it was quiet, very quiet. I had heard stories of animals leaving an area hours before an earthquake occurred, people wondering why flocks of birds were suddenly flying away in the same direction, and then rodents following in droves. It must be the same when the shedding of blood is in the air, for the world appeared suddenly empty of life.

I heard a slow scraping sound and saw Bullus draw his sword. And then I saw them.

A column of horsemen cresting a gentle rise beyond the fields, initially riding two abreast with outriders performing the duties of scouts. At first, they were hard to identify. Every horseman appeared to be carrying a lance, though I could see no banners or pennants to identify their kingdom of origin. Their column was ragged and actually a collection of small groups, which indicated they were not disciplined soldiers, which meant they were bandits. As they got closer, I saw that they wore a variety of armour – mail, scale and leather – though every rider was bare headed. The man at the front of the group suddenly raised his hand to halt his men, exchanging a few words with the rider I assumed was his deputy before re-commencing his journey towards us. My heart sank when I recognised him.

'Shamash give me strength.'

It was Spadines, the leader of the Aorsi tribe that had made its home in northern Gordyene, and who had been a close ally of first Spartacus and now Castus. The rulers of Gordyene believed the Aorsi to be valued allies, but I held them in contempt, and had done nothing to hide my opinion from their leader. He was a swarthy individual with a wild beard and even wilder hair, a roisterer, cut-throat, robber and all-round rogue. I saw a couple of riders gallop away from the now-stationary group of Sarmatians, a leering Spadines pulling up his horse a few paces from me.

'King Pacorus of Dura. What strange twist of fate brings you here?'

He glanced at Bullus beside me, *gladius* in hand, but ignored him.

'I am visiting an old friend,' I replied. 'More to the point, what are you doing here? This is, after all, Media, and the Aorsi have no business here.'

He scanned the huts in front of him.

'We are on the business of King Castus, and seeing as his brother sits on Media's throne, Akmon will not mind if we traverse his territory to please his brother.'

'What business?' I demanded to know.

'Out of courtesy and respect for your age and position, I will tell you.'

I was barely controlling my anger. He was probably my age, or thereabouts, his hair and beard streaked with grey, though his locks were thicker than mine, which annoyed me intensely for some reason. Like many Sarmatians, he wore a short kaftan that opened at the front and was wrapped across the chest from right to left. Fashioned from deerskin leather, it was dyed red to reflect his 'noble' position. His leggings were brown leather, as were his ankle boots. Over his kaftan he wore a shining scale and mail corselet, the rounded iron scales sewn to a leather backing, the mail attached to the bottom of the leather and split at the front and rear to enable him to sit comfortably in the saddle.

'I am here to escort a wedding present for the new queen of Gordyene back to Vanadzor,' he smiled.

I was at a loss as to what he was babbling about. As far as I knew, Castus was going to marry Princess Elaheh of Atropaiene, though I had no specific details as relations between Dura and Gordyene were distinctly frosty following Castus' attempt to kill Gallia's assassins, hence our not being invited to the wedding. But there was nothing of value in this region to take back to Vanadzor as a wedding gift for a queen.

'What can you possibly want with a small village in Media?' I queried. 'I doubt there is anything here that would interest Princess Elaheh as a wedding gift?'

He gave me a knowing smirk. 'How little you know, King Pacorus.'

'This old man is asking for a slap,' whispered Bullus.

'Not yet, Bullus,' I said.

'King Castus has not married Princess Elaheh,' Spadines told me. 'He has found a far more suitable bride, a woman cast in the same mould as himself.'

'Does she have a name?' I asked.

'Yesim,' he answered.

'Who?'

I had never heard of her, and try as I might, I could think of no king in the empire who had a daughter by the name of Yesim. I assumed she was a daughter of one of Gordyene's lords, which was perfectly fine. Though I was still at a loss as to why Spadines had been despatched to Media.

'We are here to take a man by the name of Klietas back to Vanadzor,' said Spadines. 'He was a difficult man to find. But King Castus has much gold and gold buys you information.'

'What does Castus want with Klietas?'

He sighed. 'To punish him for the great insolence he has displayed towards King Castus. He is to be sacrificed in honour of Yesim, in accordance with the ancient rituals of her people.'

'The time for talking is over, majesty,' whispered Bullus.

A rider suddenly galloped up to Spadines, pulling up his horse sharply. He bowed his head to the Sarmatian.

'No soldiers nearby, highness.'

'Highness?' I laughed. 'I knew things in the world are far worse than they once were, when men of honour and integrity ruled the empire and the rule of law applied to all kingdoms, but the title "highness" is only applicable to those of royal birth. Have you become a king, Spadines, or perhaps you are here to carve out your own kingdom?'

His smirking demeanour disappeared, to be replaced by a cold, hateful visage.

'The great King Pacorus, the mighty warlord who has always looked down his nose at the Aorsi.'

'With good reason,' I retorted.

'And here you are, a long way from home with no army to protect you.'

He jabbed a finger at Bullus. 'Is this all that remains of your famed foot soldiers, King of Dura? Has Dura fallen on hard times?'

Bullus growled under his breath but I held him back.

I scanned his motley collection of horsemen attired in a variety of armour either gifted or stolen, the mail rusty and full of holes, the scale armour tatty and in a state or disrepair. Only the horses were in an excellent condition. Sarmatians needed well-fed, speedy mounts to make good their escape after thieving and murder.

'How many men have you got? A hundred? One Duran to one hundred Aorsi. That is what one of my soldiers is worth.'

Bullus guffawed.

'Turn around and ride back to your master, dog,' I spat. 'For that is what you and your Aorsi are. Jackals who inflict misery on all you come into contact with.'

He drew his sword. Bullus immediately jumped to place himself between me and Spadines, shield in front of him, *gladius* poised ready to plunge into his horse's chest. The Sarmatian pointed his sword at me.

'I am a generous man, King of Dura. I will allow you and your lone soldier to leave this village unharmed. Decide now. Live or die, it makes no difference to me. But I will not return to my king empty handed.'

'How about returning to your king headless?' I quipped.

He was dumbstruck. 'You would die for a poor farmer?'

'Would you?'

He ignored me, turning his horse to canter back to his men. I too turned and walked back into the village, Bullus covering my back. I heard shouts and heard horses' hooves and knew the battle was about to begin. I tried to run but my left leg suddenly began to ache intensely, causing me to hobble towards a waiting Navid.

'Get your men out and kill as many as possible,' I shouted to him.

He turned to his signaller and issued a command, seconds later the shrill sound of the trumpet echoing around the village. Navid tossed me Horns' reins and Bullus interlinked the fingers of his hands to provide an aid to allow me to gain the saddle.

'Protect Klietas,' I told him, 'and stay alive.'

He gave me an evil grin and made for the headman's hut where Klietas and Anush were sheltering.

Twenty-seven riders prepared to attack nearly four times their number. But numbers were only part of the equation during a battle. The main thing separating my men from the Aorsi rabble was training. 'Train hard, fight easy' was the motto of Dura's army, which in turn had been the philosophy of its first commander, Lucius Domitus, a former Roman centurion I had first met in Italy. Every legionary, cataphract and horse archer received intensive training, so they obeyed orders without question on the battlefield, instinctively reacting to commands even in the white-heat of combat. In this way drills became bloodless battles and battles became bloody drills. Nothing was left to chance, and that included equipment.

When they had first encountered us, the Romans had made the fatal error of dismissing Parthians as nothing more than effete, weak barbarians with their womanly long hair and beards. Carrhae had disabused them of that notion but both armies that had fought each other on that hot, dusty plain had been highly trained instruments. Just as the Romans had simple but effective weapons in the *gladius* and *pilum*, so did we have the Scythian bow. Perfected over hundreds of years, the weapon first used by wild Scythians of the plains measured only three-and-a-half feet in length when strung. Comprising a three-element core of ibex horn between two segments of wood, its most distinctive characteristic was the extreme curvature of the end sections, which pointed away from the archer, that is, they were reflexed. Conversely, the central section is severely bent towards the archer in a deflexed fashion.

Wrapped in sinew which in turn was covered in Chinese lacquer to keep it waterproof, each bow required around six months of crafting and drying before it was ready to use. Light and compact, it was ideal for shooting from the saddle. But the instrument to propel an arrow was only half the equation. The arrows themselves were highly developed weapons. Many woods were used for arrow shafts. Birch was hard and tough, cedar was light, but Dura's soldiers were equipped with reed arrow shafts. The reeds were collected from the banks of the Euphrates and dried for two weeks before fletching and the fitting of heads. The vast majority of arrowheads were the three-winged variety, though narrower heads were also used to penetrate armour, both metal and leather. Arrowheads were bronze, a metal excellent for casting, which meant arrowheads could be mass produced. Iron was lighter and stronger than bronze, though, and was used to make narrow-pointed arrowheads that could penetrate armour, as the Romans had discovered to their cost at Carrhae.

Two lines of horse archers charged out of Vazneh, one led by me, the other by Navid. The Aorsi, leisurely cantering towards the village, were taken completely by surprise. As I had done a thousand times before, I plucked an arrow from one of my quivers, nocked it in the sinew bowstring, my legs secured in place by the four horns of the saddle I sat on, Horns' reins wrapped around my left wrist, my left hand gripping the central section of my bow.

I dearly wanted to kill Spadines but in battle you shoot the first target that presents itself, in this case a mounted spearman bearing down on me with his weapon levelled. I raised my bow, pulled the bowstring back to my ear and let the sinew slip from my fingers. The arrow hissed through the air and flew past his right ear. He howled in delight and hollered a war cry; certain he was about to skewer the King of Dura. But the ruler of Dura had other ideas. I plucked a second arrow from my quiver, strung it and released it when the Sarmatian was but twenty paces from me, the missile thudding into his chest. His horse carried on galloping, but its rider slumped in the saddle and hit the ground hard, being trampled on by those following.

Shooting a bow from a secure saddle is easy enough. Hitting a moving target while one's own horse is charging is more difficult. I slowed Horns as the horse archers behind me flanked left and right to form a line, each man slowing their mount to allow them to shoot more accurately, loosing around five arrows a minute – one hundred and thirty missiles – at the Sarmatians, who quickly took to their heels.

Navid's file had also enjoyed good shooting, dead and wounded Aorsi lying on the ground in front of them as their surviving comrades also beat a hasty retreat into the distance. I scoured the green earth for a body clad in red but saw only bodies attired in green and brown hues. Spadines lived to fight another day, it seemed. Navid's archers raised their bows in the air and began chanting 'Dura, Dura' as the Aorsi retreated out of range. Their commander galloped over, his face flush with victory and wearing a broad grin.

'We must have dropped nearly half of them, majesty,' he said excitedly.

'They might return,' I warned him. 'Get your men back inside the village. We surprised them, but they will be more wary next time.'

His eyes met mine and we both realised something was very wrong. His smile vanished when we heard the sound of hooves behind us. I turned and saw Sarmatians galloping out of the village, spears levelled and swords raised high, ready to skewer and slash at men on stationary horses.

Whether Spadines had planned a two-pronged attack on the village or whether it was another group of his men who had been scouring the countryside and had happened to appear at more or less the same time, I did not know. But I knew we were about to be dealt a cruel blow.

'Retreat!' I hollered, but it was too late. Far too late.

Some of Navid's men displayed a rare courage in not attempting to flee from the horde bearing down on them, choosing to twist in the saddle and shoot at the oncoming Aorsi. Their arrows emptied saddles but within moments they were surrounded and cut down. Others did flee, shooting over the hind quarters of their horses, as did I as we galloped away from the village. The Aorsi, ill-disciplined rabble that they were, completed the butchering of those horse archers that had remained stationary, before wheeling around to head back into the village.

I pulled up Horns and turned him.

'Follow me,' I shouted, digging my knees into his flanks to urge him back towards the village.

The Sarmatians who had surprised us were already turning back to loot the village, search for women to rape and presumably capture Klietas. That gave us an advantage, albeit a small one, as I led the wedge-shaped formation that numbered perhaps fifteen riders – nearly half our original strength. I shot an arrow into an Aorsi who was sitting on his horse using a flint and stone in an attempt to light a pitch-soaked torch, which I assumed he was going to toss on the thatched roof of the nearest hut. He stiffened and dropped the torch when my arrow slammed into his back, sliding from the saddle.

I strung and shot another arrow at a Sarmatian barking orders to some men who had dismounted and were about to burst into a hut. He too toppled from the saddle. And then the doors to the huts opened and the villagers flooded out, armed with sickles, hoes, slings and clubs.

Pandemonium followed.

We were in the centre of the village now, forming a loose circle and shooting at any Sarmatian within range, which was all of them. I saw the big Kevork haul a man from his horse and club him to death with his hammer, spurts of blood shooting into the air as he pummelled the man's skull. One villager was screaming in rage as he ran at a raider, only to collapse when the Aorsi hurled his spear and hit him in the chest. I shot the Sarmatian before he had a chance to retrieve his weapon.

I felt something go past my left ear and turned to see a Sarmatian who had been about to skewer me with his spear waver in the saddle, before tumbling to the ground, dead. I spun in the saddle to see a grinning Avedis with an empty sling. I raised my bow in thanks.

Horses were rearing up and whinnying in pain when slingshots slammed into them, some collapsing when villagers armed with abandoned Sarmatian spears thrust them into the animals. I caught sight of a man on foot running towards Klietas, who was shooting his bow but who had his back to the Aorsi. Bullus nearby was fully occupied shielding Anush and fending off a Sarmatian with an axe. I shot the man intent on killing Klietas in the back and he pitched forward on the ground. Then he staggered to his feet and stumbled on towards Klietas. I shot him a second time and he stopped. A third arrow put him down for good.

The roofs of two of the huts were on fire now, the flames crackling loudly as they gripped the dry thatch. The centre of the village had become a place of gore, covered with dead and dying horses and men. I saw Anush next to Klietas frozen in fear and horror, and witnessed another female villager have her belly ripped open by an enraged Sarmatian with a sword. He was wearing a scale-armour corselet but that did not save him from the arrow I put into his right thigh. He yelped, clutched at the shaft and plucked it out, wincing in pain as the barb at the base of the arrowhead tore at his flesh. I reached into my quiver for another arrow.

Empty!

I reached into my second quiver and that too was devoid of missiles. Had I really shot sixty arrows?

I jumped down from Horns and walked over to the bleeding Sarmatian. It had been many years since I had fought a man face-to-face with a sword on foot, and though he was wounded and I was not, I reasoned his youth and strength made us equal. I unsheathed my *spatha* and slashed at his head with the blade. He ducked and thrust his own sword at my thigh, an attack I parried with a downward cut. He circled me, hobbling but not excessively so. His maddened state was obviously blocking out the pain, though his leggings were now showing a large red patch from the arrow wound. That did not stop him charging at me, delivering a series of downward cuts from the left and right as he tried to slice open the side of my neck. I defeated each one with my *spatha*. But after I had brought up my sword a final time, he punched me on the nose, sending me reeling backwards, disorientated. I fell to my knees, my back to him.

I spun and brought up my blade to stop his own sword from beheading me. He laughed maniacally as he drew back his sword to deliver another blow. He was towering over me, I was kneeling, and he sensed victory. All I could do was hold my sword in front of me and try to anticipate the direction of his strike. That and pull my Roman dagger from its sheath with my left hand and stab down on his left boot. He emitted a high-pitched cry as he collapsed on the ground and made no further sound when Bullus drew the edge of his *gladius* across his throat. The centurion hauled me to my feet.

'Are you hurt, majesty?'

'I appear to be in one piece, thank you.'

'They've gone. For the moment.'

I looked around and saw the Aorsi had indeed gone, those still living, that is. Many of their former comrades were now corpses with arrows stuck in them, or their skulls and bodies bludgeoned by blunt instruments. Dead horses lay on corpses, bodies were draped over slain animals, and the centre of the village was painted red. There was blood splashed on the walls of huts, on the ground, on human and animal corpses, and on the faces of those who had done the killing.

The aftermath of battle is a curious phenomenon. In the cauldron of combat, men can excel themselves to achieve superhuman feats. Some, driven to a white-hot rage, can continue to fight oblivious to injuries they have suffered. Others, previously frightened and quivering, suddenly become calm and focused as they discover an inner core of iron they were unaware of, like a miner finding a rich seam of metal. Highly trained professionals will obey their officers and carry out their duties regardless of the horror unfolding around them. But for all, the aftermath is the same. Limbs become leaden and weak as bodies relax. Battle exhausts physical and mental reserves. Individuals can be possessed of a raging thirst and after hours of combat the body craves rest. But for civilians caught up in combat, it is far worse.

Klietas was going among the villagers to reassure and congratulate them. Some were shaking, others weeping, but most just stood staring into space, vacant expressions on their faces. Dura's soldiers, used to the face of battle, were already thinking about what would happen next. Navid was directing his men, all ten of them, to stack the bodies of dead horses in the gaps between huts to form makeshift barricades.

'Move.'

I heard Bullus' gruff voice and saw him shoving a dazed villager with his shield. 'If they come back, you won't have time to mope around. You'll be dead.'

They did come back, but not in the way we expected. As we frantically hauled dead horses to block the gaps between huts, throwing dead Aorsi on top of them to increase the height of the makeshift barricades, it was Spadines himself who rode back to the village. He held a sprig of ironwood in his hand, a tree indigenous to northern Media, Gordyene and Atropaiene. He approached the village with the sprig held aloft to show he wished to talk. How I wanted to give the order to shoot him down. But it was a universally accepted rule of war that one did not kill emissaries, no matter how repugnant they were.

'Put down your weapons,' I told Avedis and four others who had stones in the pouches of their slings, ready to send Spadines to the underworld.

They grudgingly obeyed my command, though Avedis' eyes were filled with rage.

I walked over to him, or rather hobbled as my left leg was throbbing with pain.

'It is considered an offence against the gods to kill an emissary of the enemy who comes in peace, and we do not want to offend the immortals, do we?'

He said nothing but gave a curt nod, staring at the figure of Spadines, now around thirty paces from the edge of the village.

'No more need to die,' he called to us. 'Surrender the man named Klietas, or show me his body, and we will leave you in peace. We have no quarrel with you. But if you do not give Klietas or his corpse up, we will burn your village to the ground.

'I will give you until the dawn to decide. A whole night to determine whether you and your village will live or die. No help is coming, but in the morning, more of my men will be here.'

He tossed the sprig to the ground, turned his horse and cantered back to his men, now making camp, the flicker of campfires decorating a hill in the distance.

'Do you believe him, majesty?' said Bullus.

'He's a thief, rapist and liar. But he is right when he says no help is coming.'

I looked around at our ragged collection of stunned civilians and tired soldiers.

'If they attack again, I doubt we will be able to hold them.'

Bullus looked over at Klietas comforting Anush.

'Our fate lies in his hands, then.'

'We are not giving up Klietas,' I stated, 'not to the bandit Spadines. Never.'

As the sun dipped in the west, we stood behind our ghastly barricades, waiting for an attack that never came. There was no wind that night but still the sounds of revelry from the Sarmatian camp reached our ears, unnerving the villagers. Navid had had the foresight to bring the camels and supplies into the village, though the pitched tents remained beyond the stream, a watercourse now beyond reach. The odds were stacked against us, that much was certain. And Klietas must have realised this, for when dawn came, our eyes red, our limbs aching and our mouths dry and foul, he had gone.

A distraught Anush came to me accompanied by an angry Avedis and a resigned Kevork, the big man's tunic stained red with the blood of the men he had bludgeoned to death with his hammer. Those corpses and others were now as stiff as wooden boards, their skin a hideous grey-white. They and the dead horses were crawling with flies, adding to the feeling of dread that weighed down on us. I saw the pregnant Anush, the anguish on her face and anger welled up inside me.

    I held her hand. 'Don't worry, I will get him back.'

Chapter 7

In their eagerness to kill us, the Aorsi had left our tents intact, which meant I could pen a letter to Akmon at Irbil while Navid sent out scouts from his depleted force to ensure the Sarmatians had departed. They returned with news that they had indeed left the area, though in a leisurely fashion, his men having seen them travelling north back to Vanadzor. He, Bullus, the remainder of his men and the villagers hastily prepared a pyre to cremate the dead, the threat of pestilence hanging over us all, as well as the nauseating aroma of burning flesh as the fire consumed the dead. The horse carcasses were butchered for meat – a ghastly thing to do but the most practical given the need for food and the fact the horseflesh could be smoked to preserve it for future consumption. The villagers would need all the food sources they could lay their hands on, seeing as the Aorsi had trampled their crops into the ground.

In my letter I informed Akmon what had happened in the north of his kingdom, urging him to send troops to guarantee the safety of Vazneh and its inhabitants. I also requested that he despatch food to the villagers, plus seeds for replanting the fields and a pair of oxen to make ploughing the aforementioned fields easier. Dura's treasury would reimburse Irbil for the expense incurred. I told the assembled villagers the same when they had cleared the centre of their settlement of dead men and horses, the former consigned to the pyre; the latter being carefully butchered. They looked a sorry sight, their clothes stained with blood and their faces dirty and ashen.

I held up the folded papyrus sheet I had been writing on.

'Your king will send soldiers, food, seeds and oxen.'

'We have no money to pay for such things,' said Avedis, bitterly.

'I will be paying for them,' I told him.

For the first time in two days, I saw the semblance of a smile on their faces and appreciative nods.

'That is very generous, highborn,' said Kevork, who had donned a leather apron to assist the village butcher carve up the horse carcasses. 'But what if the wild horsemen return?'

I glanced at Anush, her eyes red and puffy from weeping.

'They will not. They have got what they came for.'

I saw her head drop as she cradled her belly.

'But I intend to ride to Vanadzor to bring back your headman, that I swear.'

Anush looked up and had utter relief etched on her face. But Navid and Bullus were horrified. The young horse archer officer, his right arm in a sling as a result of receiving a sword cut, came over to me and bowed his head.

'With respect, majesty, we are too few to attempt a rescue mission.'

'He's right,' agreed Bullus, who looked remarkably fresh considering he had had no sleep. Adversity obviously suited him.

'Of my men, only five are unhurt and a number of the horses have also been wounded,' emphasised Navid. 'And we are very low on ammunition.'

'That is why you and they are returning to Irbil,' I told him. 'I will be going to Vanadzor alone.'

Navid's forehead creased with a frown.

'I would advise against that, majesty.'

'As would I,' said Bullus. 'If the Aorsi discover you are after them, they will kill you.'

'They won't,' I said. 'And though I am touched by your concern for my welfare, I have not fought for forty years to allow a rabble of Aorsi bandits get the better of me.'

Bullus sighed. 'I better come with you, majesty, just to make sure you don't get into trouble.'

I was going to refuse but then remembered Gallia telling me she had selected Bullus to be a member of her group of assassins because he had been part of the scratch force I had taken to Irbil to defend it against Atrax and his mercenary army. She believed the big, gruff centurion to be beloved of the gods, and while I could think of no reason why this particular soldier of Dura's army should be singled out by the immortals, who was I to query the whims of the gods? I was not so conceited to believe I was invincible or indeed would myself receive the assistance of the immortals, especially after giving away the armour I had been gifted by them.

'I accept your impertinent offer,' I said.

Navid was deeply troubled. 'I must strongly protest, majesty.'

I pressed a finger into his chest.

'Your task, your mission, is to get to Irbil as quickly as possible to give King Akmon my letter, after which you are to write to Dura to inform the queen of what has happened to her husband. Is that clear?'

Chastened, he stiffened and saluted. 'Yes, majesty.'

'You and your men will leave at once,' I said.

They took all the camels but left us a spare horse to carry our single eight-man tent, fodder and food. I watched the rather pathetic column of battered horse archers with hardly any ammunition trot away to the south, Bullus on his horse beside me holding the reins of Horns and the spare horse. I walked over to the knot of villagers, behind the charred remains of a hut the Sarmatians had set alight. I embraced Anush.

'I will return with Klietas, that I promise,' I whispered into her ear. I stepped back and addressed the others.

'The devastation and lawlessness that has been visited on your village will not be forgotten. You have my pledge that those responsible will be brought to justice, and that Klietas will be rescued to once again assume his responsibilities as your headman. Media is no longer a place of tyranny but a land of freedom, justice and the rule of law. Just as you have planted your fields anew, so has your king sowed the seeds of a new kingdom, one which will flourish to make Media once again the first kingdom of the empire.'

I turned, walked back to Horns and hauled myself into his saddle. Bullus passed me his reins.

'Fine speech, majesty. Do you think they believed you?'

'I hope so, for surely as day follows night, it is the truth.'

My plan was a simple one. We would ride north to Lake Urmia, journey along its western shore before swinging west to head directly for Vanadzor. The plan had two advantages, I hoped. First, the Aorsi, ill-disciplined rabble that they were and now flush with a victory of sorts, would make their back to Castus in a leisurely fashion. Even if they were not tardy, I hoped the second advantage would allow us to arrive at Gordyene's capital before Klietas was murdered – our horses.

The Persians had revered them, the breed being the choice of their nobility, and it was said that the great chariot of their god, Ahura Mazda, was pulled by them. The Chinese called it *Tien Ma* – Heavenly Horse – for a steed that was both beautiful and the most valuable. Horns was a Nisean, named after the town of Nisaia in the Nisaean Plains at the foot of the Zagros Mountains. But now they were bred and ridden across the breadth of the Parthian Empire.

Horns was so named because of the bony knobs on his forehead, a distinct characteristic of the breed, though his were particularly pronounced. They came in a variety of colours but the most common were dark bay, chestnut and brown. Horns was black and the rarest colour among Niseans was white, so rare that they were reserved for kings and gods, or so the saying went. All Niseans had great strength and endurance, the latter quality serving us well as we cantered along the shore of Lake Urmia.

No words were exchanged between me and Bullus for the first two hours of our journey, during which we covered at least twenty miles. When we stopped for a halt near the great lake, the sun reflecting off its glittering turquoise surface, we did so near a freshwater stream filled with bubbling, ice-cool water. Horns and the other two horses drank from the stream and while they did so we relieved them of their saddles and loads. Lake Urmia sat in a great basin surrounded by mountains, from which came runoff from the heavy winter snowfall they were subjected to. The basin itself was subject to cold winters and long, dry summers. But the meltwater that came from the mountains in spring and early summer ensured the land remained green.

We both disrobed and threw ourselves into the stream, the temperature of the water at first a shock but then refreshing as I washed the filth and grime from my body and hair. We had ridden without helmets and armour, though my bow was close at all times. But we had seen no signs of human life since leaving Vazneh, and I doubted we would be disturbed during our journey, not until we entered Gordyene, at least.

After immersing ourselves in the invigorating stream for some time, we emerged from the water rejuvenated. The sun was high in the sky now, warming the earth, though not excessively so. As I pulled on my leggings, I saw Bullus glancing at the scars on my back.

'Was it painful, majesty, the flogging, I mean?'

My mind went back to a younger Pacorus being lashed on the deck of a Roman ship, a cocky young prince of Hatra who had allowed himself and those of his men to be captured during an expedition in Cappadocia.

'Yes,' I answered, 'though the worst part was afterwards when my back felt as though it was being used as a pin cushion for a thousand red-hot needles. Not that I had any medical treatment, not until I and the rest of my men were rescued by Spartacus.'

He buckled his leather belt around his waist.

'What was he like?'

I laughed, which caught him by surprise. The same old question asked of me a thousand times over the years. When I had first been posed the question I had answered truthfully. Spartacus was just a man, a good man, an honest man, a decent man. But that answer was wholly unsatisfactory to those who wanted to hear stories of a man who had challenged the might of Rome in her own homeland. No ordinary man could have raised himself up to command an army of tens of thousands, conjured up from nothing, which defeated army after army sent against it. So, over the years I embellished the story. Spartacus became taller, broader, possessed of a keen intellect, a giant on the battlefield, both literally and metaphorically. This was certainly no lie, but neither was Spartacus a demi-god. He was a simple, ordinary man and that is why other men loved him.

'A great soldier,' I answered. 'A man who inspired loyalty, and that quality above all is what made him so great. That is why we go to rescue Klietas, Bullus. We must remain loyal to our family, friends and homelands at all times.'

'You might pay a high price, majesty.'

I put on a fresh tunic and buckled my sword belt. I drew the *spatha* and held it up.

'This was given to me by Spartacus over forty years ago. He never broke faith with his friends. Neither will I. At the very least, I owe it to Klietas to save him as he saved me.'

Bullus threw a saddlecloth on to his horse's back.

'The queen told you Castus tried to have us killed?' he said.

'She did.'

He turned to look directly at me.

'If you don't mind me saying so, majesty, there is something not quite right about him. He was angry when he found out Haya and Klietas had been sleeping together. But he sent his men to kill Klietas before he knew that. Your going to Vanadzor might not save Klietas; but it might get you killed.'

'It might get you killed, too.'

He shrugged. 'Not me, majesty.'

'And why is that?'

He grinned like an impious child. 'I've got a beautiful woman with large breasts watching over me. She saved me once, and I'm sure she will do so again.'

'Your reverence for the gods is truly humbling, Bullus.'

We rode a further thirty miles that day before leaving the glittering surface of the great salt lake to head west the next day, towards the mountains that ringed Gordyene. There was a time when the mountain passes were filled with traffic carrying goods in both directions. But that was before Parthia had even existed and now the narrow valleys were mostly empty. The air was cool and refreshing as we rode through the high peaks, many still capped with snow, though the lower slopes were carpeted with trees, mostly pine with a sprinkling of juniper and aspen. The air was thick with the smell of the evergreens, the temperature humid and heavy as we threaded our way through the trees along tracks that were hundreds of years old. People were strangers in these parts, and I wondered if the inhabitants of the region, if they were still extant, were direct descendants of the gods that walked the earth thousands of years ago.

The forests were certainly alive, with bears waking up from their hibernation, wolves that tracked us in packs but never came near, especially when we lit a fire at night, plus lynx and wild cats. We bathed in ice-cold waterfalls cascading over rocky peaks and drank from fast-flowing streams. And never once did we see any soul until we were through the mountains and into Gordyene proper.

Once, many years before, I had spent a summer and winter in Gordyene, skirmishing with its Roman garrison, which harried us out of the kingdom and chased us into Atropaiene. We nearly died of starvation and were eventually cornered by the Romans, only to be saved by the arrival King

Khosrou of Margiana and King Musa of Hyrcania. Then Gordyene had been a wasteland, but two generations later the kingdom had changed beyond all recognition. Where once there had been abandoned villages and a paucity of people, now there were large settlements filled with lots of children.

Villages are usually insular, tight-knit places that often display hostility towards outsiders. Two men riding powerful horses wearing swords and armour would invariably arouse suspicion and so we avoided any settlements, giving them a wide berth. On the fourth day of our journey we reached the Pambak Valley where Vanadzor was located. There were now black strongholds guarding the approaches to the capital, along with many villages sited along the length of the Pambak River, all surrounded by well-tended fields growing wheat and barley. The men and women in the fields paid us no heed as we rode by them. They had no need to for the whole valley was patrolled by horsemen, a party of which intercepted us before we reached the city.

I had seen them many times on the battlefield where they had been allies, but now the riders in red tunics and black leggings gave the impression of being hostile, or at least their commander did. He sat on his horse blocking our way, three of his lancers behind him in a line.

'What business do you have in Gordyene?' he demanded of us.

Our horses, clothes and weapons marked us out as strangers, and since we had only one draught horse carrying a tent and supplies, we were clearly not merchants visiting Gordyene for business reasons. Emotionless brown eyes peered at me from a face encased by a helmet with large cheek guards, his men wearing similar headgear. The officer was wearing a scale-armour cuirass of rows of overlapping iron scales riveted on to a thick hide vest, reinforced with scale-armour shoulder guards. Black leather pteruges hung from the lower edge of his scale armour to protect his thighs from sword cuts.

'I am waiting,' he said, impatiently.

'I am King Pacorus of Dura,' I informed him, 'and am here to see your king. I assume he is in the city?'

The officer blinked in surprise, momentarily lost for words. His men looked at each other and then at me. The officer saw the scar on my right cheek and then glanced at Bullus. I could read his mind. King Pacorus was a man in his sixties with a scar on his right cheek, which was always clean shaven. But where was Queen Gallia and where were the Amazons, who always escorted the King of Dura? And where was the king's famous griffin banner?

'Are we going to sit here all day?' I snapped.

'Do you have any proof you are who you say you are?' he retorted.

It was an excellent question. I realised I had nothing to prove I was indeed the King of Dura.

'Your king will verify my identity,' I told him. I reached inside my tunic and pulled out the chain holding a lock of Gallia's hair.

'I always wear this around my neck. It is a lock of Queen Gallia's hair. You have heard of Queen Gallia?'

He saw the blonde hair and I saw in his eyes that he knew the story of how Dura's king wore a lock of his wife's blonde hair around his neck. I pulled my sword from its sheath. His men instinctively lowered their lances, but the officer held up a hand to calm them.

'You know what a *spatha* is?'

'I know what a *spatha* is,' he replied.

'How many Parthians do you know who keeps a shaved face, wears a lock of blonde hair around his neck and who is armed with a Roman sword?' said Bullus in exasperation. 'You see our saddlecloths?'

I think they convinced him. The large white blankets had red griffins stitched in each corner, the emblem of Dura.

'I will take you to the city,' said the officer, grudgingly.

'The welcome in Gordyene is not what is was,' remarked Bullus, icily.

We were not taken to the city but rather escorted to the fort nearest to the capital. Built by Spartacus, until this moment I had never stepped inside one. Constructed from the same black stone used to build the city itself, up close it was an impressive affair. The fort was surrounded by a double row of ditches, the spoil from which had been used to construct the sloping rampart on which the walls and square towers at each corner sat. The entrance was a twin-arched affair, the gates plated with iron as a defence against fire and locked by a hefty crossbeam on the inside. The gatehouse had two storeys, with arrow slits on each level and what looked like a fighting platform on the roof. A huge red banner decorated with a silver lion motif fluttered from a flagstaff above the gatehouse. The fort covered a large area, its courtyard surrounded by what appeared to be barracks and stables and fronted by a squat building, the entrance to which was guarded by sentries – Immortals uniformed and equipped like Dura's legionaries.

The officer of our 'welcome party' dismounted.

'Wait here.'

He removed his helmet and marched across the dirt courtyard to what I assumed was some sort of headquarters building, the sentries snapping to attention as he passed them to disappear into the interior. I looked around and saw Immortals patrolling the walls and keeping watch from the roofs of towers, while behind us another party of horsemen trotted towards the gates. Clearly the fort's garrison comprised both foot and horse for defence and attack.

The officer reappeared with an Immortal wearing a red plume in his burnished helmet. He paced over to us and stared up at me, his expression turning from annoyance to alarm. He removed his helmet and bowed his head.

'King Pacorus. My apologies, we did not know you were coming to Gordyene.'

He turned on the officer beside him.

'You idiot, do you not recognise the King of Dura? King Castus will hear of this.'

The haughty officer's eyes bulged with trepidation.

'It is quite all right,' I said. 'I am eager to see the king. Is he in residence?'

'Dismiss your men,' ordered the fort's commander to the unfortunate officer who had stopped us. He smiled at me. 'I will escort you to the palace myself, majesty. Unless you require rest and refreshments.'

'No, we are fully refreshed,' I told him.

'Bring my horse,' barked the commander.

He said nothing further to his chastened subordinate, who slunk off to the stables with his men. A stable hand passed him and his soldiers leading a fine brown stallion with a magnificent red saddlecloth decorated with lion motifs, which the commander mounted. He rode beside me, perturbed by my lack of an escort.

'The consequence of an unforeseen set of circumstances,' I told him, not wishing to divulge I had taken part in a brief but bloody clash with the Aorsi, who were regarded as valued allies in Gordyene, much to my dismay.

'I hear you have a new queen now,' I said, changing the subject.

'Yes, majesty,' he beamed. 'Queen Yesim will make a fine wife for King Castus.'

'Yesim?' I said. 'Is she from Gordyene?'

He shook his head in horror. 'No, majesty, she is from Pontus.'

'Pontus? Then she is the daughter of King Polemon?'

'The daughter of King Laodice, majesty.'

I pulled up Horns. Laodice had been the leader of the hill men of Pontus, who were a scourge on humanity akin to the Aorsi. My heart sank at the prospect of Castus marrying the daughter of a man whose warriors had inflicted great misery on Parthia, not least when they were part of Atrax's rebel army that besieged Irbil. I sank into silence and the commander no longer engaged me in conversation, sensing my sudden frostiness.

At the palace, the commander acted as our escort after our horses had been taken from us by stable hands. Bullus look around at the bleak black stone buildings that fronted the large cobblestone courtyard.

'Something troubles you, Bullus?'

'The last time I was here, majesty, we were about to flee for our lives from the vengeance of King Castus.'

'Do not worry, you are under my protection.'

He said nothing but gave me a sympathetic look, as though anticipating my pledge might not amount to much now we were in the heart of Gordyene. My mood did not lighten as we were shown into the palace, a place of dark, cold corridors, heavy, iron-studded doors and grim-faced guards. Unlike the great palaces in Babylon, Ctesiphon and Hatra, which were spacious, light and airy places, the residence of the King of Gordyene had always been an austere place. It had been a perfect reflection of the brooding menace that had been King Spartacus.

The commander left us in the capable hands of the chief steward, a dour, thin man whose pale skin looked like it had never seen sunlight. As he showed us into our rooms, which were spartan to say the least, he informed us Castus and his queen would see me in the throne room shortly. He loitered in the doorway of my bedroom like an old crow looking for carrion.

'Fetch my clothes and armour from the stables,' I commanded, 'and those of my companion also. And some fresh goose feathers.'

'Goose feathers, majesty?'

'Yes, and make sure they are clean. Now leave me.'

He gave me a condescending smile and bowed his bony head before departing.

'Bullus,' I called.

The centurion appeared seconds later.

'Majesty?'

'Come in and close the door.'

'We have a slight problem, Bullus. As you will have heard, it would appear that the new queen of Gordyene is none other than the daughter of the bandit Laodice, who was one of your targets for assassination last year. And who was killed after the Battle of Melitene, according to Akmon.'

'When young Azar was flogged, I remember,' nodded Bullus.

'Indeed. Well, I doubt his daughter will be well disposed towards anyone associated with her father's death. So be very careful how you reply to any questions you are asked.'

'I could stay here,' he said.

'Unfortunately, Castus is no fool and he will have been informed that two of us arrived in his palace. No, we shall both meet him. I will be the epitome of courtesy and diplomacy to get Klietas back, so I ask you to not do anything to provoke Castus.'

'I'm just…'

'Just a soldier,' I interrupted. 'I know. Let us hope Castus is in an amicable mood now he has found love.'

Slaves brought our armour and helmets, which I ordered to be cleaned, along with my boots. When they had finished and when I had fastened white goose feathers into the crest of my helmet, the spidery chief steward arrived requesting we follow him to the throne room where the king and queen waited. The corridor leading to the royal chamber was dark, notwithstanding the oil lamps that hung from the walls. It resembled a prison and for some reason, a chill came over me as I marched into the throne room. It too had black walls, pillars and ceiling, though fortunately white floor tiles brightened the chamber, plus the oil lamps hanging from the pillars. In front of the wall at the far end stood a black stone dais, on which sat two individuals. Behind them, hanging on the wall, was a huge red banner embossed with a snarling silver lion.

Helmets in the crooks of our arms, Bullus and I walked over to the dais, the steward bowing his head and retreating as we did so. As we got closer, I recognised the loathsome Shamshir, the commander of the King's Guard, standing next to the dais, on the other side the figure of Prince Haytham, the youngest son of Spartacus and Rasha. We halted a few paces from the dais and Bullus bowed his head. I did not bow because I was a king like Castus. That was probably my first mistake.

'King Pacorus,' said Castus coldly, 'what an unexpected pleasure.'

'Greetings Castus,' I replied, my eyes studying the young woman seated next to him. 'I hear congratulations are in order.'

Now he smiled, beaming with delight at his new bride. She had full lips, high cheekbones, olive skin and was attractive enough, considering she had been sired by a brute. But her long black hair was arranged in a long braid that gave her a somewhat severe countenance. She was also dressed in boots, leggings and long-sleeved tunic. I bowed my head to her.

'It is an honour to meet you, lady.'

'Majesty,' Castus corrected me. 'Yesim is a queen.'

I forced a smile. 'Apologies, *majesty*.'

'Who is he?' asked Yesim, ignoring me to point at Bullus.

The centurion, attired in mail armour, silver greaves and carrying a helmet sporting a magnificent white transverse crest, cut an imposing figure in the throne room. He stood spear straight, his black eyes staring straight ahead.

Castus stood and stepped from the dais to circle the centurion.

'This, my queen, is Centurion Bullus, a member of the group of assassins sent by Queen Gallia to rid the world of Dura's enemies. He and they were my guests last year but left without saying goodbye. Perhaps he has returned to kill me.'

Shamshir took a step forward and placed a hand on the hilt of his ukku sword.

'We are here to save a life rather than take any, Castus,' I said.

The young king turned to face me.

'What life?'

'That of Klietas, my former squire who was apprehended by your Aorsi lapdogs a few days ago. By chance, or perhaps it was the will of the gods, I was visiting Klietas when that waste of a skin Spadines arrived with a horde of his thugs.'

Castus took a step forward until our faces were inches apart. He was slightly taller and broader than me, but then he was in his early twenties and I was an old man. He had crystal-clear blue eyes and dark blonde hair, a strange combination bearing in mind his mother and father both had brown eyes and dark hair. Those eyes now bored into me.

'The affairs of Gordyene do not concern Dura.'

'They do if your bandits are invading other kingdoms of the empire and abducting innocent civilians.'

Castus sneered at me. 'Klietas is not innocent.'

I smiled in an attempt at levity.

'You have a new wife, Castus. Concentrate on a new life with her and forget about Haya.'

As soon as the words left my lips I regretted saying them. I winced when Yesim spoke.

'Who is Haya?'

Castus, shaking with anger, spun and smiled at his queen.

'No one, a whore who once bewitched me.'

He turned to face me again.

'You will regret provoking me.'

He stomped back to his throne.

'You are not welcome here, King Pacorus. You will leave my palace and city forthwith, never to return.'

I stood my ground. 'Not without Klietas.'

'He will be sacrificed to the God Ma as a gift to my wife.'

'Ma?' I guffawed. 'Is there such a deity? I have never heard of him.'

'The Goddess Ma is the bringer of victory, the mother goddess who watches over us all,' said Yesim.

I admit I found the whole business of Castus marrying the daughter of a Pontic hill man ludicrous. They did not.

'I may be old,' I said to her, 'but were not your father's warriors slaughtered by the soldiers of Gordyene at Corum and last year outside Melitene? Where was your goddess then when his troops,' I pointed at Castus, 'were butchering your people?'

I heard Haytham take a sharp intake of breath and saw Shamshir glower at me. But Yesim was obviously a calculating woman for she merely shrugged.

'My people were deceived by the traitor King Polemon, who used sorcery to lure my father and his warriors to their deaths. But Ma never forgets her loyal servants and gave me a great gift and told me to take it to King Castus, which would result in my own happiness and that of my people.'

This was gibberish. Had Castus married an insane woman?

'General Shamshir,' said a smug Castus, 'fetch the great prize gifted to me by my beloved wife.'

General Shamshir? More madness. I looked in vain for Hovik, the commander of Gordyene's army and a man who was both reasonable and intelligent, two qualities sadly lacking in Shamshir.

'Where is General Hovik?' I asked, unable to hold my tongue.

'Retired,' answered Castus, leaning forward. 'He was old and the old must give way to the young, King Pacorus, it is the natural order of things. Shamshir is now head of the army and my brother has assumed the duties of leader of the King's Guard.'

I looked at Haytham. 'My congratulations, prince.'

'Thank you, majesty,' he beamed, the smile disappearing when his brother glared at him.

Shamshir was gone only for a short time, returning with two men flanked by guards. Both were solid individuals, though each had unshaved faces and unkempt hair. They were dressed in simple red tunics and black leggings – the uniform of a common soldier in Gordyene's army – though when they were bundled in front of the king, my jaw dropped in astonishment. One was Titus Tullus, the former trusty centurion of Mark Antony, latterly the commander of King Polemon's palace guard, and a man who was supposed to be dead.

'That's one lucky bastard,' whispered Bullus.

Castus looked at the sorry pair and pointed at me.

'This is King Pacorus of Dura. I believe you know him, Tullus, but you have not had the pleasure, ambassador,' he said.

They both turned to look at us.

'It is good to see you again, majesty,' said Tullus.

He had visibly aged since the last time I saw him, when he had been the commander of the execution party assigned to nail me to a cross in front of Irbil's citadel when Atrax had besieged the city. To be fair to him, he had tried to save my life, but I had been unwilling to pay homage to Atrax.

'It is good to see you, general,' I answered.

He had a cough and his eyes were sunken, indications of mistreatment. His companion, a man who looked younger than Bullus but also possessed of a martial bearing, looked kindly at me.

'It is an honour to meet the famous King Pacorus. My name…'

'He is Gaius Arrianus,' interrupted Castus, 'Roman ambassador to the court of King Polemon and currently a guest of the Kingdom of Gordyene.'

The ambassador had a square jaw, broad forehead and long nose, but the jaw was covered in stubble, his hair was uncut and his clothes entirely inappropriate for a man of his position. I was appalled.

'Have you taken leave of your senses, Castus? Do you not realise that Roman ambassadors are accorded the friendship of Caesar Augustus himself? You insult or mistreat one of them, you insult the leader of the Roman world. Release them at once.'

Castus was initially stunned by my outburst and for a moment became a worried young man, but his viper of a wife soon coaxed the cunning young king back.

'Are you going to allow him to speak to you like that in your own palace, conqueror of the world?' she cooed.

I burst into laughter. 'Conqueror of the world? Have you both been inhaling *charas*?'

They gave me quizzical stares.

'It is a resin burnt in temples,' I explained. 'and whereas it has a calming effect if inhaled in moderation, if ingested in excess it can lead to delusions.'

Yesim toyed with her braid, draped over her right shoulder.

'Were the great victories at Kayseri and Melitene a delusion, King of Dura? Was the gold paid by the vanquished to my husband a mirage?'

She pointed at Tullus and the ambassador.

'The Romans and the traitor King Polemon will pay handsomely to get these two back.'

'In my experience,' I said, 'the Romans do not take kindly to being blackmailed. I would advise sending the ambassador and general back to Pontus forthwith, along with a humble apology.'

'Apology?' roared Castus. 'I did not defeat the Romans at Kayseri and their lackeys at Melitene to meekly apologise to those I vanquished.'

'I may be old, but I seem to remember it was Kewab whose plan defeated the enemy at Kayseri and Melitene, not yours. Indeed, Kewab would not have been at Melitene had it not been…'

I stopped myself from divulging the intelligence concerning the great coalition gathering at Melitene had been gleaned by Talib and his fellow assassins. I had no desire to reveal what was Dura's sordid secret. But Castus was now intrigued.

'Had it not been for what, King Pacorus?'

'I grow tired of being interrogated, Castus,' I said, irritably. 'When Spadines and his rabble finally arrive, you will kindly turn Klietas over to me, and in the meantime, you will release these two individuals at once,' I pointed at Tullus and Gaius Arrianus.

'Who is this man to dictate to you in such an insulting tone?' sneered Yesim.

'He was a great commander once,' sniffed Castus, 'but that was long ago. I tolerate him out of respect for an old man. But his words carry no weight, my love.'

'No weight at all.'

I gave a loud groan when Spadines swept into the chamber, an impish grin on his face, which prompted equally devilish smiles to appear on the faces of Castus and his wife.

'You have him, lord prince?' asked Castus.

Spadines halted before the dais and bowed deeply to the rulers of Gordyene.

'I have him, great king, as promised.' He shot me a murderous glance. 'Despite the attempts of some to prevent my orders being carried out.'

'Explain,' commanded Castus.

Spadines proceeded to inform him about the battle at Vazneh, revealing he had lost a great many men killed and wounded, which brought a smile to my face.

'You think this is funny?' Castus accused me.

'There is much I find amusing, Castus, not least that you would entrust a mission to a Sarmatian, though as it was one of abduction, murder and destruction, I can see why you would choose Spadines.'

'You will pay for that,' seethed Spadines. 'I demand he apologises to me immediately, majesty.'

Castus looked at me expectantly.

'The day I apologise to an Aorsi is the day I give up on life,' I said.

'I demand justice, majesty,' spat Spadines.

Yesim suddenly reached over to stroke Castus' head, whispering into his ear. He nodded.

'You are right. There is much to think about. King Pacorus, you and your companion will surrender your weapons and wait in the palace until I have decided what to do with you both.'

'This is an outrage,' said Bullus, loudly.

Castus merely flicked a hand at Shamshir who ordered Immortals to take our weapons.

'Do as he asks,' I ordered Bullus, unbuckling my sword belt and handing it to the nearest soldier. Gaius Arrianus looked intently at the dagger fastened to my sword belt.

'By what strange twist of fate do you possess a parazonium dagger?' he said.

'Nothing strange about it, ambassador,' I smiled. 'It was a gift from a friend. You may have heard of him. Marcus Vipsanius Agrippa.'

Gaius Arrianus was stunned. 'You are a friend of Agrippa?'

'He was in Dura recently,' I replied, casually. 'I found him most agreeable.'

Shamshir stood in front of me and pointed towards the throne room's entrance. I took the hint and walked away from the dais.

'I hope you are the conqueror of the world, Castus,' I called, 'because the number of Gordyene's enemies is increasing by the day.'

Chapter 8

We were not marched to the cells after our audience with Castus; rather, we were placed in a wing of the palace where Gaius Arrianus and Titus Tullus had been confined. A thick oak door led to a communal area, off which were a number of small bedrooms. There were couches, tables and chairs in the communal area and each bedroom had a single bed, a small bedside table and candles for night-time illumination. But the windows were narrow and high on the walls, allowing some light to enter the rooms but small enough to prevent anyone from escaping through them.

'Refreshments will be brought to you, shortly,' smiled a gloating Shamshir.

'If you have any influence with your king, I would strongly advise you convince him to release us all at once,' I said. Gordyene's new army commander closed and bolted the door behind him.

'You are wasting your breath, majesty,' sighed Gaius, 'our new Alexander has been seduced by the twin evils.'

I flopped down on a couch, glad to take the weight off my aching feet.

'Twin evils?'

'Gold and glory,' replied Gaius, also sitting on a couch.

I indicated to Tullus that he too should sit, as I placed my helmet on the floor beside the couch.

'Arrogant little bastard wants to ransom us,' spat Bullus, 'for ten thousand talents of gold each.'

'Language, general,' Gaius rebuked him. 'You insult an ally of King Pacorus.'

'Dura's alliance with Gordyene is like a frayed rope, ambassador,' I said, 'it weakens by the day. But it is I who should be apologising to you for the ill-treatment meted out to you both.'

The door was unbolted and slaves carrying food and drink appeared, along with Immortals who kept a close eye on us as we were served wine. The slaves left fruit, bread, cheese and sweet meats, along with two jugs of wine. They also left us with fresh water, bowls and towels with which to wash our faces and hands.

'Our confinement in this palace is not unbearable,' admitted Gaius, 'aside from our loss of liberty. The hospitality of Queen Yesim and her people, on the other hand, leaves a lot to be desired.'

He told me how he and Bullus had been ambushed in the highlands of Pontus, after which their lives had been spared, though they had both been mistreated harshly. They had expected a grisly death, but instead Yesim had hauled them off to Gordyene.

'Yesim is not to be underestimated,' Gaius cautioned me. 'She essentially sold us to King Castus in exchange for food for her people.'

'Food?' said Bullus. 'Don't they know how to grow their own?'

'Unfortunately for the hill tribes of Pontus,' replied Gaius, 'many of their menfolk were killed by King Castus outside Melitene last year. But she also enchanted the young king to make herself Queen of Gordyene.'

'Not to be underestimated, indeed,' I agreed. 'I would not worry, ambassador. Before I came here, I despatched couriers to Irbil to alert King Akmon of what was happening in the north of his kingdom. They will also notify Dura.'

'I fear King Castus is unhinged, majesty,' said Gaius.

'He will kill the one you came here to save, lord,' added Tullus.

'If he does, he will face war,' I said.

Gaius' eyes opened wide with surprise and even Tullus was astonished.

'This man is dear to you, majesty?' enquired Gaius.

'He was, and indeed is, a poor farmer, an orphan who for a while was my squire,' I told him. 'He also saved my life, and for that alone I am in his debt. But even if that were not the case, I would still go to war for him.'

'For a farmer?' Tullus was amazed.

'For a principle, general,' I answered. 'All men, irrespective of whether they are born high or low, deserve the protection of the law. Without the law there is no order; and without order there is only chaos.'

'I mean no disrespect, majesty,' said Tullus, 'but you are here, alone, and at the mercy of King Castus and his bitch of a wife.'

I filled a cup with wine and took a sip. I registered surprise at the taste.

'At least Gordyene has fine wines,' said Gaius.

'I learned long ago not to prize my life too highly, general,' I replied to Titus Tullus. 'If Castus kills me, my wife will avenge me, and my eldest daughter is adviser to King of Kings Phraates.'

'The taste of victory has intoxicated King Castus, I fear,' remarked Gaius, 'and combined with the entrancing Yesim, I fear his mind has been corrupted.'

As far as I knew, Spartacus had never been cruel to his sons. But he had been hard with them, taking them on their first campaign when they were mere boys and showing them the horrors of the battlefield after his great victory at Mepsila. I doubted he showed them any affection and was quite prepared to lose Akmon when he had the effrontery to run off with Lusin. Akmon did not have a cruel streak, but the same could not be said for his brother.

I had noted how both the ambassador and Tullus had stubble on their faces, Gaius informing me that Castus only supplied shaving instruments to the pair once a week. He knew Roman men liked to keep clean-shaven faces and so denied them the opportunity to shave on a daily basis. He did the same with me that night, knowing I too did not sport a beard. He also denied me writing materials when I requested them. I found it irksome but, more ominously, these things pointed to a disturbed mind.

The next morning, after we had been treated to a fine breakfast and given fresh clothes, albeit the uniform of Gordyene's soldiers, we were escorted back to the throne room. The oily chief steward had taken away our old clothes, helmets and armour to be cleaned and polished, or so he said. I wondered if we would ever see them again. This annoyed me in particular because my *spatha* had been a present from Spartacus and my armour and helmet a gift from Castus, two friends now long dead. My humour did not improve when standing in a line like prisoners about to be sentenced, we faced a grinning King Castus and Queen Yesim. My blood boiled when Shamshir appeared leading Klietas by a rope wrapped around his young neck. He was also shackled and had a few cuts and bruises on his face. That visage lit up when he saw me.

'Are you hurt, Klietas?' I asked.

'No, majesty, I am fine,' he lied.

Shamshir turned and struck him across the face with the back of his hand.

'No talking.'

'You have had your fun, Castus,' I growled. 'Now it is time to grow up. I make this pledge now. If you kill Klietas, you will have war with Dura.'

Spadines, Shamshir and Haytham were shocked by my declaration but Castus waved a hand dismissively in my direction.

'Yes, yes, we have all heard the threats of the King of Dura before, but this one is an empty one. I could have you killed right here, right now.'

'Then why don't you?' I said.

'I am a fair man, King Pacorus,' he spouted, prompting Bullus to laugh. Castus ignored him.

'Years ago,' waxed Castus, 'I heard a story of how you and your queen travelled to a Roman city to take part in gladiatorial games.'

'Ephesus,' I said, glancing at a bemused Gaius Arrianus. 'It was a long time ago.'

'And, of course, you were a friend of the gladiator Spartacus, whom my father was named after.'

He laid a hand on Yesim's arm.

'My wife had a vision last night. She saw two men fighting in a great arena to decide the fate of a farmer, presided over by a king and queen. One of those fighting had the feet of a griffin.'

He pointed at me. 'That man was you, King Pacorus.'

He then pointed at Klietas. 'You wish to save this wretched individual? Then fight for him, King Pacorus. Let the gods decide if he should live or die. Do you accept the challenge?'

Yesim had a smug expression on her face, Castus feigning indifference. But Bullus was outraged.

'You dare talk to King Pacorus in such a manner?'

Castus chuckled. 'I will say what I like in my own palace and do as I like. I have given your king a chance to save his former squire, who was due to be sacrificed in honour of my wife.'

'My conqueror is merciful,' said Yesim, looking lovingly at her husband.

'I will take the king's place,' offered Bullus.

'Your offer is declined,' said Castus, dismissively. 'King Pacorus wants to save the farmer so much, let him fight for him.'

'I accept,' I said, 'if only to shut you up.'

'Prince Spadines will select a champion from among his people to face you in the arena,' said Castus, 'for you have consistently denigrated the Aorsi over the years, thus damaging their reputation.'

'Their reputation?' I scoffed. 'The only reputation they have is for being thieves and murderers, though granted they maintain it impeccably.'

'You have insulted me and my people long enough, King of Dura,' shouted Spadines. 'You will now face the consequences of your actions.'

Castus gave the command to escort me from the throne room, Bullus and the two Romans also being roughly bundled from the chamber.

'Rome will hear of this, majesty,' called Gaius Arrianus. 'King Pacorus is a personal friend of Marcus Vipsanius Agrippa, the second-most important individual in the Roman world.'

'I thank you, ambassador,' I said to him as we were led away, 'but I fear your words are wasted on a poisoned mind.'

At the entrance to the palace we were separated, Gaius and the other two being marched across the palace courtyard and up a set of stone steps leading to the battlements. A few minutes later Castus, Yesim, Spadines and a sheepish-looking Haytham appeared behind me, walking across the courtyard to the large, three-storey gatehouse and disappearing into the imposing structure. Shamshir stood beside me but said nothing, avoiding my eyes. Behind me a pair of Immortals stood with swords drawn. The atmosphere was oppressive, laced with the threat of impending violence.

It became more so when other Immortals began to file into the courtyard, dozens of them. Under instructions from their centurions, or whatever the commander of a hundred-man battalion of Gordyene's foot soldiers was called, the troops formed a large hollow square, each man facing inwards. Behind each Immortal stood another soldier to make two rows on each side of the makeshift square. Perhaps Castus thought I would try to escape, hence the additional security. I saw him and his wife appear on the roof of the gatehouse, giving them an uninterrupted view of the courtyard below. Shamshir placed a hand in the middle of my back to move me forward.

'Take your filthy hands off me,' I said, walking down the palace steps.

He smarted at my tone but said nothing, probably reasoning there was little point into getting into an argument with a dead man. The square of Immortals parted when I reached it, an officer bowing his head and handing me a shield and a *gladius*, though it was forbidden to call the short swords that equipped the Immortals by that name. I felt a dull ache in my left leg and smiled to myself. Whatever Castus had in store for me would not last long before my leg gave out.

I walked into the re-formed square and saw a man standing across from me, on the opposite side. He was a tall, gangly individual with a large black beard and shoulder-length hair. In one hand he held an axe, in the other a long knife. When he saw me, he raised his weapons in the air and screamed abuse at me.

'I am Abdarak, champion of Prince Spadines and you are the son of a lowborn whore.'

He mimicked an effeminate walk. 'You are a boy-lover and a eunuch who has no balls. You are a molester of horses.'

That was a new one.

'Tonight, my people will be feasting on your intestines and my king will be drinking wine from your skull.'

His inane rantings were interrupted by a blast of trumpets, which mercifully stopped him in mid-insult. As one, the front row of Immortals knelt, resting their shields on the cobblestones. After they had done so, the second row stepped forward and rested the bottom edge of their shields on the top rims of those resting on the cobbles in front, thus creating a four-sided arena. Abdarak looked up at the assembled dignitaries on the roof of the gatehouse, raising his weapons aloft. I too gazed up at the king and his guests, and then at my fellow prisoners on the battlements, who had been joined by Klietas. Castus slowly raised his arm and then chopped it down to signal the beginning of the fight.

I was a man in his sixties, Abdarak was perhaps half my age, but he made a common mistake when a younger man fights an older opponent. He ran at me in an attempt to kill me as quickly as possible. Had he given the match any thought, he would have realised the most effective tactic would be to wear me down. He was younger, stronger and possessed of more stamina than me, and the longer the bout went on, the greater the chance of him emerging victorious. Like me he wore no helmet or armour, but unlike me his face was contorted with rage as he sprinted towards me, axe held at arm's length, ready to swing it and split my head open. My options were to feint left and right at the last moment, to try to avoid his blow, to run at him and meet him halfway, or, the best option, use my shield to block the blow and thrust at his unprotected body with my sword.

The Roman shield was one of the world's greatest inventions. A curved rectangular board weighing around twenty pounds, made of three strips of wood laminated in three alternate layers, faced with hide and edged with metal, it was both a defensive and offensive tool. Held by a horizontal grip positioned in the centre of the shield, which was protected by a metal boss facing the enemy, it can be used to smash into an opponent to barge him aside or knock him over.

Seconds before Abdarak delivered his overhead axe blow I stepped forward, crouched low and caught the strike on the shield, the iron edge ripping the hide cover. I thrust the *gladius* forward low under the shield and whipped it back, slicing the side of his left calf. Raised to fury, I doubt he felt it immediately, but blood showed on his leggings as he stabbed the knife he held in his left hand forward. But I had already withdrawn, which meant he had stabbed air. I roared in triumph.

First blood to the old man.

He circled me, his arms in constant motion to confuse me.

'Your mother was a whore and your wife *is* a whore.'

Ignore the words, focus on his weapons.

He suddenly lunged forward, leading with his left hand, the point of his dagger aimed at my face. I brought up the shield to stop the knife, Abdarak swinging his axe sideways to slice open my side. But I spun left to rotate the shield to place it between myself and the axe blade, thrusting the *gladius* over the top edge to stab the point into his left shoulder. He cried out in pain.

Second blood to the old man.

I was beginning to enjoy myself against this oaf of a Sarmatian, who was now bleeding from two wounds. He came at me again with a blizzard of axe blows, chopping down from the left and right in an effort to decapitate me. But I kept moving backwards and sideways, using my shield to defeat the strikes, constantly jabbing my *gladius* forward to keep his knife away from me.

Abdarak came at me again, all rage and flailing arms, intent on hacking me to pieces in a deluge of axe and knife blows. But feral anger can only achieve so much and if an opponent can retain his composure when confronted by a wild demon, he had the upper hand. Like Dura's foot soldiers were trained to do seconds before a clash of arms, I stepped forward rather than wait to be struck, moving to my left. I shoved my shield forward to stop his axe, the iron edge smashing into the hide and wood. At the same time, I spun left to take me beyond the reach of his knife. I crouched low to thrust the point of the *gladius* below the bottom edge of my shield, the metal piercing his leggings just above the right knee.

Third blood to the old man.

I roared with triumph as he staggered back, banging the edge of the *gladius* on the front face of my shield. He was panting heavily and now bleeding from three wounds, and had I been thirty years younger I could have dashed forward and finished him off with ease. But I was old and suddenly a spasm of pain shot through my left leg. I winced in agony and my leg began to give way. Thinking quickly, I crouched down to place the bottom edge of the shield on the cobbles, so it became a rest. Another spasm of pain, this one more severe, tortured my leg and I groaned in pain.

Abdarak, seconds before looking like a beaten, bleeding man, saw my agony and drew strength from my disability. He licked his lips and smiled with relish, sensing I was helpless. I was! If I brought up my shield to defend myself, I would surely collapse to the ground. If I fell to the ground I was a dead man. I knew it. He probably knew it. So, I waited to be battered, stabbed and cut into submission. Abdarak was in no rush, wanting to savour the moments leading up to my demise. But he was also cut and bleeding and had to ration his reserves accordingly. He moved slowly towards me, axe and knife in hand. His eyes flitted from mine to the *gladius* I still gripped in my right hand, wary of the weapon that had cut his flesh.

Then, beyond the palace walls, bells started ringing.

Abdarak stopped and looked around as the wall of shields dissolved and Immortals began running in all directions, officers shouting orders at them to man the walls. Alarm bells were ringing in the city and now in the palace grounds. It could only mean one thing: Vanadzor was in peril. I gingerly put pressure on my left leg and found I could stand on it again without the need for the shield. I took three steps forward and plunged the *gladius* into Abdarak's chest. His body stiffened when the metal was driven through his ribcage into his heart, becoming limp when I yanked it out of his torso. He collapsed to the ground, dead.

'That is for calling my mother and wife whores.'

I looked around and realised I was being totally ignored as soldiers were streaming up stone steps to take up position on the walls, or were running to the armouries to be issued with javelins and quivers of arrows. I looked up at the roof of the gatehouse and saw it empty. Castus and his queen were nowhere to be seen. But then I saw Bullus, Klietas, Gaius Arrianus and Titus Tullus being escorted towards me by a burly centurion, or whatever the equivalent was called in Gordyene, and half a dozen Immortals. He pointed at my blood-smeared *gladius*.

'I will have to relieve you of that, majesty, if I may.'

His tone was conciliatory, almost apologetic. He glanced at the corpse of Abdarak.

'Fine work, if I may say so.'

I handed him the sword. 'You may.'

Bullus was grinning from ear to ear. 'You still have it, majesty.'

I fell in beside him as we ambled back to the palace, around us organised chaos as the palace walls were filled by fully armed soldiers.

'That was a clever ruse, majesty,' said Gaius, admiringly.

'Ruse?'

'Feigning injury to lure him into a false sense of security.'

I laughed. 'Alas, ambassador, the injury is real. An old leg wound courtesy of an enemy arrow shot many years ago, a

Parthian arrow, I might add. What you saw was an old man waiting to be struck down, before the gods intervened.'

Bullus looked around. 'I can't see her.'

'Who?' I asked.

'The beautiful lady with the large breasts.'

I rolled my eyes and addressed the commander of our escort party.

'I take it the alarm is not a drill.'

'No, majesty, it is not a drill.'

'Then what?'

'At this point in time, majesty, I know as much as you do.'

We were taken back to our quarters in the palace, which were eerily quiet while outside pandemonium reigned. Slaves brought us refreshments and the serpent-like chief steward appeared to enquire if I wanted medical attention. I said no and asked him what was going on, but he merely feigned ignorance, bowed in a fawning fashion and departed in haste. As I collapsed on a couch and gratefully accepted a goblet of wine from Klietas, who had assumed the duties of squire once more, my mind raced with theories, eventually coming to the only logical conclusion.

I looked at Gaius sitting opposite. 'I assume the governor of Syria is on the way at the head of several legions to rescue you, ambassador.'

He raised his eyebrows in surprise. 'I very much doubt that, majesty. The governor would make an appeal to

Ctesiphon to intercede for my release first, and only after that had been turned down would force be considered, and only then on the specific orders of Augustus himself.'

'The Armenians?' offered Tullus. 'They have enough reasons to despise King Castus.'

Gaius discounted the notion. 'King Artaxias may indeed despise young Castus but having been mauled by the Parthians on several occasions, and latterly by Gordyene, I doubt he has the appetite to repeat the experience.'

The chief steward reappeared with slaves holding my clothes, armour, helmet and sword.

'King Castus requests your presence in the throne room, majesty,' he squeaked, 'after you have eaten and changed, of course.'

I pointed at the ambassador and Tullus.

'Fresh clothes will be brought for my companions, too,' I told him, 'and anything else they require.'

'It shall be done, majesty,' he replied, almost bent double as he grovelled before me.

'And bring a physician to attend to my squire's wounds.'

Klietas, one eye purple from being struck, protested.

'I am fine, majesty.'

'No, you are not,' I snapped, 'you have been abducted and beaten.'

'A physician will be summoned, majesty. Is there anything else?'

'A large-breasted woman?' grinned Bullus.

'Not now, Bullus,' I said.

'You may inform King Castus I will attend him shortly,' I told the steward, sipping at my wine. 'You may go.'

'Castus is sweating,' gloated Bullus, emptying his goblet and holding it out to Klietas for it to be refilled.

'You are impertinent, Bullus,' I said, 'but entirely right. Let's make him sweat a little longer.'

After I had finished my wine and sampled a few of the palace's pastries, which were a little hard, I changed into my fresh clothes and armour, strapped on my sword belt and examined the goose feathers in my helmet's crest. I then left for the throne room, an honour guard of Immortals commanded by the same centurion who had escorted us from the courtyard accompanying me along the palace's dour corridors, the pain in my leg having mercifully subsided. When we arrived at the throne room, Castus gave the impression of being a worried man, pacing up and down in front of the dais, his calculating queen seated on her throne eyeing me suspiciously. She I ignored as I walked up to a flustered Castus.

'Do you know anything about this?' he babbled.

'About what, Castus?'

He pointed at the wall.

'An army of horsemen is approaching Vanadzor from the east, led by the ingrate King Ali of Atropaiene. You know him?'

'The lord high general of the empire,' I said, casually, 'of course. He is a fine man.'

Castus stopped to glower at me. 'A fine man? He brings an invading army into my kingdom and you call him a fine man?'

'King Ali is not given to rash actions,' I remarked, looking at Yesim. 'He must have been greatly provoked to take such action. I wonder what provoked him?'

Shamshir and Haytham stood by the side of the dais and they both shifted uneasily on their feet, hinting they knew the reason for Ali's invasion. Fortunately, Spadines was not present. Perhaps he was sobbing over the body of Abdarak. I sincerely hoped so.

'You will go to King Ali and request he and his army withdraw from Gordyene,' Castus said suddenly. 'You know him; I do not. I have no wish to embroil Gordyene in an unnecessary war.'

I looked behind me left and right.

'Did you not hear me, King Pacorus?' said Castus, testily.

'My apologies,' I replied, 'I thought you were talking to a low-ranking officer or a slave by the tone of your voice.'

He smarted at my words.

'You send your Sarmatian dogs into Media to murder and destroy, you abduct my former squire, you imprison a Roman ambassador and, finally, you make me fight in a gladiatorial contest to amuse your new wife.

'Why should I help you, *boy*?'

His eyes filled with anger and his wife and Shamshir gave me murderous looks, made worse by the smug expression I was wearing. He had revealed he needed me, and I was relishing the power I had over him in that moment. I decided to be magnanimous and not let him squirm.

'I will help you, Castus. Though my aid is dependent on certain conditions being met.'

His eyes narrowed. 'What conditions?'

I held out my helmet and examined the goose-feather crest. The tension in the room was rising by the second.

'First, you will release Klietas to me. Second, you will also release Gaius Arrianus and Titus Tullus to me. Third, you will pledge, here, in your own palace, to keep your Sarmatian dogs out of Media. And, finally, you will swear on your honour to never again threaten the life of Klietas, or do harm to his wife, his children or his property.'

Before he could answer, an officer of the King's Guard entered the chamber, marched up to the dais, saluted to Shamshir and handed him a note. The army commander read it, frowned and handed it to Castus. The king tossed it to the ground.

'I agree to your damned conditions. You will leave at once to meet with King Ali.'

'Please,' I smiled.

'What?'

'Say please.'

He was shaking with anger, made worse by the fact he needed me, and he knew it. Yesim looked as though she about to spring from her throne to rip out my throat, which made me even happier.

'Will you please ride to King Ali and convince him to turn around and go back to Atropaiene?' he asked.

'It will be a pleasure, majesty.'

The note Castus had tossed to the floor was a reconnaissance report informing him King Ali's force was a mere fifty miles from Vanadzor, closing fast on the capital. It had invaded Gordyene north of Lake Urmia to advance on the city from the northeast. It was feared advance parties of horsemen might have been sent ahead to raid the Pambak Valley, hence the alarm bells being sounded in the city.

I returned to the quarters I shared with the other captives to inform them they would soon be free to leave the palace, and indeed Vanadzor. However, I suggested they stay with me until I had spoken to King Ali personally.

'I trust Castus to keep his word, but I do not trust Spadines, the more so because I killed his champion.'

'He could easily kill all of us riding in one group, majesty,' said Bullus.

'Good point,' I agreed. 'I will have Castus provide us with an escort.'

We rode from the palace that afternoon in the company of Prince Haytham and a score of King's Guard, plus packhorses carrying tents and supplies.

As we rode through the Pambak Valley I was gripped by a sincere desire to avoid bloodshed between Gordyene and

Atropaiene. The valley, surrounded by tree-covered hills and filled with thriving villages, had not seen war for nearly four decades, since the time when Surena had rid the land of Roman occupation. No, that was incorrect. It had seen more violence briefly when grief and power had corrupted Surena, leading to Orodes bringing an army into Gordyene, which won a great but costly victory before the walls of Vanadzor. And now another Parthian army was approaching the kingdom's capital.

Haytham was nineteen now, his rectangular face framed by thick, long hair as black as night. He was shorter than both his brothers but more muscular and had a stolid disposition. Despite his age, he was already a veteran of numerous campaigns and it was testament to his dependability and talents that Castus had made him commander of the élite King's Guard.

For the first hour of the journey no one spoke, the jangling of horse saddlery and the clop of hooves on the hard dirt track being the only sounds. Haytham stared directly ahead, probably embarrassed by his brother's behaviour towards me and Gaius Arrianus. My observations of him in the palace suggested he was uncomfortable with his sibling's actions. Eventually, I grew tired of the silence.

'Before we encounter King Ali and his army,' I said to him, 'can you think of a reason why the lord high general of the empire would wage war against Gordyene?'

'You will have to ask him, majesty,' he replied.

'I am asking you,' I said, forcefully. 'I have known Ali for a long time, and he is not given to making rash actions. Did Castus ever meet his daughter, Princess Elaheh?'

'No, majesty. Yesim appeared at Vanadzor before the princess' arrival. My brother was enchanted by the daughter of Laodice.'

'More fool him,' remarked Tullus behind us, 'though the bitch's scheming saved my life and that of the ambassador.'

'Queen Yesim is certainly a force to be reckoned with,' conceded Gaius, 'but I fear she will drag Gordyene into a war it cannot win.'

'A war with Rome?' I asked, concerned a woman from the Pontic hill tribes might plunge Parthia into yet another war with Rome.

'I doubt Augustus will sanction hostilities against Parthia, majesty,' he said, 'especially as you have engineered our release. No, I was thinking of the war that will be waged against Gordyene by other Parthian kingdoms if King Castus continues to behave in an unpredictable manner.'

'I did warn him against marrying Yesim,' added Haytham, 'as did Treasurer Khalos.'

'Khalos?' I queried.

'One of my father's most trusted advisers,' replied Haytham. 'He had engineered the marriage between Castus and Elaheh. His reward was to be sent to Melitene to be the ambassador there.'

'And Hovik?' I asked.

Haytham sighed. 'The general was retired when he too voiced concerns over the marriage to Yesim.'

'I can only assume King Ali has taken the insult to his daughter very badly,' surmised Gaius, 'hence his desire to punish Gordyene.'

It was a plausible explanation but still seemed an extreme reaction to a slight against a daughter. Had Castus raped the girl, then Ali's decision to march to war would have been understandable. But the pair had never met and in such cases where a marriage contract is wilfully broken, a financial penalty is usually agreed upon. Castus certainly had enough gold to pay what amounted to a fine, so as we trotted out of the Pambak Valley I was still at a loss as to why Ali had brought the army of Atropaiene into Gordyene.

On the second day of our journey, Haytham's spirits dipped when we encountered a large party of horse archers led by a man with a hideously scarred face by the name of Ulvi, a lord of Gordyene whose lands were in the path of the invading army. Most nobles in this part of the kingdom lived in stone strongholds perched on rugged hillsides overlooking fertile valleys that provided an abundance of crops, game and timber. The windswept mountain meadows were usually devoid of life in the autumn and winter, though in the spring and summer many villagers took themselves and their flocks to the high regions to live in felt tents and graze their animals on the lush foliage.

Ulvi wore his hair and beard long like a wild man of the mountains that his ancestors had been, and perhaps he still was. He wore a cuirass of thick black leather and carried a sword at his hip, his men wearing no armour and like him no headgear. He smiled and bowed his head when he recognised Haytham, his scars shaping his face into the vision of a hideous demon when he did so. Indeed, for a moment I thought it was the demon Pazuzu riding at the head of a column of horsemen so disfigured was his face.

'Greeting, highness,' he said in a deep voice, 'it is good to see you.'

Haytham extended a hand to me.

'It is good to see you also, Ulvi. This is King Pacorus of Dura, who has come to speak with King Ali.'

Ulvi was surprised and the horsemen immediately behind him began to talk to each other in an animated fashion. Ulvi's ugly face again twisted into a smile-cum-demonic leer.

'The army of Dura is here? Praise the gods.'

'Alas, no,' I told him. 'Merely its king. However, King Ali is an old friend and I hope to convince him to withdraw back to his kingdom.'

'You have news of King Ali's whereabouts, Ulvi?' asked Haytham.

The lord nodded. 'Around a day's ride east of here, highness. All horsemen, very many of them.'

'How many?' I enquired.

Ulvi turned and beckoned a rider forward, an individual who looked like he had been dragged feet-first through a thicket. His horse, a brown mare, by comparison, had a shining coat, immaculate mane and tail and a muscular frame.

'This is one of my best scouts. Tell King Pacorus what you told me, Agar.'

Agar smiled and bowed his head to me, suddenly slapping the side of his face to kill a fly on his skin. Probably one among the colony living in his beard.

'I tracked them for two days, highborn, before they had reached the great lake. There are at least fifty thousand horsemen, plus hundreds of camels carrying supplies. They are moving slowly, highborn, as a precaution against ambushes.'

'Then we must move more quickly,' I said, 'to intercept them before they reach Vanadzor.'

'Have they plundered the land?' asked Haytham.

Ulvi shook his head. 'I moved my people and their animals to higher ground, highness, but thus far King Ali has refrained from destroying villages and crops.'

That was something, at least, but fifty thousand horsemen were a force to be reckoned with, not least because they were led by the lord high general of the empire, who in theory could call upon all the other kingdoms to supplement the army of Atropaiene should he so desire. Castus, like Surena and Spartacus before him, would wait until the enemy was in the Pambak Valley before offering battle, using the professional army of Gordyene to defeat the enemy, after which what remained of Ali and his men, isolated and far from home, would either be destroyed or harried by men such as Ulvi and his retainers all the way back to Atropaiene. At least that was the theory.

Ulvi and his men led us along unknown tracks through forests of beech, oaks, elms and maples, above us the air rumbling with thunder to announce a deluge of rainfall that freshened the air and invigorated the senses. Ulvi sent out parties to hunt deer for our evening meal, riders returning with carcasses draped over their horses.

Before the sun had set, we made camp just off the track near a fast-flowing stream filled with ice-cold water. There was no space among the trees on the hillside to pitch tents so Ulvi and his men collected firewood and fashioned shelters from branches they chopped from trees with their axes. When dusk came a myriad of campfires flickered among the elms, around which were groups of men turning venison on spits, the pleasing aroma of cooking meat filling the forest. Before the rain it had been fresh, but with the coming of night the temperature dropped markedly to cool the air and mist the breath.

We sat huddled round raging campfires wrapped in thick woollen cloaks and feasting on freshly cooked meat, washed down with wine. Klietas ensured our fire was fed at regular intervals and fussed around us to keep us fed and watered. I sat in the company of Bullus, Gaius and Tullus, the centurion and former centurion swapping war stories and discovering a soldierly bond between two former adversaries. I had warned Bullus not to divulge that Gallia wanted the commander of King Polemon's palace guard dead, not least because for some strange reason I did not wish Gaius to know Dura sanctioned assassination.

'What will you report to Rome when you return?' I asked the ambassador.

'That I was captured by the barbarian hill tribes of Pontus, sold to King Castus and rescued by the King of Dura, a man whom I was privileged to meet and who saved my life.'

'That is very generous of you,' I said.

'It is the truth, majesty. I have no doubt I and General Tullus would have met the same fate as your former squire. Queen Yesim is full of poison and King Castus is besotted with her, a combination that bodes ill for Gordyene.'

'Augustus might desire retribution against the king who imprisoned his ambassador and friend,' I suggested.

'Augustus will have no need to punish Gordyene, majesty,' he said.

'Why is that?'

'Because other Parthians will do that for him. After all, is that not the reason we are camped in a forest eating meat and drinking wine? So, you will try to convince King Ali of Atropaiene not to attack Gordyene?'

'I hope to convince King Ali to turn around, yes.'

'You are probably the most influential man in all Parthia, majesty, the man who humbled Rome and forged the Parthian Empire into the mighty instrument it is today.'

'I fear you overestimate me, ambassador.'

The flames highlighted his now clean-shaven square jaw and broad forehead, for a moment reminding me of Marcus Licinius Crassus, a man I had fond memories of, despite him being my enemy. He was far from his mansion in Sinope, and among wild horsemen of Parthia, but propped up by his saddle wrapped in a thick blanket and a thick cloak, he looked relaxed and indeed at home. It comforted me to believe he felt safe and secure in my company, or perhaps it was nothing to do with me but was rather Roman arrogance that led him to believe no one, not even the unhinged King Castus, would dare harm him. I had met many Romans but this one did not appear to be imbued with the unshakeable belief, akin to a religious conviction, that Rome's destiny was to rule the world. But then, this 'Roman' was actually a Greek.

'I thought all Rome's ambassadors were Roman,' I said. 'But you are Greek.'

'I was fortunate in being sent to Rome by my parents to further my education and career, majesty, which brought me to the attention of Augustus and set me on the path that led to Pontus and now Parthia.'

'We will soon have you back in Pontus, ambassador,' I said, 'as soon as my business with King Ali is concluded.'

'I believe you were also lord high general of Parthia, majesty.'

'Three times.'

'Perhaps there will be a fourth,' he said.

I rubbed my aching left leg. Sleeping out in the open was definitely a younger man's pursuit.

'I have retired from military affairs, ambassador, or at least have attempted to. But war is a jealous lover, it seems, who is reluctant to release me from her embrace.'

In the morning, all my other limbs joined my leg in aching, as Klietas assisted me in rising to my feet and walking to the stream where dozens of men were washing the previous day's grime from their bodies. Others were standing naked under a waterfall at the site of another stream further into the forest. After the horses and had been watered, fed and rubbed down, we settled down for a breakfast of cured meat, biscuits and cheese that the King's Guard had brought from Vanadzor.

Ulvi sent Agar ahead with a couple of riders to scout the vicinity, knowing Ali and his soldiers were close. They returned after an hour to report the King of Atropaiene was indeed near – in the next valley. Haytham, worry etched on his young face, gave the order to mount up but I queried the command.

'It might be prudent if I and my companions spoke to King Ali first, Haytham. Wait here until we return. After all, your brother did entrust me with the mission of resolving this dispute.'

I thought it wise not to inform him the only reason I wanted him along was to safeguard against Castus sending horsemen to butcher us. On the orders of Queen Yesim, of course. Haytham hesitated.

'Time is of the essence, prince.'

'Very well,' he reluctantly conceded.

I hauled myself into Horns' saddle, Klietas, Bullus and our two Roman companions doing the same.

'Agar will show you the way, majesty,' said Ulvi.

Our dishevelled scout led us high into the forest before we descended towards a wide plain flanked by tree-lined slopes on either side. Streams cascaded from the slopes and the grass on the valley floor was thick and lush. Dew clung to those areas of greenery still in the morning shade as the sun rose slowly in a clear blue eastern sky. As we rode downhill, gaps in the trees gave us a panoramic view of King Ali's encampment occupying a large area in the middle of the valley. I pulled up Horns to take a closer look and smiled. It was a far cry from the marching camps of Dura's army, and indeed those of Rome's legionaries.

In appearance it resembled a huge, sprawling tent city: a collection of brightly coloured tents of varying shapes and sizes, the largest being the royal pavilion in the centre, though for some reason there appeared to be three large pavilions. Behind them was a vast fenced-off area that housed the horses of the royal bodyguard of what I assumed was King Ali's élite, a patchwork of wood and canvas windbreaks forming stalls and stables for the animals. A host of squires and slaves were darting around like an army of ants, tending to their masters and their horses, digging latrines, cooking food, feeding and mucking out horses. Mobile armouries were repairing armour and sharpening weapons. The army's other horses were corralled in fenced-off areas beside the tents of their owners, while camels had been herded into other temporary stabling areas.

Parties of horsemen were patrolling the valley around the camp, and it was one such party that intercepted us when we left the trees to ride towards the tent city. The four horse archers directed their mounts immediately towards us when they spotted us, each rider plucking arrows from their quivers to nock in bowstrings. I held up both arms and told the others to do the same.

'Keep your arms up and make no sudden movements,' I warned them.

Moments later they confronted us with bows primed but not aimed at us.

'I am King Pacorus of Dura and wish to speak with King Ali. Take me to him at once,' I commanded.

The horse archers looked at each other in confusion. They saw my four companions and looked behind us for signs of other horsemen, for everyone knew that King Pacorus had a bodyguard of women warriors called Amazons.

'Are you deaf?' I snapped in irritation, lowering my arms. 'Put down your arms,' I told my companions.

'Are you going to escort us to King Ali or shoot us?' I asked the young bare-headed commander of the soldiers.

'I will take you to my commander,' he sniffed, 'who will determine your fate.'

We cantered back to the great camp and then it suddenly struck me. The commander and his men were wearing white leggings and green tunics – the colours of Hyrcania's army.

'You are soldiers of King Scylax?' I asked as we entered the camp.

'Yes,' he answered, pulling up his horse in front of a large round tent decorated with the insignia of a Caspian tiger. The officer jumped down from his horse, strode over to the tent and disappeared inside. A couple of minutes later he reappeared with an older man with grey in his beard and hair, which was still thick and long. He too was wearing a green tunic and white leggings, though his tunic was fringed with gold and he wore a pair of expensive boots. He blinked in the sunlight as he peered up at me, his eyes opening wide in amazement. He struck the younger man across the face with the back of his hand.

'Idiot! This is indeed King Pacorus.'

He bowed his head. 'Forgive me, majesty. We had no warning of your arrival.'

I did not recognise him. 'Have we met?'

'No, majesty. But I accompanied King Musa on numerous occasions when he visited Ctesiphon when you were lord high general.'

'His son is here?'

'King Scylax is with King Ali and Prince Khosrou, yes, majesty.'

My heart sank. 'Khosrou is here as well?'

'Yes, majesty, along with twenty thousand of his father's horsemen.'

That explained the three large pavilions I had spotted earlier, though not what a combined army of Atropaiene, Hyrcania and Margiana was doing in Gordyene. For what would Scylax and particularly King Khosrou, the aged ruler of Margiana, a kingdom that lay far to the east, be doing sending troops to invade Gordyene? The air smelled of horses, camels and leather as we rode deeper into the camp, the sounds of hammers striking red-hot horseshoes on anvils filling our ears. Racks holding vertical *kontus* shafts stood outside tents, in front of them squires seated on stools stopped their cleaning of armour and leather to stare up at us.

We were taken to the pavilion of King Ali, a huge structure with a roof supported by wooden poles and surrounded by a canvas wall to restrict entry. Guards in the colours of Atropaiene – yellow tunics and red leggings – halted us at the entrance, the commander of our escort explaining who I was. Outside the pavilion was a tall flagpole, from which hung the banner of the kingdom – a golden shahbaz on a red background, though unfortunately as there was no wind the large standard hung limply in the morning air. A runner was sent to the pavilion and we were invited inside the enclosure.

Slaves took our horses and guards came from the pavilion to escort us into King Ali's mobile palace.

The pavilion probably confirmed everything Gaius had been taught about effete Parthians. We left grass to tread on crimson and yellow carpets and rugs interwoven with gold and silver thread. Expensive draperies covered the insides of the pavilion's walls, decorated with hunting scenes and mythical beasts, chief among them the shahbaz. It was a huge bird reported to still inhabit the high peaks of the Zagros Mountains, though I had never met anyone who had actually seen one. Shahbaz means 'king of falcons', though it was much larger than the ordinary bird of prey.

My companions were left to sit on couches with golden feet in the shape of eagle talons. I reached the inner sanctum of the pavilion, which was attended by slaves and watched over by guards armed with short spears to more easily wield in the king's tent. I was shown into Ali's private compartment, a section at the end of the pavilion where the king slept and received guests.

'Pacorus. By what strange twist of fate do you find yourself in this godless land?'

He looked every inch the lord high general of Parthia, dressed in rich red leggings edged with gold, a yellow silk tunic and a sleeveless dragon-skin armour cuirass of overlapping silver scales stitched on to a leather vest. He walked up to me and clasped my forearm.

'I have recently been a guest of King Castus,' I replied, 'who asked me to negotiate on his behalf. You look well. I trust Queen Elham and your children are also prospering.'

He extended an arm to indicate I should relax on a large couch positioned in the cosy chamber I had been shown into. He sat on a couch opposite, leaving two others vacant.

'They are all well. Indeed, my eldest son, Bagoas, is with me.'

I placed my helmet on the carpet. 'I remember when he was but a small child. How the years fly by.'

He reminded me of his father Aschek with his thick, black curly hair and hooked nose that dominated his thin face. But when I had first sat down with his father I was young and eager. Now I was old and tired.

'I have asked the others to come,' said Ali, accepting a gold rhyton of wine. A slave bowed and presented a tray holding another to me. Ali held up his rhyton.

'To Parthia.'

I raised my rhyton. 'Parthia.'

'You ride alone, without Gallia, Pacorus? Who are the others with you?'

'A Roman ambassador, a Pontic general, a farmer from Media and a soldier from Dura.'

He gave me a bewildered look.

'As you said, Ali, a strange twist of fate.'

As I had great respect for him and had no wish to try to deceive him, I told him the full story of my trip to Ctesiphon and then to Media, followed by the unfortunate events in Vanadzor.

'And you still wish to negotiate on his behalf?' asked Ali.

'For him, no. To avoid war, yes.'

'That might be easier said than done, Pacorus.'

We were interrupted by the arrival of Scylax and Khosrou, the former embracing me, the latter bowing his head deferentially. The namesake of his father, the prince of Margiana was a tall individual with a brooding face, thin eyebrows and narrow black eyes. His sharp nose gave him a somewhat fearsome appearance, but he was affable enough.

'How is your father?' I asked him.

'Old and irritable, majesty. He desperately wanted to join our expedition, but alas his great age means he can no longer ride a horse.'

'How old is he?'

'Eighty-three.'

'He is an example to us all.'

Scylax, son the late Musa, was also tall, though more muscular. His heavy brow gave him a serious, almost morose, appearance, though like Khosrou he had a full head of hair and thick beard. They both accepted wine and reclined on couches as Ali told them my story. At the end of the sorry tale Scylax shook his head.

'Even if Castus had not committed his other crimes, his treatment of you, Pacorus, would warrant us laying waste to his kingdom.'

I grew alarmed. 'Other crimes?'

'Humiliating my daughter,' began Ali, 'allowing his Sarmatian allies to plunder the north of my kingdom at will, refusing to curtail their activities when I demanded he do so, as well as encouraging them to raid into Hyrcania and Margiana.'

I was astounded. 'The Aorsi have been raiding Hyrcania and Margiana?'

Ali chuckled. 'Would that the Aorsi were the only Sarmatian tribe. When Surena invited them into his kingdom all those years ago, they were admittedly a useful bulwark against the Romans and Armenians. But times have changed, Pacorus.'

He sipped at his rhyton. 'Now that Castus has forbidden them to raid into Armenia, they amuse themselves with plundering my kingdom. Worse, they have encouraged the other Sarmatian tribes to try their luck against northern Parthia.'

'The Sauromatae, Siraces, Iazyges and Roxolani now infest the regions west and east of the Caspian Sea,' Scylax informed me.

'From where they either join their Aorsi allies or undertake raids against Hyrcania and Margiana,' added Khosrou.

'As lord high general, Pacorus,' said Ali calmly, 'it is my duty to protect the empire, from both external and internal enemies. Laying aside the gross insult to my daughter, at least for the moment, Castus needs to have his wings clipped.'

'If he will not apologise to Ali, rein in his Sarmatian dogs and pay compensation in gold to each of our kingdoms for the damage they have caused,' said Scylax, 'then we will lay waste to the Pambak Valley.'

I stared into my wine, thinking of how arrogant and deluded Castus had become, and how his new wife would continue to pour poison into his ears. There was scant hope Castus would apologise for anything, let alone dip into his precious gold reserves to pay any compensation. And I could tell the men I now sat with would not back down from their threats. War was a distinct possibility, though technically it had already begun as an invading army was on Gordyene soil.

And yet…

'I ask you all to withdraw your forces,' I pleaded, 'before blood is spilt.'

'Blood has already been spilt,' growled Ali. 'The villages of my kingdom raided by the Sarmatians have become lifeless places, Pacorus.'

'It is the same in Hyrcania,' added Scylax.

'And Margiana,' said Khosrou.

'If Castus was summoned to Ctesiphon, ordered to control his allies and commanded by Phraates himself to pay you compensation in gold; would that be an acceptable compromise?' I asked.

'Why do you protect this puppy, Pacorus?' said Scylax. 'This man who has humiliated you, insulted you and now sends you to us like a slave doing his master's bidding?'

Ali frowned at his ally. 'Your words are ill considered, Scylax.'

The King of Hyrcania's thin lips clenched together, but then he nodded.

'I meant no disrespect, Pacorus. You were a friend of my father and have been Parthia's guardian for longer than I have walked the earth. But Castus is rotten to the core. Marrying the daughter of the man who was an enemy of the empire proves he has taken leave of his mind.'

'I care nothing for Castus,' I said, 'but I have spent my life defending Parthia and I have no stomach to see it being ripped apart once more because a foolish young man has allowed his loins to rule his head.'

Ali laughed. 'We are all guilty of that at one time or another, Pacorus.'

He looked at his two companions-in-arms.

'Out of respect for you, Pacorus, I will agree to your proposal. But only because you have suggested it, and only on the understanding that Castus will pay us all reparations.'

'And get rid of his Sarmatian allies,' added Scylax.

'If my father were here, he would also agree to the terms proposed by King Pacorus,' said Khosrou, 'so great is the respect he has for the king and queen of Dura.'

'Let it be so, then,' agreed Scylax, 'though to encourage Castus to be a good boy, we will keep our army close to Gordyene's border. If you have no objection, Ali.'

'No objection at all, my friend,' smiled Ali. 'Sixty thousand horsemen will hopefully quicken Castus' journey to

Ctesiphon. I will have a scribe compile a letter after this meeting. What about you, Pacorus?'

'I will take the letter and hand it to Prince Haytham, who is nearby.'

Scylax's eyes narrowed. 'Perhaps we should capture him and force him to fight Hyrcania's champion, and then send his head back to his brother.'

Khosrou roared with laughter and Ali rubbed his hands together.

'Tempting.'

I was appalled. 'I will deliver the letter and hand it to Haytham, and impress upon him the urgency of the situation.'

'What about the Roman ambassador?' asked Ali, changing the subject.

'I will escort him to Syria via Dura,' I replied. 'From there he can make his way back to Pontus. Castus was going to ransom him and his companion for a great deal of gold.'

A mischievous glint appeared in Scylax's eye.

'Perhaps we should let him do that. Then he would find a Roman army knocking at his palace gates as well.'

'That is precisely why I want to get him back to Roman territory as quickly as possible,' I said. 'Not that the Romans want a war.'

'I never thought I would hear those words,' said Ali. 'The Romans not wanting a war. What is the world coming to?'

Gaius Arrianus spent an enjoyable morning being shown around the huge camp, discussing subjects ranging from the equine heritage of Parthian horses to the different types of arrows carried in the quivers of horse archers. He had an enquiring mind, a military mind, and seemed at home in an army camp. He informed me he had experience of military command, having fought at Actium on the side of the then Octavian.

'I have heard you met Mark Antony, majesty.'

'First in Syria and then when he invaded Parthia, yes. That was, let me see, twelve years ago. I liked him. My wife did not.'

'He insulted Queen Gallia?'

I chuckled. 'Far from it. He was charm itself when he met her. But she was in a testy mood that day and wanted to use him for arrow practice. I persuaded her it was better to swap him for something precious.'

'What was that, majesty?'

'The mother of the son who is causing all of us so much anguish at this time.'

An officer of King Ali's bodyguard interrupted our tour of the camp, requesting I accompany him to his liege's pavilion. I left Gaius in the capable hands of one of Ali's dragon commanders and rode to the king's living quarters. The son of Aschek handed me a letter signed and sealed by himself, Scylax and Khosrou, setting out their grievances, all the actions Castus should take to avoid war, including his attendance at Ctesiphon 'as soon as the high king summons you'.

I went to take the letter, but he held on to it.

'We are only offering Castus this olive branch because you asked it of us, Pacorus. I pray Castus will receive it with the solemnity and respect with which it was written.'

'I pray to Shamash that will be so, my friend.'

'Are you sure you don't want an escort?'

I smiled. 'I will take just one with me.'

Bullus had a face that could sour milk as we rode at speed back to the forest we had left that morning, his square jaw set solid. When we neared the treeline, we slowed the horses and he shook his head a couple of times. It was warm and humid, sweat running down my neck and face. I used a cloth to wipe away the perspiration, catching sight of Bullus mumbling under his breath. I pulled up Horns.

'What is the matter, Bullus? Spit it out, for pity's sake.'

'You are the King of Dura,' he said through gritted teeth, 'not some errand boy to do the bidding of other kings.

I reached into one of my saddlebags and pulled out the rolled papyrus scroll.

'Do you know what this is?'

'A letter,' he said, dismissively.

'This, centurion,' I said slowly, 'is a document that might avert a very costly and bloody war in northern Parthia. And if my being an errand boy means there will be peace instead of war, then I am quite prepared to assume the role. Now, where is that wretched track?'

I heard a whistle and my eyes were drawn to what looked like a scarecrow sitting on a horse, one gesticulating to us with its arm. It was Agar. He said nothing as we followed him into the humid forest, the air thick with the aroma of pine, our horses making little sound as they trod on ground covered with moss and brown pine needles. After an hour we reached Haytham's camp and I handed the prince the letter signed by two kings and once prince.

'There will be peace,' I told him.

He smiled with relief, but I held his eyes.

'*If,*' I continued, 'your brother fulfils the obligations set down in that letter. If you have any influence with Castus, I strongly advise you use it to avert war. There are sixty thousand soldiers but an hour's ride from this camp, who are about to withdraw back to Atropaiene. But they are not just from that kingdom but also from Hyrcania and Margiana. Those three kingdoms can easily muster twice that number if forced to do so.

'You understand, Haytham?'

He swallowed. 'I understand, majesty.'

I hoisted myself back into Horns' saddle, Bullus' dark eyes observing Haytham with a mild contempt.

'You must impress upon Castus that the war he seems intent on starting is one he cannot win,' I said, tugging on Horns' reins, 'whatever his wife may think.'

I was in a bullish mood as we left his camp to retrace our steps through the forest, the scruffy and silent Agar being our guide once more. Fate had brought me to Gordyene, and the gods had blessed me by being in the right place at the right time to be a peacemaker. I said a silent prayer of thanks to Shamash for his divine guidance.

'You want to know what I think, majesty?' said Bullus.

'Not really.'

'I think Castus is already thinking of new conquests and fresh glory, and all the words in the world won't change that.'

But it was not Castus and his delusions that shattered my world but devastating news from Hatra.

Chapter 9

The army of invasion quit its camp and headed east, towards the border of Gordyene and the eastern shore of Lake Urmia, where it would remain until Castus agreed to the conditions in the letter I had delivered. Ali, Scylax and Khosrou felt cheated, that much was apparent. But if they bore me any ill will they did not show it or bear me any resentment. And if they were bored by the stories I told them of the time when their fathers had been great warlords in the defence of Parthia, they did not show that either. The sun was warming the earth, a war had been avoided and I believed it had been the will of the gods that had directed me to Media to seek out Klietas, which had led to my journey to Gordyene.

But the gods are fickle, and fate is a wheel that is in perpetual motion. On a dazzlingly beautiful morning by the shore of Lake Urmia, the surface of the water glittering like a thousand mirrors reflecting the sunlight, a sweat-covered courier riding an exhausted horse arrived at the camp, his arrival prompting an urgent request from King Ali for me to attend him in his pavilion. When I walked into his audience chamber his face was ashen, his eyes moist. Scylax and Khosrou stood with heads bowed, consciously avoiding my eyes. I saw the parchment in Ali's hand and knew something was terribly wrong.

'Pacorus, dreadful news has arrived from my capital. King Gafarn is dead.'

I saw his mouth move as he spoke to me afterwards, but I did not hear him. Nor Scylax or Khosrou who offered their condolences. The news hit me like a hammer. Gafarn, the man I had known all my life, first as a master, then as a fellow slave and finally as a brother and fellow king, was gone. After I had recovered from the terrible news, my first thought was to get to Hatra as quickly as possible to comfort Diana.

Ali provided me and my companions with spare horses to quicken our journey, Gaius Arrianus and Titus Tullus electing to accompany me to Hatra. I agreed as from Hatra they could journey in safety to Roman Zeugma. We covered sixty miles each day, swapping horses regularly and watering them in the many springs and streams that blessed King Akmon's kingdom, not bothering to visit Irbil to pay our respects but pressing on to Assur, the city beside the Tigris that was the gateway to eastern Hatra. We reached the city on the fourth day, five individuals covered in dust with dirty clothes and faces and aching limbs, nearly toppling from our spent horses when we rode into the governor's courtyard.

Assur, mighty stronghold on the west bank of the Tigris, was administered by Lord Rodak, a nephew of Lord Herneus, the former governor, now commander of Dura's army and resident in Hatra. Rodak was a gruff, no nonsense individual but unlike Herneus had a full head of hair and thick beard. The moment he was informed we had arrived at his mansion, he took charge of the situation. We were shown to bedrooms where we were bathed, massaged with invigorating balms and fed foods that would replenish our spent reserves – fruits, dates, eggs, seeds, rice and yoghurt. We were denied wine in favour of water, which produced much grumbling from Bullus and Tullus. But at least we felt human again and mercifully the bath and massage had prevented my left leg from seizing up.

There was no banquet that evening. Food was served to my companions in their rooms, after which they retired early as I was determined to leave Assur at dawn the next day to reach Hatra by the afternoon. I dined with Rodak so he could bring me up to date on the dreadful events that had engulfed the kingdom. Rodak had a somewhat severe countenance and a face that wore a frown better than a smile. As such, he was perfectly suited to provide a summary of the awful events that had taken place recently.

'The king's leg ulcer returned with a vengeance, majesty. There was nothing the physicians could do to halt the spread of infection.'

'Poor Diana,' I whispered, morosely. 'Alone with her grief.'

He looked surprised. 'Have you not heard, sire? Queen Gallia is at Hatra.'

I looked up at him. 'Gallia is at Hatra?'

'As soon as she heard of the king's death she rode to the city, with her Amazons.'

I picked at the food laid out before me. Fish caught earlier in the Tigris and served on a bed of rice were arranged on long silver dishes. Kebabs of freshly cooked chicken were arranged in neat lines on a gold platter, surrounded by dishes filled with butter, olives, yoghurt, cheeses and both spicy and mild sauces. Other dishes held bread, biscuits, pastries, cakes and fruits. But I had no appetite.

A slave came forward to refill my rhyton.

'Prince Pacorus has been notified of his father's death?'

'Yes majesty. But the prince is currently fighting in the Zagros Mountains against incalcitrant tribesmen. It may be some time before word reaches him of the king's death.'

The Zagros Mountains began on the Mediterranean coast inland from Antioch and extended east before curving southeast to take them all the way to the Persian Gulf. As well as snow-capped peaks, cliff faces and glaciers, the mountains were home to huge forests, lush valleys and windswept steppes. The massive oak forests were home to numerous tribes, including the Bakhtiari, Uxians, Cosseans, Mardians and Kashqai. These nomads were a law unto themselves and paid no taxes to the kingdoms they happened to live in. But they traded with towns and cities and many of their young men, wanting more than a meagre existence in the uplands, took service in Parthian armies. Occasionally, a tribal chieftain would declare himself a god and lead his people against their Parthian overlords, prompting retaliation.

Prince Pacorus, the son of Gafarn and Diana and heir to Hatra's throne, had been made protector of Elymais in the wake of King Silaces' death at the Battle of Ctesiphon. Silaces had married a slave, a beautiful woman by the name of Cia who had borne him a son, though after the king's death. Cia was not from Elymais nobility and was thus very isolated and at risk of being killed by an ambitious local lord, her infant son, too. The decision was therefore taken to install the prince as their protector to quash any rebellions, and to facilitate the rule of Queen Cia until Prince Silaces came of age. And by all accounts, judging by the lack of any rebellions in the six years since, he had made a splendid job of his task. But then Pacorus was the archetypal Parthian hero. He was brave, handsome, undefeated in battle and a prince of Hatra, one of the oldest and most traditional kingdoms in the empire. He had married the beautiful Arezu, the scion of a wealthy and influential Hatran family, who had borne him two sons: Varaz and Orodes, who were now princes of Hatra. And now Pacorus was King of Hatra, or would be once he had been crowned in the city's Great Temple.

The next morning, the sun still a pale-yellow ball hanging low on the eastern horizon, Rodak bid us farewell in the mansion's courtyard. He gave us fresh horses to ride the last leg of our journey to Hatra, our own mounts being fatigued after the forced ride from Lake Urmia.

'I have will them sent on to you after they have been rested and examined for any loose shoes, majesty,' he told me.

He also gave us an escort of a dozen horse archers, all wearing white tunics, their red saddlecloths emblazoned with a white horse head motif in each corner. They all wore *shemaghs*, as did we, though Gaius was curious as to why they were necessary. During the ride from Lake Urmia through Media the terrain had been alternately rocky and green, but as we ventured further south the landscape changed to one of desert. And in the desert one needs a *shemagh* as protection against blowing dust, and to keep the sun off the head, neck and face. Bullus and I also had floppy hats as sun protection, but dust was also a problem.

The road from Assur to Hatra was well-trodden, being used by thousands of camels and horses each year as camel caravans on the Silk Road transported their wares east and west. The horses' hooves kicked up immense amounts of fine particles into the air, which on windless days hung around to tickle the back of the throat and irritate the eyes. For a short journey it is not a problem; but four hours in the saddle requires prior planning.

As we cantered along the dirt road that was already filling with caravans, I reflected on the life of Gafarn, the Bedouin child who had been captured by my father during a raid against his people and brought back to Hatra as a slave. Many children would have been overwhelmed by such a trauma, but Gafarn had a quick wit and easy-going manner that soon ingratiated him to my mother, who suggested he become my personal slave. Life as a slave in Hatra's palace was bearable enough. For an intelligent slave made a companion to the king's only son, it resulted in a life of relative ease. Until we were captured in Cappadocia Gafarn was always a slave, albeit one who could be very free with his tongue and became de facto a member of the royal family, like a loyal dog. All that changed when we were taken to Italy as slaves.

Gafarn instantly became a friend, confidant and de facto brother, our bonds made stronger by the triumphs and perils we faced together. By the time we had escaped Italy to return to Parthia he *had* become my brother, which was recognised by my father when he made Gafarn legally part of Hatra's royal family. And when I had departed for Dura, Gafarn became the heir to my father's throne. With Diana by his side, he had been made king following my father's death fighting Narses, had raised two sons, had maintained Hatra's wealth and power, and, most impressive of all, had earned the loyalty and respect of the kingdom's nobles. Not bad for a Bedouin slave.

I slowed my horse when I spotted the high walls of Hatra shimmering in the distance, a long line of camels on the road from the huge caravan park sited outside the city making their way towards Assur and the east. None would go as far as China, or indeed the eastern kingdoms of the empire. At the various *caravanserai* along the way, the precious goods carried on the backs of the camels would be sold to other caravans for onward shipment.

'Is something wrong, majesty?' asked the commander of the horse archers after removing the *shemagh* from over his mouth. He was looking at the legs of my horse to check for any signs of lameness.

'No, I am fine and so is my horse.'

I had slowed my mount to delay entry into the north of the city where the royal quarter was located. Fear suddenly gripped me, and I did not want to see Diana, because a part of me believed that if I did not see her then the death of Gafarn would not be real. The cowardly part. I gripped the reins tightly and dug my heels into my horse's sides.

What kind of man are you, Pacorus? One of your oldest friends needs you. His wife needs you. Your wife needs you.

We cantered across the wooden drawbridge spanning the water-filled moat at the city's northern gates. Guards on the bridge snapped to attention and archers on the battlements atop the gatehouse stood down when they recognised a party of their own horse archers and perhaps the man wearing a cuirass of Roman armour leading them. The leader of the dust-covered horse archers reported to the officer of the watch at the gatehouse, who sent a rider to the palace to announce my arrival. The officer left his office to pay his respects, bowing his head and keeping it bowed as I rode on.

I had forgotten how big and imposing Hatra's palace and its adjoining stables and barracks were. They were like a city within a city, fed by endless cool water from beneath the earth. Even the royal stables had running water to nourish the horses and keep the buildings and spaces around them clean. We rode by the stables and passed a company of the Royal Bodyguard – a hundred cataphracts riding white horses, all the animals wearing gleaming scale-armour suits that covered not only their bodies and necks but also their heads. Metal grills covered the horses' eyes and their tails had been plaited.

Each rider was wearing a scale-armour cuirass of burnished, overlapping steel plates that dazzled in the sunlight, arms and legs being covered with tubular steel armour. Hatra's cataphracts wore open-face helmets, each one decorated with a large white plume, the company commander's headgear decorated with a second, red plume. He and the others held a *kontus* in their right hands, the shafts painted red and topped with a long, thin blade designed to pierce armour. They also had butt spikes for driving into the ground during pauses in battles, and for inflicting injuries on enemy flesh. Each cataphract was also armed with a sword, mace, axe and dagger. The officer and his men did not give us a second glance. They were nobles and the sons of nobles in the finest army in all Parthia, or so they believed.

And then we were in the great square itself. Located between the Great Temple dedicated to Shamash and the palace, it was paved with well-dressed white stone slabs. The iron-shod hooves made a clattering sound as the horses trotted to the foot of the palace steps and slaves rushed forward to take our reins. I saw figures come from the palace to stand at the top of the steps. I had a lump in my throat when I saw Gallia, who gave me a wan smile. I slid off my horse and walked up the steps. I saw the grim Herneus beside my wife and Adeleh, my sister, on his other side. I looked for Diana, but she was not present. Presumably she was locked in her bedroom, grieving.

Gallia looked deathly pale, her eyes red and puffy from crying. When I reached the top of the steps she collapsed into my arms.

'Oh, Pacorus, it is so good to see you.'

The death of Gafarn had obviously affected her deeply. I had not seen her looking so fragile and vulnerable in years. I planted a gentle kiss on her forehead.

'I'm glad you are here. How is Diana faring?'

Still holding me tight, she began to sob quietly. Adeleh, dressed in the simple white robe and sandals of the Sisters of Shamash religious order she belonged to, stepped forward and whispered in my ear.

'Diana passed away yesterday, Pacorus. She is in the embrace of Shamash now.'

I was numb and just stared at my little sister in disbelief. Her hair cut short and devoid of makeup as laid down in the rules of her order, her brown eyes were full of sorrow at being the first to inform me.

'Dead? How?' I stammered.

Gallia pulled away from me, tears streaming down her cheeks.

'A broken heart, Pacorus. One day she was fine physically, the next she had passed away. It was that quick.'

They were both buried in the Crypt of the Kings beneath the palace, a dark, forbidding place that was the realm of the dead rather than the living. My mother and father were both interred there, though my father had been cremated after his death at the Battle of Susa, the ashes being returned to Hatra afterwards to lie beside the white marble sarcophagus of my mother. Each sarcophagus was prepared during the reign of the incumbent king and queen, so that when they died a resting place in the cool, vaulted chamber would be immediately available. The marble effigies lying on top of each sarcophagus also portrayed the ruler and his queen in their prime, not as wizened shadows of their former selves.

I stood with Gallia and Adeleh before the final resting places of our friends, the effigies looking exact replicas of Gafarn and Diana. I looked at the sculpted marble and expected them to speak: a kind word from Diana, a witty quip from Gafarn. I felt a tear course down my cheek and felt Gallia gripping my arm tightly. We said nothing for what seemed like an eternity. It was deathly quiet in the crypt, which was entirely appropriate. I felt the weight of history on my shoulders.

'Castus has married the daughter of Laodice, the dog who ruled the hill tribes of Pontus,' I said. 'She is a poisonous bitch who has corrupted the mind of the young King of Gordyene.'

'Harsh words for a holy place, brother,' Adeleh berated me.

'Would you say forcing the King of Dura to fight as a gladiator against a Sarmatian for the amusement of said bitch harsh, sister?'

Gallia's jaw dropped.

'What was left of your escort returned to Dura and gave me a full report concerning the Sarmatian attack on the village,' she told me, 'which was foolhardy of you, Pacorus. But I had no idea you would be mistreated by Castus. Klietas is dead?'

I turned away from the tombs of our friends to look at her. In her grief, she had not spotted my former squire accompanying me. But then, his *shemagh* was covering his face.

'He is alive and in this palace,' I said. 'He rode with me from the north, along with a Roman ambassador named Gaius Arrianus and…'

I hesitated to mention Titus Tullus, one of her targets marked out for death. I sighed. She would know he was in the palace also soon enough.

'And?' she asked.

'Titus Tullus,' I answered.

Her eyes widened and then narrowed.

'Who is Titus Tullus?' enquired Adeleh.

'Someone my wife wants dead,' I informed her, 'though I am hopeful she will hear my plea that his life should be spared.'

'How is it you arrived here in the company of a Roman ambassador and a former Roman centurion?' asked Gallia.

'They were ambushed in the hills of Pontus following the great victory at Melitene,' I said, 'and both captured by the aforementioned queen of darkness herself.'

Adeleh gave me a quizzical look.

'Queen Yesim, wife of King Castus and also queen of the hill tribes of Pontus,' I explained. 'She is a calculating bitch because she marched her captives off to Gordyene and sold them to Castus to buy food for her people.'

'What did Castus get out of it?' asked Gallia.

'Aside from a venomous wife, two captives he was determined to sell back to the Romans for a tidy amount of gold,' I said. 'You can see how they are well matched. However, King Ali, King Scylax and Prince Khosrou spoiled his plans.

'I will explain later.'

I laid a hand on each marble sarcophagus before we left the crypt. The stone was cool to the touch and made me shiver.

'Farewell, my friends,' I whispered. 'Until we meet again.'

Hatra was in a state of limbo. The city markets still bustled with activity, the army still drilled and sent out patrols, priests and priestesses still performed their holy rituals and accepted offerings from a devout populace, and the trade caravans continued to fill the road going to and from the city. But the only topic of conversation from the seediest brothel and inn to the wealthiest table was: when would Prince Pacorus and Princess Arezu be returning to the city? For Hatra without a king and queen was considered inauspicious, and every day that passed without someone sitting on the city's throne was considered an ill-omen.

I walked into the throne room and looked around the cavernous chamber. Guards flanked the dais where two wooden thrones stood empty, behind them a red banner emblazoned with a white horse head motif. Sunlight flooded in from the windows positioned high in the walls on either side of the hall to illuminate the chamber. The guards observed me but did not move as I walked over to the dais, white marble tiles beneath my feet and the walls painted white to make the hall light and airy. I stepped on to the dais and eased myself into Gafarn's throne, soon to be his son's. It was the first time I had sat on Hatra's throne, but it was much like my own at Dura: hard and uncomfortable.

The doors of the chamber opened and Herneus marched in, striding up to the dais and bowing his head. He held out a folded piece of parchment to me. I saw the imprint of a four-pointed star in the wax. I laughed.

'I am not king, Herneus.'

'No, majesty, but you are a king, and at this present juncture the only one we have got.'

I took the parchment, broke the seal and then stopped.

'This is from Queen Cia, who might be informing us Prince Pacorus has been killed in the Zagros, his life ended by a spear wielded by some filthy barbarian in some nameless mountain valley.'

'That would mean his eldest son Varaz would become king,' said Herneus, matter-of-factly.

I opened the letter and read the words.

'It appears the prince has not been killed but is still in the Zagros Mountains after having concluded a peace treaty with the Uxians. He will then ride directly for the capital to pick up his family and thence to Hatra. He and they should be here in three weeks.'

'Will you stay to receive him, majesty?'

I thought about the army encamped by the shore of Lake Urmia and the plea to Phraates that Ali would be sending to Ctesiphon to summon Castus to the high king's residence.

'I may be called away before then Herneus. In the meantime, have the city criers announce Prince Pacorus is returning to Hatra. That should calm any nerves.'

He bowed his head, turned and marched from the chamber. In truth, I had little desire to stay in Hatra. The palace reminded me of my dead friends and made me feel morose. I hoped a letter would arrive from Ctesiphon so I could leave the city of my birth and escape the gloom that hung over it.

I would indeed be leaving Hatra, but not in a way I could have foreseen.

Chapter 10

When my father had been Hatra's king, meetings of the royal council had been held in a small room beside the throne room. He and the others of the august assembly sat round a large rectangular table to discuss matters both important and trivial. How history repeats itself. I too now sat in his chair, the one used by his father before him and latterly by King Gafarn. It was old and the arms were chipped and in need of repair. That it had not been restored I put down to superstition, or something similar. I had to laugh, which did nothing to brighten the mood of those gathered at the table with me. There was Gallia, her eyes filled with fury and an expression of granite-like hardness. Opposite her sat Aspad, the city governor, a gaunt and serious individual with sunken eyes and a long beard that accentuated the narrowness of his face. Next to him sat Manu, High Priest of the Great Temple. He was a large, loud man with a large head and hands who wore a flowing white robe decorated with gold sun symbols. A man of immense power, he ruled over the spiritual lives of the city and kingdom. And then there was Herneus, his crown and face completely devoid of hair and his clothes like him: unfussy and entirely functional.

    I had convened an emergency session of the council even though strictly I had no power to do so. But such was the gravity of the situation Hatra now found itself in, there was little choice. The dire news had first reached Herneus via his nephew at Assur, and he had immediately informed me. That news I now shared. I sighed, stood and walked over to the large map of the Parthian Empire painted on wooden boards fixed to the wall. I pointed at Lake Urmia.

'The army that invaded Gordyene intent on retribution has been destroyed. King Ali has been wounded but made it back to his capital, though with few troops. The gods be praised, King Scylax and Prince Khosrou also reached the city of Urmia safely.'

'King Castus has gone too far this time,' lamented Manu, closing his eyes and shaking his huge head.

'It was not King Castus that ambushed the Parthian army,' I said, 'but a large horde of Sarmatians, according to the scribe who was taking down King Ali's words, an army that has invaded Parthia from across the Araxes.'

'No army can cross the Araxes in the spring, majesty,' said Herneus. 'There are no bridges over the river and in the spring, much of its length is a fast-flowing torrent.'

'There is only explanation,' seethed Gallia, 'one that sticks in my craw but must be true, nevertheless. This Sarmatian army was already in Gordyene before the spring, on the invitation of King Castus.'

'What do the Sarmatians want with Parthia?' asked Aspad.

'Slaves, gold and plunder,' I answered.

I traced a finger from Lake Urmia south towards Ctesiphon.

'The centre of the empire lays exposed like a lamb to a wolf. I assume the Sarmatians are currently sweeping south like a plague of ants. They will dally in Media to gorge themselves on that kingdom's rich pastures, which will give us time to organise a response. Which is why I have called this meeting. I need Hatra's army.'

Herneus glanced at the imposing Manu, the high priest looking reflective.

'I have sent word to Dura for my horsemen to ride here with all speed,' I told them, 'but I need Hatra's horsemen also.'

'May I ask for what purpose, majesty?' requested Herneus.

I pointed at Assur on the map.

'The Sarmatians will overrun Media, that much is certain, and will head for the nearest crossing point over the Tigris. Here, at Assur. If they get across the river, Babylon and Hatra will be at their mercy.'

'The bridge should be destroyed,' said Manu. 'It is, after all, only wood.'

Lucius Varsas, my quartermaster general, had built a pontoon bridge to span the Tigris at Assur, a marvel of engineering that allowed the trade caravans to cross over the river all through the year. Manu was right: it could be torched.

'If we destroy the bridge, we deny ourselves a crossing point over the Tigris,' I told him. 'Destroying the bridge must be a last resort.'

I looked at him and then at Herneus. Both were critical to whether I could muster and lead Hatra's army to support my own, which I expected to arrive within three days. Herneus, despite his rather austere appearance and manner, was from one of the most prestigious Hatran noble families in the kingdom. Without his support, the Royal Bodyguard for one would not obey me. Manu wielded enormous power in the city. His blessing, and by implication that of Shamash himself, would make my task much easier.

'As soon as Prince Pacorus arrives, he will assume command of Hatra's army,' I emphasised. 'But we cannot afford to do nothing until he arrives.'

Manu spoke first. 'It can be no coincidence that a son of King Varaz is in the city at the moment we lose our king and queen and a great threat against the kingdom manifests itself. I believe you were sent to us by Shamash himself, King Pacorus, and therefore I endorse your request.'

Herneus stared at the map and exhaled loudly.

'Without a general muster of the kingdom's lords, Hatra can supply only six and half thousand horsemen. How many soldiers will come from Dura, majesty?'

'Twelve thousand,' I answered.

'Plus a hundred Amazons already in the city,' added Gallia. Herneus tilted his head at her in acknowledgement.

'If sixty thousand Parthians could not stop these Sarmatians,' said the general, a frown creasing his brow, 'what chance will only eighteen and a half thousand have?'

'They will give us time, Herneus,' I said. 'Time to allow my foot soldiers to get here and time for the high king to muster the forces of Babylon, Susiana and indeed Elymais. He has a fine general in Satrap Otanes. It will also give Lord Orobaz time to muster the lords and their men.'

Herneus left the meeting to organise the march of the army to Assur, calling all his senior officers together to inform them they would be under the temporary command of King Pacorus, formerly prince of Hatra, until their king-in-waiting returned from Elymais. When he, Aspad and Manu had left I sat staring at the map on the wall, a slave offering me a rhyton of wine. I accepted, as did Gallia.

'Sarmatians,' I spat. 'What were the gods thinking of when they created that race of vagrants?'

'More to the point,' said Gallia, 'such a large number of horsemen could not have crossed the Araxes without the knowledge of Castus, unless the Aorsi have turned against him.'

I poured scorn on the idea.

'Spadines and Castus are as tight as a pair of horizontal catamites. It makes no sense.'

'What?'

I drank some wine, stood and walked over to the map.

'When Castus received news Ali and his allies were approaching Vanadzor, he panicked. That is the only reason I am alive.'

She sipped at her wine. 'So?'

I tapped my finger on the map where Vanadzor was located.

'So, if he knew he could call upon a horde of Sarmatians to reinforce his own considerable army, why would he be so alarmed at the approach of Ali's force?'

'He is still young, Pacorus,' she said. 'It is no small thing when the lord high general of the empire is approaching your capital with a large army.'

I shook my head. 'Perhaps.'

'Whatever the reason, he will have to account for his actions. His treatment of you and his allowing the Sarmatians into the empire must be held to account, Pacorus. You realise this?'

I turned to look at her. 'Everyone must be held to account. That should be the motto of the Amazons instead of, what is it?'

'Behind every man there is a stronger woman,' she replied. 'And are we not all answerable, Pacorus, to the laws of man or those of the gods?'

I walked back to my seat.

'Some have a very strict notion of the idea of accountability.'

'I hope we are not going to argue about things past,' she said.

I retook my seat. 'I don't want Titus Tullus harmed. You had your chance to kill him and missed it. There will be no other.'

Her eyes narrowed and she pressed her lips together. I had seen that expression before but the appearance of an officer of the palace guard interrupted her. He bowed his head to Gallia.

'Apologies, majesty, Governor Aspad requests your presence in the throne room on a most urgent matter.'

Like many things in Parthia, Hatra had been heavily influenced by Greek civilisation. The soldiers of the city garrison wore Greek-inspired uniforms – full-face bronze helmets topped with white plumes, leather cuirasses overlaid with iron scales and leather greaves protecting their shins and lower legs. Their round wooden shields were faced with bronze, upon which were engraved horses' heads, and their weapons comprised six-foot long thrusting spears and swords. Not the short sword favoured by Rome, Dura and Gordyene, but the *kopis*, a curved weapon with a single cutting edge. It was light and fast in skilled hands, well deserving its nickname of the 'kitchen knife from hell'.

The officer, helmet in the crook of his arm, bowed, turned on his heels and walked from the office into the throne room. We followed, to be greeted by the sight of two girls standing before the dais, behind them Aspad and four guards with spears levelled at their backs. Gallia passed me and marched to the dais, sitting in what had been Diana's throne and waiting for me to sit beside her.

'We found these two girls in the guest quarters of the palace, majesty,' Aspad reported. 'They say they are Amazons.'

I studied the pair, each wearing a cloak with hood, soft shoes, tight-fitting tan leggings and a white tunic. They looked vaguely familiar though I could not place them. Aspad held out a hand. One of the guards walked forward to place two wicked-looking daggers in his palm. Aspad showed them to us. Gallia ignored them.

'They are Amazons,' she said, 'and you will release them to my custody immediately.'

Aspad smarted at her terse words. She may have been a queen, but he was a lord of Hatra, the commander of the garrison who was entrusted with the safety of the city, the king and queen when they were in residence, and any guests that may be in the palace. He took his duties very seriously and was not about to release two individuals who had no business being in the palace's guest quarters, let alone caught carrying weapons.

'With respect, majesty,' he said, 'whether they are Amazons or not, they had no business being in the guest quarters of the palace. As you are the commander of the Amazons, may I enquire why they were in the guest quarters?'

'I do not have to explain myself to you, Lord Aspad,' said Gallia, prompting the two girls to smirk.

I pointed at them. 'You will answer the question.'

They both looked too young to be Amazons. The smaller one looked very young, her heart-shaped face framed by straight black hair that was plaited in the Amazon style. The other one, taller with a willowy frame, had a round face and brown curly hair. It was she who spoke to me in a soft voice.

'We were ridding the world of the enemies of Dura, majesty.'

'They must die,' said the other, causing Aspad to frown and Gallia to smile.

'Who must die?' I demanded to know.

The girlish one looked at me with her dark eyes, eyes that appeared devoid of emotion.

'Titus Tullus, majesty.'

'To harm a palace guest is a capital offence, majesty,' Aspad reminded me.

I nodded. 'I am well aware of the laws of this city, governor. And you are right, harming a guest in the palace warrants the death penalty.'

The two girls swayed on their feet and their cockiness evaporated.

'As Titus Tullus still lives.' Gallia looked at the governor. 'He is still alive?'

'Yes, majesty,' replied Aspad. 'But…'

'But nothing,' she snapped. 'Parthia is in great peril and I need every soldier I can get my hands on, as does the empire. If it makes you feel any better, I apologise for the over-zealous diligence of my Amazons. I hope you can forgive me.'

Gallia was old now but still capable of employing charm to win her arguments. Moreover, Aspad was aware she had been his dead queen's closest friend and that she had always been a staunch defender of Parthia's interests. Finally, he was aware that Hatra had bigger things to worry about than two errant girls, even if they had been intent on inflicting death on a guest. He stood rigidly to attention and bowed his head.

'The prisoners are released to your custody, majesty.'

He bowed his head to me, about-faced, ordered the guards back to their stations and strode purposely from the chamber. Though he did not surrender the two daggers. The two girls exchanged sly grins, which I found annoying. I stood and stepped down from the dais, facing the younger-looking Amazon.

'Name?'

'Azar, majesty.'

I turned to the other one. 'You?'

'Yasmina, majesty.'

I remembered what Bullus had told me about the band of assassins sent north.

'The kill order on Titus Tullus has been rescinded.'

I looked back at Gallia, expectantly.

'It is as the king says,' she said, icily.

'Report back to your commander,' I told the girls. 'The palace is out of bounds to all Amazons.'

They bowed their heads and departed, looking a little too smug for my liking.

'Try to keep your assassins under control.' I complained. 'And I meant what I said about Titus Tullus. The thought of murdering a guest in this palace disgusts me.'

'All right,' she said, rolling her eyes.

'Your Amazons will have more than enough people to kill when they encounter the Sarmatians,' I told her.

'How do the Sarmatians fight?' she asked.

It was an excellent question, one I had to admit I had no answer to. I had seen the Aorsi many times on the battlefield and they had never impressed me, being used as bait for more disciplined forces or for mopping-up operations. As far as I knew they had no tactics, but the invading horde was obviously very different, having scattered King Ali's army with what appeared to have been relative ease.

'I have no idea,' I admitted. 'Perhaps we could send your pair of female assassins to gather some intelligence on the enemy.'

There is an old saying that there is no rest for the wicked. It came to mind later that day when we had retired to our quarters after a sombre evening meal, both of us reflecting on the loss of Gafarn and Diana, which in truth had yet to fully sink in. It had been worse for Gallia who had been with her closest friend when she had passed from this world into the afterlife, and I knew that part of her was numb with grief.

'I will be glad to be away from here,' she said morosely. 'There are too many ghosts in this palace.'

'I agree. Let us hope Pacorus and his wife do not feel the same way.'

She looked at me with eyes filled with pain.

'They have children, and the young are a powerful antidote to the spectres of old age and death. I was thinking about Rubi earlier.'

I scratched my face. 'Rubi?'

'The girl we rescued from slave hunters in Italy, near the town of the same name.'

'The half-mad girl. Yes, I remember. There's a name that echoes down the decades.'

Gallia walked over to the open wooden shutters leading to a large balcony that overlooked the palace gardens. White doves were settling down for the night in dovecotes and ostriches still strutted around the lawns, kept clean of their droppings and those of other birds by slaves on their knees equipped with trowels, dustpans, brushes and bowls of water.

'She was happy here.'

I remembered the hissing, snarling she-demon who seemed to have a particular disliking for me, notwithstanding I was there when she was freed from a hideous death.

'She and your mother spent hours in those gardens,' she sighed. 'So many ghosts.'

A knock at the door interrupted her sombre musings.

'Lord Herneus requests your presence in the throne room urgently, majesties,' said a muffled voice.

The officer of the guard accompanied us to the throne room where an agitated Herneus was pacing up and down. A knot tightened in my stomach. The commander of Hatra's army was usually unflappable and it was a cause for concern to see him in an agitated state. Such was my preoccupation with his demeanour that I failed to see two other individuals standing near him, until I heard Gallia's voice.

'Haytham?'

I was stunned to see the brother of Castus standing in the throne room, next to him the imposing figure of Lord Orobaz, the governor of Nisibus and the most powerful and influential noble in the kingdom. Herneus stopped and pointed at the prince.

'Tell their majesties what you told me.'

Haytham looked as sheepish as he had done in the throne room of his brother, his eyes flitting between me and Herneus.

'We are waiting,' snapped the general.

'Prince Spadines and his Sarmatians are going to attack northern Hatra,' he said in haste.

'Why?' asked Gallia. 'Why should the King of Gordyene attack the land of his closest ally? It makes no sense.'

'Alas, majesty,' said Haytham, 'sense is a rare commodity in Gordyene these days. Queen Yesim had a vision that Castus would rule the lands from the headwaters of the Euphrates to the Caspian Sea, and my brother is determined to turn her vision into reality.'

'Does he not know that the king and queen of Hatra are not yet cold in their graves?' I raged.

Haytham, his face ashen, nodded. 'It is because of their deaths that he seeks to take advantage of Hatra's weakness.'

'Hatra is not weak,' growled Herneus, 'as your brother will soon discover.'

'Castus has taken leave of his senses,' said Haytham, 'as you can attest to, majesty.'

He was looking at me, but I had no time for his words.

'Why are you here, Haytham? Are you part of your brother's mad schemes, or perhaps you too have been seduced by the witch he married?'

'I came here because his actions will lead to the ruin of Gordyene, majesty,' he answered, 'even with the support of Tasius.'

'Who?'

Haytham swallowed. 'The chief of the Sarmatian tribe called the Roxolani, which wintered among the Aorsi before raiding Atropaiene recently.'

'Allow me to bring you up to date, prince,' I said. 'Your Sarmatian friends destroyed King Ali's army and are at this moment moving south, plundering the kingdom of your other brother as they do so.'

Haytham's head dropped. 'I told Castus it was a mistake inviting them into Gordyene. He would not listen.'

We listened as he recounted the whole miserable tale. Of how, a few years before, Spartacus had invited warriors of a Sarmatian tribe called the Siraki into his kingdom to support his invasion of Armenia. 'Invited' was the wrong word because Spartacus had paid them gold in return for their services, which included burning not only Roman wagons and supplies, but also Armenian villages. It was easy work for their leader, a man called Akka, who returned to whatever wind-lashed land he called home with saddlebags full of gold and many slaves. The Siraki, a comparatively small tribe, had much interaction with the larger Sarmatian groupings, which included the Roxolani, a much larger tribe whose leader, Tasius, was lured south by the prospect of gold, plunder and slaves. And an easier life. When Castus learned through Spadines that Tasius was intent on plundering Parthia, he saw an opportunity to further his own ambitions. The Aorsi guarded Gordyene's northern frontier, after all. Why should not the Roxolani fulfil the same function to the south, east and west?

I was initially lost for words. Gallia appeared remarkably calm after Haytham's revelations, but perhaps they paled beside the loss of Gafarn and Diana.

'How many people has this bandit, this Tasius, brought with him?' I demanded to know.

Haytham bit his bottom lip.

'Spit it out, for Shamash's sake,' said an irate Herneus.

'One hundred thousand,' came the reply.

Gallia was no longer calm; neither was I.

'One hundred thousand?' I said, shocked. 'And your brother has invited them to stay?'

Haytham nodded.

'If we may address the matter immediately at hand, majesty,' said Orobaz.

It was the first time the lord of northern Hatra had spoken. He did so in a calm, measured manner. He was dressed in silk and wore expensive soft leather boots. His sword had a silver horse head pommel and was held in a red scabbard with silver decoration.

'Nisibus and the surrounding area are in danger,' he looked at Herneus, who nodded.

'The army will be riding north tomorrow, my lord.'

I was taken aback. 'What? No. Hatra's army is to march east when my own army arrives, to safeguard the river crossing at Assur.'

'My nephew will burn the bridge if the Sarmatians get close, majesty,' said Herneus.

'Alas, majesty,' smiled Orobaz, 'there is no river to protect northern Hatra from being plundered, unlike at Assur.'

'The army has already been committed to the east,' I said.

'This new information changes everything, majesty,' remarked Herneus. 'I cannot in good faith take the army east when the north of the kingdom is in danger.'

'The matter is not open to debate,' I retorted angrily.

'Until the son of King Gafarn assumes his position, majesty,' said Orobaz, 'the kingdom is under the control of the royal council. Dura has no authority in Hatra.'

I was taken aback by his effrontery and was tempted to order his immediate arrest. But Herneus, in a symbolic gesture, moved to stand beside Orobaz.

'There are many villages and estates around Nisibus, majesty,' said Orobaz. 'There is only one bridge across the Tigris at Assur, which can be burned if the enemy appears.'

'The defence of the north is more pressing, majesty,' insisted Herneus. 'And presumably High King Phraates is mustering an army to fight the Sarmatians.'

'I hope so,' said Haytham.

We all looked at him.

'Why?' I demanded to know.

'Because that is where the Sarmatians are heading.'

'For Ctesiphon?' Herneus was confused. 'It has no strategic worth.'

'But it has gold, lord,' said Haytham.

I threw up my arms. 'Your father was obsessed by gold and so is your brother. And now, thanks to that obsession a plague of Sarmatians has descended on the empire.'

I pointed at Haytham. 'You are coming with me.'

'Where, majesty?'

'To Assur, we leave in the morning, with all the troops from Dura.'

I waited until he shuffled up to me before I grabbed his tunic and shoved him towards the doors to the chamber.

'Move.'

'You will depart for Assur still, majesty?' Herneus called after me.

'Yes, draw up an order for your nephew to place all his resources at my disposal. Unless that has to be ratified by the royal council, too?'

'Don't be churlish, Pacorus,' Gallia beside me scolded me.

'And when my horsemen arrive from Dura,' I said loudly, 'have Governor Aspad direct them on to Assur where their king, queen and one hundred Amazons are holding back one hundred thousand Sarmatians.'

'Churlish,' repeated Gallia.

I did not blame Orobaz and Herneus. Nisibus, the second city of the kingdom, had been built in the middle of a huge plain at the base of Mount Masius, one of the mountains in the Taurus range. The lower slopes of the mountain are covered in deciduous and conifer forests and the plain itself is lush and blessed by favourable winds and nourishing rains. It was where the royal stud farms that bred horses for Hatra's army were located, along with the countless farms that grew the crops that fed both Nisibus and Hatra. To lose such a gem would seriously weaken the kingdom, perhaps fatally.

I ordered a guard to be placed outside Haytham's room that night to ensure he did not abscond from the palace, though where he would go now he had burned his bridges with Castus I did not know, and cared even less.

'You should not be angry with Haytham,' said Gallia. 'He has given us prior warning of the Sarmatian attack.'

'I am going to kill Spadines,' I pledged, 'and all his wretched tribe of cockroaches. Where are you going at this late hour?'

She stood at the door to our bedroom, my old childhood sleeping quarters, with a hand on the handle.

'Something I need to do before I forget. Have you considered Gaius Arrianus and Titus Tullus?'

'Considered them?'

She tut-tutted. 'Now that Nisibus is in danger, they cannot go into northern Hatra to reach Zeugma. They will have to travel to Dura and on to Zeugma along the western bank of the Euphrates. I will arrange it.'

'Ah, very thoughtful of you.'

She opened the door to walk into the corridor illuminated by oil lamps.

'I always am, Pacorus.'

Chapter 11

I had hoped to ride to Assur with sixty-five hundred of the finest horsemen in all Parthia, including fifteen hundred cataphracts. The next morning, the sun shining down on the great square in front of Hatra's palace, just over a hundred figures on horseback greeted me as I descended the steps of the palace to reunite with Horns. Herneus' nephew had sent him back refreshed and re-shoed, as promised, and now he would take me back to Assur. One hundred Amazons stood in two lines on the square and at the end of the first line Bullus, Klietas and a crestfallen Haytham sat on their horses.

I hoisted myself into the saddle and took the reins passed to me by a stable hand who had brought Horns from his night-time quarters. I patted him on the neck and waited for Gallia to mount up beside me. Hatra's cataphracts and horse archers, all professional soldiers, would be forming up on the square after we had left for Assur. Normally they would already be arrayed prior to departing for Nisibus, but Herneus had deliberately delayed their muster to avoid rubbing salt in my wounded pride.

The general stood at the foot of the steps with a sheepish-looking Aspad and an indifferent Orobaz. Gaius Arrianus and Titus Tullus, both fully restored to health and attired in fine clothes as befitting their rank, stood with them. I nudged Horns forward and leaned down towards Herneus.

'I have sent word to Dura for my horsemen and foot soldiers to march straight to Assur. They will not stay in the Hatra. You have sent word to your nephew?'

'Yes, majesty.'

'Good luck in the north.'

I turned Horns to walk along the line of dignitaries, halting him at Gaius Arrianus.

'Well, ambassador, here is where our journeys part. An escort will accompany you both to Dura from where you will be able to reach Syria. Though if you have the time, I would recommend a trip to Palmyra.'

Gaius bowed his head.

'It has been an honour to meet you, majesty. You can be assured that I will inform Augustus himself of your great service to his ambassador. And be assured Rome will honour its commitments.'

Strange words to end on, but then these were strange times. I smiled at Titus Tullus.

'Safe journey back to Pontus, general. I would advise avoiding its hills and mountains. They appear to be filled with rebellious tribesmen.'

'Have no fear, majesty, I won't be making the same mistake again. I am glad we are parting as friends rather than enemies.'

'As am I, general.'

I turned Horns and directed him towards the exit from the square, the honour guard of foot soldiers drawn from the garrison lining the outside of the quadrangle standing to attention as we trotted past them. The camels carrying our tents, supplies and ammunition had deposited liberal quantities of dung on the stone slabs, which would be removed before the muster of Hatra's professional horsemen. After they had left for Nisibus, the deposits of their horses and camels would also be removed and the stone slabs washed clean. I reflected that my life and that of a slave and stable hand were not that different. Like them, I had been shovelling the same detritus for years.

We reached Assur dirty, thirsty and drenched in sweat, having covered the route to the city without a halt. We had ridden for four hours through the hottest part of the day and were glad to slide off saddles and dunk our heads in water troughs to refresh our roasted bodies and brains. Gallia ordered Minu to see that the Amazons were allocated quarters in the barracks of the governor's mansion, while she and I immediately conferred with Rodak.

'You wish to lie down, majesty?' he asked us, concerned the journey had fatigued us. It had.

'No, find us fresh horses and accompany us to the bridge.'

It was with difficulty I hauled myself into a fresh saddle once more, my back aching like fury. But I maintained a brave face, as did Gallia, who was watching Klietas removing his saddle from his horse.

'He elected to stay with you?'

'He did,' I said.

'He still desires Haya?'

'He has a new woman now, called Anush. She is pregnant.'

I thought of rampaging Sarmatians plundering Media and my heart sank.

'Or was.'

Gallia looked at me. 'Was?'

'She might be dead, skewered on the end of a Sarmatian spear.'

She pointed at a hot and panting Haytham.

'What about him?'

'He is here to atone for his brother's crimes.'

'What a mess,' she lamented.

'What a mess, indeed.'

We rode to the bridge spanning the Tigris in the company of the governor and his second-in-command, a rather dour individual who did nothing to improve the mood. Already the road from the east that carried the trade caravans was strangely silent, the news of the Sarmatian incursion having resulted in the traffic on the Silk Road fleeing back to Esfahan.

We halted at the western end of the bridge across the Tigris, a marvel of engineering constructed by Dura's quartermaster general. It comprised a row of boats, or pontoons, secured by anchors to the riverbed arranged side-by-side, over the top of which was a roadbed comprising wooden beams lashed together and topped by a road of wooden planks nailed to the framework. Below it the waters of the Tigris flowed with a fast current, the river swelled by the spring meltwaters coming from the mountains far to the north. We walked our horses on to the bridge, and I caught sight of brushwood piled high on each side of the roadway.

'You are ready to fire the bridge?'

Rodak nodded. 'Yes, majesty.'

'You have scouts out, searching for the Sarmatians?'

Another nod. 'Thus far, they have reported no sightings.'

'They are probably too busy plundering Media,' said Gallia.

It was around seventy miles northeast from Assur to Irbil – a two-day ride. Castus must have supplied information to his new friends concerning crossing points over the Tigris. I wondered why the Sarmatians had not yet shown their misshapen faces.

'The bridge is not to be burnt,' I ordered. 'We will hold it until my army arrives.'

'And Hatra's army,' added Rodak.

Herneus had obviously omitted to mention in his missive to his nephew it would not be coming any time soon.

'Hatra's army has been called away to Nisibus,' I informed him.

He looked alarmed. 'We have insufficient soldiers to hold the bridge, majesty.'

'How many men do you have?' I asked.

'Fifty horsemen and a hundred foot soldiers,' he replied. 'It would be prudent to fire the bridge now, majesty.'

'We need the bridge, Rodak, so we will hold it until reinforced.'

In front of us was the structure in question, just over three hundred paces in length and eight paces in width to allow two wagons to pass each other with ease. The Tigris was around two hundred paces wide at Assur, being fordable in autumn and winter when the sun baked the earth and the level dropped. But this was the end of spring and the river was raging, which would prevent the Sarmatians crossing downstream or upstream.

I scanned the opposite riverbank, either side of the bridge. It was open and flat on account of the date palms having been felled to provide timber for the pontoon bridge, and to give the garrison of Assur guarding the river crossing clear fields of vision. Lucius Varsas had thought of everything, having cut timbers to leave stumps that had been sharpened to provide another impediment to hostile forces, channelling them into the bridgehead. Further upstream and downstream the riverbanks were fringed with dark-green date palm groves, interspersed with orange trees.

'We need to block the far end of the bridge with overturned wagons,' I told Rodak, 'in front of which we will plant rows of sharpened stakes to create an impenetrable semi-circle of defences around the bridge.'

'It is too late for that,' said Gallia, pointing at the eastern end of the bridge where a single black figure shimmered in the haze.

It was barely recognisable, and I had to squint to see it. I felt a familiar knot tighten in my stomach and the hairs on the back of my neck stood up. It could have been anything – a camel, a gazelle, a person on foot – but my instincts told me otherwise and my instincts were seldom wrong.

'Sound the alarm, muster every horse archer and get those wagons,' I said to Rodak. 'The Sarmatians are here.'

He peered at the shimmering figure. 'It is just one man, majesty.'

'No, they are here.'

Gallia turned her horse and began cantering back to the city gates.

'I will stay here,' I called after her, 'bring plenty of arrows.'

Rodak bowed his head and followed, leaving me alone at the western end of the bridge. I told Horns to walk forward on to the structure, quickening his pace to canter across the wooden planks. And all the while the black, hazy figure remained where he was. When I had neared the eastern end of the bridge, however, the figure had become larger, more distinct. Whoever it was now approached the bridge, a figure on horseback around a hundred paces away. I pulled up Horns and drew my bow from its case, plucking an arrow from one of the two quivers fixed to the left side of my saddle and knocking it in the bowstring. The horseman stopped when he saw me arming my bow.

I walked Horns forward and halted him at the end of the bridge. He grunted and chomped on his bit, scraping the boards with his front right leg. I patted his neck.

'Easy, boy.'

He probably sensed the threat of violence in the air and the calm before the storm of battle. There was no wind, only flies, heat and piles of baked horse and camel dung on the road that forked a short distance inland from the bridge. The fork heading north led to Irbil; the one to the east all the way to Esfahan, some five hundred miles distant. The other horseman re-commenced his advance, walking his beast forward to come within range of my bow. I clutched the weapon in my left hand but kept it at arm's length on my left side, curious to take a closer look at a Roxolani tribesman.

As the figure got closer I was surprised to see a woman dressed in a tan upper garment that resembled a kaftan, with tight-fitting leggings of the same colour. Her long black hair was loose, and a long dagger or sword hung on her left side. She held the reins of her horse in her left hand and what appeared to be a coil of rope in her right. She was around forty paces away, maybe less, and had now halted, peering past me to examine the bridge and the town of Assur beyond. I brought up my bow and aimed it at her. She hissed at me, turned her horse and galloped away in a cloud of dust.

Another cloud of dust announced the arrival of reinforcements, comprising Gallia, her Amazons and Rodak and his fifty horse archers, plus Bullus and Klietas driving two four-wheeled carts. They were overturned on the eastern end of the bridge, in line with the water's edge below. In this way, enemy troops would not be able to use the riverbank on either side to outflank our makeshift defences. Bullus supervised the siting of the overturned carts, walking up and down behind the sweating and complaining garrison horse archers, *gladius* and shield in his hands.

'Put your backs into it, you miserable dogs, or else the enemy will be eating your livers for supper.'

I looked into the sky. The sun was still high above us – it would be hours before we would be eating our suppers. Gallia supervised leading the horses to the western end of the bridge, to put them beyond enemy arrow range but still close enough if the barricade was overrun and we had to make a dash for Assur. Rodak kept glancing behind him at the town, the gates of which were now slammed shut and the walls lined with spearmen.

'The brushwood should be doused with oil, majesty,' he said. 'If the Sarmatians overrun us, there will nothing to stop them riding to Hatra and beyond.'

I turned to look at the brushwood piled into each of the pontoons on either side of the roadway below us.

'We hold the bridge,' I told him.

He became frustrated. 'I must protest, majesty. If we burn the bridge, the Sarmatians have no way of crossing over the river. My first duty is to Hatra.'

I squared up to him. 'Your first duty, your only duty, is to obey me, Rodak, nephew of Herneus. However, if you do not have the stomach for the fight, you are free to ride back to your mansion in the town.'

He smarted at the insult but kept his tongue in check.

'My men should defend the wagons, majesty,' he said at length.

I looked at the overturned wagons laid side by side, their undersides facing east to employ their wheels as additional obstacles to the enemy. Behind them stood a row of eight Amazons, the maximum number of archers that could stand in a line on the bridge. My original plan was to create a semi-circular defence around the eastern end of the bridge composed of overturned wagons and stakes. But that had been rendered redundant by the appearance of a lone Sarmatian woman. Where there was one, there were many. And so, a hundred and fifty archers stood on the bridge, ready to repulse whatever the invaders threw at them.

The time before battle is the worst, when the waiting allows the mind to fill with endless possibilities of what will happen when the fighting begins. Fortunately, we did not have time to dwell on our fate. No sooner had I given the order for the Amazons at the wagons to withdraw to allow Hatra's archers to have the honour of standing in the first line of defence than did the enemy appear. We heard them first, the rumbling sound of hooves striking hard ground, causing arrows to be nocked in bowstrings.

I was standing beside Gallia, just behind the archers positioned behind the wagons, Bullus on my left and Minu on Gallia's right, when they came into view – a rabble of hollering horsemen waving spears and axes in the air, galloping full tilt towards the wagons. It was a fearsome sight and was designed to strike dread into us, to make us flee for our lives before they reached the wagons.

'Keep your nerve,' I shouted.

'Find your targets,' called Gallia.

'Arrows,' warned Minu.

I looked into the sky to see black missiles arching upwards and then down towards us. Not many – perhaps only half a dozen at most – but enough to cause us all to instinctively crouch down to make ourselves as small a target as possible.

Thud, thud, thud. The arrows slammed into the planks. A high-pitched scream. One struck an Amazon. I glanced behind to see a woman clutching her left leg, an arrow stuck in it. Another rushed to her to assist her in getting to the other end of the bridge, from where she could ride a horse the short distance to the town for medical aid.

Gallia shot her arrow, which hissed through the air to strike a horse in the front of the Sarmatian throng, the beast collapsing and throwing its rider to the ground. Then the air was filled with hisses resembling a nest of vipers being disturbed. Horses reared up, arrows in their bodies. Riders were struck and tumbled from their saddles. Others, arrows in their torsos, slumped in the saddle and turned their horses around to limp away.

The Hatrans at the wagons were shooting arrows with abandon, the Sarmatians having been stopped in their tracks by the wagons. For no horse will charge at a solid obstacle. But then a flurry of spears came from their ranks, killing half of those behind the wagons and two more standing a few paces back from them. A second hail of spears that killed four more was followed by a hail of Parthian arrows that brought down more than a score of Sarmatians and forced the others to withdraw. They left a pile of dead horses and men behind, all in front of the barricade to add to the obstacle the enemy would have to surmount in order to take the bridge.

Klietas shoved a water bottle in my face. I held it and took small swigs. I saw him looking behind us at Haya, resplendent in mail armour and helmet, with her file of Amazons on the bridge some way back. I handed him back the water bottle.

'Concentrate on keeping yourself alive. You still lust after her?'

'Majesty?'

'Haya.'

'No, majesty. I have a wife.'

He suddenly looked dejected. I gripped his arm.

'Castus will have sent soldiers to safeguard her and the others in your village. Have no fear.'

He looked cheerier. 'Yes, majesty.'

'Listen. You do not have to stand on this bridge with us. Why don't you go back to the town? If the enemy breaks through here, they will not bother to besiege Assur. You will be safe.'

He was shocked at the suggestion.

'No, majesty. You rode to my aid and Gula would never forgive me if I were to abandon you in your hour of need.'

I thought of all the poor farmers who had been butchered over the years when armies had criss-crossed Parthia, and the ones who had probably been killed by the invading Sarmatians. I smiled at him.

'I thank you for your loyalty, Klietas.'

'Look sharp, here they come again.'

The authoritative voice of Centurion Bullus diverted my attention back to the barricade, which was about to be assaulted by men, and women, on foot. Armed with axes, spears and a few swords, there must have been upwards of three or four hundred walking towards the bridge. Seemingly undeterred by the heap of dead horseflesh and humans to their front and wearing nothing that could protect them from the arrow storm they would walk into, they appeared fearless, determined and wholly reckless.

They were led by a huge man with a tattooed face carrying a two-handed axe, who suddenly raised his weapon and raced forward. A great cry came from the Sarmatian ranks and the whole mob charged.

'Now,' shouted Gallia.

The arrows of the Amazons were shot high into the sky, so they would fall like rain drops on the Sarmatians, a second and third volley being strung and loosed before the arrowheads of the first peppered the enemy. It was a sight both beautiful and terrible to behold as black slivers fell from the sky to strike flesh and bone, cutting down ten, twenty and more of the enemy every five seconds. Sarmatians clutched forlornly at arrow shafts stuck in them, stumbling and falling, those behind tripping on the bodies of their comrades. Some looked up and were killed instantly when an arrow pierced their eye sockets and the metal heads penetrated their brain.

And still they advanced.

They were relentless, stepping and stumbling over their dead to reach the barricade, Amazons shooting arrows at an almost vertical trajectory so they would fall on the Sarmatians thrusting spears and chopping with their axes at the men at the wagons. Dismounted horse archers, they had only daggers to defend themselves at close quarters and suffered accordingly. I saw one, two, three collapse, their heads split open by axes or their faces disfigured by spear points.

I grabbed Rodak's arm. 'Get some of your spearmen here, otherwise we are lost.'

He gave me a curt nod and ordered one of his men to run back to the horses and fetch more men. The soldier took to his heels as though all the demons of the underworld were after him.

I released my bowstring to shoot a Sarmatian who had been hoisted on top of one of the wagons, the arrow slamming into his belly, causing him to flop back down from whence he had come. Another man scrambled up on to a wagon. I shot him, too. A woman, a screeching banshee wielding a long knife, scrambled over a wagon and stabbed one of Rodak's men. I hesitated. Two arrows struck her in the chest, and she was gone.

'Getting soft, Pacorus?' asked Gallia beside me, nocking another arrow.

I saw Bullus at the barricade, using his shield as a defence and thrusting with his *gladius* in a series of deft moves. Next to him was Haytham, wielding his own sword with aplomb, stabbing Sarmatians in the face, chest and belly as they appeared in front of him. But they were only two and around them Assur's horse archers were going down with alarming speed.

'Line,' shouted Gallia, kneeling and hauling me down to my knees.

Four other Amazons knelt beside us and six more stood behind us.

'Rapid shots,' commanded their queen.

Quivers slung over our shoulders, we shot seven arrows a minute at the Sarmatians attempting to scale the wagons.

Twelve archers loosing a combined total of over eighty arrows a minute.

Then the enemy was gone. Assailed by a storm of arrows that literally swept them away from the barricades like a brush sweeping leaves, they retraced their steps back to where they had come from. My elation at having thrown them back was tempered by the sad realisation I could not rise from a kneeling position.

'Come on, old man.'

Gallia, herself slowly rising to her feet, assisted me to my own, around us Amazons and what was left of Rodak's horse archers raising their bows and cheering their victory. But twenty of his men were either dead or wounded and three Amazons had been slain by enemy arrows.

The arrival of fifty spearmen from Assur raised spirits further, especially as they were accompanied by slaves carrying water bottles and food. It was late afternoon and though the heat of the day was now subsiding, it was still hot and airless and after our exertions, many men and women took the opportunity to lie on their backs and gasp for air.

Bullus, rivulets of sweat coursing down his granite-like face, came over to me. The hide covering his shield was torn, the metal rim dented and the central boss showed battle scars.

'That was close,' he panted.

He looked at the spearmen from Assur – men equipped with wicker shields faced with hide, helmets and only long knives for close-quarter fighting.

'Is that the best we can call on?'

'I'm afraid so.'

'It's at moments like this that makes me appreciate what we have at Dura.'

'Dura will be here, Bullus,' I told him, 'we just have to hold a little longer. My horsemen are on their way, and close behind, the Durans and Exiles.'

He cocked his ear to the north. 'What's that?'

It was chopping. Barely audible at first but gradually increasing to arouse everyone's attention. Tired men and women hauled themselves to their feet to look north, staring at the great expanse of date palm grooves that filled the eastern riverbank. From where there came the sound of what seemed like an army of woodpeckers furiously at work.

'Even Sarmatians have a basic understanding of mathematics,' I lamented.

'Majesty?'

I pointed at the wagons decorated with dead bodies, both Parthian and Sarmatian.

'The end of the bridge is a chokepoint, Bullus, which can be held by a comparatively small number of troops.'

I then turned and pointed at the bridge behind us.

'But this bridge is over three hundred paces in length, and if I had an overwhelming superiority in numbers, I would construct rafts to allow my soldiers to float down the river to assail the bridge along its whole length.'

'Clever,' said Bullus, admiringly.

'Not a word I thought I would ever associate with Sarmatians, but yes. Clever.'

I called Rodak to me. 'If the Sarmatians are going to assault the bridge with rafts, then we need more men. Call for volunteers. Anyone who is able to use a spear, axe or knife.'

He looked up and down the bridge. 'Perhaps it is time to fire the bridge, majesty.'

'No. We need it. And if we are overrun and it is captured by the enemy; it can be recaptured at a later date. If it is burnt, then we lose a valuable crossing point over the Tigris.'

He was right but so was I, and in truth there was a part of me that was reluctant to destroy something that had been created by Dura's engineers. Perhaps it was vanity, but I was not prepared to see something go up in flames because of a tribe of Sarmatians, however large.

The bodies of enemy dead were left on the other side of the wagons to impede attacking Sarmatians, those of our own slain being removed for cremation. The chopping did not lessen as the light began to fade, and when the sun had left the earth the palm groves further upstream were illuminated by what appeared to be a thousand torches. The Sarmatians obviously had the bit between their teeth and were determined to create a fleet of rafts by daybreak. I felt tired and dirty and would dearly have loved to depart for the governor's mansion to bath, be massaged and sleep in a soft bed. Instead, I could look forward to grabbing perhaps a couple of hours' sleep on the planks of the bridge before battling the Sarmatians again on a new day.

Rodak had sacks stuffed with straw and blankets brought from the town to allow us to sleep in shifts, plus more ammunition from the garrison's armoury. Full quivers were issued to Assur's archers and the Amazons, after which Rodak reported to me and Gallia, the queen swathed in a thick blanket, for the night sky was cloudless and the temperature had dropped considerably.

'That is the last of the ammunition, majesty,' he said. 'Three quivers for each archer.'

'Ninety arrows each,' remarked Gallia. 'The loss of Hatra's army works against us by the hour.'

After the governor had made his excuses and left, cooks brought us hot soup cooked on pans over braziers brought from the town. She did not say anything while she was consuming the soup, dipping pieces of bread in the thick, tasty broth. But when she had finished, she spoke.

'Phraates will want Castus' head for this.'

I sighed. 'I know. There is no way he will be able to extricate himself from the great harm he has inflicted on the empire.'

I looked at Haytham nearby, seated on a barrel cleaning his sword.

'His life will be forfeit, too. Phraates will not allow a sibling of Castus to inherit Gordyene's throne.'

'Exile, then,' said Gallia.

'Exile, yes.'

'What about Akmon?' she asked. 'Phraates will not wish to remove a man who has proved an excellent king of Media, but one who is also brother to both Castus and Haytham.'

'That is something for Phraates to worry about, not me.'

'And then there is the separate matter of Dura avenging Gordyene's treatment of its king,' she said ominously. 'Such insults cannot and will not be tolerated.'

'I will be honest with you. I do not wish to see the death of the son of Spartacus and the grandson of the man of the same name. If it comes to it, I will lobby for Castus and his snake of a wife to be exiled from the empire.'

'That will not do, Pacorus. We do not want another Atrax lingering like a bad smell just beyond Parthia's borders.'

'I am just glad Gafarn and Diana are not here to witness the tragedy that is unfolding,' I said, rather pathetically.

A line of torches leaving Assur provided a merciful distraction and all chatter on the bridge ceased as eyes turned to the reinforcements tramping out of the town. Tired Amazons and horse archers smiled and slapped each other on the back at the sight of more soldiers to stiffen our defence. Even Bullus was impressed. Until the reinforcements marched on to the bridge.

They were led by Rodak, now mounted, and a coterie of Assur's lords, all men with grey beards and thinning hair who had seen too many dawns. They led a few hundred old men, boys and slaves, the latter at least in their prime. Rodak jumped down from his horse and bowed to me. I noticed he had changed his clothes and now sported a fine scale-armour cuirass that glittered in the torchlight.

'Reinforcements, majesty, as promised.'

Gallia smiled when slaves rushed forward and went down on all fours beside the horses to allow their old, fat masters to use them as dismounting aids. Rodak saw my disappointment.

'Alas, majesty, some lords left Assur with their horsemen as part of the general muster called by my uncle, riding directly to Nisibus.'

The lords left in Assur assembled behind the governor, waiting expectantly. They were all armed with swords and held bows in their hands, manservants holding full quivers.

'Thank you for answering my summons,' I said to them. 'That chopping sound you can hear is the enemy cutting down trees to make rafts, which they will float downriver to the bridge tomorrow morning.'

'It is already tomorrow, majesty,' said a lord with a huge belly and a long beard.

'The night passes quickly,' I smiled. 'I have to tell you the enemy greatly outnumbers us. But I am confident we can hold out until Dura's horsemen arrive.'

'Just like at Surkh,' grinned one of the lords.

I walked up to him. He was a tall, rotund individual with hardly any hair, though a full beard.

'You were at Surkh?'

'Yes, majesty,' he grinned, 'a commander of horse archers in your father's army. I was slimmer and had more hair in those days.'

I laughed. 'Didn't we all. Well, we were victorious on that day and I have every confidence we will triumph today.'

Bullus was less confident, his initial examination of our reinforcements leaving him less than impressed.

'Most are either too old or too young, and the slaves for the most part look horrified, like someone who has been handed a bag of venomous snakes.'

Shards of light were lancing the eastern sky to announce dawn breaking. It was very cold and I was shivering, rubbing my numb hands together to return some feeling to them.

'Do your best,' I told him.

A token force of garrison troops was left in Assur, the rest lining the bridge, facing north where the rafts would come from. The current was still strong, and I hoped that would work in our favour by making the rafts hard to control on the river. On the other hand, the flow would bring them to us quicker.

The gods give with one hand and take away with the other.

Bullus interspersed the troops from the garrison with the volunteers, placing those with any military experience in the front rank and ensuring they at least had a helmet, spear and shield. The latter was not the stout items of equipment used by Dura's legionaries, but it was roughly comparable in size. Made of wicker and faced with leather, it was easy and inexpensive to make, easy to repair, light and offered protection against slingshots and arrows. Where it fell down was at close quarters where spears, swords and axes could penetrate the wicker and literally chop it to pieces.

There were no chopping sounds now, only the creaking of the bridge as the pontoons were moved by the river current. I placed Haytham at the wagons with ten spearmen and the same number of archers, just in case the enemy used the threat of an assault from the river as a decoy to lure us away from the barricade. Whatever his faults and complicity in his brother's madness, he had acquitted himself well enough the day before. I offered him my hand. He took it.

'Keep yourself alive, Haytham. And try to hold the bridge.'

'Yes, lord.'

He drew his sword and I realised it was an ukku blade, produced of the semi-magical metal found only beyond the River Indus in the east.

'Make sure you keep hold of that sword. I would hate to think of a Sarmatian swinging it from his mangy horse.'

'I will, lord.'

I walked slowly from the wagons along the bridge, in front of the rank of spearmen that now lined it. Behind them stood archers from Assur and Amazons from Dura. I tried to smile at every man and woman who stood gripping a spear and clutching a shield. There were around five hundred of them, of which only around eighty were professionals. The rest were old men, boys and slaves, the latter a mixture of house servants in excellent clothes and shoes, the rest manual labourers in more threadbare attire. I stopped at one slave, a handsome man in his early twenties wearing a fine white linen tunic edged with red, loose red leggings and a pair of soft leather shoes. My eyes were drawn to the hand gripping his spear, which had manicured nails.

'You are a slave?'

'Yes, highborn. Mascius, tutor to the children of my master and mistress,' he answered in perfect Greek.

'Where is your master?'

'Gone to Nisibus, highborn.'

'What do you teach your master's children, Mascius?'

'Reading, writing, poetry, music and magic.'

'Magic?'

He smiled, revealing a row of even white teeth.

'Yes, highborn, magic tricks to amuse them between lessons.'

I looked at the river.

'I don't suppose you can make the Sarmatians disappear?'

'Highborn?'

I slapped him on the shoulder. 'It doesn't matter. I am glad you are here with us, Mascius.'

I laid a gentler hand on one youth, perhaps sixteen years old or less, who was clearly terrified, shivering with fear. I glanced past him to see the helmeted Yasmina standing behind him. I moved in closer so no one else would hear.

'You see that young lady behind you?'

He turned to stare at the Amazon and nodded.

'If things get too heated, take cover behind her. She has killed more men than I have, so you are in good hands.'

His eyes opened wide in amazement and he took a second look at the stern-faced Yasmina.

'It's true,' I assured him. 'Have courage.'

Courage, the most precious commodity on the battlefield, and the rarest. Those who have not fought in battle, and there were many standing on this bridge, believe that all soldiers are magically infused with bravery. But the truth is, soldiers put more faith in their training and their comrades than in their personal stock of courage. Only the deluded and insane believe that courage alone can win battles. Therefore, soldiers take greater comfort in faith. Faith that the gods they worship will keep them safe on the battlefield, and faith in their comrades, training and equipment.

'Here they come.'

I heard the warning and the trumpets of the garrison's signallers and looked north. To see a crowd of individuals upstream, pushing rafts out into the river. One, two, five, ten, twenty. Simple structures comprising felled tree trunks lashed together, on which stood groups of Sarmatians clutching axes, spears and bows. None carried shields and only a smattering wore helmets. I caught sight of a large individual clutching a two-bladed axe – the man who had led the attack the day before. More rafts pushed off from the riverbank, filling the river with square platforms that were paddled into mid-stream and towards the western bank, after which they drifted downstream towards us.

I stood in the centre of our thin battle line at the mid-point of the bridge, next to Rodak, behind me Gallia and Minu. I was the only person in the front rank clutching a bow. Rodak was equipped with a sword and wicker shield, those elderly lords among the spearmen the only others equipped with swords.

The Sarmatians began shouting and screaming in our direction in an effort to intimidate us, raising their weapons in the air and shaking them at us. I had seen such displays many times before and they no longer unnerved me. It was very different for the many who were facing the trial of combat for the first time, though. I turned to Gallia.

'Shut them up.'

'Amazons,' she called. 'Loose.'

Ninety-five woman stepped forward through the front rank, selected their targets and began shooting, arrows whooshing through the windless air to strike bodies. The shooting was measured and unrushed, every missile finding its target. Yelps and screams came from rafts and individuals began collapsing into the water. I shot an arrow at the nearest raft, around fifty paces away, the missile striking a man holding a spear in the chest, causing him to spin and topple into the water. I strung another arrow and shot the man who has been standing next to him, who collapsed on the raft.

The volleys of the Amazons, who had been joined by Assur's archers, were reaping a cruel harvest but the rafts were closing on the bridge fast. They were not in a line or lines, more groups of rafts, and they would strike the bridge haphazardly, but when they did the Sarmatians would clamber over the pontoons and then attack our line.

The raft in the Sarmatian vanguard now held only dead men and women, having been the focus of our arrows. But the other rafts still carried more living than dead, and now they smashed into the bridge, one disintegrating as it did so, its occupants falling into the river to be swept under the bridge and downstream. But the others did not break apart and now their occupants leaped on to the pontoons to attack us. I slung my bow behind me and drew my sword.

Rodak deflected an enemy spear point with his shield, the metal failing to pierce the hide facing, thrusting his sword forward into the Sarmatian's face, specifically his mouth. The man recoiled and fell into the water below. Another Sarmatian chopped down at his face with an axe, the governor bringing up his shield sharply to block the blow before stabbing the man in the belly with his sword.

The man on my left collapsed, a spear in his belly, the Sarmatian holding it grinning with relish as he twisted the shaft to increase the victim's agony. I cut down with my sword and severed the Sarmatian's right hand gripping the pole at the wrist, the stump pumping blood after I had done so. The man gazed, open mouthed, at his wound before being killed when I rammed the tip of my *spatha* though his chest.

The Sarmatians were swarming on to the bridge now, spearmen fighting deadly duels in an effort to keep them at bay. The air was rent with pitiful screams and cries as bodies were ripped open by axe and sword blades and spear points.

'Down, Pacorus.'

I heard Gallia's voice and instantly obeyed, a second after I had done so an arrow hissing over my head to strike a Sarmatian gripping an axe before me in the belly. Another to my left chopped down at me with his axe but I blocked the blow with my sword, the wooden haft striking the edge of the blade. I pulled my Roman dagger from its sheath and thrust it upwards into his groin. He let out a blood-curdling shriek and doubled over, falling from the bridge when I kicked him over the side.

Our line had been broken, the bridge becoming the venue for a number of separate fights as groups of spearmen and archers tried to hold back the Sarmatian tide. I picked up my bow at Gallia's feet and searched for targets, Rodak beside me, his sword smeared with blood and his shield looking the worse for wear. Minu and Haya joined us, the young women's file of nine forming a circle, in front of which were Rodak's second-in-command and around ten of his spearmen.

'We need to sweep the bridge,' I shouted. 'Form wedge and head for the barricade. Move.'

Rodak took up position at the tip of the wedge, Gallia and me flanking and slightly behind him as he walked forward. A Sarmatian, having just butchered a hapless slave with his axe, turned his head and staggered backwards as I shot him in the side. Gallia shot a Sarmatian woman hollering like a demented person, silencing her instantly. We continued walking towards the wagons, two hundred paces away, or thereabouts.

Parthian spearmen, slaves, old lords and boys eagerly joined our group when we saved them from being sliced open or thrown into the water, plus Amazons who had been defending their own small groups. Soon, there were several dozen with us, with only me, Rodak, Gallia, Minu and Haya at the tip of the spear. We shot our bows and those behind us shot theirs to maintain a continuous volley of arrows that cut down every Sarmatian in our path.

Our pace slowed when we were forced to step over the dead and dying, our footing becoming precarious as we slipped on the blood-splattered planks. I shot a woman in the back – not my proudest moment – who was grappling with an Amazon, Gallia's warrior shouting in triumph as she pushed the dead woman away from her, bloody knife in her hand.

And then we were at the wagons where Haytham and his ragged band still held the barricade. His head bleeding from a gash and his scale armour missing a few plates, he raised his gore-covered sword in acknowledgement.

'Watch out!' I shouted, seeing a Sarmatian suddenly appear on top of the wagon above him.

Without thinking he spun and slashed his sword diagonally at the enemy's legs, the keen edge of the ukku blade slicing through both limbs just under the knee. The Sarmatian toppled backwards from whence he came, his lower legs falling forwards to land at Haytham's feet.

We had linked up with the young prince at the barricade. But behind us stood a thick press of Sarmatians between us and the western end of the bridge.

Gallia showed me her empty quiver.

'What now?'

Chapter 12

Half of Rodak's spearmen were dead, more than half of the volunteers had also fallen and the governor's archers were almost all gone. Fortunately, due to their training and the fact they were armed with swords and daggers in addition to their bows, most of the Amazons still lived, though a few had nasty cuts and bruises. Worse, they were almost all out of arrows, as was I.

'Well?' demanded Gallia.

The battle had been a bruising affair not only for us but also the enemy, the Sarmatians having lost a great number of men and women in their efforts to wrest the bridge from our control, which in truth they had achieved. However, they were also tired, and I could see as they formed into a group behind the big man with the two-bladed axe, many were hobbling, and others had arms hanging limply by their sides. If not broken then fractured or badly sprained.

'Bullus,' I called, praying to Shamash he still lived.

Battered, bruised and in a testy mood, he pushed his way through what was left of us to report to me. The crest on his helmet was damaged, the hide of his shield had been torn and he was sweating profusely. But he appeared not to have a mark on him. He stood to attention and saluted.

'The queen wishes to know how we are going to get across the bridge to reach the safety of Assur, Bullus. I am at a loss, but I thought you might have a few ideas.'

He turned to look at the menacing group of Sarmatians being marshalled by the big brute with the axe, around forty paces away.

'Pig's head, majesty,' he said, 'though the chances of it working with what we've got are low.'

The pig's head formation was used by Rome's legions to devastating effect on the battlefield. It involved forming foot soldiers into extremely close order to create or exploit gaps in the enemy battle line. On a bridge only a few paces wide, it would be reduced to one man forming the tip of a very narrow wedge to literally cut a path through the Sarmatians.

I looked at a perplexed Rodak, who had picked up a new wicker shield.

'Essentially a wedge formation.'

Bullus pointed his *gladius* at the Sarmatians who were now in a compact mass, the big brute in vanguard, gripping his axe with both hands.

'May I make a suggestion, highborn?'

All eyes turned to the figure of Mascius, the well-dressed slave with manicured hands, who by some intervention of the gods had managed to survive the bloodbath. He had lost his helmet and but retained his spear and wicker shield, which had taken a few blows. Bullus screwed up his face at the attractive young man.

'Make it quick,' I said.

'It would appear we are about to be attacked by a large number of the enemy,' he began.

'We have ourselves a military genius among us,' remarked Bullus, caustically.

'Continue,' I said, glaring at Bullus.

'Why do we not use one of the wagons as a blunt instrument to force our way through them, highborn?' suggested Mascius.

'That might just work,' said Gallia.

One of the wagons was tipped back on its wheels and manhandled towards the Sarmatians by willing slaves, glad to no longer have to participate in the fighting. There were bodies on the bridge to impede its movement it was true, but now we had a battering ram to force our way through the enemy throng.

The bridge had been built to allow two wagons travelling in opposite directions to pass each other, so there was room for three spearmen to lock shields and level their weapons on each side of the wagon, plus a pair of Amazons sheltering behind shield bearers to ride on the wagon itself, who began shooting immediately.

'Heave,' I called, slaves gripping the sides and rear of the wagon to push the vehicle forward.

Then the Sarmatians charged, a wild, disorganised rush that gave the appearance it would overwhelm us.

'Stand firm,' shouted Bullus, standing behind one of the spearmen beside the front of the wagon, shield resting in the soldier's back to ensure he did not abandon his position. I stood beside the centurion, my wicker shield also 'supporting' the back of the spearman in front of me, *spatha* raised and poised horizontally.

The two Amazons in the wagon – Haya and Minu – had been given all the remaining ammunition, and they continued to shoot furiously, an arrow leaving each bowstring every eight seconds. It took the Sarmatians around ten seconds to reach us, but by then the pair had shot over twenty arrows, each one striking a target and taking the sting out of the enemy charge. But they still hit us with a force that stopped us in our tracks, spears and axes thrusting and chopping at the spearmen either side of the wagon.

Bullus was like a human scorpion, his *gladius* jabbing back and forth like a deadly sting, stabbing at enemy faces over the shoulder of the spearmen in front of him. The spearmen themselves, as they were trained to do, kept their shields tucked tight to their bodies and thrust their spears into the target in front, withdrawing the point to stab another enemy soldier behind after the first man had fallen. Their spears were around seven feet in length, allowing them to be manoeuvred relatively easily in confined spaces.

The spearman in front of me had killed the first Sarmatian who had attacked him, a second thrusting his own spear at his belly, the point going into his wicker shield and getting stuck. He released it, pulled a knife and lunged at the Assur soldier. But I also lunged my *spatha* over his shoulder and into the Sarmatian's left shoulder, forcing him back.

'Heave.'

I heard the cry and saw the wagon move forward once more, Minu and Haya still shooting their bows at point-blank range into the enemy mass. A mass that had lost its momentum and was now faltering. The Sarmatians had no shields, headgear or armour and were suffering accordingly. They were essentially light horsemen and women totally ill-suited to fighting on foot in confined spaces.

'Heave.'

The wagon trundled forward a few feet, momentarily stopping when one of the front wheels hit a dead body, moving again with a mighty effort from those pushing it.

I thrust my sword over my companion's shoulder again, the point glancing off the side of a Sarmatian face, cutting the skin and forcing him to flinch. I jabbed at him once more and this time the *spatha*'s tip went into his eye. He staggered backwards.

The other Sarmatians were giving ground; they were no longer hacking and thrusting at us. Rather, they were retreating. I gave a shout of relief when I saw their leader, the big brute with a large axe, lying dead on the planks in front of us, an arrow lodged in his right eye socket.

The wagon stopped. There was a small pyramid of dead preventing its movement, no matter how many people tried to manhandle it forward. It was stuck fast and unless the pile of dead was removed would go no further. But there was no need to push it any more. It had done its job. The Sarmatians, having lost their leader, were now streaming back to the rafts to make their escape.

We let them go. Haya and Minu were nearly out of arrows and were physically drained, flopping down in the wagon and panting for air. I slapped the spearman in front of me on the shoulder.

'Well done.'

He turned, his face ashen, his eyes bloodshot. He looked like a demon had sucked the life out of him.

'Thank you, majesty.'

Few spoke as we walked slowly across the bridge, barely casting Sarmatians paddling furiously on rafts a second glance as they passed us in the water below. I embraced Gallia and together we trudged back to Assur. In a touching scene, Klietas placed an arm around Haya to comfort her and provide support. Rodak, physically shattered, walked with his head down, while Haytham still looked reasonably fresh after his exertions. As was Mascius, who was walking behind us.

'We are in your debt, Mascius,' I told him, 'and you now have a tale to tell the children of your master.'

He was visibly shaken by what had happened and the scene of horror around him. I had long become used to the sights and sounds of the battlefield, though I still found the smells – urine, faeces, vomit and blood – disagreeable. But for a pampered house slave, the sight of corpses with entrails hanging from their sliced-open bellies, limbs nearly severed, and skulls smashed and reduced to unrecognisable bloody messes, must have been truly traumatic. Blood was everywhere. It never ceased to amaze me how much blood a body contained. Ripping open a stomach with a blade was like slicing a bulging water skin. Blood gushed from the wound or spurted like a fountain if a limb was severed or a head cut open. Mascius was holding a cloth to his nose. Bullus slapped him on the back.

'Men shit themselves when they die. You'll get used to it.'

'I have no wish to get used to it, master.'

'Most sensible,' I said. 'I too had resolved not to participate in the sport of war, and yet here I am, once again walking in the blood of my enemies.'

'It is your fate, lord,' said Haytham behind Mascius.

'My curse, more like,' I muttered under my breath.

That afternoon, Dura's horsemen arrived.

A long line of horses, camels and riders filled the western horizon as twelve thousand mounted troops rode to Assur, kicking up a huge cloud of dust. In addition to Azad's dragon of cataphracts and Sporaces and his five dragons of horse archers, Kewab brought his three thousand horse archers and the same number of horse archers that had ridden with Karys from Mesene in the aftermath of the sycophant Sanabares becoming the king of their kingdom. They were now exiles in Dura. Karys was dead and though their families dreamed of a return to their homeland, I feared their stay in Dura would become permanent. Nevertheless, they and Kewab's men were battle-hardened veterans who were significant force multipliers on the battlefield.

When Rodak had organised the collection and cremation of the bodies on and around the bridge, Sporaces sent out patrols to scout the eastern bank of the Tigris, giving strict orders his men were not to engage any Sarmatians they encountered for fear of being overwhelmed. They returned with news that the wild horsemen of the northern steppes had seemingly vanished.

Over the course of two days my body was restored to a semblance of full health by a succession of baths, massages and sleep, during which Chrestus and Dura's foot soldiers arrived, together with Talib and his scouts. The commander of the army was in a foul temper when I convened a council of war in the governor's mansion the day after his arrival, during which he vented his anger. Despite being early morning, it was already a hot day, the sun roasting the army now in a marching camp located to the north of Assur, so it could draw fresh water from the Tigris rather than sip from the river that contained the town's waste flowing downstream.

Chrestus smashed his fist on the table, causing Kewab to squirm with embarrassment and Mascius, whom I had invited to attend, to jump. The slave sat next to me at the governor's highly polished table.

'I have to tell you, majesty, that the army is spitting blood over your treatment in Gordyene, and there have been near-mutinous grumblings during the march here.'

I was shocked. 'Mutiny' was not a word I had heard when describing Dura's army.

'Explain,' I demanded.

Chrestus ran a hand over his shaved crown.

'The boys are asking why we are marching east when we should be heading north, to Gordyene.'

'My men were wondering that, too,' said Azad.

'As are my dragon commanders,' added Sporaces.

'Enough!' I barked. 'An army is not a debating society. It obeys orders, my orders.'

'The men gathered at this table have a right to know why the army is not being used to right the wrongs committed against its king,' said Gallia, her eyes full of mischief.

Chrestus was delighted and even Kewab, who I thanked the gods had not yet left for Egypt, appeared thoughtful.

'The empire itself is under threat,' I said to her, 'and that outweighs the wrongs done to one man, even if he is a king.'

Chrestus guffawed. 'The Sarmatians are no threat to anyone, majesty.'

'They are when there are one hundred thousand of them, Chrestus,' I told him. 'At this juncture they are torturing Media, but soon they will turn their attention to Ctesiphon.'

Kewab was confused. 'There is nothing of strategic value at Ctesiphon, aside from King of Kings Phraates, who can depart at a moment's notice.'

'But the gold in his vaults cannot,' I said, 'and that is what the Sarmatians are after.'

'May I ask how you know this, majesty?' enquired Kewab.

I told him about the appearance of Haytham at Hatra, his revelations concerning the ambitions of Castus and the invitation given by the King of Gordyene to Tasius for him and his people to settle on Parthian lands, not all of them in Gordyene.

'He's clearly insane,' said Chrestus, dismissively. 'We would be doing the empire a favour removing him from power and chopping off his head. Ignorant little bastard.'

'He is not a bastard,' Gallia chastised him. 'His parentage is impeccable.'

'Apologies, majesty,' said Chrestus. 'I had great respect for King Spartacus and Queen Rasha, but as far as I am concerned, his son has forfeited any respect after the insult to my king.'

'He has been intoxicated by a woman,' I sighed.

'Like Paris and Helen,' said Mascius.

Everyone looked at him, Chrestus glaring at the impudence of… Of who?'

'Who are you?' he asked bluntly.

'This is Mascius,' I answered, 'whose idea to use a wagon as a shield and battering ram saved our hides on the bridge. I asked him to join us so he could see the inner workings of Dura's army. As a reward for his advice.

'You are not the only one who has used the analogy of Helen of Troy and Prince Paris to our present situation, Mascius.'

'Who are they?' asked Chrestus, eyeing Mascius with mild contempt.

'The central characters in Homer's *Iliad*,' smiled Kewab. 'You should read it sometime, Chrestus.'

'It is a splendid work,' agreed Mascius, 'though if I am honest, master, I prefer *The Odyssey*.'

Kewab looked thoughtful. 'As an examination of loyalty, kingship and the trial of the human spirit, I would agree. Mascius. However,…'

'However, we have a war to win,' interrupted Chrestus, rudely.

'Wars are not only won on the battlefield, general,' said Kewab. 'As *The Iliad* illustrates.'

'This one will be,' growled Chrestus.

I ignored him. 'How many Greeks besieged Troy, Mascius.'

'Around fifty thousand, highborn,' answered the slave. 'But the Trojans were safe behind the walls of their city. At least until the Greeks thought up a clever ruse to deceive the Trojans.'

I smiled. 'Just as we are behind the Tigris. We will wait until Hatra's army arrives and then move across the river to give battle to the Sarmatians.'

'How long will that be?' asked Chrestus.

'I have no idea,' I told him, 'but we are not moving across the river without the Hatrans.'

'What of Media, Pacorus?' asked Gallia.

'Media is, alas, the sacrificial lamb on which the Sarmatians are feasting,' I said. 'But thanks to Dura, Irbil now has stout walls and will easily withstand a siege, if indeed the Sarmatians have bothered to besiege it. But Media's suffering buys us time, and at the moment that commodity is more precious than gold.'

I provided a summary of how the Sarmatians had seemingly brushed aside an army of sixty thousand Parthians near Lake Urmia.

'I have no idea how many survived the battle, though I do know a wounded King Ali made it back to his capital, as did King Scylax and Prince Khosrou.'

'King Ali is a very competent commander,' said Kewab. 'That would suggest the Sarmatians caught him by surprise.'

'We will not be falling for the same trick,' I told him. 'Not until we know more about this Tasius and his army.'

'And Gordyene?' enquired Chrestus.

'One enemy at a time, general,' smiled Gallia.

While Talib and his scouts rode across the river to collect information on the Sarmatians, and Sporaces sent patrols of horse archers north and south along the western riverbank of the Tigris, we waited for Hatra's horsemen to arrive. I received regular reports from Governor Aspad concerning what was happening around Nisibus. Herneus and Orobaz had mustered their horsemen and were waiting to surprise Spadines and his horsemen. Spadines and his rabble of riders had appeared north of Nisibus. Herneus and Orobaz had scattered the Sarmatians with ease. Spadines had fled back to Gordyene. The lords of Hatra were chafing at the bit to invade Gordyene. Orobaz had reined them in. Herneus was riding back south after his 'great victory'. The missives from Aspad were a welcome relief from the tedium of waiting in the dreary, sun-bleached town of Assur.

The nephew of General Herneus bowed his head and placed a folded sheet of papyrus on my desk, or rather his desk as I had requisitioned his office during my stay in his town. It was secured by a wax seal bearing the imprint of a horse's head – the sigil of Hatra.

'Another letter from the Governor of Hatra, I assume?' I said.

'It came from the south, majesty, not the north.'

I broke the seal with interest. I read the words and handed him the letter.

'Prince Pacorus, soon to be King Pacorus, will be here in the morning.'

It had been some time since I had seen the dashing and brilliant heir to Hatra's throne, the natural-born son of Gafarn and Diana who was the epitome of a Parthian prince. Handsome, brave, undefeated in battle and for several years the guardian of the widow Queen Cia of Elymais and her infant son Prince Silaces. Everything he touched turned to gold: he had married a beautiful Hatran noblewoman from a powerful family, who had born him two healthy sons to ensure his line would continue. More importantly, he himself was born in

Hatra, an event that instantly washed away the 'sins' of his parents, who had both been slaves in their younger years.

I was shocked when he rode into the mansion's courtyard. We all aged but he looked at least ten years older than his thirty-six years. With him were two hundred horse archers from Elymais, each rider wearing a blue tunic, baggy white leggings and a red headband. Pacorus himself wore a magnificent dragon-skin armour cuirass whose silver scales dazzled in the sunlight, as did his burnished open-faced helmet decorated with white plumes. Everything about his appearance was designed to impress, from his glittering armour to his expensive sword with a silver pommel in the shape of a horse's head, and its red scabbard decorated with white ivory horse heads.

He gave Gallia a tired smile and they embraced lovingly, Hatra's new king noting the presence of Chrestus, Sporaces, Azad and Kewab behind me. I too embraced him.

'I grieve with you, Pacorus,' I said.

He sighed. 'I knew this day would come, but I thought it would be many years in the future.'

'None of us know the day or hour we will leave this world,' I said. 'Perhaps that is best.'

'The gods take advantage of our grief, uncle, for why else would they send a plague of Sarmatians to torture us in our hour of desperation? Before I forget.'

He turned and beckoned the commander of his escort forward, the man snapping to attention and handing him a papyrus scroll. Pacorus handed it to me.

'A summons to Ctesiphon, uncle. My congratulations.'

I took the scroll with trepidation. 'For what?'

'You are the new lord high general of the empire in King Ali's absence due to injury. And the high king summons you to Ctesiphon.'

I groaned, broke the seal and began reading the words. I saw the first line – *To my dear friend, King Pacorus of Dura* – and my heart sank. I read the rest and handed the document to Gallia. She laughed.

'There's life in the old dog, yet.'

'Very droll,' I muttered.

The loss of his parents weighed heavily on Pacorus, that and a sense of guilt from being away from them for long periods during his tenure as lord protector of Elymais. The feast given in his honour that night by Rodak was a subdued affair, the shadow of the deaths of Gafarn and Diana, and the Sarmatian threat, hanging over us all. Chrestus and Kewab had both known Gafarn and Diana for many years, as had Sporaces and Azad. Gafarn had never been an aloof king or one for protocol, which endeared him to the senior officers of Dura's army. And both he and Diana had been Companions, which ensured there was a close bond between them and Dura.

'Alas there is no such bond between myself and my nephew,' lamented Pacorus later that evening as he perused the small pile of letters written by Governor Aspad, which provided an account of the defeat of Spadines and his Sarmatians at Nisibus. He looked at Prince Haytham, who had joined us in the governor's office at my invitation.

'You are certain your brother ordered Spadines to attack northern Hatra?'

'Yes, lord.'

'And that Castus invited this Tasius into the empire?'

'Certain, lord.'

Pacorus closed his eyes and held his head in his hands. The silence in the governor's office was oppressive. Haytham looked distinctly uncomfortable. Pacorus opened his eyes.

'Castus has sealed his own fate. Even if I were to forgive his transgression, Atropaiene, Hyrcania and Margiana will want revenge.'

'Scylax and Prince Khosrou are unhurt?' I asked.

'They are both licking their wounds at Hecatompylos, uncle.'

He smiled. 'Waiting for orders from the new lord high general.'

'Where is Arezu?' I asked, changing the subject.

'She and my sons remained in Elymais. There is no point putting them in danger, not with a hundred thousand Sarmatians at large in the centre of the empire.'

He looked at Haytham. 'Hatra is in your debt, prince, and will support your claim to Gordyene's throne.'

'I have no claim, lord,' said Haytham.

Pacorus gave him an evil leer. 'You do when Castus is deposed as king, along with his wife. Gordyene has declared war on Hatra, and Hatra will answer with fire and sword.'

'As the new lord high general,' I said, 'I would advise we concentrate on the immediate threat, for if we do not rid the empire of the Sarmatians, then who sits on Gordyene's throne will be irrelevant.'

Before I left for Ctesiphon the next morning, I was accosted by Kewab who had been pondering on how we might deal with the Sarmatians, suggesting a novel plan that I would present to Phraates. My namesake declared his intention to remain at Assur to await Herneus and his troops. I begged him not to take them across the river but to wait until I had returned. He begrudgingly agreed, though the thought of Media becoming the Sarmatians' plaything weighed heavily on his mind.

'In the name of Shamash,' I said to Gallia, 'do not let him engage the Sarmatians alone, and do not be tempted to join him if his sense of honour gets the better of him. We are Parthia's best hope of rectifying this situation. At the moment, its only hope.'

'What if the Sarmatians come to us?' she said, an evil glint in her eye.

I hoisted myself into Horns' saddle. 'Then burn the bridge. We don't want them rampaging through Hatra, and then Dura. I will return as quickly as possible.'

'Give my love to Claudia.'

I nodded and nudged Horns towards Pacorus standing with Rodak.

'Kewab has come up with an interesting idea,' I told him. 'But to succeed it depends on this Tasius abandoning his common sense. You should speak with him.'

He nodded. 'I will, uncle. Safe journey.'

My escort comprised a company of horse archers commanded by Navid, whom I was delighted to discover was in one piece and looked none the worse after his adventure at Klietas' village and subsequent flight to Dura.

'It is good to see you again, Navid.'

'And you, majesty. I was disgusted to hear of your treatment in Gordyene.'

'Well, at least we are both still here to tell our tales. And we are embarking on a new adventure.'

He flashed a smile. 'To invade Gordyene, majesty?'

'No, to rid the empire of tens of thousands of Sarmatians.'

'I hope I have enough arrows,' he grinned.

Chapter 13

'Are you mad?'

Phraates sat open-mouthed behind his huge mahogany desk, staring at me in disbelief. I sat opposite him, along with Claudia and Adapa, the commander of his bodyguard. Two of that bodyguard – two burly Scythian axe men – stood behind the high king. They wore blank expressions, unlike their master who had bristled at the idea he should enter into negotiations with the Sarmatian leader Tasius.

Phraates began fiddling with the golden arrow he liked to carry around with him. He stopped and pointed it at me.

'Just to clarify, King Pacorus. You are suggesting I ask this brigand Tasius to come to Ctesiphon, the same man who has invaded my empire at the head of one hundred thousand horsemen?'

'Yes, highness.'

His lips pursed. 'Did you fall from your horse on your way here?'

I was taken aback, somewhat.

'Highness?'

He began playing with the arrow once more, swapping it from hand to hand.

'I merely ask because you seem to be spouting gibberish, one of the symptoms indicative of having fallen from a horse.'

'I can assure you I have not fallen from my horse, highness.'

The arrow was pointed at me a second time.

'Then please explain why the lord high general of the empire is advocating I grovel at the feet of this barbarian invader?'

'To lure him south, highness,' I replied. 'To encourage him to do so, I would advise offering to pay him a large amount of gold as a sweetener to begin negotiations.'

This time he dropped the arrow on the desk, staring at me with incredulity. He then turned on Claudia.

'I hope I will not regret being convinced by you to create your father lord high general, despite his age.'

Claudia remained calm and collected, long used to her master's outbursts and mood swings.

'My father would not suggest such a thing without very good reasons, highness. Is that not correct, father?'

I stood and walked over to the finely crafted map of the Parthian Empire painted on wooden boards attached to the wall. I pointed at Ctesiphon.

'We lure the Sarmatians south, away from Media where their horses and camels can graze to their heart's content, to the barren landscape of Susiana.'

Phraates was unimpressed. 'That is your strategy? To deprive their animals of fodder while I pay them gold? To invite them south is pure folly, King Pacorus. There is nothing to stop them invading Susiana and Babylon if they are invited here. No, I will not do it.'

I understood his reluctance to endanger Susiana and Babylon, two kingdoms he had close ties to, being the realms of his father and mother respectively, even if he murdered Orodes. I put the idea out of my mind. There was no proof, only the wicked tongue of Claudia suggesting it was so.

I pointed at Assur. 'My army is here, highness.'

'It is not marching to Ctesiphon?' said Phraates with alarm.

'No, highness. It waits at Assur for Hatra's army.'

'Then it will march south,' said Phraates.

I shook my head. 'No, highness. The idea, or rather Kewab's idea, is to dazzle the Sarmatians with the prospect of gold, which will allow us to strike across the Tigris to attack them in the rear.'

'While leaving Ctesiphon defenceless,' remarked Phraates, coolly.

I looked at the handsome, strapping Adapa.

'What is the garrison of Ctesiphon?'

'A thousand soldiers, majesty,' he answered.

'The walls of Ctesiphon are strong. They can easily withstand a short siege until our plan is put into operation.'

Phraates' jaw dropped.

'I have spent a great deal of time and gold restoring Ctesiphon to become the glittering heart of the Parthian Empire, King Pacorus. It is a place of beauty, wealth, religion and power, not some dreary stronghold held by a garrison of ruffians.'

'It is a credit to you, highness,' I said.

'But you want to use it as bait,' smirked Claudia.

'Yes,' I answered honestly.

Phraates was appalled. 'No, no, no, no, no. I will not have foreign barbarians desecrating the beating heart of Parthia.'

I tried to keep my temper, but it was becoming difficult.

'Highness,' I began, 'this is the quickest way to rid the empire of the Sarmatians, and believe me I wish to see them gone as much as you, more so truth be told. But I must crave your indulgence if we are to rid the empire of the Sarmatian plague.'

I tapped the map. 'Ctesiphon, Susiana and Babylon all have garrisons and well-maintained walls. The Sarmatians cannot take them.'

'And nor will they, King Pacorus,' announced Phraates. 'As we speak, Satrap Otanes is gathering an army at Susa to the west. King Silani of Persis is marching north to join him, and I have requested that Queen Cia send horsemen to Susa as a gesture of support.'

He suddenly looked at me with a kindly expression.

'My condolences regarding King Gafarn and Queen Diana, by the way. I know you and Queen Gallia were close to them. The empire has lost two fine servants and we share your grief.'

I bowed my head to him. 'Thank you, highness.'

He began tapping a finger on the table.

'Claudia has informed me of your humiliation in Gordyene, and the other base actions committed by King Castus.'

I looked at my daughter. 'Has she?'

'Mother keeps me fully abreast of developments,' she said.

'I have a mind to make Kewab the new King of Gordyene,' said Phraates, 'once the present predicament has been dealt with.'

'Castus has a younger brother, highness,' I reminded Phraates.

He waved a hand at me. 'He can be killed. Gordyene is becoming a liability. Its kings provoke needless wars with Armenia, which drives the Armenians into the arms of the Romans. King Castus has shown nothing but ingratitude since we sent Kewab to assist him defeat the coalition raised against him last year. He humiliates the King of Dura and now invites a Sarmatian host to plunder the empire. Such behaviour cannot be tolerated.'

I was glad I had left Haytham at Assur. Phraates pointed his wretched arrow at me again.

'You do wish for Kewab to remain in Parthia, do you not?'

'I do, highness, but…'

'But nothing, King Pacorus. It is decided. Kewab will be made the ruler of Gordyene. At least that will keep him happy and deprive the Romans of his services.'

'And the Sarmatians, highness?' I probed. 'Can I ask your indulgence in enticing them south?'

For some reason, we both looked at Claudia, my daughter as usual wreathed in black robes, making her look out of place in a palace filled with gold, silver, ivory, stucco and white marble. But she was not the only one seemingly out of place. The Scythian axe men who guarded Phraates in the palace were hewn from very different base materials than the attractive, well-dressed courtiers, officials and priests that graced Ctesiphon's palace and temples. There was probably more gold hanging from the ears and draped around the necks and limbs of the noblewomen of Phraates' court than in Dura's vaults. Claudia pointed at the two axe men standing like statutes behind Phraates.

'According to legend, the Sarmatians are the offspring of Scythian men and Amazon women. This means they should not be underestimated. King Ali and his allies made that mistake at Lake Urmia. I believe we have but one chance to rid the empire of them. We must be cautious and spring our trap at the right time. As Kewab appears to be a military genius, I would advise supporting his scheme.'

'If we could expedite the speedy arrival of Satrap Otanes and King Silani, highness,' I said, 'it will increase our chances of success substantially.'

Phraates nodded. 'I agree. I will send a letter to Susa recommending the virtue of haste. And I also reluctantly agree to your scheme. But know I will hold Dura responsible for any damage inflicted on Ctesiphon by these barbarians.'

Afterwards, I walked with Claudia through the palace, courtiers and officials bowing their heads not only to me but also to my daughter, a sure sign of her power and position at the high king's right hand.

'Mother told me about your ridiculous escapade in Media. After all these years, father, you are still trying to save the downtrodden of the earth. Have you ever considered that the poor, the dispossessed, the diseased and the insane are part of the gods' plan for the world?'

'For your information, I merely wanted to speak to my former squire.'

'The beggar from Irbil, whom you raised up to a station he did not deserve, and then lavished him with land, which he threw back in your face? Does such a wretch deserve the time of Parthia's most revered king? You should have let him be sacrificed in Vanadzor. At least his life would have amounted to something.'

'His life *has* amounted to something,' I insisted.

'Phraates is quite right when he states Castus must be punished. Forcing the victor of Carrhae to act like a slave for his amusement will not do, not at all.'

'I'm glad you hold my life in such high esteem, Claudia,' I teased her. 'I need you to get Phraates to write that letter to Tasius. We need to lure him and his people south.'

'There is no guarantee the Sarmatian leader will ever get it, father, even if Phraates writes it.'

'Oh, he will receive it.'

'How can you be so sure?'

'Because I will be the one delivering it.'

Claudia raged at me not to be foolish and Phraates was more convinced than ever that I had received a blow to the head that had unhinged my senses. But I was determined to see this Tasius for myself, to get the measure of the man. And in truth, I did not hold my life that dear. I had seen many friends die over the years, some of old age, many on the battlefield. I remained. But with each death a part of me had been chipped away and now I was tired. To place myself in danger was an irrelevance. I had chosen that path long ago and knew the consequences well enough.

Phraates wrote the letter.

'They will kill you, majesty.'

Adapa, the leper returned from a living death, stared up at me, squinting in the sun that made Ctesiphon's grand buildings around us more dazzling.

'Nothing ventured, nothing gained, commander.'

He gripped Horns' reins.

'Do not go, majesty. For the sake of your daughter.'

An expressionless Claudia stood beside Phraates at the top of the stone steps leading to his vast palace, behind them white-robed priests from the Temple of Marduk chanting prayers to beg the god for his protection for my mission. I leaned over and laid a gentle hand on his.

'I appreciate your concern for me and my daughter, Adapa, but we both serve the empire and we both know the risks involved in carrying out that service.'

He released the reins and looked past me, at Klietas mounted on his horse holding the reins of two camels loaded with a tent and supplies.

'You will take only one man with you?'

'He's a good man.'

Navid had been distraught when I informed him he would not be accompanying me north to meet the Sarmatian leader and deliver the high king's invitation. But what use would a hundred horse archers be against a thousand times their number?

Phraates had a bemused look on his face when I bowed my head, turned Horns and trotted from the palace down Ctesiphon's replica Processional Way. Purple-clad guards watched us trot through the impressive gatehouse and out into the barren terrain that surrounded Parthia's jewel in the desert. I smiled when I saw a party of slaves on scaffolding cleaning the white stone used to face the walls of Ctesiphon. An overseer was watching their work but was not shouting or using a whip. I surmised he was an engineer or architect managing cosmetic work rather than a sadistic brute. Ctesiphon's slaves lived a better life than many free commoners.

Initially we travelled north along the Tigris, passing prosperous villages surrounded by fields of barley, watered after the Tigris had burst its banks. Reservoirs collected the meltwater to ensure the crops had enough water until they were harvested, though the initial flooding often caused immense damage to the land and settlements. Unlike in Dura, no one had thought of, or bothered with, erecting flood defences to control the waters in spring.

'I have something to tell you,' I said to Klietas as we cantered north.

'Majesty?'

'I have not been totally honest with you regarding your village.'

'I do not understand, majesty.'

'You remember I sent Navid to Irbil with a request for King Akmon that he send troops to Vazneh to protect the villagers.'

'Yes, majesty.'

'Well, the truth was that I sent an urgent request to your king that he send soldiers to take the villagers back to Irbil until such time as it would be safe to return. Dura will pay for their upkeep, but I did not trust the Sarmatians not to return and finish their murdering.'

He was beaming from ear to ear. 'May Gula bless you with long life, majesty.'

'May she bless the both of us, Klietas, for as day follows night, we will need the protection of the gods where we are going.'

I pulled up Horns. 'You can return to Ctesiphon if you wish. I do not compel you to accompany me.'

He had volunteered to ride with me to the Sarmatian host the moment I had mentioned it to him, insisting Gula had guided him to me to perform such a mission. I pointed out that I had visited *him*. But he retorted the goddess had planted the idea in my mind before I had thought of it. I did not have the time to argue with him, and in any case I found his company agreeable enough. But now I felt guilty accepting his offer to attend me. I had no idea what sort of reception we would receive. Having saved Anush, I had no desire to make her a widow.

'The goddess wishes me to accompany you, majesty.'

I was going to ask if she had conversed with him but thought better of it. We had both been privy to strange and otherworldly happenings in recent years, so I saw no need for flippancy.

We rode fast, the need for urgency was paramount, leaving the lush, humid environment adjacent to the Tigris to head directly north into the barren desert. It was two hundred miles as the raven flew between Ctesiphon and Irbil, the first half of which was sun-blasted desert. Nothing thrived in the sandy, dusty flat lands, aside from scorpions and snakes. The light grey and brown soils covering the area were easily disturbed, throwing up clouds of dust that irritated eyes and throats. Our faces were covered with *shemaghs* but the fine particles still found a way into our clothing and hair.

We rose before dawn broke to ride for two hours at speed before the heat of the day bore down on us. In the hottest part of the day we dismounted and led our horses on foot. The camels carried our water skins, the beasts fortunately being able to subsist for days without liquid refreshment. Our clothes were soaked with sweat and our horses tramped along with heads down as the heat increased. In such an unforgiving environment, rationing one's energy becomes imperative. There is no idle chatter, no unnecessary exertions, only a steady pace forward. One is alone with one's thoughts and mine turned to Gafarn and Diana. It was only now, in the searing heat of a deserted landscape, that the enormity of their loss struck me. It was like a mythical beast was plunging its claws into my stomach and playing fast and loose with my entrails with its talons. I felt sick, angry and lost. It seemed entirely appropriate I was in such bleak terrain because it suited my mood. A part of me also wanted to jump into the saddle and ride. Ride away from Dura, from Ctesiphon and all the responsibilities that burdened me. To live out the rest of my days in the Alborz Mountains far to the north where no one would disturb me. Around me the desert shimmered in the heat, giving the illusion I was flanked by huge expanses of water.

'It is your destiny to be the last one standing.'

I heard Gafarn's voice but thought it a cruel illusion, like the mirages of water to the left and right. I therefore kept my head down.

'Dear Pacorus, death is only a temporary fence to keep us apart.'

I heard Diana's voice and wept.

'I'm sorry.'

'For what?'

'For not being there.'

'You have always been there, Pacorus,' she said, 'for us, for your kingdom and for the empire.'

'I wanted to say goodbye.'

Gafarn laughed. 'Here we are. So, say it now.'

'Leave him alone,' said his wife.

My eyes stung with tears. 'I wish, I wish it could have been different.'

'Different how?' asked Gafarn. 'I liked being a king. It certainly beat being your slave, or a slave of the Romans for that matter. And if it had been different, Diana might have still been a kitchen slave in Capua.'

'All lives come to an end, Pacorus,' said Diana.

'Even yours, faster than you think if you continue on your present escapade,' sniggered Gafarn.

'Is that a prediction?' I asked.

'Merely an observation.'

'Do not underestimate him,' said Diana.

'Who?'

'The Sarmatian. He is not the ignorant barbarian you desire him to be.'

'Anyway,' said Gafarn, 'we can't linger here all day speaking to you. We have better things to do and you have an empire to save.'

I was alarmed. 'It's that serious?'

'Oh, yes. And don't refuse Claudia's gift.'

'What gift?'

There was no answer, only the sound of my heavy breathing as I tramped across the hard-packed dirt. I glanced behind me to see Klietas following. I looked around and saw nothing save the hazy deception of lakes of cool, clear water.

I was glad to leave the blistering heat and grating dust behind when we reached the more temperate environment of southern Media on the morning of the third day. It was still hot, but the landscape changed colour from brown to light green and then a darker shade of the colour as we entered a land fed by countless streams and springs.

I dismounted and knelt beside one such spring by the side of the road, dunking my head in the clear water. Horns sipped at the side of the pool and Klietas took the opportunity to douse his head and wash away the dust and grime of the desert. I flopped down on my back and gazed up at a sky, devoid of clouds.

'Lord,' I heard Klietas say.

'I am resting,' I answered.

'Lord!'

There was concern in his voice. I raised myself up and looked in the direction he was pointing. To see four horsemen observing us.

I slowly rose to my feet.

'Do not make any sudden movements,' I told Klietas. 'Stay calm.'

The riders sat stationary on their horses for what seemed like an age, observing us but making no offensive movements. Eventually, I decided to take the initiative, pacing towards them.

'I am an emissary of King of Kings Phraates and wish to be taken to Chief Tasius,' I called to them.

Loathe as I am to admit it, the Sarmatians and Parthians were both descendants of the Scythians, so spoke the same language. There were regional accents and dialects, of course, but Parthian and Sarmatian could converse with each other with ease. In response to my announcement, the riders nudged their horses forward. The beasts were smaller than our own, with longer manes and tails, though their riders used the same four-horned saddles found throughout Parthia. Their weapons comprised lances tipped with large iron heads and knives. I saw no bows among them, or swords. One among the group, a man with straggly hair and a wispy beard, looked me up and down.

'Who are you?'

'I told you. I am an emissary of King of Kings Phraates, sent to deliver a message to Chief Tasius.'

'What message?' he asked curtly.

'I do not know. I am merely the messenger who carries a letter.'

He extended an arm. 'Give me it.'

'Are you Tasius?'

'No.'

'Then it is not for your eyes.'

He levelled his spear at my face. 'Perhaps I should take your eyes.'

I yawned. 'Are we going to stand here all day? I have a message from the ruler of the whole Parthian Empire. If it is not delivered he will be angry and gather a mighty army to fight the Sarmatians. Are you going to risk that for the sake of reading some words before Tasius does? Can you read?'

He glared at me and for a moment I thought he was going to drive his spear point through my face. But instead he moved the point closer to my eyes in a petty display of machismo but then returned the shaft to a vertical position and turned his horse.

'Follow us,' he ordered.

He and the others were a cheerless lot, not speaking as we rode through southern Media. Our escort led us in a northeasterly direction, towards a stone-built mansion that had previously been a stronghold of one of Media's lords, but which was now in Sarmatian hands. On the way, we rode through a deserted village, which I thought had been plundered but on closer inspection turned out to be perfectly preserved.

Most odd, given the Sarmatian predilection for rape, murder and looting.

When we reached the mansion, which was surrounded by a strong wall, we were shown into the building. Guards had been posted at the entrance to the mansion and by doors inside, but the rooms and corridors appeared pristine and the furniture and statues were still in place. Again, I found this most odd. Slaves were still cleaning floors and waiting on the top table when we were shown into the dining room, a splendid chamber with intricate murals of hunting scenes painted on the walls and dragons seared into the wooden ceiling. We were both herded in front of the table where a man with a large head and round face was stuffing meat into his mouth. He had thick brown hair and a well-trimmed beard and was obviously a man of some wealth, his red leather jacket having a sheepskin trim. He stopped eating when we stood in front of him.

'Who's this?' he asked in a deep voice.

'We found them on the road, lord,' said the man who had threatened me. 'The old man says he has a letter from a Parthian king for Chief Tasius.'

The man at the table wiped his hands on a cloth and leaned back in his chair to study us. He looked at me long and hard, his eyes resting on my sword.

'Why would a courier carry a sword?'

'These are dangerous times,' I replied.

He pointed at Klietas. 'This is your slave?'

I made a mistake when I answered. 'He is a free man who volunteered to accompany me.'

My interrogator stood and slowly walked around the table.

'Expensive boots, a sword and a scar on the right cheek, a clean-shaven cheek.'

His leggings were the same colour as his jacket, which was fastened by a red leather belt with a gold-plated buckle. He too wore a sword, which was held in a red scabbard decorated with gold plaques. He was obviously a man of some importance.

'May I see your sword?' he enquired.

I drew my weapon and handed it to him. He examined the straight blade and grip before handing it back to me and bowing his head.

'I know of only one man who carries a Roma *spatha*, has a scar on his right cheek and keeps his face free of growth despite being a Parthian. A man now in his sixties who fought beside my friend King Spartacus in Media, Armenia, Pontus and Galatia.'

He had me at a disadvantage.

'Have we met?'

'Not until now, King Pacorus, for you are surely he, are you not?'

I saw no reason to lie. 'I am.'

He clapped his hands together and laughed.

'I am Lord Akka of the Siraki tribe and I had the honour of fighting with your nephew a few years back. Sit, please, take the weight off your feet.'

He returned to his chair and ordered another two to be brought.

'Leave us,' he told the man who had brought us to the mansion.

I did not like Sarmatians, but I had to concede this Akka was an excellent host, notwithstanding the meagre fare we were fed on, which consisted of meat and milk, plus the mansion owner's stock of wine. He also put his feet on the table when he began to wax lyrical about his people.

'The Siraki and Aorsi are small tribes, but the Roxolani are a different prospect altogether.'

'Why are you and they here?' I asked, trying to chew on a piece of meat that was more gristle than muscle.

He emptied his cup. 'Gold, land and horses, lord.'

He suddenly took his feet off the table and looked at me with deadly seriousness.

'Lord Tasius has assured King Akmon that our stay in his kingdom is only temporary, and has promised him there will be no looting, destruction of property or taking of slaves. Well, maybe a few. Young and pretty girls, of course.'

'Naturally. May I ask which land Lord Tasius and you have in mind?'

'The land south of the Araxes River between Lake Urmia and the Caspian Sea,' he informed me.

'None other?' I said, thinking of the failed Aorsi attempt to seize northern Hatra and the city of Nisibus.

He flashed a mischievous smile. 'That will do for the moment.'

'King Ali of Atropaiene might have something to say about that.'

He laughed. 'He did, and we sent him packing at Lake Urmia.'

I gave up trying to eat the meat and sipped at my wine.

'What of King Castus?'

Akka shrugged. 'What of him?'

'He was the one who extended an invitation to Lord Tasius, was he not?'

Another shrug. 'Gordyene has always been a good friend to the Sarmatians. May I ask you a question, lord?'

I nodded.

'What is the message you carry from your high King?'

'I have no idea,' I answered, truthfully.

After our meal we were shown to the guest bedrooms, Akka ordering slaves to prepare baths to refresh our tired bodies. No guards were placed on our rooms and we were free to come and go as we pleased. I found this more disconcerting that if we had been treated like prisoners, as it pointed to the Sarmatians feeling very comfortable in their new surroundings. Despite Akka's words, I began to fear that eastern Media had already been added to the land coveted by the Sarmatians.

Klietas was of the same opinion, and while I was grooming Horns in the stables and checking his shoes for any loose nails, asked a question that I too had pondered.

'Where is King Akmon, majesty? He would not have stood idly by while his kingdom was invaded.'

I examined the steel shoe and the foot it was attached to. Foot problems were one of the most common causes of lameness in horses, remedied by keeping a mount's feet in good condition.

'I too have been wondering that, Klietas. I can only surmise that King Akmon has been waiting to see how events unfold before making his move.'

'I do not understand, highness.'

I finished examining Horns' feet.

'Well, I am sure King Akmon received word of the defeat of King Ali at Lake Urmia, which would have made him cautious to commit his army against the Sarmatians. In addition, his northern lands might have been raided by the Aorsi, or even his brother's troops.'

I slapped him on the arm. 'But at least Anush and the rest of your people are safe in Irbil, which has strong defences.'

'Praise Gula,' he said.

'Praise Gula, indeed.'

The next day, refreshed after having spent a night in a comfortable bed, we rode on in the company of Akka and a score of his soldiers. I was relieved to see no pillars of smoke on the horizon indicating burning villages, and the settlements we did pass by were undamaged, albeit deserted, their inhabitants having fled from the Sarmatians, or enslaved. And the orchards and vineyards around them were as yet undamaged, as were the fields. But the land was strangely quiet, being devoid of people in villages and traffic on the roads. As we rode on, the feeling of dread hanging over me increased.

After two hours of travel, the sun once again shining down from a cloudless sky, we began to encounter patrols of horsemen. The feeling of dread was magnified when I saw them, each one accoutred in either leather or horn scale armour. The latter was manufactured by splitting horse hooves into small plates, which were shaped and bored with holes for laces and then sewn to a hide backing. Curiously, the armour of the patrol that intercepted us was painted blue, as was the identical armour worn by the soldiers' horses. As Akka and the commander chatted to each other, the men of the patrol maintained two straight files and their spears did not waver. Their initial appearance indicated well-trained soldiers, far from the disorganised rabble we had defeated at the pontoon bridge.

The feeling of dread increased when our new escort led us into a great plain where the Roxolani tribe had made what I hoped was its temporary home. As far as the eye could see were wagons: heavy, four-wheeled vehicles pulled by oxen, pairs of the beasts grazing near each wagon. On top of each wagon was a felt tent and around each vehicle were grazing goats, which produced milk and cheese, and meat when they became old or lame.

Eventually, we reached a wagon that looked much like the others, having a simple felt tent covering and four solid wooden wheels. The only thing that marked it out as different from the rest were guards ringing it, though there were still goats tethered to its sides.

There were no stable hands to take our horses and so I left Klietas holding the reins of Horns and his own horse and walked with Akka to the rear of the wagon. I took with me a tubular leather case containing Phraates' letter to Tasius, the commander of the horsemen with blue armour instructing us to remain at the bottom of the wooden steps leading to the rear of the wagon until summoned. He reappeared moments later.

'I must take your sword and dagger, lord.'

I unbuckled my belt and handed him my weapons.

'I must ask you to reveal what is in the case, lord,' said Akka.

I unfastened the top and extracted the rolled papyrus letter with a wax seal bearing the bull of Babylon.

'No snakes, or hidden daggers,' I smiled.

He took the letter from me.

'Come with me, lord.'

I followed him up the wooden steps into the back of the wagon-cum-tent, which was remarkably snug inside. The boards were covered with carpets and there were couches on both sides. The interior was subdued in lighting but cool and far from musty. The 'tent' comprised a wooden frame over which was laid an off-white felt cover.

'Welcome, King Pacorus. I am Tasius.'

My eyes were averted from admiring the simple yet sturdy construction of the tent to an individual who stood to greet me. He was smaller than me and trim, his face narrow with a sharp nose. Two things stood out about him: his armour, which comprised sheets of iron on his arms and around his torso; and what appeared to be bone fragments in his long, reddish hair. Like the interior of his tent, his beard was neat and tidy.

Tasius sat on one of the couches lining the side of the tent and extended an arm to indicate I should sit on the other opposite. I did so and Akka passed the chief of the Roxolani the letter. He broke the seal and read the words. At least he was literate, which was a good start. Akka stood by the entrance, beckoning forward women carrying trays holding silver cups and a wine jug. Their confident demeanour and clothing of long leggings, soft leather shoes and kaftan-type tunics indicated they were not slaves. They served us wine and departed, Tasius barely noticing them as he perused Phraates' letter. When he had finished, he took a sip of wine and looked at me.

'Why would your high king send a great warlord to deliver his letter? Has he run out of slaves?'

'He has many slaves, and many soldiers.'

'He proposes I go to Ctesiphon where we can enter into negotiations, though he is vague as to what will be discussed there.'

He tossed the letter to the floor.

'Your high king must believe I am a witless barbarian, King Pacorus. Why else would he invite me to walk into a trap?'

My heart sank but I tried to put on a brave face.

'Lord Tasius, I sincerely believe King of Kings Phraates desires to reach an accommodation with you.'

'He wants us gone, King Pacorus, and perhaps a part of him would be willing to give me a great deal of gold to usher us on our way.'

He smiled to reveal perfect white teeth. 'But no king gives up either his gold or parts of his kingdom freely. I therefore ask myself; why would he sit down with me, who desires both?'

'I am not privy to the decisions of High King Phraates.'

He took another sip of wine.

'You may think me ignorant when it comes to Parthia, King Pacorus, but I have not led my people south without first collecting intelligence regarding what they may face.

'The land we currently occupy is green and well-watered. But to march south would be to enter a land of desert where the animals we depend on would perish.'

He sipped at his wine again.

'And then there is the matter of the River Tigris.'

'The Tigris?'

He smiled at me. 'You are a wily old fox, King Pacorus. A while ago, a reconnaissance in force was worsted trying to capture a floating bridge across the Tigris.'

I gave an indifferent shrug.

'A few survivors made it back to us,' said Tasius, 'and what they reported was most interesting. They spoke of deadly female archers defending the bridge, all wearing armour and helmets.'

My heart began to sink.

'I know from Lord Akka and Prince Spadines that your own wife has a bodyguard of female warriors called Amazons. That indicates that you and your queen were most eager that the bridge should not fall.'

I took a large gulp of wine. Tasius looked thoughtful.

'Let us suppose I take my people south to meet your high king. They will suffer in the heat and desert. Meanwhile, an army marches across the wooden bridge and attacks us in the rear, while another army, perhaps led by Phraates himself, assaults us frontally.'

He nodded. 'It is what I would do. Phraates must come to me, King Pacorus. He must prostrate himself before me and then we will talk.'

'And if he refuses to do so?' I probed.

'Then we stay here and enjoy the hospitality of Media.'

It was Tasius who was the wily fox, and as we continued to chat about nothing in particular, I realised that he was indeed not a foe to be underestimated. Despite his somewhat fierce appearance, he possessed a calmness borne of supreme, unchallenged authority. But even the most calculating mind can be taken by surprise, and so it was when one of his warlords interrupted us to bring news a Parthian army was approaching from the south. I too was taken by surprise, which Tasius noticed.

'It would appear your high king has changed his mind since he sent you on a fool's errand, King Pacorus.'

Chapter 14

I had no idea why Phraates had sent troops to engage the Sarmatians. Perhaps he thought I was dead. Perhaps he *wanted* me dead. More likely, his cunning mind hoped to use my visit to Tasius as a deception to mask his plan to attack the Sarmatians and win all the glory for himself.

Tasius remained calm when he was informed that a Parthian army was closing from the south. But he had the letter from Phraates burnt in front of me and placed me and Klietas under armed guard. He could have had us both killed on the spot for breaching the rules of diplomacy, though I doubted the Sarmatians put much store in them, if they even knew what they were. But he did not and though we were placed in a covered wagon, which was guarded by sentries, my instincts told me we were not in any danger. This depressed me even more, for it pointed to Tasius being supremely confident he could defeat the force sent against him.

The next morning the plain was alive with activity, and after a breakfast of milk and cured meat, Tasius himself came to visit us, along with a host of his warriors. He was dressed in his metal armour and wore a metal helmet with huge cheek guards and a nasal guard, resulting in most of his face being covered.

'King Pacorus, I hope you slept well.'

'As well as can be expected.'

'I would like you to ride with me today. As a student and practitioner of war, I think you will find it most enlightening. You may bring your slave along, as well.'

Horns and Klietas' horse were brought to us and we gained our saddles. Our weapons had also been returned to us, along with my armour and helmet. I checked the case fixed to my saddle to see if my bow was in its place. It was. Tasius noted my relief.

'We are not thieves, King Pacorus. The bow is special to you?'

'It was made in a land far from here many years ago. It is an old companion and a reminder of happier times. He is not my slave, by the way.'

'Mm?'

I jerked a thumb behind at Klietas.

'He is a free man who volunteered to accompany me.'

There were around two hundred horsemen in two files behind us, each one wearing similar armour to their lord and carrying lances and swords. I surmised they were his bodyguard. His standard comprised a metal head resembling a dragon mounted on a wooden pole, behind the head a red fabric body that writhed when the wind blew through its jaws. I patted Horns on the neck, noting his coat shone after someone had groomed him. I assumed he had also been fed and watered.

After I had fallen in beside him, Tasius nudged his horse forward and Klietas and the soldiers of the chief's bodyguard followed. Around us, thousands of horsemen and women were heading south. At first, I thought they were just a disorganised mass, akin to the Aorsi and their ill-disciplined warriors. But my prejudice had blinded me to the obvious, and a closer examination of the columns of horsemen riding parallel to our own two lines revealed bodies of troops moving in a disciplined manner, forming files and not breaking formation. I also noticed there was no shouting, no bravado or sounding of horns or trumpets, just an ominous rumbling as thousands of horses pounded the verdant earth of Media.

'I have heard of your animosity towards slavery, King Pacorus,' said Tasius, who gave the appearance he was on a leisurely pleasure ride.

'If you had been a slave, you would understand,' I said, glancing left and right in an effort to take in everything that was occurring around me.

'If you have any questions, please feel free to pose them,' he said.

I came straight to the point. 'How do the Roxolani fight?'

'With discipline,' he replied. 'You may think nomads are uncouth barbarians. But the open steppe has allowed us to perfect our tactics, as you will soon discover.'

'Discipline and organisation,' I said.

'That is correct, King Pacorus, allied to aggression and never allowing an enemy to rest. Just as we do not allow a prey to escape on a hunt, so we press our attacks until the enemy has been destroyed.'

I thought of my own highly trained soldiers.

'What if the enemy attacks you?' I said.

'Then we have a worthy prey.'

It soon became apparent why Tasius was reluctant to take his warriors south to the desert around Ctesiphon. His troops were marshalled by means of signal flags, which in the dust thrown up when thousands of horses were pounding the dirt and sand of the desert would be hidden by dust clouds. In the grassland of Media, however, there were no such problems.

It was no accident the Roxolani had selected this part of Media for their base. The abundance of water, grazing and a landscape of gently undulating terrain made it ideal for manoeuvring large numbers of horsemen. And the Sarmatians had many riders.

When officers reported to Tasius that their scouts had reported the Parthians were nearing the Sarmatian host, he gave orders for his units to deploy into battle formation. It felt surreal to be among an army that was about to engage a force of Parthians, but I believed that whoever led my kinsmen would triumph over the Sarmatians. I glanced behind me to see horsemen flanking left and right to form ranks of horsemen, which advanced past us to create a battle line. The separate formations, which I estimated to number around five hundred each and which were widely spaced, kept moving forward.

In each formation the first two lines of Sarmatians were armoured horsemen – both rider and horse wearing rows of horn scales and the soldiers wearing leather helmets. Each rider carried a lance and a short dagger, which I was informed was called a *culter*. I doubted their horn-scale armour would offer much protection against the arrow storm that would engulf them when the Parthians attacked. The arrow storm that would also engulf me and Klietas!

But there was no arrow storm.

Parthian tactics were simple enough: use horse archers to annoy and harass an enemy, prior to wearing him down with blizzards of missiles, surrounding him and shooting his demoralised formations to pieces. Then the cataphracts would be unleashed to seal victory. Mobility, missiles and shock action combined to destroy an enemy. It had worked on many occasions, most notably at Carrhae when Rome's legions had been humbled. But here, on a grassy plain in Media, it was different.

The Roxolani formations deployed in five lines – two of armoured lancers and three of light horsemen behind. It was the latter who started the battle by galloping through the stationary lancers to assault the Parthian centre, comprised of cataphracts and mounted spearmen from Persis and Susiana.

Light horsemen wearing no armour against steel-clad riders equipped with a *kontus*, sword, axe and mace. It would be no contest. And *was* no contest, because the Sarmatians speedily withdrew when the Parthian centre advanced, galloping back through the lines of their own armoured horsemen. But then the Parthians themselves stopped, which I found confusing. Why did they not press their attack? A *kontus* would easily go through horn scales. But then it became clear.

The Sarmatians kept extending their battle line on both wings, continually overlapping the flanks of Parthian horse archers opposite. By means of basic signals conveyed by flags, the Sarmatian battle line became longer and longer. In response, the horse archers from Susiana and Persis rode away from their centre to try to outflank the Sarmatians. But they were the ones being outflanked. I saw horsemen wearing yellow tunics and blue leggings – the colours of Persis – disappear to the right, while on the left the horse archers of Susiana – red tunics and tan leggings – also disappeared into the distance.

The soldiers of Otanes and Silani shot their bows and brought down Sarmatians, but not in enough numbers to even make a small dent in Tasius' horde. And all the while the Sarmatian chief sat calmly on his horse, observing the stand of colours opposite: banners showing an eagle in its talons and the black head of a bird god on a yellow background. It was a bizarre experience, both being among enemy troops observing a Parthian army across no-man's land and sitting stationary on Horns in the midst of a battle with no fighting going on around me, or within sight.

The cataphracts and stand of banners opposite suddenly began to diminish as the soldiers of Persis and Susiana retreated. I understood why they had done so, even though it brought a lump to my throat to see Parthians withdraw without washing their weapons in enemy blood. They were in danger of being surrounded. Perhaps they were already surrounded.

Once more, Tasius sent the three lines of light horsemen forward to harry the cataphracts, keeping his hundreds of lancers under tight control. He knew in a one-to-one fight his armoured horsemen would fare badly against Parthian cataphracts, but he also knew no commander worth his salt would allow his best troops to be surrounded. And I knew Otanes and Silani were too competent to allow that to happen.

And then the cataphracts were disappearing into the distance in rapid retreat. It was now that Tasius, sensing victory was his, unleashed his lancers. There was a flurry of flag signals followed by hundreds of riders breaking into a canter and then a gallop, the ground trembling beneath their hooves. Tasius looked at me, fire in his eyes.

'Is this the best Parthia has got?'

Surrounded by his iron-clad bodyguard, we cantered across the greenery. On each wing, far into the distance, Sarmatians under iron control were literally running rings around Parthian horse archers. I silently prayed to Shamash they had managed to escape, though the squires, slaves, farriers and civilians accompanying the army of Otanes and Silani were not so lucky. I fought back tears when we reached their camp, a sprawling collection of brightly coloured tents, carts, camel parks, temporary stables, field workshops and pavilions. Shamash in his mercy had spared me the anguish of seeing the camp being plundered, so my eyes did not bear witness to seeing unarmed men and women being cut down by Sarmatian lancers or hear their cries as lances skewered bodies and men raped women and girls. But the sight was horrific enough.

I heard Klietas weeping behind me as we trotted through the carnage, bodies sprinkled over the ground, all bloody, many mutilated, all dead. Not all had perished, though. Cowered and beaten women, former slaves of Persis and Susiana and all naked after being raped, were being led away back to the Sarmatian camp. I took a crumb of comfort from seeing dead teenage boys in armour – squires – with weapons in their white hands. At least they had died fighting.

The final ignominy was when Tasius' warlords began dumping captured banners before him, tossing bird-god and eagle standards on the ground in front of him. I could feel his eyes on me as they did so, the honour of Parthia being trampled on in a scene I never thought I would bear witness to. The Roxolani had destroyed an army drawn from Atropaiene, Hyrcania and Margiana, and had now scattered a force made up of soldiers from Persis and Susiana. They had forced Akmon to take refuge behind Irbil's defences and treated his kingdom as their own.

As Tasius basked in the acclaim directed at him, I realised I had been completely forgotten in the celebrations. I sat next to the Roxolani chief, who was within striking of my sword. I could have pulled my *spatha* and ended his life there and then. I did not do it. Why did I not kill him? A part of me wanted to believe that if I could chop the head off the snake the rest of the body would wither. But I knew nothing about this chief.

Did he have sons or a chosen successor? If so, killing him would achieve nothing, aside from making me feel better before I too was cut down. But there was another reason. To do such a base thing to one who had shown me hospitality and courtesy would be dishonourable. I therefore sat in silence and watched the Roxolani celebrate another victory over a Parthian army.

During the ride back to the Sarmatian camp, the banners having been burnt on a pyre to symbolise the futility of Parthian efforts against him, Tasius informed me of my fate.

'You will return to King of Kings Phraates, King Pacorus, and tell him the Roxolani shall make Media its new home. King Akmon will be allowed to leave Irbil with his family, after which Irbil shall be my capital.'

Thoroughly deflated after having witnessed the triumph of his warriors earlier, I merely nodded.

'He will also pay me a sum of gold to welcome me into his empire,' he carried on, 'the exact amount to be determined when I have had time to think more.'

'And if Phraates refuses your terms?' I asked wearily.

'Then we will seize the Silk Road,' he replied.

The threat chilled me to the bone. The silk transported from China through the empire to the Roman world and Egypt was the lifeblood of Parthia. The main artery ran east through Aria and Drangiana via Esfahan and on to either Hatra and then Zeugma, or south through Dura and Palmyra. Any interruption of trade would have serious consequences not only for my own kingdom, which would be unable to maintain its army at its current strength, but also for Hatra, thus threatening the two kingdoms that acted as the western shield of the empire. In short, Tasius' declaration represented the greatest threat to Parthia since Crassus' invasion nearly thirty years before.

That night I sat with Klietas in a covered wagon, both staring at each other while outside the Sarmatians celebrated long into the night. There was much revelry and with good reason. The Roxolani had done something no foreign army had ever achieved: defeated two Parthian armies in quick succession. I suddenly felt very old and helpless.

'What will you do, majesty?' Klietas asked me.

'Return to the only things I can rely on in this world. My wife and Dura's army.'

I fell asleep when the din outside began to finally subside, the dawn casting the interior of the tented wagon in a subdued light that fitted my mood entirely. The side of the wagon being hit with a blunt instrument woke Klietas with a start.

'Chief Tasius wishes to speak with you, King Pacorus.'

I emerged from the wagon bleary eyed and aching, the morning warm and heavy with the scent of wood smoke. Around me men and women were moving around in a lethargic fashion after their over-indulgence the night before. How I wished the horizon was lined with Dura's army. Without having the chance to wash or shave, I was escorted to the wagon of Tasius where I found Horns and Klietas' horse being held by two of the chief's bodyguard. My former squire trailed after me, gawping at the seemingly endless Sarmatian encampment. Nearby, women were milking goats and young children were running around and making mischief. A pale-faced Akka appeared, his red coat unfastened and his eyes bloodshot. He belched.

'Apologies, majesty, too much drink last night.'

He reeked of alcohol and was unsteady on his feet.

'Lord Tasius will see you now, majesty,' said an officer of Tasius' bodyguard, who at least looked fresh and alert.

Klietas waited by his horse while I talked to the Roxolani leader. The interior of his wagon did not smell of wine and he himself looked as though he had not indulged in the previous night's debauchery.

'You recall our conversation yesterday about my proposal, King Pacorus?'

'You mean your demands,' I said.

He scratched his nose. 'Demands, proposals. It amounts to the same thing. Media is now the land of the Roxolani. To facilitate a peaceful transition of ownership, you will kindly instruct Phraates to give me forty thousand talents of gold, payable within a month.'

I could have argued with him, convinced him that Phraates would never agree to such a sum. But I knew Phraates would not pay him anything anyway, and so I meekly nodded and promised to pass on his demands, eager to be away from both him and his tribesmen.

'I look forward to meeting with you again in the near future, King Pacorus.'

I forced a smile. 'I will count the days.'

To be fair, he did not gloat about his recent victories or say anything to belittle me. Indeed, he made his demands sound reasonable, which was even more galling. Tasius was as far removed from the boorish, unintelligent Spadines as one could get, and that made him a dangerous foe. He was not to be underrated. But the question I asked myself when I rode away from his wagon was: could he be speedily dealt with before he and his tribesmen made Media their permanent home?

Chapter 15

I rode straight to Assur where I found a huge marching camp holding Dura's army and the forces of the new king of Hatra. The fortified camp resembled another town that had sprung up immediately north of Assur, so large was it. A patrol of horse archers intercepted us before we reached the pontoon bridge, the young officer recognising my black leather armour and Roman helmet decorated with goose feathers. He was initially perplexed as to why his king was on the eastern side of the Tigris.

'Have you encountered any Sarmatians?' I asked.

'No, majesty. We have encountered barely anyone.'

'Any news from Irbil?'

'No, majesty.'

Gallia did have some news about Irbil, having ordered Talib to send scouts across the Tigris and ride to Media's capital. When I presented myself at the command tent we both shared when on campaign, and after I had washed and eaten something, she summoned my chief scout so he could report in person. She noticed my downcast expression as I sat in a chair waiting for him to arrive.

'They are very good.'

'Who?' she asked, flopping down in a wicker chair opposite.

'The Roxolani. I was a guest of their leader for long enough to ascertain they are formidable foes.'

I told her about the defeat of Otanes and Silani. She seemed unconcerned but was appalled Phraates had endangered me.

'He should have waited until you had returned to Ctesiphon before sending an army to intercept the Sarmatians. And anyway, is that not a decision you should be part of, seeing as you are his lord high general?'

I too was unconcerned. 'I had forgotten how duplicitous Phraates could be. He probably thought he could win all the glory for himself. Alas for Silani and Otanes. I pray they escaped with their lives.'

Talib had always been slim but he seemed to wither with age. Now in his thirties, he looked at least ten years older. I wondered if he and Minu had yet to get over losing their child, and also whether their bodies were too battered and worn out to conceive again.

'It is good to see you, majesty,' he said, giving me a rare Agraci smile.

'And you, Talib. How is Minu?'

He looked askance at the enquiry. He had always been a remote individual, a true offspring of the desert, and had never been one for small talk. He obviously found my question about his marriage intrusive.

'Well, majesty,' he said, curtly.

'Sit, tell me about Irbil.'

He pulled up a chair and an orderly served him and us some wine. Two of his best scouts had ridden along the eastern bank of the Tigris before making a dash for Irbil. They found a city deluged with refugees and surrounded by a great host of Media's soldiers. They were granted an audience with Akmon, at which the king informed them he was waiting for news of our intentions before he launched his own attack against the Roxolani, reasoning a two-pronged assault would stand more chance of success. He was right, but coordinating such an attack would be very difficult, if not impossible. One thing was certain, though, if action was not taken against the Roxolani soon, the refugees in Irbil would starve, and Tasius and his people would cement their stay in Media, which in turn might lead to more Sarmatians flocking into the empire.

'We need to act fast,' I told the assembled war council later in my tent, Talib relating to its members what he had told me earlier.

'You are right about acting speedily, uncle,' said Pacorus, now King of Hatra following a hasty coronation service in the city's Great Temple the day before. 'There are over forty thousand soldiers and civilians in this camp, to say nothing of the thousands of horses, mules and camels. They will strip Assur's granaries dry if we delay.'

Supplies were being ferried from Hatra on a daily basis, but not enough to sustain Hatra's fifteen hundred cataphracts, three thousand squires and ten thousand horse archers, to say nothing of the entourage of slaves and the civilian camel drivers of the ammunition train. Dura's army marched with enough food and fodder for three months of campaigning, but it too could not stay at Assur indefinitely.

'We must defeat the Roxolani alone,' I told them.

Kewab raised an eyebrow. 'Having already defeated two Parthian armies, majesty, what tactics do you propose to use so this army may avoid suffering the same fate?'

Gallia screwed up her face in annoyance at his impudence, but he was an accomplished general who had little time for niceties in the face of an emergency. In any case, it was a fair question.

'We use the legions to form a hollow marching square,' I said, 'inside which will be our horsemen.'

I saw Chrestus doing calculations in his head.

'Problems, Chrestus?' I asked him.

'It will be a square with very thin sides, majesty.'

I looked at Lucius Varsas, Dura's quartermaster general.

'The siege engines will stay here, as will the slaves and servants.'

I smiled at the other Pacorus. 'And the squires will remain here, also.'

Pacorus frowned. 'That is most irregular, uncle.'

I knew Hatra's Royal Bodyguard liked to have a small army of slaves and squires to keep it looking immaculate and to attend to its every need. But I saw little point in dragging thousands of non-combatants along who would have to be fed and protected, and who would be of no use against the Roxolani when it came to battle.

'These are irregular times, nephew.'

'Perhaps we should wait until High King Phraates sends us reinforcements,' said my nephew.

'There will be no reinforcements,' I stated. 'I saw with my own eyes the defeat of King Ali and Satrap Otanes, who were foolishly committed by Phraates before I returned from negotiating with the enemy.'

'You were lucky you weren't executed for Phraates' treachery,' said Chrestus, bluntly.

'Why would Tasius cut off my head,' I smiled, 'when he needed me to convey to Phraates his new demands.'

'Which are?' asked my nephew.

'The Kingdom of Media,' I said, 'which is to be the new home of the Roxolani tribe. Plus, forty thousand talents of gold as a welcoming gesture.'

There were sharp intakes of breath. Everyone knew surrendering Media would be akin to a dagger through the heart of the empire.

'Tonight, I will write to Phraates explaining the current state of affairs,' I said, 'and in the morning we will cross the Tigris to rid Parthia of this plague of Sarmatians.'

After the meeting, I asked Pacorus to stay, eager to convey my sorrow regarding the death of his parents. Klietas hovered around us, topping up our cups of wine. The great weight of his grief and the sudden burden of kingship in difficult circumstances had dimmed Pacorus' handsome features somewhat. But he had been raised a prince in Hatra, and from my own experiences I knew that from an early age it would have been drilled into him that service to his kingdom and Parthia was his goal in life. That grief and loss were but temporary aberrations to be endured with stoicism. And so it was now.

'They lived long and happy lives, uncle, and for that I thank Shamash. It is my duty to ensure the kingdom they left to me continues to prosper. Phraates was a fool to commit forces before you returned.'

'As usual, it is Dura and Hatra that has to save his arse,' sneered Gallia. 'We should burn the pontoon bridge and let the Sarmatians seize Ctesiphon, just to teach him a lesson.'

Pacorus said nothing but merely toyed with his cup of wine.

'Phraates is high king,' I said. 'Contrary to popular opinion, he is not a god. He therefore makes mistakes, as do we all.'

I looked at her, unblinking. She knew I was alluding to her assassins, but she shrugged.

'Phraates makes more than most.'

'I cannot believe my nephew invited these Sarmatians into the empire,' said Pacorus, unwilling to indulge in a debate about Phraates' suitability for being high king.

I laughed. 'I can. Gordyene has always been apart from the empire, and its rulers have always encouraged that view. To Castus, seduced by his new wife into believing he is a modern-day Alexander the Great, it makes perfect sense to encourage more Sarmatians to join the Aorsi in being his allies.'

'He will have to account for his actions,' said Pacorus. 'We must remove him and replace him with Haytham.'

I shook my head. 'Phraates intends to make Kewab King of Gordyene.'

'I thought he will be leaving for Egypt,' said a surprised Pacorus.

'So did I,' added Gallia.

I drank some wine. 'That was his intention, despite my lobbying Phraates to give him a position commensurate with his abilities and service to Parthia. However, the recent emergency has swayed Phraates' mind and now he wants Kewab occupying the throne in Vanadzor. Will that present a problem for Hatra?'

'Kewab is a man of exceptional talents,' he replied. 'Hatra would have no problem with him ruling Gordyene. What does he say on the matter?'

'He does not yet know of Phraates' offer,' I told him, 'and I would appreciate you not mentioning it to him until Phraates has written down his promise.'

'My husband does not trust the high king not to renege on his offer,' smiled Gallia. 'Once the emergency has passed.'

Pacorus looked thoughtful. 'As he is ignorant of the offer of kingship, why then has not Kewab already left for Egypt?'

'Because he is a man of integrity and honour,' I said, 'which even if he had few military skills, would make him worthy of high office in Parthia.'

'What of Haytham?' asked Pacorus.

'The best he can hope for is exile,' I answered. 'Phraates is too vindictive to allow a legitimate claimant to Gordyene's throne live in the empire. He has told me he wants Haytham dead.'

'I would be willing to give Haytham sanctuary in Hatra if he so desires,' stated Pacorus.

'He would not be safe from Phraates' assassins,' I warned.

Pacorus shook his head. 'What is the world coming to?'

I looked at Gallia. 'A question I have often asked myself, nephew.'

He excused himself soon after, Gallia also leaving me to spend time with her Amazons, her mood distinctly frosty after my references to her own band of assassins. She would calm down after a couple of hours telling her Amazons how they were the guardians of the empire and the actions of a select few of them beyond the empire's frontier had made them heroines.

I dismissed Klietas and settled down to write the letter to Phraates. The hour was late, outside there was little sound. Despite the thousands of troops camped around my command tent there was an atmosphere of calm serenity in the air. I began to write on the papyrus, the oil lamp on the table providing light. I informed Phraates of the new demands of

Tasius, how I had witnessed the defeat of Silani and Otanes, and that I prayed they still lived. I begged him not to despatch any more forces against the Roxolani and declared my intention to immediately cross the Tigris and engage the Sarmatians before they could do any more damage to Parthia.

I signed my name and waited for the ink to dry, the hairs on the back of my neck standing up and my palms becoming sweaty. I heard nothing to indicate anything was awry, but my instincts screamed at me to act. In a blur I stood, pulled my *spatha* from its scabbard and spun around.

To see a Scythian Sister standing before me.

I recognised the thick, golden hair and in the pale-yellow light of the oil lamps could just about identify her emerald green eyes.

'Saruke,' I said in surprise.

She was the mistress of poisons sent by Claudia to instruct Gallia's Amazons in their nefarious arts; a tall, slender, beautiful practitioner of murder. She glanced at the sword point inches from her gracious neck.

'Are you going to kill a servant of the gods?'

I slid the blade back into its scabbard.

'I did not realise you journeyed here with the army.'

'I did not. I have just arrived.'

I wondered how a lone woman was able to infiltrate a guarded camp, all the entrances to which were sealed during the night. And I assumed she was riding a horse. Perhaps she rode a griffin and flew over the ramparts.

'I have a gift for you, majesty,' she said, 'may I sit?'

I offered her my chair and pulled up another. She saw the letter to Phraates and smiled.

'The high king has locked himself in his bedroom after he received news of the defeat of the army he sent to battle the Sarmatians. He is in the pit of despair.'

'Claudia told you this?'

She nodded. I poured wine into a cup and offered it to her. She looked around the tent.

'Your quarters are sparse compared to the great pavilions favoured by the other kings of the empire, majesty.'

'They suffice.'

She took the cup and tipped it at me.

'To Parthia.'

She lifted the cup to her full lips and sipped at the liquid, her eyes not leaving mine.

'What brings you here, lady?'

She put down the cup.

'You march to fight the invaders?'

'Tomorrow.'

'You cannot defeat them on your own.'

She reached into her black robes and placed a thick gold ring on the table.

'You will need this.'

I lifted it from the table and examined it. The shank was wide, and it had a square head, in which had been engraved a strange beast: a winged monster with a lion's head and an eagle's body. It was obviously an expensive piece of jewellery and recently created judging by its pristine condition.

'The engraving is that of Anzu, the winged servant of the sky god Enlil,' she told me. 'It is from the time when only the gods walked the earth and humans did not exist, when the riverbeds of the Euphrates and Tigris existed but were not yet filled with water.'

I held up the ring. 'This is centuries old?'

'Millenia,' she replied.

I drank some more wine.

'Anzu was so large that when he flapped his wings he caused huge storms. You will need his help to defeat the Sarmatians.'

I turned the ring over in my fingers.

'Put it on, majesty,' she said.

I did as she requested and braced myself for a surge of immortal energy to flow through my body, to rejuvenate me so I would feel young again. I inhaled deeply, anticipating the air to be charged with the power of the gods. I closed my eyes and waited for the spirit of Anzu to infuse my being. Nothing happened, and after a few moments my leg began to ache. I opened my eyes and saw Saruke looking at me with a bemused look on her face.

'One more thing, majesty,' she said. 'The armour you were gifted by the gods. You gave it away?'

'I did, to Kewab.'

'It was not yours to gift to anyone. It was given to you and you alone. But have no fear, it will be returned to you.'

'It will?'

'All will be revealed.'

She stood, bowed her head and walked towards the entrance.

'Will you not stay here tonight? I will arrange quarters to be made available for you.'

She sniffed the air. 'Your camp reeks of soldiers, leather and sweat. I will find a place in Assur.'

I stood. 'Guard!'

Seconds later two Exiles rushed in, one a centurion, swords drawn.

'At ease. This lady is to be escorted to the camp's entrance and thence to Assur.'

'Begging your pardon, majesty,' said the centurion, 'the gates to the town will be closed.'

'They will be open,' insisted Saruke.

Alerted by my raised voice, Klietas rushed in from his sleeping compartment, knife in hand.

'It is fine, Klietas,' I said.

Saruke looked at him, studying his bear's claw necklace.

'Your wife and son are safe in Irbil.'

'I, I have no son,' he stammered.

She walked from the tent. 'You will, bear slayer.'

The comment caused Klietas' spirits to soar and he began pacing up and down with an idiotic grin on his face. I sighed and poured him a cup of wine.

'Sit down, you will wear out the carpet.'

He did so. I handed him the cup.

'Do you think she tells the truth, majesty?'

'I would swear by it.'

He closed his eyes, a look of utter relief on his face. Touchingly, he was clutching the bear's claw necklace.

'I am pleased for you, Klietas, truly.'

He opened his eyes and took a gulp of wine.

'Thank you, majesty.'

'You should get some sleep, dawn must be only a few hours away.'

But I could tell he was too excited to think of sleep. I, on the other hand, was ready for bed. I stretched out my arms.

'Well, I am a lot older than you and require sleep.'

A guard entered the tent and saluted.

'Satrap Kewab requests an audience, majesty.'

At this hour? Was I the only one in need of sleep?

'Show him in.'

Klietas quickly drained his cup, fetched another and filled it as Kewab entered and bowed his head. Klietas retreated a few feet with the wine jug.

'What brings you here at such a late hour?' I asked the satrap, keen to emphasis the unsociable time.

'Apologies, majesty, but I received your note and came as quickly as I could.'

'My note?'

He produced a papyrus sheet and placed it in front of me. I was most surprised to see a missive requesting Kewab to return the armour I had gifted him, not least because although it was indeed my handwriting on the parchment, I had not written it.

'When was this delivered?' I enquired.

'About an hour ago, majesty.'

He placed the armour on the table. It must have been Saruke who had forged the letter, but the mystery then deepened.

'A most curious thing, majesty,' said Kewab. 'The armour no longer fits me.'

I looked at the immaculate, shining silver armoured cuirass.

'Oh?'

'Strange as it sounds, it appears to have shrunk,' said Kewab.

I picked up the cuirass and examined the silver scales. It was as light as a feather. The scales were still perfectly flush horizontally, starting from the top the rows overlapping slightly the ones below to provide maximum protection. I told Kewab to sit. I told Klietas to take the armour to my sleeping quarters. He started whistling as he did so.

'I wanted to thank you for being here,' I told him. 'I know you must be thinking of Egypt.'

He looked serious. 'I am thinking only of bringing this campaign to a successful conclusion, majesty.'

Ever the professional.

'Well, with your help, I am sure it will be a success, Kewab. You miss Egypt?'

'My memories of Egypt are not happy ones, majesty, whereas those of Parthia are the opposite. But…'

He hesitated.

'But your wife is eager to return.'

He appeared embarrassed. 'She is from an ancient family, majesty, who held great power and commanded great respect in Egypt. When I was fighting the Kushans, she had a taste of her former life. She wants to taste that life again.'

'I do not blame her. She is ambitious for you.'

How I dearly wanted to tell him he was to be king of Gordyene. But I did not want to tempt fate. If I told him, his life might be snatched away to spite me. So, I kept silent. He sighed.

'Well, it is late. I will see you in the morning, majesty.'

He took his leave and I was free to retreat to my bed. Gallia returned soon after Kewab had left, no longer in a prickly mood. In our sleeping quarters, she saw the armoured cuirass identical to her own hanging on a frame.

'Kewab returned it to me,' I told her.

She spotted the ring on my finger.

'What's that?'

I told her of the clandestine visit of Saruke, the forged note and the armour that no longer fitted Kewab.

'Try it on. The armour, try it one,' she said.

I did so. It fitted like a second skin. A sharp stabbing sensation shot through my leg.

The gods give and they take away.

The army marched just after dawn, the camp remaining extant as just over thirty-three thousand soldiers tramped out of its entrance and crossed the pontoon bridge to rid the empire of the Sarmatian plague. Rodak was left in charge of the camp, which was garrisoned by five thousand squires and a detachment of Hatra's foot soldiers, sent by Governor Aspad on the orders of his king. Also left behind were the slaves that attended Hatra's Royal Bodyguard and the dozens of others who cooked meals, erected tents and field stables, dug latrine trenches and served their masters. For the young nobles of the Royal Bodyguard, not to be attended and squired was a novel and not particularly welcome experience. But needs must.

The Durans and Exiles marched six abreast across the bridge, singing songs of glory, bawdy ballads about whores and girlfriends, and filling the air with obscene threats directed at the Sarmatians. Their morale was high and they were eager for battle, Chrestus having deliberately spread news of my mistreatment at the hands of Castus and Tasius to encourage the thirst for vengeance. I sat on Horns in my shining silver scale-armour cuirass and accepted their acclaim as they marched past, raising my sword in salute when the golden griffin of the Durans and the silver lion of the Exiles passed me by. Gallia, similarly attired, also saluted them, taking off her helmet and beaming with delight when they whooped and whistled. Behind her the Amazons sat impassively on their steeds, ignoring the invitations to dismount and wrap their lithe limbs around lusty legionnaires. 'Tomorrow we might be dead', 'you are only young once,' and 'I'm hung bigger than the king's stallion' were popular calls.

Dura provided the bulk of the army, Azad's cataphracts marching in full armour, their visages covered by full-face helmets, each *kontus* flying a white pennant sporting a red griffin motif. How they must have envied Sporaces' horse archers attired in only white tunics and tan leggings, but with the Sarmatians only two days' ride away, I did not want Parthia's last hope to be surprised.

No one envied Kewab's battle-hardened veteran horsemen in their sun-bleached tunics and leggings, leather armour and helmets. But in their case appearances were indeed deceptive, and his three thousand horsemen were worth twice that number on the battlefield, perhaps three times as many under their Egyptian commander. He saluted us as he passed at the head of his men.

'When are you going to tell him he is to be King of Gordyene?' asked Gallia after he had passed by.

'Not until the campaign is over,' I said. 'I want his mind focused on the here and now. After all, what use is a crown if its wearer is dead?'

The exiles from Mesene, the last link with Nergal and Praxima, had a special place in both our hearts. They numbered three thousand, all horse archers, but every one a professional soldier trained by my old friend the former King of Mesene. I ordered the Amazons to draw their swords and hold them aloft when the horsemen of Mesene rode by, the horse archers responding by raising their bows to us.

Talib and his scouts, plus those of Hatra, had left camp before dawn to reconnoitre the route ahead, and we also had patrols of horse archers far and wide acting as a screen for the army. Nothing was going to be left to chance on this campaign. Hatra's nobles were already bending the ear of their new king concerning my battle plan before we had barely left camp. The idea of hiding behind foot soldiers in a giant square was anathema to them, not least because in Hatra foot soldiers were regarded as only slightly better than slaves. Real soldiers fought on horseback, from a position where they were figuratively and literally head and shoulders above their social inferiors. They were also acutely aware that many of Dura's foot soldiers were former slaves, and despite also knowing that Dura's two legions had never been bested on the battlefield, the thought of allowing such men to be their guardians appalled them. In answer, I reminded them I was lord high general of the empire, appointed by King of Kings Phraates himself, and if they had any objections they should take up the matter with the high king himself. Once he had left the sanctuary of his bedroom, of course.

We had left the scorpions and siege engines at Assur but still had hundreds of mules and three and half thousand camels that made up the ammunition trains of Dura and Hatra, which together with the need to erect a marching camp each night, slowed our rate of advance to twenty miles a day. This further infuriated Hatra's Royal Bodyguard, which believed a rate of advance of at least twice that was more honourable. After two days of listening to their grievances transmitted to me via King Pacorus, it made me give thanks to Shamash that I was not King of Hatra.

The days were hot and getting hotter, spring having given way to summer. Each day the sun beat down from a cloudless sky without interruption. As we headed west at least the terrain changed from one of hard-packed dirt to a grassier landscape, made possible by the freshwater springs and streams that the gods had blessed Media with. And which the Sarmatians coveted as it provided grazing for their tens of thousands of horses. But their invasion had resulted in a land denuded of people and their livestock. We marched by abandoned farms and villages and empty fields. Only the crump of thousands of marching foot soldiers, the trundling of wagons and the clops of horses' hooves broke the ominous silence hanging over Akmon's kingdom.

I chose to ride near the vanguard, Gallia beside me, the Amazons behind us, the sun high in the sky and the air hot and dry. There was not a hint of wind and sweat was trickling down my neck. I absently turned the gold ring on my finger and kept glancing into the sky.

'What are you searching for?' asked Gallia.

'Mmm? Nothing.'

She rolled her eyes and turned to Klietas.

'I was happy to hear your wife is safe in Irbil. I hear you will have a son.'

'Yes, majesty,' he beamed. 'I will call him Pacorus, if the king has no objections.'

'He has no objections,' I said, looking up at the sky.

'What are you searching for, majesty?' he asked.

'A giant bird,' said Gallia, prompting Klietas to peer into the sky.

But a giant of another kind was approaching, Talib galloping up to me to report that his scouts had detected the Sarmatians closing from the east.

'How many?' I asked him.

'Enough to fill the whole horizon, majesty.'

Chapter 16

I peered to the east, to the yellow-hued Zagros Mountains in the distance, their snowy peaks glistening in the sun. I glanced at the gold ring on my finger and twisted it, hoping for… For what?

'Pacorus.'

Gallia's voice was laced with irritation. I turned away from the Zagros to see Chrestus, Kewab and King Pacorus had also been alerted to the news the Sarmatians had been spotted and had ridden over for a final briefing. I forgot about myths of giant lion-headed birds and the help of the gods.

'We stick to the agreed plan,' I said. 'Discipline and determination with rid Parthia of this plague. Shamash be with you all.'

They nodded and turned their horses, Talib walking his steed over to Minu to share an embrace before the clash of arms.

'Pacorus,' I called.

He halted his pure white stallion. 'Uncle?'

'Please impress on the fine lords of your bodyguard the need for restraint.'

He smarted at the implication. 'They will obey their king.'

In the time following, the still air was rent with trumpet blasts as over thirty thousand soldiers changed formation to adopt the great square that would be our formation to battle the army of Tasius. Much as Hatra's nobles would have loved to lead the charge to scatter the dirty barbarians polluting the soil of Parthia, they were under strict orders to wait until the time was right. In the battle sequence, they were last in line.

Our first line of defence was made up of the Exiles and Durans – ten thousand foot soldiers forming the four sides of our square. Each century was divided in half to number four ranks instead of eight, thus doubling its frontage but weakening its depth. In this way each cohort of split centuries had a width of just over one hundred and fifty paces – five cohorts side-by-side extended for three-quarters of mile. There were gaps between each cohort to allow horsemen to charge from the square. The same gaps would hopefully be inviting to the Sarmatians, who might be tempted to direct their armoured horsemen towards them. But if they did they would be shot to pieces by the horse archers taking up position behind the cohorts.

On the grassy, almost flat terrain the great square took shape, each side made up of five cohorts, behind them companies of horse archers, and behind them, with the camels of the ammunition train, mules and carts, the cataphracts of Hatra and Dura.

Gallia was watching the square take shape, ahead of us Sporaces' horse archers deployed to 'dance' with the enemy if the Sarmatians got too close while we were organising our deployment.

'Remember Carrhae?'

'Yes, I was there, you may recall.'

She looked at the square taking shape with admirable efficiency.

'That day, we were the ones shooting at a square of Romans, and now we will be a target for enemy horsemen.'

'The difference being, my sweet, the Sarmatians have few horse archers, so we do not need to worry about being under a deluge of arrows.'

She was unconvinced. 'What if this Tasius deliberately kept you from seeing his horse archers, Pacorus?'

I had not thought of that, but I was not unduly worried.

'Our square has missile power, whereas Crassus put his faith in his legionaries.'

'It is too late to change anything now,' she said, pointing to the east.

A detachment of white-uniformed horse archers was cantering towards us, and as it got closer, I saw it was led by Sporaces. He pulled up his horse and saluted.

'The enemy is closing, majesty, divided into many formations that appear to be equal in size.'

They were the same tactics used against Silani and Otanes.

'Armoured horsemen in front?'

He nodded. 'Yes, majesty.'

'Very well, withdraw your companies and get them inside the square.'

He saluted, turned his horse and galloped away, followed by his men. Minu had removed the wax-coated sleeve covering my griffin banner to allow it to flutter in the wind. Unfortunately, there was no wind, so it hung limply on its pole. The sun was still beating down from a cloudless sky, making us all sweat in our armour, though at least my cuirass was feather-light, unlike the mail protection worn by the Durans and Exiles, standing in their ranks waiting for the battle to begin.

I rode over to where Bullus stood with his century, Gallia and the Amazons following. The grizzled centurion had become something of a legend and was regarded as a lucky mascot by the rest of the army. As a result, everyone wanted to serve alongside Centurion Bullus, though it was certainly not because of his charm or cheery words. As usual, he was standing in front of his men, marching up and down with vine cane in hand, tapping shields and arms to highlight infractions.

'Stay sharp. Eyes front and no talking in the ranks.'

He turned when his men and others in nearby units began banging the shafts of their javelins on the insides of their shields. He stood to attention and saluted when I pulled up Horns in front of him.

'Come to try a bit of real fighting, majesty?' he grinned.

'I will have to decline your kind invitation, Bullus. I have a battle to direct. Keep yourself alive; this campaign is not over.'

He raised his cane. 'You can be sure of it, majesty.'

'She is alive, Centurion Bullus,' Klietas behind me called to him.

Bullus looked none the wiser.

'Anush,' said Klietas, 'she is in safe in Irbil. And I will have a son.'

'My day is complete,' shouted Bullus. 'Look lively.'

He was pointing to where horse archers were galloping towards the gaps between cohorts. Behind them, still at a distance but closing, bodies of horsemen, a great many of them all in a line.

The Sarmatians were here.

I raised a hand to Bullus and waited until the horse archers had entered the square, then commanded the Amazons to follow them. Gallia pulled her bow from its case and her women did the same. Out of the corner of my eye I saw the griffin banner ruffle. A few seconds later it began to billow as a wind picked up. I followed the Amazons into the square, halted Horns and turned him so I could see the Sarmatian host. I heard trumpets sounding and whistles blowing and knew legionaries and horse archers were readying themselves to receive the enemy's assault. Then I heard Klietas, wonderment in his voice.

'Majesty.'

'Not now, Klietas.'

'But, majesty.'

Annoyed, I spun in the saddle. And saw a truly breathtaking sight.

At first, I thought it was dust tornado on the horizon, a great brown cloud in the sky. But it could not have been a tornado because it was high in the heavens, separated from the ground, and it was descending rather than ascending. And then I saw it transform into the shape of a giant bird filling the sky. I blinked and the vision was gone, replaced by the huge brown cloud once more. Everyone was looking at it in wonderment and had forgotten about the tens of thousands of Sarmatians deployed to our front, their disciplined formations of horsemen extending left and right as far as the eye could see.

The cloud changed formation as the wind blew it along, eddying and spinning like autumn leaves in a breeze. And then we heard the buzzing and realised it was not leaves but insects, millions of them.

Locusts!

The wind picked up and suddenly they were above our heads, almost within touching distance, an incalculable number of them, blocking out the sun and making the earth go dark. Horses whinnied in fear and men clutched lucky talismans as they stared, open-mouthed, at the unholy spectacle. Klietas gripped his bear's claw, I caressed the lock of Gallia's hair and my wife did the same with Rasha's hair hanging around her neck.

They are reddish-brown in colour, with bright wings, and when the sun's rays catch them it appears the sea has been transported into the sky. But the vast myriad of insects had momentarily blotted out the sun as they passed over us, driven by a wind blowing in the Sarmatians' faces. I had to remind myself that one locust is but a tiny insect that you can catch and crush in your hand, but this vast, dense cloud of them had the power to wreak appalling destruction.

And then the wind abruptly ceased and the Sarmatians disappeared as the maelstrom of locusts enveloped them. I checked myself and Horns for signs of locusts but could not see even one. Everyone was doing the same, looks of disbelief on their faces when they realised not one locust was on their body, face or horse. I saw the gold ring on my finger and understood.

I raised my bow and dug my heels into Horns' sides.

'Every horse archer to me.'

He bolted through a gap between two cohorts and headed for the swarm of locusts around four or five hundred paces ahead. I heard trumpet blasts and hooves pounding the ground behind me and smiled. Pulling an arrow from one of my quivers, I nocked it in the bowstring and shot the missile. I saw the arrow arch into the sky and disappear in the swarm. I pulled up Horns around fifty paces from what appeared a dense, moving wall of locusts and loosed another arrow into the swarm. Gallia halted beside me and the Amazons began spreading out into line either side of us. Klietas pulled up his horse and nocked an arrow in his bowstring.

There was a sudden gush of wind and the liquid-like wall of locusts began to recede, to reveal men in horn-scale armour frantically trying to brush away the tormenting winged insects, calm their frightened horses, and a combination of both. The last thing on their minds was the lines of Parthian horse archers forming to their front almost within touching distance.

'Pick your targets,' shouted Gallia, her voice barely audible in the buzzing that hurt our ears.

I saw a man remove his helmet to shake out the locusts that had wormed their way inside it. I shot him with an arrow, knocking him from his saddle. I shot the man next to him and the man behind him, selecting targets with ease from close range as the locust swarm continued to move east, propelled by a gentle wind. Either side of me, Amazons were doing the same, adding lethal hisses to the incessant buzzing as arrows shot through the air, each one finding a target. And either side of my wife's bodyguard, stretching into the distance, more and more companies of horse archers from Dura and Hatra were leaving the square to join us in shooting helpless Sarmatians from their saddles.

The locust swarm moved slowly, as though the wind itself was being directed by a supernatural force to allow us to shoot as many enemy soldiers from their saddles as possible, while at the same time allowing us to replenish our ammunition from the camels that now came from the square to take up position behind the companies of horse archers. And all the while, as we walked our horses forward among the bodies of the dead Sarmatians we had killed, not one attack was launched against us. Not one arrow was shot at us, not one spear was thrown at us or one axe hurled at us.

As Sarmatians appeared as they exited the swarm, which continued to be blown east, they were shot. Not all were killed instantly. Some tumbled to the ground with arrows lodged in their shoulders or bellies, the iron heads having penetrated the horn scales of their armour to inflict wounds with varying degrees of severity. But all died when they were shot a second, third or fourth time. And then we were shooting individuals with no armour and I realised we had penetrated to the third and fourth lines of the Sarmatian formation we had been battling.

Individual Roxolani, driven mad by the locusts, were running around on foot, weeping and clutching at their clothes that were infested with insects. They too were shot down. Horses maddened and terrified by the locusts, their owners now dead, bolted towards us to escape the swarm, our own mounts also giddy with trepidation as they walked towards the seething cloud of locusts, which fortunately was always moving away from us. But they now had to thread a path through ground littered with dead Sarmatians, though no locusts. I stared at the ground with disbelief to see no insects were feasting on the lush grass. I touched the ring on my finger and gave thanks to Shamash for the miracle he had gifted me, and Parthia.

The battle was not entirely free of unwelcome interruption, however.

Unable to contain their frustration with having to stand idle while their social inferiors were winning all the glory,

Hatra's cataphracts pleaded with their king to be allowed to uphold their honour. Pacorus, also wanting to win his first victory as their king, readily acquiesced to their request. He led fifteen hundred cataphracts from the square to plunge into the locust swarm, the cream of Hatran society disappearing into the brown cloud to plunge their long lances into Sarmatians, and then go to work with their swords, axes and maces.

I rode to the ammunition train to pick up two fresh quivers where I was accosted by Azad, helmet pushed up on his head.

'The lads are unhappy, majesty.'

I knew what was coming. 'Oh?'

'They have been putting up with a lot of sarcastic comments from Hatran nobles about who are the best horsemen in Parthia, that sort of thing. And now they are forced to sit by and watch the Hatrans win all the glory.'

I handed the camel driver my empty quivers and slotted the two full ones on to my saddle.

'You have my permission to prove the Hatrans wrong, Azad.'

He was gone in an instant, his signaller blowing his trumpet to alert the cataphracts, who had exited the square and were formed up in company-sized wedge formations, ready to be unleashed against the enemy.

A cataphract charge is a truly wondrous sight: men in full armour riding horses attired in steel and leather making the earth tremble as they canter across the ground, every *kontus* being lowered in unison and gripped on the right side of every horse prior to being thrust into an opponent. This charge was not made at the gallop as Azad's men were traversing ground covered with bodies, but it was still a sight to swell the chest of any Parthian.

We had unleashed a deluge of arrows at the Sarmatians, but the cataphract assault drastically reduced the volleys of missiles shot at Tasius' warriors, who had mostly fled from us anyway. The great swarm of locusts had also moved on, propelled by a gentle wind to the east, which suddenly changed direction to a southerly breeze. I thought nothing of it. We had won a great victory and inflicted huge losses on the Roxolani, who were still suffering at the hands of the cataphracts. Dura's steel fist would be doing murder with their ukku blades, which would be cutting through horn and iron scales with ease. I wondered if Tasius himself had escaped the slaughter.

It was three hours before Azad returned, he and his men in high spirits after their orgy of violence. He recounted how they and he had pursued the Sarmatians for miles, cutting down any who attempted to stand and fight, slaying those who attempted to give themselves up, and hacking at anything with their swords until they no longer had the strength to wield their weapons. They and their horses blown, their armour and that of their steeds splattered with blood and gore, they reluctantly headed for camp. By the time they and Hatra's cataphracts walked into the marching camp being created by the Durans and Exiles, many literally as they led exhausted horses on foot, the sun was dipping on the western horizon. Using their entrenching tools was the only work the frustrated legionaries did that day, much to their disgust.

At dusk, the sun a massive blood-red ball in the west, a rider in a blue tunic and grey leggings rode into camp with a message from King Akmon, stating he and his army were approaching from the north. The victorious day was complete. In the morning, we would join forces with Media's king and drive the Sarmatians from Parthian soil.

No one slept that night, the sounds of revelry filling the air until the first shards of light lanced the eastern horizon to announce a new day, a glorious day in Parthia's history when barbarian invaders would be driven from the empire.

Despite my age and ailments, I felt remarkably fresh when Klietas served me and Gallia breakfast in the morning, my former squire wearing a broad grin as he placed figs, olives, biscuits, cured meat and diluted wine before us.

'Well, Klietas,' I said, 'we will soon have you back with Anush. You can ride to Irbil today, should you so desire.'

His smile disappeared. 'I would rather stay here, majesty, until the fighting is over.'

'I doubt there will be much fighting,' said Gallia, 'not after yesterday.'

'The appearance of the locusts was a miracle, majesty,' said Klietas.

Gallia smiled and I touched my gold ring.

'It certainly was,' I agreed.

'You are both beloved of the gods,' he announced.

I had to admit I believed he was right. We enjoyed the basic fare on offer. It was hard to not grin like Klietas, especially when Chrestus appeared with the casualty lists. I told him to pull up a chair. Klietas poured him a cup of watered-down wine.

'Fifty wounded in total, none dead,' he reported. 'Of those, five reported to the medical tents with rashes and inflammations due to insect bites.'

'This must be the most one-sided victory we have ever enjoyed,' I said.

Chrestus nodded his head. 'It is, indeed, majesty. Azad thinks the disc of victory commemorating our triumph should bear a locust and nothing else.'

'An excellent idea,' agreed Gallia.

'We should not get carried away,' I cautioned. 'The Sarmatians have suffered a grievous loss, but they have not been wiped out. We will continue to pursue them until we have chased them out of Parthia.'

'I'll tell that to the cohort commanders,' said Chrestus, 'who are aggrieved to say the least that they were bystanders yesterday.'

A sombre mood came over me and I remembered that dealing with the Sarmatians was only one half of the problem needing resolving.

'They will get their fair share of fighting, I can promise them that.'

Chrestus drained his cup and stood.

'After the Sarmatians, then.'

There was no wind as the army marched out of camp under an angry sun, Talib and his scouts riding out to reconnoitre ahead, others being sent to link up with Akmon and his Medians. We gave the ghastly battlefield to the east a wide berth, ravens and vultures already feasting on dead flesh and making dreadful cawing sounds that made one shudder.

'Yesterday locusts, today birds,' mused Gallia, peering towards the black flocks descending from the sky to go about their awful work.

We met up with Akmon and his army three hours later, the young king wearing a smile as he greeted us and congratulated us on our victory. He also congratulated Pacorus on his ascension to Hatra's throne and apologised for his brother's actions in general, and in northern Hatra in particular.

'You have nothing to apologise for, lord king,' said Pacorus, still flushed with his triumph the day before. 'Hatra considers Media its staunch ally and its king and queen close friends. I trust the queen is well?'

'Very well, thank you,' replied Akmon. 'It is good to see you, brother.'

Haytham riding behind us tilted his head at his brother. It had been a difficult time for the young prince of Gordyene, having fled his homeland to report Castus' intention to unleash his Sarmatians against northern Hatra. Despite his revelation, which gave Hatra time to prepare counter-measures against

Spadines and his Aorsi, Haytham was regarded with mistrust by many in the army, not least the Hatrans.

'My sword is yours, Akmon,' he said.

'You will always have a home in Irbil, brother,' Akmon told him.

Joro, the white-haired commander of Media's army riding beside his king, growled in a disapproving manner but said nothing. A stickler for tradition, rules and regulations, he would never dream of openly contradicting his king, but I had no doubt that in private he would have words with his king about the inadvisability of offering sanctuary to Haytham.

To change the subject, I provided a summary of the previous day's events, which delighted Akmon but caused the worry lines on Joro's face to deepen. After a further hour of travel, we understood why his expression was so glum.

The locusts had devoured everything.

First consuming the grass and leaves, they then moved on to the branches of trees and everything hanging from them. The vineyards and orchards that traditionally surrounded Media's villages were stripped bare, the bark being eaten away to leave trees devoid of any green so that they resembled white skeletons. Every bush had been eaten quite bare and the grass around them had been devoured so totally that it appeared the land had been scorched by fire to leave the ground devoid of life. We rode into a wasteland stretching into the distance, which we would have to traverse to harry the Sarmatians. The dreadful realisation began to dawn on me that the Roxolani would have to flee Parthia as quickly as possible, for their horses, goats and oxen would have no grass to graze on, no fodder to keep them alive. The gods had answered my prayers and had sent Anzu to strip the land bare. We had won a great victory, but the people of Media who had fled their homes to escape the Roxolani would be unable to return to their villages. To do so would mean starvation. They would probably starve anyway, for I doubted Akmon would be able to find enough food to feed the refugees who filled his capital.

The army was halted, and a speedy gathering of the kings convened. We sat on stools on the bare earth and pondered our next move.

'We cannot now march after the Sarmatians,' I said, 'at least not with the whole army. With no foliage to graze on, our supplies will soon be used up, and we have a campaign in Gordyene to wage before returning home.'

'We must pursue the Sarmatians,' insisted Akmon. 'Northern Media is still recovering from the depredations my father inflicted on it, and now the eastern half of the kingdom has been literally stripped bare by locusts. What is to stop the Sarmatians withdrawing north into Gordyene to recuperate?'

'He has a point, uncle,' agreed Pacorus. 'After butchering so may Sarmatians, it would be a great pity to let the others live to fight another day.'

I stood and peered at the bare, devastated landscape stretching north as far as the eye could see, and also extending east into the distance.

'How many troops did you bring with you, Akmon?' I asked.

'Ten thousand horsemen,' he replied with pride.

'And how much fodder?' I probed.

He blushed. 'None, for I expected…'

'You understandably expected to be able to graze your horses on the lush grass of Media,' I interrupted. 'Look around you, my lord. There is nothing to sustain livestock as far as the eye can see.'

They knew as well as I that the tens of thousands of Sarmatian horses would quickly weaken with no grass to graze on. The gods designed horses to be constant eaters. Their stomachs, being relatively small compared to their size, cannot handle large amounts of food. That being the case, they require constant access to quality pasture or hay. One of the reasons Tasius led his men into Media was due to its verdant pastureland, watered by countless springs and streams. Now that pastureland had vanished. Horses accustomed to grazing on the endless grass of the northern steppes would quickly become jittery at having no food. After a few days they would become jaundiced, with a yellow tinge to their eyes and gums. They would also become stressed, which would result in ulcers. After a few days more, a rider would be able to see his mount's rib and hip bones, and notice that his flanks had sunk in a little. In this weakened state, the Sarmatian horses would be unable to carry armoured riders, let alone wear their own suits of horn-scale armour.

'We have fodder, uncle,' said Pacorus, casually. 'We could send a small force, say two thousand horse archers, to harry the Sarmatians.'

'That will not suffice,' I told him. 'Tasius is no fool and even with his army decimated, he will easily be able to deal with such a puny force. Even if his horses are on their last legs. He is not to be underestimated.'

Pacorus exhaled loudly. 'Then what, uncle?'

'We must let King Ali and Atropaiene deal with the Roxolani,' I answered.

'Ali is wounded; he might even be dead for all we know,' retorted Pacorus, irritably.

I too was losing my temper. 'And perhaps not. I will send a courier to Urmia to request Ali, or his son Bagoas, to muster all the men they can to harry the retreating Sarmatians, to pick off stragglers and generally give them no peace.'

'Hardly an honourable way to conduct war, uncle.'

I threw up my arms in despair.

'Perhaps you wish to issue a personal challenge to Tasius, Pacorus, to settle the future of Parthia in a single duel?'

'As King of Hatra, uncle, I will decide what is best for my kingdom, and the empire.'

'But you are wrong,' I smiled. 'As lord high general, my decision is final, nephew, unless you wish to challenge my authority.'

He looked away from me. 'As you command, uncle.'

I assumed a pacifying tone. 'If we wish to prevent further Sarmatian incursions into the empire, we must deal with Gordyene, which gives them encouragement and sanctuary.'

I turned to Akmon. 'Will you join our campaign against Castus?'

'Yes,' he answered without hesitation. 'My brother needs to be taught a lesson.'

I did not tell him or Pacorus that Castus would be removed from power and probably killed, that the army contained the man whom Phraates himself wanted to see on Gordyene's throne, and who I also wanted to reward with a crown. If Castus and his deranged wife died, what did I care? Gordyene had become a cancer in the body of the empire and had to be cured. And the only way to cure a cancer was to cut it out.

The Durans and Exiles went to work creating a camp on the edge of the newly created wilderness, and I sat down to write a letter to King Ali, a conciliatory note apologising for stealing his position, assuring him that it would be restored to him as soon as he was able to ride in the saddle again, 'as I find the rank akin to a poison chalice', and explained the situation after our pleasing encounter with the Roxolani. I pleaded with him to muster as many men as he could to send against Tasius, being careful not to be drawn into a battle. 'The land has been denuded of foliage, and this being the case, the Roxolani's animals will soon be in a weakened state. In such circumstances, the tactics of the hyena are most useful.' I finished by saying 'we were going to deal with Gordyene once and for all'.

Talib selected one of his best men, a stick-thin Agraci who was so gaunt that a gust of wind could have snapped him in two, but whom my chief scout assured me could ride for days without rest, water or food.

'He sounds just the man, Talib, for he will be riding through a wasteland. The post stations will all be empty and devoid of supplies, I have no doubt, so give him two spare horses so he can reach Urmia as quickly as possible.'

The empire's posts stations, sited thirty miles apart, ran in more or less straight lines between the capital of each kingdom. But if the Roxolani had not plundered those between Irbil and Urmia, then the plague of locusts certainly would have. I sealed the letter and passed it to Talib.

'It is important this reaches Urmia.'

'You can depend on it, majesty.'

'You might be interested to know that the rest of us are heading for Gordyene, Vanadzor to be exact.'

His thin lips cracked a smile.

'King Castus will regret abusing his friends and allies, majesty. You sow what you reap.'

'You and your scouts will be the eyes and ears of the army, Talib. Castus might try to ambush us in the mountain valleys before we reach Vanadzor. I don't want to give him any easy victories.'

Another smile. 'Do not worry, majesty, we know the routes into Gordyene like the backs of our hands. We have traversed them many times over the years.'

'Then we were allies; now we are enemies,' I reminded him.

'You will kill King Castus, majesty?'

I was taken aback by his unusually blunt query. But I had forgotten that Castus had threatened not only his life but also that of Minu. He thus had a very personal reason for wishing to know the fate of the King of Gordyene.

'Castus seems to be actively bringing about his demise himself,' I answered cryptically.

I sent Navid and a party of horse archers back to Assur with instructions for Lucius Varsas to march with those left behind, plus his siege engines, to Irbil and there await our arrival.

The first part of the campaign had ended. The second part was about to begin.

Chapter 17

Irbil was once again filled with refugees, just as it had been when we had defended it five years before. Then, the city had been besieged by Prince Atrax and his Pontic allies and I had nearly lost my life. Now, no army ringed the capital and the Sarmatians were beating a hasty retreat out of Parthia, but the sight of bedraggled men, women and children huddled on streets, in doorways and in market squares made me want to weep. I took a crumb of comfort from the strong walls that now ringed the city, and the verdant terrain surrounding the capital. At least for the moment the refugees were being fed from the abundance of crops, fruits and milk produced by that fertile soil, but many would be unable to return to their homes and I wondered how long Akmon would be able to feed them.

Food was the chief topic of conversation when he convened a meeting in his palace in the calm surroundings of the city's citadel perched high on the stone mound in the middle of Irbil. Lusin had wanted to allow refugees into the hallowed streets and alleyways of the citadel itself, but was successfully resisted by the lords and priests who lived in the royal quarter and served in its temples. She toyed with her chestnut curls as we discussed matters at hand, looking positively glowing in her pregnant state. Her first child – Spartacus, now a year old – was a healthy baby with a strong pair of lungs, screaming the walls down and causing Joro to frown in disapproval before his nanny was ordered to take him back to his nursery.

Now summer had arrived, we convened in a small room adjacent to the neat and tidy palace garden, slaves having opened the shuttered doors to allow the sunlight and fragrance of flowers to enter. The citadel had its own water source: underground springs bringing cool, fresh water to fill the ponds filled with goldfish and power the fountains. Brightly coloured parrots sat on bird tables, pecking at the slaves feeding them. It was a scene of soothing calm; war and famine appeared but abstract notions. The more so as we nibbled on delicious pastries and sipped at gold rhytons in the shape of crouching dragons filled with expensive wine. But Joro brought us back to reality when he presented the bleak situation Media now found itself in.

'Our scouts have returned from the east with news that the devastation caused by the plague of locusts extends all the way to Lake Urmia and on to the Araxes. They report seeing dozens of abandoned wagons and ravens feasting on dead oxen and horses in the wake of the Sarmatian withdrawal.'

'What of the Sarmatians?' I asked.

'They are flooding across the Araxes into eastern Armenia, majesty,' reported Joro.

'Shamash be praised,' I said.

'How long will it take for the kingdom to recover from the locusts?' asked Pacorus.

Akmon and Lusin looked at Joro expectantly, but the aged general merely shrugged.

'No one knows, majesty, there have been no instances of such a large number of locusts descending on Media. Ever.'

I felt uncomfortable and, for some strange reason, moved my hand wearing the gold ring under the table. I suddenly felt responsible for Media's woes. I *was* responsible, was I not? The guilt weighed heavily on me.

'Gordyene has food.'

We all looked at Haytham sitting beside his brother.

'Food was the reason we are in this mess,' he continued. 'If it had not been for Yesim's need for food to feed her people, she would have never visited Vanadzor to barter her prisoners for food. Perhaps we may…'

'No,' I said. 'I know what you want. A promise from Castus to supply Media with food in exchange for him keeping his throne. I think not. At this juncture, he will be lucky to keep his head.'

'If you kill my brother, lord,' said Akmon, 'then Haytham will become King of Gordyene, as he will be the rightful heir. It will be for him to decide his kingdom's fate.'

Gallia looked at me with a smug expression, knowing, as did I, that Kewab would be made King of Gordyene. This would also lead to Haytham being exiled, for no king could tolerate a legitimate claimant to his throne living in his kingdom. I suspected that Phraates might send assassins to murder Haytham once he was in exile, just to tidy up loose ends. What a mess it all was.

'Does Castus have to die?'

Lusin's voice was laced with sadness but I felt no remorse for wanting him dead.

'The lord high general has ordered that he has to pay with his life for his crimes,' said Pacorus, clearly still resentful over my terse words with him.

I took a bite of honey cake.

'Castus has threatened my subjects, humiliated me, waged war on northern Media, which led to the deaths of your people, lady. He invited Sarmatians into Parthia, which has led to thousands of Parthian deaths near Lake Urmia and will be likely to lead to thousands more fatalities when winter comes, and Media is unable to feed the thousands of refugees packed into this city.

'His actions have led to Parthia facing its greatest crisis since Crassus' invasion.'

'Who is Crassus?' asked Lusin.

Pacorus laughed and I suddenly felt very old. Was Carrhae now mere ancient history, to be mentioned only by scholars and old men?

'A dangerous Roman,' said Gallia, 'who desired to conquer all Parthia. We stopped him from doing so.'

'Crassus paid with his life for his ambition,' I told Lusin. 'If Castus is allowed to retain his throne, let alone his head, then we will face endless Sarmatian incursions, encouraged by Gordyene's king. This I cannot allow to happen.'

I looked at Akmon. 'I understand if you do not wish to march north with us.'

The king looked at his general.

'Media will not stand by and watch other kingdom's fight on its behalf, majesty,' stated Joro.

'My brother will be expecting us,' said Haytham. 'There are many places where we can be ambushed.'

Fighting our way through the mountain valleys of Gordyene did not fill me with relish, but it would have to be done.

Pacorus was wearing a smug expression.

'It might interest you to know, Haytham, that I have arranged for a diversion to keep your brother amused while we advance on his capital.'

I was intrigued. 'What diversion?'

'I have contacted Lord Orobaz at Nisibus and commanded him to lead an army into southern Gordyene, during which it will make a lot of noise and lay waste to wildlife, villages and forests. This will hopefully hold Castus' attention while we are mounting the real invasion.'

'That will make our task easier,' I said.

Pacorus scratched his noble nose.

'You are not the only one with a comprehensive military knowledge, uncle.'

I ignored his barb. 'Dura will send food supplies to Media, and after Castus has been deposed, Gordyene will also be sending food to Irbil. This should alleviate the kingdom's immediate problems.'

'I will make it so, lord,' nodded Haytham, prompting Gallia to shake her head.

I left the meeting thoroughly depressed, knowing that the forthcoming campaign would be bloody, notwithstanding Hatra's well-thought-out diversion, and would result in the death of at least one of Spartacus' sons, perhaps two. They were the sons of the infant we had carried out of the Silarus Valley all those years ago. I hoped my lord would forgive me.

At least the reunion between Klietas and Anush was a happy event, the pregnant wife of my former squire thanking me profusely for saving him, her and the surviving villagers of Vazneh. On the orders of Lusin, she and they had been lodged in the citadel and the queen had taken a personal interest in ensuring Anush received proper nutrition and was attended by midwifes to ensure her pregnancy proceeded smoothly. For an illiterate commoner from northern Media, the experience was overwhelming. But it pleased me to see some good come out of a wretched situation. I took comfort in their simple desires and pure love for each other and reasoned that as long as there was a place for individuals such as Klietas and Anush, Media and Parthia would thrive.

'This is where we say goodbye, Klietas. I have something for you.'

I handed him a leather pouch filled with coins.

He began shaking his head but I took his hand, placed the pouch in his palm and closed his fingers around the soft leather.

'Take it, with thanks and gratitude. You and your family will always have a home in Dura, should things not work out here.'

Anush, tears in her eyes, threw her arms around me and kissed me on the cheek. She froze when she realised she had touched a king, something technically punishable by death. I laughed and kissed her back.

'I will pray for the safe delivery of your child, Anush. Shamash keep you both safe.'

The army was already on the march, Lucius, his siege engines, the squires and the civilians having journeyed from Assur to link up with the legions, horse archers and cataphracts. Now the force was joined by Akmon and five thousand horsemen, half the number he had taken east to link up with us. I had urged him to keep the rest at Irbil under the capable command of Lord Soter, just in case there were roving bands of Sarmatians still at large.

It was a sombre group of commanders leading the army north from Irbil at the head of over thirty-eight thousand soldiers and a formidable siege train. The banners of the three kings – the red griffin of Dura, the white horse's head of Hatra and the silver dragon of Media – flew proudly in the pleasant breeze, but Akmon rode in silence, Pacorus had receded into

Hatran haughtiness, and I was resentful. Time after time I had declared my intention to retire from the politics of the empire, yet I was continually, unwittingly dragged back into the cauldron of war and the affairs of Parthia, despite my protestations. I felt like Sisyphus, the Greek king of legend who was punished by the gods for his craftiness by having to push a large boulder up a hill, only for it to roll down when it neared the top. Sisyphus then had to start again from the bottom of the hill, a cycle of endless struggle that he would have to repeat for all eternity. Sisyphus had tried to trick Zeus and had been justly rewarded, but what was the crime I had committed to warrant me being punished with endless strife?

It is just over one hundred miles from Irbil to Vanadzor – five days' marching – and for every one of those days I agonised over the fate we would be inflicting on Gordyene and its king. Akmon and Pacorus kept their counsel, which darkened the mood further. At least we were untroubled by ambushes as we threaded our way through the ancient forests nestling in the valleys and mountainsides of southern Gordyene.

Talib and his men scouted the tracks and forests, searching the pines for any signs of the enemy. Because of the narrowness of the tracks, the army was forced to use several routes at once, the columns joining together to establish camp in the afternoon, long before the sun disappeared behind the high peaks in the west. I comforted myself with the knowledge that most of the forest floors were festooned with a dense undergrowth of brambles, ivy and other creepers. This foliage would not hinder small parties of ambushers but would seriously disrupt large formations of troops. So, we crept on unimpeded through southern Gordyene like a giant crab inching its way towards the city it would eat. Our advance was not entirely without resistance, though.

On the evening of the fourth day, Vanadzor a mere two days' march away, Chrestus presented himself at my tent with a man in tow. His companion wore a cloak with a hood and was dressed in scuffed boots and leggings that had seen better days. I wondered why Chrestus had brought a trader down on his luck to me, until the man removed his hood.

'General Hovik,' I said in surprise.

'A general no longer, majesty,' he replied, bowing his head to me and Gallia who entered the tent after inspecting the Amazons.

She repeated my words. 'General Hovik.'

'He has been searched for weapons, majesty,' said Chrestus.

'I doubt the general is here to assassinate me or the queen,' I said. 'Please sit, general.'

As he removed his cloak and did so, an orderly poured him wine. Chrestus stood over him menacingly, hand on the hilt of his *gladius*.

'Take a seat also,' I told my own general.

Hovik, whose tunic was in no better condition than his leggings, drained the cup of wine. He ran a hand through his thinning brown hair that was heavily laced with grey.

'Castus sent you?' enquired Gallia, accepting a cup of wine.

'No, majesty, I am here of my own volition. I will come straight to the point. I beg you not to attack Vanadzor, for the sake of the history of the collaboration and allegiance between Dura and Gordyene.'

I sipped at my wine slowly, examining his weathered face and tired eyes. I had always respected Hovik greatly, both for his abilities and honesty.

'I know you were dismissed from your position, general,' I said.

'A black day for Gordyene,' added Gallia.

'And believe me when I say I regret having been forced by Castus to march against him. But his actions leave me no choice. In the absence of King Ali due to injury inflicted on him by your king's allies, High King Phraates has appointed me lord high general. I have specific instructions to take punitive action against both Gordyene and its king.'

'Gordyene has a fine army, majesty. Many men will die,' he said, glumly.

'Castus should have thought of that before he married a mad woman, invited the Sarmatians into Parthia and encouraged them to conquer Media,' I retorted.

'Is there no way to avoid bloodshed?' he pleaded.

'None,' I said harshly.

'General,' said Gallia. 'If we were to turn this army around, Castus would interpret it as weakness, which would only embolden him to be rasher in the future, to see himself as the man who could defeat other armies without even having to fight them.'

He finished his wine and stood.

'Then if you will excuse me, I will be on my way.'

'Stay with us tonight at least, general,' I offered.

'Thank you, majesty, but no.' He pulled his cloak around him. 'When I was a young lad I carried a spear in the army of King Balas, and I was a horseman when Surena freed Gordyene from the Romans. Now my kingdom is in danger again and I will fight beside my king.'

'You will die,' I said.

'Most likely, majesty, but I will do so with a clear conscience.'

He bowed, turned and walked from the tent into the night air.

'Do you want him placed under armed guard, majesty?' asked Chrestus.

'No, see him safely on his way. A loyal soldier should always be given the chance to die for his king.'

That night I went to bed utterly depressed.

The next morning, I summoned Haytham to my command tent, which would soon be dismantled and loaded on to a cart as the army continued its march north towards

Vanadzor. The sun still shone fiercely but the Kingdom of Gordyene was not as hot as the lowlands of Mesopotamia. The land was fertile and watered by many mountain streams. The forests were packed with animals – brown bears, wolves, lynx and wild cats – and the valleys were home to many settlements. The scouts reported those that lay in our path had been abandoned, their inhabitants having either fled to the capital, sought refuge in neighbouring valleys, or moved to higher ground to wait out the campaign. It saddened me to think Parthians were causing such disruption, which is why I decided to make a direct appeal to Castus.

The words of Hovik had struck home, especially when he had mentioned Balas and Surena. King Balas had been a close friend of my parents and Surena had been my former squire. Indeed, his life had to a certain extent mirrored that of Klietas. Both had unexpectedly entered my life, both had saved my life, and both left Dura to make their own way in the world. I had been deeply saddened when Orodes had led an army to the gates of Vanadzor to fight a rebellious Surena. But here I was, doing exactly the same. I was determined to break the cycle.

The prince of Gordyene, just twenty years of age, stood before me in his scale armour cuirass, black leggings and red tunic – the uniform of Gordyene. Gallia stood nearby, also in armour and buckling her sword belt.

'I have decided to give your brother one last chance to save his capital from destruction,' I told him. 'I want you to ride to Vanadzor and persuade Castus to relinquish his crown. As I am feeling generous, I will allow him and his bride to depart Gordyene to seek a new home beyond Parthia's borders. Perhaps the Roxolani will offer him a wagon so he can live among his friends and allies.'

Haytham looked relieved. 'I will be delighted to do so, majesty. You are a generous and great king.'

'Make sure my generosity is not abused, Haytham. You are the only one standing between peace and bloodshed.'

He bowed his head to me. 'I will not fail you, majesty.'

He rushed from the tent, eager to be the one to save his homeland from destruction. He had betrayed his brother's plans to allow the Hatrans to save Nisibus and the north of their kingdom, and that betrayal had weighed heavily on him. I had never questioned him about why he had left his brother's side, but in truth I was grateful for him doing so for it had prevented Spadines and his Aorsi from taking Nisibus.

'You have made a grave mistake, Pacorus,' said Gallia.

'How so?'

'Castus is made of the same material as his father and grandfather, his blood grandfather. He will see your gesture as weakness and will use it to motivate his people to fight harder. All you have done is thrown more tinder on the fire.'

'You know what we are walking into, Gallia, don't you? A blood fest, an orgy of killing. The Romans killed Balas and Orodes killed Surena. I do not wish to be remembered as the man who killed another ruler of Gordyene, not least because he is the grandson of the man I loved, and whose son I swore to protect.'

She walked over and gently cupped my face with her hands.

'You are a good man, Pacorus, an honourable man. But not everyone shares your view of the world or possesses your morals. By his actions, Castus has revealed his true nature. He will refuse your offer.'

'I had to make it,' I said, rather pathetically.

She kissed my cheek. 'I know.'

The army's rate of advance slowed as we neared the Pambak Valley where Vanadzor was located. The valley itself is long and narrow and running through it is the river of the same name, a torrent in springtime when filled with melt water, a narrow, fast-flowing watercourse the rest of the year. The maximum width of the valley is around half a mile, making it ideal for defence, surrounded as it is by tree-covered hills, through which run streams filled with cool, clear water. The southern and eastern regions of the valley are densely forested with beech and oak, the north and west less so but still enough of an obstacle to channel an army into the valley floor. The valley itself is some twenty miles in length, which meant we had to adopt a dense formation to avoid being strung out too much, thus inviting ambushes.

Chrestus was in an agitated mood, looking left and right up at the hills on either side as we advanced east through the valley to approach Vanadzor from the west.

'It's too quiet,' he complained, casting glances left and right.

Ahead of us were companies of cataphracts, beyond them horse archers, on the flanks more horse archers and behind us the legions marching in two columns, between them camels, carts and mules carrying supplies, plus Lucius' siege engines. The rearguard was formidable, comprising cataphracts and many companies of horse archers. Scouts hovered around the army like flies around freshly laid dung to detect any signs of the enemy. Thus far, they reported seeing nothing.

I had informed Akmon and Pacorus of Haytham's ride to the city with my olive branch, which his brother had approved of. Pacorus had been less committal, still harbouring a desire to see Castus punished. I reasoned with him that removing him as king and sending him into exile was more desirable than reducing Vanadzor to ashes.

'My brother will see sense,' Akmon assured us.

'Sense and your brother have been strangers up to now,' said Pacorus. 'I see little reason for that to change.'

'He has been seduced by Yesim,' said Akmon, 'his mind is not his own.'

Pacorus scoffed at the notion.

'Seduced? A king who allows his wife to interfere in the affairs of his kingdom is clearly mentally deficient.'

'Is not Cia queen of Elymais?' asked Gallia. 'Does she not rule that kingdom?'

'On the advice of those more qualified than herself, yes,' answered Pacorus. 'And she is glad to be guided by wiser heads.'

'Tell me, Pacorus,' said Gallia. 'Do you consider women to be inferior to men?'

'Not inferior, aunt, just not suitable to wield power. The world is ruled by men, after all.'

'Indeed,' agreed Gallia. 'But who rules the rulers?'

Chrestus laughed, to the chagrin of Pacorus. The budding argument was halted by Talib galloping up. He bowed his head to me, ignoring Pacorus and Akmon, to the annoyance of the former. He momentarily glanced at Akmon.

'Your presence is requested, majesty.'

'Requested by who?' I asked.

'Something you should see, majesty,' he answered evasively. 'I would not ask if it were not urgent, majesty.'

I looked at Gallia, who shrugged.

'Very well, Talib, lead on.'

He turned his horse and galloped away. I followed. We rode through Hatra's cataphracts and Dura's horse archers advancing at walking pace, joining up with three of Talib's Agraci scouts who followed close behind as we rode east at speed. My eye caught sight of something standing upright in the ground in the middle a great patch of grass. I slowed Horns, realising immediately what it was. My heart sank and my head dropped. Talib and his men halted their horses to allow me to approach the totem alone. I halted Horns and slid off his back twenty paces from the pole, peering beyond it to see the Pambak stretching into the distance. Empty. I sighed and walked up to the pole, on the top of which was mounted the severed head of Haytham. Blood was running down the staff and on the prince's forehead was carved the word 'traitor'.

I closed my eyes and despaired.

Castus would fight. And many men would die before his fate was decided.

Chapter 18

I told Akmon in person that his brother was dead. His knees nearly buckled under him, but he managed to retain his footing and dignity long enough to compose himself. Drawing himself up, slightly shaking, he thanked me for informing him Haytham had been killed and told me mourning him would have to wait until the campaign was over.

Ending the campaign was the chief topic at the council of war held the next morning, the kings and Gallia assembled in my command tent where we listened to Kewab give us a precis of the obstacles we faced. Using wooden blocks placed on the table we ate at and held meetings around, he explained what we already knew, but nevertheless what he wanted to remind us of. He pointed to one block in the middle.

'Even if it was not guarded by strongholds to the east and west,' he pointed at four blocks on each side of the central block, 'Vanadzor itself has strong walls and a sizeable garrison. And the palace itself is a formidable citadel.'

We all nodded, being familiar with the defences of the Pambak Valley, waiting for Kewab to reveal how we would crack those defences, defeat Gordyene's army and bring Castus to justice.

'There are eight strongholds outside the city,' continued Kewab, 'four to the west, four to the east, each pair spaced two miles apart along the valley. The valley itself is only half a mile in width, which is the distance between each pair of strongholds.'

'Each stronghold is self-sufficient,' said a morose Akmon, 'with its own water supply, storeroom, stables and armouries.'

'So how do we deal with them?' I asked.

'We ignore them,' replied Kewab, much to my surprise. 'Each stronghold has a garrison of five hundred men.'

He looked at Akmon for confirmation. The King of Media nodded.

'Castus' best troops are his Immortals. If he ties up four thousands of them garrisoning his strongholds, he has already fatally weakened his field army.'

Pacorus stared at the table.

'We too will have to weaken our army to ensure the garrisons of the strongholds to the west of the city do not sally out to strike us in the flanks or rear.'

Kewab nodded. 'We need not worry about those strongholds to the east of the city, majesty, and can easily assign dragons of horse archers to guard against what you fear.'

Pacorus looked up at him. 'I fear nothing, satrap.'

I rolled my eyes but Kewab merely smiled.

'I meant no offence, majesty.'

'Carry on, Kewab,' I said, shaking my head at Pacorus.

Kewab pointed at the block representing Vanadzor.

'We strike at the capital, we breach its walls using Dura's siege engines and force King Castus to give himself up. However, I believe he will lead the under-strength Immortals against us before we reach Vanadzor, which will play into our hands and perhaps make the capture of the city unnecessary.'

'What makes you so sure?' Gallia asked him.

'Because, majesty, due to the success of Gordyene's army last year against Rome's allies in Cappadocia, Castus now believes that army is invincible. He has allowed us to enter his kingdom unopposed, Hatra's diversion doing its job, but now he has us in a valley where we cannot use our superiority in horsemen to outmanoeuvre him.'

'It would be preferable to meet Castus in the field,' I said, 'rather than battering our way into Vanadzor, with all the attendant horrors that will ensue. Whatever our views of Castus, Gordyene is still a Parthian kingdom and one that occupies a strategically important position. If it is fatally weakened, both Armenia and Rome will seek to exploit the situation, of that I have no doubt.'

We fell into silence, staring at wooden blocks on the table, each of us considering how it had come to this. The appearance of Chrestus diverted us from our thoughts, the general pacing crisply up to me and bowing his head.

'Scouts report the army of Gordyene is approaching, majesty, foot and horse.'

'How may foot and horse?' I asked.

'All the Immortals, flanked by a few thousand horsemen,' he replied.

Kewab was surprised. 'All the Immortals, are you sure?'

Chrestus nodded. 'Can't be certain, but Talib has campaigned with the soldiers we are about to fight and he knows them and his job.'

'It would appear you have underestimated King Castus, satrap,' Pacorus said to Kewab. 'He appears to believe he can brush us aside like a horse swats away flies with its tail.'

The King of Hatra stood. 'He will soon be disabused of that notion.'

The Durans and Exiles were eager to get to grips with the Immortals, both to decide once and for all who were Parthia's best foot soldiers, and to avenge the humiliations heaped on their king, and by extension themselves. They marched out of camp with a steely determination on their faces and resolution in their step. Around them, horse archers rode out to form a screen to mask the deployment of the legions, behind which the cataphracts formed up in their companies. In the centre of the rapidly forming battle line was a stand of banners, a coterie of kings, and one queen.

The Durans and Exiles adopted a formation of five cohorts in the first line and five behind, in what the Romans called *duplex acies*, with the second line cohorts offset to the left of those in front of them. In this way they covered the half-mile span between the two strongholds, though leaving enough space between the stone citadels and their flanks so any arrows shot from the battlements would fall short. Talib and his men, plus Hatra's own scouts, were crisscrossing the ground to provide as much intelligence about the enemy as possible. They reported the battlements of each stronghold were filled with soldiers, whetted spear points glinting in the angry blue sky.

'The Immortals will soon fill the gap between the two strongholds to seal the valley, majesty,' he told me.

Pacorus was impatient. 'We should send the cataphracts forward before they do so.'

'It's too late,' I told him. 'The Immortals will merely form shield walls, against which the horses of the cataphracts will be reluctant to charge at. And even if they do, they will head into a blizzard of javelins just before impact which will destroy their momentum.'

'It is worth the risk,' said Pacorus, angrily.

'No, it is not,' I said. 'The Immortals have scorpions like my own legions, and a scorpion bolt can go through scale armour with ease.'

'Then what?' he demanded.

I turned and beckoned Sporaces to attend me.

'Send forward the horse archers to shower the Immortals with arrows,' I told him when he was adjacent to me.

He saluted. 'Yes, majesty.'

'After the horse archers have forced the Immortals to halt and adopt *testudo* formations as a defence against out arrows, the Durans and Exiles will attack,' I informed Pacorus and Akmon. 'I would appreciate the assistance of Hatra and Media in this effort.'

It took time to organise nearly twenty thousand horsemen into four formations, each one numbering five thousand men, every individual carrying two full quivers of thirty arrows. In an act of churlishness, Pacorus insisted that Hatra's ten thousand horse archers be on the right flank – the place of honour on the battlefield. On the left were Sporaces' men and Akmon's horse archers.

The ammunition trains came forward to be nearer the horse archers to make re-supplying them with full quivers easier. I also rode forward with Pacorus and Akmon, our respective bodyguards trailing, to follow the battle that was about to begin more closely. Horns, sensing the tension in the air, began tossing his head up and down in impatience, eager to join the fray. I patted his neck.

'Easy boy.'

The sight of the legions advancing always made me tingle, the sun reflecting off thousands of javelin points and helmets, ten thousand soldiers marching in perfect unison, as though a single mind was directing each and every one. Even facing the prospect of death or serious injury their discipline never faltered. Train hard, fight easy. On the flanks of the two legions, thousands of horse archers, deployed in their companies, were trotting forward. Once the legions had halted around four hundred paces from the enemy, the horsemen would deploy in front of the Durans and Exiles and then gallop forward in files, wheeling their horses to the right some fifty paces from the Immortals. The rider at the head of each file would shoot his arrow just before he wheeled to the right, stringing and shooting another arrow as he galloped along the front of the enemy line, then turning his horse right again to withdraw from the Immortals. He would swing in the saddle and shoot a third arrow over the hind quarters of his horse just before the rider following him blocked his view of the enemy.

Some ninety-five companies of horse archers were now deploying in front of the legions, each one ready to shoot an average of one arrow every ten seconds – a total of five thousand, seven hundred arrows raining down on the Immortals every minute. Even for veteran troops, such a withering storm of arrows would take a physical and mental toll. And then they would be hit hard by the Durans and Exiles before they had time to recover.

Trumpet blasts brought my attention back to the centre of the enemy battle line, which, to my great surprise, was moving. Backwards!

'The Immortals are retreating.'

I heard Gallia's words but did not believe them. But my own eyes did not deceive me, and I saw the divisions of mail-clad foot soldiers, cast in the same mould as Dura's legions, showing their backs to us as they retreated.

'You can run, but there is nowhere to hide,' spat Pacorus beside me. 'Now we have them.'

Sporaces and the commander of Hatra's horse archers were professionals and I saw riders galloping from their respective knot of senior commanders to relay the order that I would also give: all companies to deploy to the flanks. I clench my fist when I saw horse archers break formation to head towards gaps that had suddenly appeared between the retreating Immortals and the strongholds that had anchored their flanks. Castus had garrisoned those strongholds but what use were soldiers manning walls when his Immortals were about to outflanked by thousands of horse archers? If our own horsemen managed to get behind the Immortals, Castus' men would face being shot at from the flanks and rear while being attacked head-on by the Durans and Exiles. I had no doubt Castus' own horsemen were behind the Immortals, but they too would be shot at by our horse archers flooding into the expanding gaps between the retreating Immortals and the strongholds.

And then the gates of those strongholds opened.

We sat in silence, unable to tear our eyes away from the horrible spectacle as horsemen flooded from the strongholds, smashing straight into the flanks of the dense formations of horse archers cantering past.

A horse archer is most effective when operating over large open spaces, where his speed and manoeuvrability can be used to optimum effect. When attacked at close quarters by horsemen armed with spears and swords and equipped with shields, he is terribly vulnerable.

And so it was now.

Gordyene's medium horsemen, attired in red tunics, black leggings and scale-armour cuirasses, smashed into the horse archers and went to work with their spears, swords and axes. They were greatly outnumbered by the horse archers, but the latter wore no armour and carried only swords as a back-up weapon. Within minutes, hundreds had been knocked from their saddles by spears as Gordyene's horsemen got among them and then went to work with their swords. Company commanders ordered their men to withdraw, signallers relaying their commands. But the horse archers had to run the gauntlet of hundreds of armoured riders slashing left and right with their swords and axes after they had used their spears to skewer our riders.

'Send forward the cataphracts,' shouted Pacorus to no one in particular, his body quivering with rage and frustration.

'No,' I said firmly. 'They will only get caught up in the chaos on each flank. We must trust the commanders on the spot to extricate their troops.'

They did so with difficulty, and many horses with empty saddles joined the throng of now disorganised and weakened companies making their way back to safety. Mercifully, Gordyene's medium horsemen did not follow. But while they had been causing mayhem and murder among our horse archers, the Immortals had about-faced to return to their original positions. The gates of the strongholds were slammed shut, the Immortals had been unharmed in the battle on the wings that had worsted our horse archers, and from their perfectly aligned and full-strength divisions galloped red-uniformed horse archers.

Just as we had intended to pepper the Immortals with arrows, so did Gordyene's horse archers now gallop through the gaps between the divisions of Castus' foot soldiers to unleash volleys against the Durans and Exiles. I did not worry unduly about this albeit unwelcome development. Dura's legionaries had been under volleys of missiles before and instantly adopted the formation to defeat them: the front ranks kneeling, the second and subsequent ranks hoisting their shields above their heads to form a wall and roof of hide and wood that easily absorbed the shower of arrows raining down on them. The horse archers would not stray too far from the Immortals, not with three thousand cataphracts lurking behind the cohorts of the Durans and Exiles.

An angry and sweating Sporaces rode up and saluted.

'I cannot tell you how pleased I am to see you,' I said to him.

'How glad *we* are to see you,' Gallia corrected me.

He gave her a weary smile. 'The companies are reforming, majesty, but we lost many men to the spears of the enemy horsemen. I did not realise Shamshir was such a good general.'

I thought of the repellent head of Gordyene's army and discounted the notion, then remembered Hovik visiting me.

'Shamshir is an imbecilic sycophant. This is Hovik's work, of that I am sure,' I said.

The whooshes to our front proclaimed volleys of arrows being shot at the legionaries, but with the now depleted companies of horse archers reforming to the rear of their flanks, I was not unduly concerned. If Castus wished to waste his arrows, I was more than happy to let the shields of my Durans and Exiles be his pin cushions.

'What now, uncle?' Pacorus pressed me.

I tapped my nose. 'Castus has played his hand and given us a bloody nose. But he can only use his stronghold trick once, and once his horse archers have exhausted their ammunition, our own will ride forward to keep the heads of the Immortals down prior to the Durans and Exiles attacking.'

Talib appeared, winking at Minu holding my standard behind me. He bowed his head to me.

'They are dummies on the battlements of the strongholds, majesty.'

This did nothing to sweeten my nephew's humour.

'Dummies?'

'Smoke!'

We all turned to where Akmon was pointing, at the stronghold anchoring the Immortals' right flank, from which came thick smoke. The black pillar rose into the sky, to be followed by a second pillar of smoke coming from the other stronghold.

'Castus is firing his forts?' said Akmon in disbelief.

A chill went down my spine.

'No, they are signals.'

Pacorus laughed. 'To whom?'

The answer was revealed a few minutes later when one of Talib's men, a swarthy individual in tatty black robes, galloped up and reported to his lord, ignoring the three kings and one queen in close proximity.

'Many horsemen approaching from the west, lord.'

Talib remained calm. 'Who?'

The man spat out phlegm right in front of my nephew's horse.

'Aorsi and others, probably the lords of King Castus.'

Pacorus was appalled, though not about the appearance of the enemy behind us.

'Is this how you conduct yourself in front of your king? I have never seen such disrespect.'

He drew his beautiful sword and pointed it at the Agraci scout.

'Arrest him.'

Two of the gilded officers of his bodyguard walked their horses forward.

'Halt!' I said loudly. 'Dura's scouts are in my service, not Hatra's. If the Royal Bodyguard wants to do something useful, it will join Dura's cataphracts in dispersing the new threat that has appeared behind us.'

Pacorus looked at me in disbelief.

'You are sending the cataphracts against a rabble of Aorsi and Gordyene's lords?'

I had had enough of his petulance and arrogance. I pointed behind me.

'Our camp containing our supplies, siege engines and tents is two miles distant. It is currently protected by squires only. And then there are the hundreds of camels of our ammunition trains between us and camp, which will be easily taken if the rabble, as you so dismissively call them, reach them. So yes, Pacorus, I am sending the cataphracts against them.'

'Azad!'

The commander of my cataphracts came forward. I instructed him to lead his dragon against the approaching threat.

'Media's cataphracts will join them,' said Akmon, wheeling his horse to the right to follow Azad.

I looked at Pacorus. 'Hatra's cataphracts can remain here, the safest place on the battlefield, should they so desire.'

The insult stung the two officers sporting white plumes in their burnished open-face helmets, both forgetting about the Agraci scout and looking imploringly at their king. Pacorus gave me a hateful glance and turned his white stallion, white being the colour of all the horses of Hatra's Royal Bodyguard. I smiled when he plucked a *kontus* that had been thrust into the ground behind him from the soil, the two officers following.

'I see you have not lost your talent for diplomacy,' said Gallia dryly.

A succession of trumpet blasts announced that three thousand cataphracts had about faced and were cantering west to meet the Aorsi and Gordyene's lords, who if they had any sense would quit the battlefield and flee back to the hovels they had come from.

'Thank you, Talib, you and your men have once again saved our arses,' I said.

'White smoke.'

Our attention was diverted from the departing cataphracts back to the forts, from which was coming columns of white smoke, not black.

'The enemy horse archers are retreating, majesty,' said Talib.

He was right. The shooting had ceased, and the companies of red-uniformed horse archers were riding back through the divisions of the Immortals, which now charged.

They did not have to advance far, for unbeknown to all of us, General Motofi, their commander, had used the volleys of his horse archers to mask the movement of ten thousand foot soldiers forward. So, when they assaulted the Durans and Exiles, they did so from less than a hundred paces. I thanked Shamash that my own foot soldiers were highly trained, for if they had received the Immortal assault from a stationary position, they would have suffered heavy casualties. Instead, Dura's centurions led their legionaries forward without waiting for orders to even the odds.

Thousands of men screamed their war cries and hurled their javelins, the air suddenly filling with thousands of spears as the first two ranks on each side hurled them forward, followed by a second volley when the third and fourth ranks also threw their javelins. What sounded like a blade being scraped along a rock face followed as the front ranks smashed into each other, soldiers identically armed and equipped using their short swords to stab at enemy faces, groins and necks.

It was carnage.

As the front ranks stabbed at each other and those behind waited for men in front to either fall or advance, the five, sixth and subsequent ranks hurled their javelins at the enemy. There was a constant criss-crossing of javelins in the air, the heads either slamming into shields, earth or finding flesh. The thin metal shafts bent on impact, making them impractical for further use. Now the air was filled with the familiar sounds associated with close-quarter combat: screams, yelps, roars and a constant tapping noise as *gladius* blades struck shields, helmets and other sword blades.

I saw Chrestus and his senior officers riding up and down the line, shouting encouragement to his men and issuing orders. On the flanks of the legions were our battered horse archers, uncommitted, and I knew that behind the Immortals were Gordyene's own horse archers, and behind them Castus and his King's Guard and Vipers. Castus had made me commit our cataphracts by offering his lords and Aorsi allies as bait. His Immortals were grinding their way into the Durans and Exiles and the battle was heading for a stalemate. But if we were stopped from advancing on Vanadzor and laying siege to the city, the scales of war would tip in Castus' favour. We could not remain in his kingdom indefinitely, and the longer we did so without having destroyed his army, the weaker we would become.

'Castus has out-witted us.'

Gallia put into words what I was thinking. He had planned his battle to perfection. And yet…

I turned to Minu. 'Send one of your Amazons to fetch Kewab. With haste.'

Kewab, Parthian satrap, native of Egypt and soon to be governor of that ancient land, for surely now the prospect of him becoming King of Gordyene had probably vanished. Unless…

The complete commander, attired in a simple white tunic and scale-armour cuirass, appeared moments later, saluting both me and Gallia.

'Majesty?'

'We are facing a stalemate,' I told him. 'But you and your men can provide the key to unlock the enemy's position.'

He and his horsemen had been guarding the ammunition trains and had formed our reserve. More prickly commanders would have refused such a 'lowly' responsibility. But Kewab was a general who knew how battles could ebb and flow, making even supposedly insignificant formations the keystone of success, or failure. So it was now.

'I am going to pull back the legions,' I told him, 'to lure the Immortals forward and thus create gaps between their flanks and those wretched forts.'

He nodded. 'And you wish me to lead an assault into one of those gaps.'

'Yes. Your men are armed with lances as well as bows. Well, at least half of them. Get behind the Immortals and create a barrier with your lance-armed men to prevent Castus using his horse archers and King's Guard assisting his foot soldiers.'

I pointed to our left flank. 'I will follow you with my own horse archers.'

He was shocked. 'You, majesty?'

'I am not yet in my dotage,' I told him. 'Now go. The battle now rests on your shoulders, Kewab.'

Gallia pulled her bow from its case and grinned at me.

'Just like the old days, eh?'

'Just like the old days.'

I dug my heels into Horns' side and rode over to where Chrestus was directing his own personal battle.

'We are struggling to hold them,' he told me bluntly.

'Pull the Durans and Exiles back,' I ordered him, 'we are going to mount an outflanking manoeuvre, but to do so we need an exposed flank.'

He relayed the command immediately, wishing me good fortune as I rode away with Gallia and the Amazons towards the left flank. I ignored Hatra's horse archers on our right flank, knowing their commander would not budge until he received authority from his king, who was leading his cataphracts against enemy horsemen. But I hoped that when the legions pulled back, he would spot the opportunity to lead his companies through the gap. I had no time to worry about Hatran sensibilities.

After being told of my plan, Sporaces marshalled his companies once more, perhaps four and a half thousand, maybe less. The commander of Media's horse archers, a handsome young man obviously of great wealth judging by his blue saddlecloth edged with gold and his dragon-skin armour, rode up and bowed his head.

'I request permission to join the attack, majesty.'

'I am not your king,' I replied.

'My king would wish his soldiers to assist his friend and ally, majesty.'

'Very well, ensure your men have full quivers.'

He bowed his head and rode back to his blue-uniformed units.

'There's a sight we don't see often.'

Prompted by Gallia's words, I turned in the saddle to see the Durans and Exiles falling back, the second-line cohorts doing so impeccably, what was left of the first line of each legion disentangling themselves with difficulty from the divisions of the Immortals they had been battling.

What an unholy mess.

There was a succession of sharp cracks as the scorpions of the second-line cohorts began shooting, their crews picking their targets carefully to avoid hitting their comrades in front. The machines attached to centuries in the front line had either been captured or disabled in the fighting. At least the scorpions of the Immortals had not been brought into play on account of the speedy attack mounted by Castus' foot soldiers in the wake of our cataphracts having to depart to deal with the threat to our rear.

Kewab marshalled his horsemen into long columns, at the front of which were his eastern veterans. Behind them came the red-uniformed exiles from Mesene, all professionals who had been trained by my friend Nergal. For a moment a great wave of sadness washed over me when I looked round and saw none of my friends present. They were all gone, either dead or retired, mostly the former.

'Pacorus!'

I heard Gallia's sharp tone and snapped out of my self-pity. I gripped Horns' reins and urged him forward. Gallia and the Amazons followed, passing company after company of horse archers. To our right the Durans and Exiles were still slowly withdrawing, the Immortals, having first re-dressed their mangled ranks, following. They were delayed by the heaps of dead and dying at their feet – the result of the brutal mêlée that had taken place earlier. But they advanced nevertheless, and in doing so moved beyond the forts that had rendered them splendid service thus far. And there it was – an inviting gap through which we would ride.

To either glory, or death.

Over fifteen thousand horsemen galloped through that gap, all carrying four or more quivers of arrows, for it would be too dangerous for the ammunition trains to follow us. Once more the Durans and Exiles had halted and were again locked in deadly combat with the Immortals. Of necessity, the plan was simple: Kewab and his three thousand easterners, reinforced by Mesene's horse archers, would head straight for Gordyene's horse archers standing behind the Immortals, either scattering them or, more desirable, killing them. Meanwhile, I would wheel the horse archers of Dura and Media right to take them behind the rear divisions of the Immortals. We would then shoot volley after volley of arrows at those divisions in a battle of attrition until our ammunition was spent.

Gallia had poured scorn on the notion we could shoot the Immortals to pieces.

'They carry shields identical to our own foot soldiers. They will merely adopt a *testudo* formation.'

She was right, but even if only one in ten arrows found its mark, we could still kill several hundred Immortals. And Kewab's lancers, working closely with the horse archers of Mesene, would hopefully reap a richer harvest against Castus' horsemen. It was a gamble. Better that than doing nothing.

Horns strained at the leash as he thundered down the ranks of the Immortals, whistles and trumpets sounding to halt and turn their rear divisions. I saw soldiers frantically manhandling scorpions to turn them around to face the new threat that had appeared behind them. I glanced over to my left to see hundreds of Kewab's men charging away from us.

I peered at the fortress that had anchored the left flank of the Immortals, hoping to see white-uniformed horse archers coming from our own right flank – the horsemen of Hatra. I saw nothing and cursed. Their commander would obviously not move without direct orders from his king. So, thousands of Hatran horse archers stood idle while we fought like demons.

Kewab's attack bought us time to halt, face right and shoot at the Immortals from a stationary position. Nine thousand stationary horse archers shooting from a static position can unleash a lot of arrows, and with a high degree of accuracy. But all company commanders had been issued orders that they passed on to their men: no rapid shooting, search for targets, do not waste arrows.

The first to die were the scorpion crews, though not before some had shot iron-tipped bolts at the dense ranks or horsemen less than fifty paces away, skewering horses and knocking them to the ground. But the crews were exposed and were shot multiple times by archers. There was a loud, continuous whooshing sound as thousands of arrows were shot at the now locked shields of the Immortals. We shot not at the shields but at their edges and tops, hoping a bronze head would force its way between shields locked together.

I shot arrow after arrow at the wall of shields in vain, the metal heads thudding into the hide-covered wood and turning individual shields into pin cushions. But it did not matter because we had diverted the attention of the second-line divisions of the Immortals from the battle being fought by those in the first line. And the longer we pinned them down, the greater the likelihood of those in the first line faltering. Chrestus would be able to exchange his battered and depleted first-line cohort with the fresh, full-strength ones behind, and tilt the battle in his favour.

I heard the roar of war cries and shouted in triumph. But then stopped and cocked my ear. They were coming not from the front but from my right, the direction we had ridden from. Gallia and the Amazons had heard it, too, and they ceased shooting and peered in the direction of the tumult, other companies doing likewise. I looked at her and we both knew what it was heralding was nothing good.

'Reform,' I called, 'wheel right.'

The Amazon signaller sounded her trumpet and within seconds Gallia's bodyguard had wheeled right and formed into two files.

'With me!' I shouted, digging my knees into Horns' flanks to urge him forward.

We retraced our tracks, Sporaces and his companies doing likewise. But it was too late.

They came flooding from the trees that blanketed the northern hillside of the Pambak Valley, a screaming horde of men and women carrying spears, axes, knives and slings. And it was the latter doing the most damage to the mounts of Dura's horse archers. The Pontic hill men, and women, were just a screeching mob, widely spaced and totally devoid of any semblance of discipline. But they had achieved surprise and were possessed of a feral courage, literally hurling themselves at mounted soldiers and stabbing at bellies of horses with their weapons.

They were Yesim's' people, dressed in rags, many barefoot and all devoid of headgear. I had seen and killed many Pontic hill men over the years, but this was different. They had caught us totally by surprise and washed over us like a great barbarian wave. The companies nearest the gap we had ridden through had already been overwhelmed, warriors and their womenfolk stabbing at unhorsed men and their animals in a dreadful scene.

'Wedge!' shouted Gallia, reins wrapped around her left wrist and leaning forward in the saddle.

The Amazons flanked left and right and began shooting, creating a swarm of arrows in front of us to scythe down everything in its path. But Yesim's people were not just in front. They were to the left, right and behind us. They were everywhere, thousands of them.

'All-round defence,' ordered Gallia.

The Pontic barbarians were like ants around us, difficult to kill but enormously irritating. In response, companies of horse archers became disorganised, ran into each other and their horses reared up when hill men screaming war cries stood in front of them. Many of Yesim's people were shot down and trampled on in the chaos, but we had to get back through the gap, which was swarming with hill men darting around like flies, adding to the confusion and resulting in an ever-growing press of humans and horses.

The Amazons provided a rallying point, companies flocking to my griffin banner. I ordered their commanders to lead their men back through the gap, which though occupied by scattered groups of hill men, showed no signs of constricting. Arrows and sling shots were hissing through the air. Riders were going down after being hit by sling shots, though at least the swirling throng of humans and horses made it as difficult for slingers to identify targets as it did for our own archers.

Sporaces, thankfully still alive and unhurt, reported to me, shaking his head at the chaos around us.

'We tried, majesty.'

'That we did. Now we have to extricate ourselves from this mess.'

A shrieking hill man, axe in hand, ran towards us, only to be hit by two arrows shot by Haya and Gallia behind me, the missiles thudding into his unprotected chest. He fell to his knees and swayed to and fro, dropping his axe and staring in our direction with vacant eyes. He disappeared when trampled on by a column of horses, their riders wearing leather armour – Kewab's men.

The area became even more crowded as more and more of the satrap's riders, plus the red-uniformed horse archers from Mesene, headed for the gap. For the moment, the hill men around us disappeared as they were either speared, shot down or trampled on by the Egyptian's horsemen.

The satrap himself appeared moments later, accompanied by a bodyguard of his soldiers. He saluted to me and nodded to Sporaces.

'We inflicted losses on their horse archers, majesty, but as soon as I heard about the attack from the woods, I withdrew my men.'

'You made the right decision,' I told him. 'Did you see Castus?'

'We saw a red banner beyond the horse archers but not the king himself.'

'Get your men to safety,' I commanded. 'I am sorry.'

It suddenly occurred to me that he would not now be King of Gordyene. Castus had fought us to a standstill, his army was still intact, and he would be able to renew hostilities in the morning. I felt a blow to my belly and saw a round stone fall to the ground beneath me. A slinger had obviously identified me and had hit me. My cuirass had stopped the shot and dissipated its power. Kewab and Sporaces both wore looks of concern.

'I live to fight another day,' I said. 'Time to depart.'

Yesim's people, having forced us to retreat, were themselves withdrawing, back to the trees where they had been hiding. They left hundreds of their comrades behind in the valley, which was now carpeted with human and equine corpses. I took comfort in the fact the Immortals were also shuffling back after their titanic battle with the Durans and Exiles.

No one was fighting now or making blood-curdling threats to the enemy. As if by mutual consent, both sides had stopped hacking at each other and made no attempt to interrupt the other's withdrawal from the field of honour. I had no idea why it was called so, being an arena of horror, fear and tragedy. Once I had lived to make war; now I shied away from its intoxicating allure and saw it for the great deception it was. Or perhaps I was just too old and my wrinkled eyes had seen too much bloodshed over the years. But those eyes did not deceive me. I saw men limping back to camp, others, too wounded to stand, being assisted by one or two comrades. Others, life draining away from them, lay on the grass gripping the hands of their friends, desperate not to die alone and forgotten. At that moment, if any man had told me this was glory, I would have struck him down.

Our horse archers and Kewab's lancers had escaped through the gap and were trotting back to camp, glancing behind to ensure Castus did not have one last trick to play on them. But just as we were tired, hungry and thirsty, so were his soldiers drained of energy. It was quiet now, aside from the mournful cries of injured men crying out for water, or their mothers. They were vastly outnumbered by the dead, who did not speak.

Gallia and the Amazons cantered on, but I pulled up Horns when something caught my eye: a bright flash that lasted but a split-second. It was probably the sun reflecting off a spear point or sword, but whatever it was, I halted Horns and turned in the saddle. I saw a group of Immortals standing in line, watching me. I looked around for more of their comrades but saw none. Most odd. There were six of them, and in unison they rested their shields on the ground and removed their helmets.

I nudged Horns towards them and sheathed my sword. Time stood still and the valley emptied as I beheld long-lost friends. In the centre stood a tall individual with cropped hair – Spartacus. Beside him, a squat, dark-haired man with a deep scar down the right side of his face – Akmon, Spartacus' deputy in Italy. I recognised the long face of the German Castus, the long black hair of Vagharsh, and the fierce, black-haired warrior we had once crossed an ocean to save: Burebista. And at the end of the line stood a thickset man with a chiselled face and narrow black eyes. My friend, my general and the man who had moulded Dura's army into a powerful instrument: Lucius Domitus.

They attempted no speech and made no gesture. They just looked at me and in that moment I understood. I could never defeat Castus because in fighting him I was battling everything I had tried to build and held dear. Gordyene's army had been created in the image of Dura's legions. They were a mirror image of each other, and no one could reach into a mirror and grab a reflection.

'I understand,' I called to them.

The decision had been made. We were going home.

I bowed my head to my friends, tugged on Horns' reins and followed the Amazons back to camp. I looked back only once but saw no trace of them.

Chapter 19

Pacorus did not take my decision well. After five years of being the de facto ruler of Elymais and now the actual ruler of Hatra, he had grown accustomed to giving orders, not receiving them. Hatran princes and nobles were by their very nature often prickly and recalcitrant subordinates, all with a keen nose when it came to their honour being questioned or damaged. It did not help that he and his cataphracts, together with those from Hatra and Media, had enjoyed an easy victory against the Aorsi and Gordyene's lords, scattering them without having to break sweat and pursuing them for several miles to the east. Which was the whole point.

'While you were taking part in a glorified hunt,' I told him, my leg aching like fury and other parts of my body complaining in apparent solidarity, 'we were engaged in a more taxing engagement.'

He drank some more wine, his temper rising.

'Castus is finished,' he spat. 'One more battle and we will be feasting in Vanadzor.'

I closed my eyes and sighed.

'One more battle and my legions will be down to half-strength. They have lost one in ten dead and wounded already. Dura's horse archers lost nearly as many casualties, as did those of Media. I assume your own horse archers suffered casualties, notwithstanding their tardiness.'

Pacorus rolled his eyes. 'Soldiers die in battle, uncle. I assume Gordyene also suffered losses.'

A stern-faced Chrestus sitting beside me, nodded. 'Several thousand, majesty, by all accounts, especially when King Pacorus got behind the Immortals.'

An orderly poured Kewab some wine into his cup. The Egyptian looked tired, his face drawn and his hair unusually unkempt. Then again, it had been a hard day for all of us. Pacorus looked at him.

'And you, satrap, what would your estimate be of enemy losses?'

'Our flank attack in the afternoon caught them by surprise and my men inflicted some losses on the enemy's horse archers before they withdrew. But I would say in the hundreds rather than thousands, and my men suffered three hundred dead when the hill men came from the trees.'

'Joro informed me Media's horse archers suffered a similar number killed,' remarked a downcast Akmon, no doubt still thinking of the base murder of his younger brother.

'It comes down to a simple matter of attrition,' said Pacorus casually. 'Castus has less men than we have, his lords and Sarmatian allies have been defeated, and his field army has been weakened. If…'

I held up a hand to him. 'I will not see it weakened any further. Gordyene's army is a formidable instrument, but if it is destroyed, the Romans and Armenians, or indeed the Sarmatians, will take advantage and de-stabilise the whole of

Parthia's northern frontier. I will not do it, and my decision is final.'

'Then you have failed,' said Pacorus harshly.

'I can live with failure, Pacorus,' I told him. 'But I cannot live with destroying something I have spent my entire life trying to maintain.'

'Which is what?' he demanded to know.

'A strong and free Parthia.'

'Castus will never forgive you, lord,' said Akmon.

'Dura will never forgive Castus for his treatment of its king,' stated Gallia. 'Gordyene lost many sons today. Do we really want to make more widows and grieving mothers tomorrow?'

'Media does not,' said Akmon solemnly. 'And I do not wish to lose another brother. I too will be taking my soldiers home in the morning.'

Pacorus fell into a sullen silence. He knew that without Dura's legions, his own soldiers would be vulnerable in enemy territory without a marching camp to rest in each night. I was expecting him to unleash a withering verbal volley against me.

'You are lord high general, uncle,' were his only words before retiring for the night.

Later, lying beside Gallia, I told her about my vision on the battlefield, of how I had seen Spartacus, Domitus and others we had both fought beside in Italy.

'It was a sign and you were right to interpret it the way you did,' she told me. 'In any case, I have no appetite to see Vanadzor stormed and sacked.'

'Me neither. I doubt Pacorus will forgive me.'

She hugged me. 'Hatran honour can be most inconvenient. Killing Aorsi and Gordyene's lords and their retainers was obviously not enough to quench Pacorus' thirst for glory.'

'To a Hatran lord, reputation is all. They probably consider it an insult they had to fight nothing more than Aorsi and low-born chiefs from Gordyene.'

Satisfying Hatran honour was Pacorus' top priority during the following days, while the rest of the army rested and kept Castus' army pinned in the Pambak Valley. The day after the battle, both sides sent parties back to the site of the fighting to search for wounded. There was no further bloodshed as medics searched the carpet of corpses for any still living. Their investigation was mostly futile, though I thanked Shamash that one of the few brought back to camp was Centurion Bullus.

The moment I heard he was in one of the medical tents I went to see him. I could have wept at the sight that greeted me. The man in the cot was a pale imitation of the gruff, sturdy fighting machine I was used to. His frame was the same size, of course, but his cheeks and eyes were sunken, his face was deathly pale, and his torso was wrapped in bandages. He was sleeping when I arrived, so I pulled up a stool and waited for him to open his eyes. His breathing was shallow and I feared he might not live to see the evening.

'He should live.'

I turned to see Sophus, the Greek head of the army's medical corps, standing over me.

'Don't get up,' he said irreverently.

'He looks poorly.'

There was a roll of his blue eyes, unusual for a dark-haired, olive-skinned Greek.

'Having a number of wounds and laying out all night without water will do that, majesty. But his wounds are fortunately superficial and when he wakes he can be given water to refresh his body. By the bruising on his chest, I believe he was trampled on, so I suspect a few cracked ribs.'

The tent was filled with wounded men with what appeared to be non-serious injuries – sprained and broken arms, wrists and legs – the other medical tents accommodating those with lift-threatening and fatal injuries, such as head and belly wounds. Bullus opened his eyes.

'Ah, the hero returns to us,' said Sophus sarcastically. 'The king will attend to your needs.'

With that he was gone. I stood, walked to a table holding jugs of water, filled a wooden cup and returned to the cot. I lifted Bullus' head and pressed the cup to his lips.

'Gentle sips,' I told him.

He emptied half the cup.

'Thank you, majesty.'

'How do you feel.' It was a stupid question.

'Like I have been stamped on by a giant. Did we win?'

'A draw. I decided not to renew hostilities today, luckily for you. What do you remember?'

He thought for a moment. 'Huddling under our shields while being under an arrow storm, and then being hit by the Immortals. After that, it was a hard slog at close quarters for what seemed like hours. I must have tripped over something or someone, lost my footing and got crushed in the press.'

He moved his arm and winced.

'The doctor informs me you have some cracked ribs, so it's rest for you for the next few weeks, though I am afraid you will have to endure riding on a wagon for a few days, until we get to Irbil.'

'Castus lives to fight another day, then?'

'He lives to another day, Bullus.'

He and his army might have escaped destruction, but the Kingdom of Gordyene was not so lucky. Pacorus directed parties of horsemen to scour the countryside to the west and north of the Pambak Valley, not for food, for we had enough supplies for the march back to Media, but to plunder the land. It was wanton destruction, pure and simple. Villages were torched, crops destroyed and livestock killed. Pacorus was a seasoned veteran when it came to fighting hill tribes, and he used that knowledge to maximum effect. After a couple of days, pillars of smoke could be seen to the north and west, and captives were brought into camp. I went to see him after he had returned from leading a raiding party, he and his senior officers enjoying wine and good food around a great rectangular table set up in his large pavilion. When I was shown into the dining area, all conversation ceased.

Pacorus raised his jewel-encrusted rhyton to me.

'Uncle, how kind of you to visit. Make room for the King of Dura.'

A slave brought a chair for me to sit in at the far end of the table, facing my namesake. Other slaves were serving the young nobles at the table cooked venison, freshly killed earlier. They carried on eating but their looks told me I was an unwelcome guest, which saddened me.

'Have you eaten, uncle?' asked Pacorus.

A slave poured wine into a rhyton placed before me.

'I have, thank you. I am here on another matter.'

He placed his rhyton on the table. 'What matter?'

'There are a number of captives in camp, natives of Gordyene?'

'There are, and there will be more before we reach Media's border.'

The officers banged their fists on the table to show their approval.

'We are not here to capture slaves,' I told him.

'I thought we are here to punish King Castus, the man who authorised his Sarmatian dogs to plunder northern Hatra. Such insolence cannot go unpunished, uncle. Besides, the captives we have taken no longer have homes to go back to, or crops to gather in.'

The officers sniggered like children. Pacorus took a sip of wine.

'Hatra is not some helpless child to be cowered and abused, uncle. Gordyene will discover that it has made a powerful enemy, one who will no longer be counted as its ally.'

'Here, here,' said the officers.

'I would ask you to show restraint, Pacorus,' I pleaded, 'notwithstanding Gordyene's ill-advised aggression.'

'Just as individuals have to be responsible for their actions,' he said, 'so do kings. By his actions, Castus has put himself outside the family of Parthian kings. He and his kingdom will discover it is cold outside that grouping.'

'What of Media?'

He reacted with surprise. 'Media? It is a valued and trusted ally of Hatra, which is committed to protecting not only its own northern border, but that of Media also.'

He leaned forward. 'Will Dura support Hatra and Media if those two kingdoms are attacked by Gordyene in the future?'

Every one of his officers turned to stare at me, unblinking, with hardened expressions and resentment in their eyes. Why did they resent me? Perhaps they thought their king should be lord high general instead of me. Maybe they believed I was too old to command an army. More likely, they resented me for questioning their taking of slaves. They knew Dura, and its queen in particular, was opposed to slavery. But in Hatra and every other Parthian kingdom aside from Dura, slavery was a fact of life, an integral part of the functioning of cities, towns and households. I knew that when Gallia and I were gone, slavery would creep back into Dura itself. Eszter and Dalir had slaves in their desert mansion and as for Claudia, she cared not if every person in the world was enslaved as long as the gods were appeased and revered.

'Dura does not forget its pledges,' I answered, 'but neither will it be drawn into a conflict without end.'

He gave me a magnanimous smile.

'We are going home, uncle, are we not?'

We left the Pambak Valley two days later, Castus' army having marched from Vanadzor to usher us on our way. But we still outnumbered him and his lords and Aorsi allies had lost many men and women to the great cataphract charge, which had drawn away our steeled fist. So, while thousands of horse archers formed our rearguard and acted as flank protection, the wounded were loaded on carts, the siege engines were disassembled, their constituents also loaded on carts; and the army retreated. The rate of march was slow, partly to guard against ambushes and attacks from Castus' troops, but mostly because Pacorus was insistent he and his horsemen should carry on their campaign of reprisal against just about everything he and they came across. They even killed wild animals and birds, not just for food but because they wanted to slay anything living in Gordyene. It was a thoroughly miserable time and I was glad to reach Media, as was Akmon, though he feared for his kingdom's future.

'With Castus having ejected us from his kingdom,' he said, 'he will be emboldened to attack Media once more, especially after the damage that has been inflicted on Gordyene.'

'I would not worry about Castus,' Gallia said to him, 'he will have other things to concern himself with.'

I assumed she was referring to Hatra's desire to continue the war with cross-border raiding, which would certainly divert Castus' attention away from Media but would hardly make him less aggressive.

'Hatra intends to launch reprisals against Gordyene for the Aorsi attack against Nisibus, Akmon,' I told him.

His head dropped. 'Castus will not sit back and take such provocation lightly.'

Gallia reached over to lay a hand on his arm.

'The gods will protect Media.'

Once more, I thought it an odd thing for her to say but gave it little credence. What troubled me more as we began the last leg of our journey back to Irbil was the empty land we marched through. The terrain was green and fertile, but villages were deserted and overgrown, a consequence of Spadines' assault on Vazneh, which had prompted Akmon to order the evacuation of the land south of the frontier with Gordyene. Whereas eastern Media was devoid of all life due to the locust plague, northern Media was empty of people. It was a truly depressing sight, as were the camps of refugees surrounding Irbil itself when we reached it. It appeared the city was besieged by a great army, an army of refugees that was stripping the city of its supplies of food.

After a tearful reunion between Akmon and Lusin and a parade by Media's returning soldiers through the city, Akmon ordered proclamations be read in all the camps, stating the north was secure and people should return to their homes without delay. Whether they would do so remained to be seen. Lucius, my quartermaster general, came up with a plan that would not only encourage the refugees to return to their homes, but which would also strengthen Media's northern frontier. I invited him to the palace to explain his scheme to the king and queen, plus General Joro. Pacorus, eager to get back to Hatra, had already departed, but in a touching gesture had promised to send a thousand camels loaded with food to Irbil once he had returned to his capital where his wife and sons were waiting for him.

We sat in the white-painted gazebo in the garden to the rear of the palace, drinking fine wine and nibbling on slices of fruit and grapes and breathing in the air scented with pine and cedar. Royal gardens were designed to symbolise paradise and the four elements: sky, earth, water and plants. They incorporated cypress trees – associated with the Tree of Life – and evergreens such as cedar and pine to symbolise the continuity of the royal line. Fountains and ornamental ponds gave life not only to the fish swimming in them and the plants they watered, but also to the royal family who lived in the palace. Symbolism was combined with practicality. Thus, shady and wide-leaf trees such as rowan, sycamore and aspen were also present to bring welcome relief from the sun.

The aged Joro, hair as white as snow, stood behind his king and queen as Lucius explained his notion, being interrupted by the radiant Lusin before he started.

'Will you not sit, general? I feel as though I am a child again about to be chastised by my tutor.'

Joro cleared his throat and sat himself down, tipping his head to his queen.

'That's better,' she smiled. 'Now, General Varsas, tell us about your idea.'

Lucius, crop haired and clean shaven, looked directly at the queen, which Joro found irritating. In his eyes women had no idea about military affairs, which is why he viewed units such as the Amazons with a barely concealed contempt.

'A basic principle of defence, majesty,' began Lucius, 'is deterrence. But at the moment, Gordyene is not deterred from sending raiding parties into northern Media. That being the case, I propose the construction of a number of forts spaced at twenty-mile intervals, between which will be watchtowers.'

Joro was unimpressed. 'Watchtowers will not stop raiding parties, general.'

Lucius turned away from the queen.

'No indeed, lord, but messages can be passed quickly between watchtowers by means of flags, torches and smoke. In this way, the nearest fort, which would contain a garrison of horsemen and foot soldiers, would be quickly alerted.'

'There is a fatal flaw in your plan, general,' smiled Joro, the first time I had seen his face wear such an expression. 'Your watchtowers would be very vulnerable and could be burnt with ease.'

'No, lord,' replied Lucius. 'For one thing they would be made of stone, be five times the height of a man, therefore could not be burnt. The entrance will be on the first upper floor by means of a ladder, which would be pulled up when the garrison was not entering or exiting.'

'How many men would staff each watchtower?' asked Akmon.

'Five men should suffice, majesty,' said Lucius. 'The soldiers would sleep on the upper second floor, just below the outside gallery from where they could look out in all directions.'

'I would like you to build these watchtowers,' said Lusin.

Lucius looked at me.

'General Varsas will be delighted to oversee the construction of both the towers and the forts,' I said.

'Will Dura be providing the soldiers to garrison these forts and watchtowers?' asked Joro.

It was a good question. Media had few professional soldiers aside from the garrison of Irbil, and they were needed to man the impressive walls that had been built by Lucius.

'I will leave the walking wounded here,' I replied, 'which amounts to three hundred legionaries. To these I will add a further two hundred, which equates to a cohort. Enough to staff the watchtowers and forts. In addition, I will also leave five hundred horse archers here to man the forts. A thousand soldiers, General Joro.'

He smiled graciously. 'That would be most acceptable, majesty.'

'I intend to make Centurion Bullus commander of these troops,' I announced, 'once his ribs have healed.'

Lusin was delighted. 'The hero of the siege of Irbil. His family must come to live in the citadel. Does he have a family?'

'He has a son, majesty,' I said, not wanting to tell her the child was a bastard.

'And a wife?' she asked.

'Alas, they have yet to be married,' I answered.

Joro cleared his throat in disapproval but Lusin would not be deterred.

'His son and woman will come to Irbil and Lord Bullus will marry her in the temple in the citadel.'

'Quite right,' smiled Akmon.

Gallia raised an eyebrow. 'Lord Bullus?'

'A centurion is a rather lowly station for such an important position,' said Akmon. 'Bullus should have a rank commensurate with his authority and reputation.'

'Reputation?' I said.

'Bullus is a Median hero, lord,' Lusin told me, 'who is beloved of the gods.'

I thought of the coarse, thuggish Bullus and his relish for killing.

'He will certainly administer northern Media with an iron hand,' I conceded, 'though he may ruffle a few feathers doing so.'

'Alas, lord,' said Akmon, 'there are no lords in the north of my kingdom to ruffle. They either died fighting my father or fighting for Prince Atrax.'

'I can think of one,' said Lusin, reaching over to clutch her husband's hand. 'We should make Klietas a lord.'

Joro's smile disappeared instantly.

'I would advise against that, majesty.'

'Why is that?' asked his queen.

'Klietas is a commoner, an orphan who is the son of commoners who has no wealth, no land and no heritage. To make such a man a lord would debase everything that nobility stands for.'

'And what does it stand for?' demanded Lusin.

Joro stroked his white beard. 'Continuity, majesty, and stability. The men who serve in the king's bodyguard are the sons of those who served King Darius and King Atrax the senior. And their grandfathers fought for King Farhad.'

'You are right, general,' nodded Akmon, 'but as a counter-argument, I would contend that exceptional circumstances demand radical measures. I am no religious expert, but I wonder if, Media having lost so many lords, the gods are inviting us to create new ones to fill the vacuum.'

'And Klietas has proved he has noble attributes,' added Lusin. 'It is surely no coincidence he and King Pacorus crossed paths, and he went on to save the king's life. I think the gods wish Klietas to be made a lord.'

She paced a finger to her fulsome lips.

'In any case, Klietas turned his back on a life of ease and luxury to serve Media. Is that not correct, lord?' she asked me.

I thought of the hovel Klietas had been living in when he was a Duran farmer, albeit one with promising prospects.

'Yes, majesty.'

She clapped her hands together. 'So, it was the will of the gods he returned to us. He should therefore be rewarded, for we do not want to offend the gods, do we, General Joro?'

Joro was totally perplexed but had neither the inclination nor interest to argue with his queen.

'No, majesty.'

Queen Lusin had her way, and two days later we stood in the Temple of Shamash with the fine lords and ladies who lived in the rarefied atmosphere of the citadel to bear witness to Klietas being made one of their own. My former squire, dressed in a simple blue tunic, grey leggings and barefoot, was kneeling in front of the altar with his head bowed. Standing him before him was a stern-faced high priest dressed in a white robe, upon which had been stitched slivers of gold to make his attire glitter in the sunlight. And there was a lot of sunlight.

The main entrance to the temple faced east to welcome Shamash as he began his journey across the heavens each day, its white-stone walls and gold-leaf covered double doors presenting a deliberate brilliance to the world. The doors had gold handles and the interior of the temple was filled with the heady aroma of burning cassia and myrrh, incense being burnt to make the Sun God feel welcome and enable mortals to more easily converse with immortals. Large windows allowed sunlight to flood into the interior, and white marble tiles and columns supporting the arched cedar roof accentuated the light to create a dazzling effect that made everyone squint. The effect was deliberate to emphasise that no matter how rich or powerful the congregation, they were but mere bedazzled mortals in the presence of Shamash. The tall, imposing high priest was framed by the large gold disc behind the altar, engraved to represent the rays of sun.

Anush, dressed in a beautiful blue dress loaned by the queen who stood next to her, looked overawed to be in such a grand building among her social superiors. But her piety and deference probably made her the most religious among this august throng. I smiled when I saw her close her eyes and begin to pray, mouthing words as she opened her soul to the Sun God.

Gallia and I jumped when the high priest began to talk in a booming voice.

'You are in the presence of Shamash, Lord of Light, the all-seeing king of the heavens, giver of life, who sees and hears all.

'Who gives this man to be made a lord of Media?'

Akmon, wearing a suit of dragon-skin armour that caught the sun's rays to create an image of a shimmering demi-god, which was the idea, stepped forward.

'I, Akmon, rightful King of Media, do present Klietas of Vazneh to you, High Priest Castor, intermediary between the realm of men and Shamash, the Sun God and protector of Media and its people.'

Castor stepped forward and placed his hands on the top of Klietas' head.

'Repeat my words, Klietas of Vazneh.'

The high priest began to recite the oath of loyalty, which Klietas repeated word for word.

'I, Klietas of Vazneh, swear to you Akmon, King of Media, that from this hour I will be faithful to you with regard to your life, and the members of your family, in good faith and without deception. And I will help you to hold, have and defend against all men and women who might wish to seize or deprive you of property and land.

'Before Shamash in this holy sanctuary and before these witnesses, I will be true and faithful, and love all which He loves and shun all which He shuns, according to the laws of the Sun God and the natural order of the world He has created. Nor will I ever with will or action, through word or deed, do anything which is unpleasing to Shamash or my king, on condition that they will hold to me as I shall deserve it.'

Castor stepped back and held out a bony hand to Klietas.

'Take my hand and rise up a Lord of Media. Rise up, Lord Vazneh.'

Klietas rose unsteadily to his feet, totally overwhelmed by his surroundings and the proximity of so many lords and ladies, plus his king and queen. Castor turned to walk to the altar, before which was laid a sword in a scabbard, a leather belt, a scale-armour cuirass and a pair of expensive leather boots.

'Step forward, Lord Vazneh, to arm and armour yourself so you may go forth to do the king's bidding.'

I had no sons, but I felt like a father to Klietas as he put on the boots, armour and sword and received the kiss of fealty from Akmon, Lusin threading her arm in Anush's, to lead my former squire's wife to Media's newest lord. He had come a long way since I first clapped eyes on a scrawny half-starving orphan waiting to die at Irbil. I thought he had made a mistake leaving Dura, doing so only because Haya had deeply wounded him. But I now realised Shamash himself had taken an interest in Klietas and had decreed that he should return to his homeland. Now he was a lord in the north of that land, perhaps the only lord, around which a new Media would be built. With Dura's help.

The gods are infallible and we can never hope to unravel their thoughts.

Lusin took a keen interest in the recovery of 'Lord' Bullus, moving him into the palace and assigning a royal physician to his care to speed his return to health. Before we left for Dura I went to see him. His room was large and airy, with frescoes of dancing dragons on the walls, a large bed, couches and a table for reading and writing at. The patio doors decorated with gold leaf opened into the royal garden and Bullus had his own personal slave to fetch and carry for him.

I found him propped up in bed wearing a blue silk robe, his chest still bandaged. He looked bored to distraction and totally out of place. But at least he cheered up when he saw me.

'I have a surprise for you,' I said, pulling up a chair.

His eyes lit up. 'You've come to rescue me from this gilded prison, majesty?'

'Alas, no. But in addition to your promotion to cohort commander, King Akmon is going to make you a lord. My congratulations.'

'The gods save me.'

'The queen has informed you your wife and child are to be brought to Irbil.'

'She's not my wife, majesty.'

'Ah, well, that is another thing someone should have told you about. Now that you are moving in polite society, the king and queen felt you should be married. Appearances, you see.'

He sighed. 'Well, at least I will be up and about soon, and then I can go north and become a soldier once more.'

'Navid will be commanding the five hundred horse archers to accompany your cohort,' I told him. 'Try to keep him under control.'

He laughed, then winced when the movement hurt his ribs.

'I will, majesty.'

'And take care of Klietas and his wife. I'm too old to keep coming back to Media to save his hide.'

I stood and extended an arm. We clasped forearms.

'And you take care of yourself, Bullus. No heroics.'

'No heroics, majesty, I promise.'

We left Media stronger than we had found it, or at least had weakened Gordyene sufficiently that it would no longer pose an immediate threat to Akmon's kingdom. And the Roxolani had been driven out of Parthia, though at a high cost. Now, at long last, we were going home.

Chapter 20

The army made a leisurely march back to Assur, the legions no longer singing as they tramped along the bone-hard road under a fierce summer sun. They had their equipment strapped to a *furca* – a pole around four feet in length with a crossbar – to which was attached an entrenching tool, cloak, water bottle and food bowl. Their helmets dangled from the front of their belts, their javelins were shouldered and their shields carried on their backs under the *furca*, the former supporting the latter. In an emergency, the kit could be dumped, helmets put on heads and shields and javelins made ready for battle in no time at all. I had a feeling the legions were in a mood for bloodshed after the disappointment of Gordyene.

'The legions appear sullen,' I said to Chrestus.

'They feel they have been robbed of victory, majesty,' he replied, swatting away a fly with his hand. 'And they were wondering why we dragged the siege engines all the way to Vanadzor without using them.'

'An army is not a society of friends and equals,' said Gallia brusquely. 'Commanders issue orders and soldiers obey them.'

But I was in a more reflective mood and I saw no reason to keep Chrestus in the dark.

'I did not have the stomach for further bloodshed, and no enthusiasm at all for battering down Vanadzor's walls and killing Gordyene's king, for I am certain Castus would never have allowed himself to be taken alive.'

'I remember when King Spartacus visited Dura for your sixtieth birthday celebrations, majesty,' said Chrestus, 'when things got a little heated.'

Gallia guffawed. 'You mean when Spartacus made a fool of himself? I remember that evening. What a child he was.'

'It's easy to love folly in a child,' I smiled. 'Carry on, Chrestus.'

'Well,' continued the general, 'I remember him squaring up to me and saying that one day the Immortals and our legions would face each other in battle. I told him I prayed such a day would never come. But it did. But we will also never know which of the two was the best. Gordyene's Immortals or Dura's legions.'

'What is your opinion, Chrestus?' asked Gallia.

'We would have overcome them, eventually, majesty,' he answered.

'Technically, our campaign was a great success,' opined Kewab. 'We defeated the Sarmatian menace, inflicted damage on Gordyene and its army, and avoided a costly and time-consuming siege of Vanadzor. And we have taken measures to strengthen Media's defences.'

'You are truly a man who views a cup as half-full rather than half-empty, Kewab,' said Chrestus.

I exchanged glances with Gallia. If Kewab knew the truth concerning the throne of Gordyene, he would not be so positive about a campaign that should have ended with him being crowned King of Gordyene. I had denied him the chance to become a king, and now he would leave Dura to become the governor of Egypt. Such is fate. The arrival of Talib interrupted my musings, my chief scout bowing his head and handing me a letter.

'From Princess Claudia, majesty,' he informed me. 'She is in Assur.'

The town was around twenty miles away – a two hours' ride on horseback. I broke the seal and opened the papyrus, Gallia looking intently at the yellow document, Talib and Minu exchanging smiles.

Father

I am at the dreary town of Assur, awaiting your urgent arrival on a matter of high import for the empire. Please come as quickly as you can, if only to save me from the boorish conversation of the governor. And bring Kewab.

Claudia

I passed it to Gallia and pointed at Kewab.

'You are with me, satrap. We have urgent business in Assur.'

'May I enquire as to the nature of said business, majesty?'

'If I knew, I would tell you, Kewab.'

'I'm coming too,' said Gallia, turning to Talib. 'You are welcome to accompany your wife back to Assur if you wish.'

He flashed a smile. 'Thank you, majesty.'

'You have command of the army, Chrestus,' I said. 'Make camp on this side of the river tonight. There is no need to rush our return to Dura.'

'Yes, majesty.'

We rode with the Amazons to the pontoon bridge across the Tigris and crossed it to arrive at Assur as the afternoon sun was beginning to set in the west, turning from a brilliant yellow to a calmer orange as it did so. We found Claudia waiting for us in the governor's courtyard, standing beside the dour Rodak. My daughter had an annoyed expression on her face and began rebuking me as soon as I had alighted from Horns.

'Have you been on a leisurely detour, father? Perhaps you should get a faster horse.'

She walked past me to embrace Gallia, and then bowed to Kewab.

'Welcome, majesty.'

Kewab was bemused, as was I.

'We are in no mood for your dire attempts at humour,' I snapped.

'I am here on the orders of King of Kings Phraates, father, to inform Satrap Kewab that he is to be made King of Carmania.'

I was astounded, as was Kewab, who nearly fell off his horse.

'Carmania?'

'A kingdom in the east of the empire, father, directly south of Sakastan, and now in dire need of both a king and internal order.'

When we had retired inside the governor's residence, Claudia informed us more fully of developments in the east. Of how King Phanes, the mad ruler of Carmania, had poisoned his entire family at a lavish banquet, before killing himself by climbing up to the roof of his palace and throwing himself off. In the days prior to the fateful feast, he had apparently been telling everyone that he had grown a pair of wings, which were of course invisible to all save himself. When courtiers had laughed in his face, thinking he was joking, he had had them and their families impaled in the palace grounds. No one was sorry to see the back of Phanes, but he had killed his son Babak, who had been the de facto ruler of the kingdom.

'With Babak gone,' said Claudia, 'Carmania has descended into civil war. King Salar and my sister are very concerned about their southern frontier.'

Salar, my son-in-law, was King of Sakastan, and the last thing he needed was chaos to the south of his realm, especially as his kingdom bordered Kushan lands to the east.

We reclined on couches and were served wine by slaves, Rodak's chief steward fussing over us. Claudia batted away a silver tray holding honey cakes.

'Time is of the essence. If Carmania descends into chaos, the Kushans will undoubtedly take advantage to place one of their supporters on the throne.'

'You are forgetting one thing, daughter,' I said casually. 'Kewab is to be the governor of Egypt.'

My daughter's visage hardened. 'The choice between becoming a Parthian king or a Roman lapdog? No choice at all, I would have thought.'

'That is for Kewab to decide,' I smiled.

But Claudia knew much about Kewab and played her hand superbly. She looked at the satrap.

'Of course, Menwi would become Queen of Carmania and your children would instantly become princes, the oldest guaranteed to inherit your throne when you leave this world, as would his eldest son, and on and on.'

I honestly believed Kewab was not an overly ambitious person, in as much as highly talented people do not need to devote much time to furthering themselves, as their genius seems to attract rank and power. But Menwi was an altogether different prospect, as I had discovered. She was ambitious, and probably hectored him incessantly about how he was unappreciated by Parthia, which is probably why he was so happy when on campaign. He may or may not have put much store in titles, but Menwi would not be able to resist the offer of becoming a queen.

'If Parthia has need of me, princess,' said Kewab, 'then I will not desert the empire.'

I stood and embraced him. 'This is a great day for Parthia.'

I did not lie.

For the previous ten years Kewab had proven himself a great commander, perhaps the empire's greatest. He had single-handedly fought the Kushans to a standstill, devised the battle plan that had saved our arses when I had allowed an army to be caught at Kayseri, which had routed the enemy, and had then aided Castus in achieving a crushing victory over an enemy coalition outside the town of Melitene. The Egyptian graduate of Dura's Sons of the Citadel scheme had excelled expectations beyond anyone's wildest dreams, and I thanked the gods he would be staying in Parthia.

'I assume you will be writing to the Romans to inform them of your decision, majesty?' said Claudia.

'I hope they will not be too disappointed,' reflected Kewab.

'I'm sure they will be amply compensated, is that not correct, mother?'

Claudia gave Gallia a mischievous grin but my wife's jaw locked rigid.

'Have more respect in the presence of your parents,' she hissed.

Claudia switched her attention back to Kewab.

'High King Phraates wishes for you to be crowned at Ctesiphon before you and your family travel to Carmania, majesty. If that is convenient.'

'It would be an honour, princess,' smiled Kewab.

'You are most gracious, majesty,' said Claudia, displaying a deference I never thought her capable of. Clearly, the years at

Ctesiphon had honed her political skills, as well as her capacity for skulduggery.

'I wonder if I might have a few moments in private with my parents, majesty,' she said softly.

Kewab, as gracious as ever, rose and bowed to Gallia and then me.

'Of course. If you will excuse me.'

'You don't have to bow to us, Kewab,' I said, 'you are a king, or soon will be. We are your brother and sister now.'

He blushed. 'Yes, majesty, thank you, majesty.'

'You can go, too,' Claudia said to Rodak.

Rodak took his leave like a chastened child being told to go to his room.

'Idiot,' hissed Claudia before he had shut the door to the room.

She clicked her fingers and pointed to her rhyton, indicating it should be topped up. A slave rushed forward and did so. She picked up the drinking vessel and settled back in her chair.

'So, the Sarmatians have been sent packing with their tails between their legs, Phanes is thankfully dead, his crown will pass to one far more capable, who will make the east of the empire strong, and Castus is still King of Gordyene. The gods have been kind.

'May I have the ring back I loaned you, father?'

I pulled the gold ring from my finger and handed it to her.

'I had no idea I would wreak devastation on Media.'

Claudia rolled her eyes.

'You did not, father, not unless you have turned into a god. It was divine help that aided you in your battle against the Sarmatians.'

'I was not talking of that,' I snapped.

'Oh, then what?'

'Your father grieves for the thousands who might starve as a result of the locusts having stripped eastern Media bare,' said Gallia.

Claudia was unmoved. 'The needs of the empire outweigh considerations for the welfare of commoners. The Sarmatians represented a grave threat to Parthia's very existence. I hear you met their leader, father.'

'Tasius? Yes, I found him both intelligent and dangerous.'

'All the more reason to get rid of him and his people as quickly as possible,' said Claudia.

She giggled. 'Phraates was near panic when Silani and Otanes were defeated so soon after King Ali, King Scylax and Prince Khosrou were beaten. Once again, you saved the day, father.'

'I assume from your irreverent tone that Silani and Otanes are alive, or at least I hope they are,' I said.

'Oh, they are alive,' replied Claudia. 'They made it back to Ctesiphon with most of their army intact, if not their pride or honour.'

She looked at me with an evil glint in her eye.

'Phraates was considering dismissing Ali from his position of lord high general and awarding you the position until you die.'

I groaned. 'If you have any influence with Phraates at all, you will dissuade him from doing so.'

She sipped some wine. 'Have no fear, father, I convinced him you are too old and your mind is too addled for such a demanding position.'

Gallia laughed. 'What it is to have a loving daughter.'

'Kewab will be lord high general in the future,' mused Claudia, 'after he has had time to settle into his new position, of course. So, in a way, father, your influence will still be safeguarding the empire.'

It was an indication of Claudia's influence and power at Ctesiphon that two hundred Babylonian lancers, all dressed in gleaming dragon-skin armour and wearing purple plumes, had escorted her to Assur. She was also accompanied by a large retinue of slaves, camels carrying her pavilion, and a hundred Scythian axe men to guard said pavilion when it was pitched for the night. More significantly, she had been given a copy of Phraates' personal seal to write letters on the high king's behalf, should she be so inclined. It was a visible sign of the trust Phraates placed in Claudia, though knowing the high king's cunning nature, he was also courting the support of the Scythian Sisters, who wielded immense influence throughout Parthia.

In an insult to Rodak, who for whatever reason Claudia had quickly grown to despise, she slept not in his residence but in her pavilion pitched by the side of the Tigris north of the town. South of Assur, the river was full of the stinking effluent produced by its residents and was to be avoided at all costs. That night I visited her in her plush mobile palace, waited on hand and foot by beautiful female and handsome male slaves. They contrasted sharply with the fierce and ugly Scythians who stood sentry around the tent, one of whom barred my way after I had left Horns at the temporary stables made of canvas and wood where the Babylonians' horses were also quartered.

'Name?' he grunted.

I regretted not bringing a party of Amazons with me, who were instantly recognisable throughout the empire.

'Pacorus of Dura, father of Princess Claudia.'

He looked me up and down. 'Wait here.'

The other axe man with him gripped his huge two-handed weapon in a menacing fashion while his companion disappeared inside the pavilion, reappearing moments later and holding open one of the entrance flaps.

'You may enter, lord.'

Inside, I walked on soft, plush carpets, was welcomed by a smiling slave no older than thirty wearing a silk tunic that would not look out of place on the body of a king, and found Claudia sitting behind a mahogany desk in a huge chair with arms carved in the shape of cobras. In her black robes and in the half light of oil lamps on stands either side of her, she looked malevolent and far from the carefree woman we had seen earlier.

'Sit, father.'

The slave pulled up another high-backed chair and placed it in front of the desk. I took the weight off my feet.

'The Sisters are aware of the great service you have rendered the gods and Parthia, father,' she said solemnly.

'I have always tried to do my duty.'

'We heard of the treatment meted out to you at Vanadzor and were appalled. That Castus should treat a great servant of the immortals and the empire in such a way was reprehensible.'

'I survived,' I said, attempting levity.

'Do you want Castus and his whore wife dead, father?'

I flinched at her words. I knew the Scythian Sisters were sorceresses, so why not assassins? After all, had not Gallia's assassins been tutored by Saruke, Dura's resident poisoner?

'No,' I said firmly. 'I have always fought for a world where justice and the rule of law are held sacred above all things. Murder is murder, no matter how you dress it up.'

She gave a gentle shake of the head. 'You fight for a world that will never exist, father.'

'That may be, Claudia, but the gifts you and your sisters have been given should not be used to settle petty disputes.'

She laughed. 'All disputes are petty, father, in the eyes of the gods. But the immortals do not regard insults and humiliations meted out to one they favour as petty, far from it.'

'I cannot speak for the gods, only myself. Castus and Yesim are not to be harmed, not in my name, in any case.'

She pointed at me. 'You prefer to kill people yourself, instead of allowing others to do it? I understand. You were, after all, going to remove Castus and put Kewab on Gordyene's throne. Castus dying in the defence of Vanadzor would have satisfied your sense of justice and honour, I suppose.'

I stood and refused the offer of wine from a nubile female slave.

'This conversation is at an end.'

'Nothing ever ends, father, as Castus will discover.'

I rounded on her. 'You are forbidden to kill him, or his wife.'

She held up her hands. 'They will not die at our hands, I swear.'

'It is just a game to you, isn't it?'

'Not just a game, father, the *great* game. A game without end.'

There were times when I could have cheerfully wrung her neck, but Claudia was not entirely callous. She wrote letters on the high king's behalf to Atropaiene and Hyrcania requesting they send grain to Media 'for the relief of that kingdom, which was raped by the marauding Sarmatians', and she also promised that Babylon and Susiana would also send supplies to Akmon. Together with Hatra's promised aid and the food I would send from Dura, the people of Media might just make it through the winter.

She and Phraates were obviously anxious for Kewab to be crowned as quickly as possible, so she was insistent that he return with her to Ctesiphon. She had already sent a letter to Rsan charging him to arrange for Kewab's family to be escorted to the high king's residence 'without delay'. In an emotional scene, Kewab got to say goodbye to Dura's army, which I paraded in its entirety on the morning of his departure. The Durans and Exiles cheered him as he rode beside me and Gallia as we trotted among the cohorts, then took to banging the flats of their swords against the front of their shields and chanting 'Kewab, Kewab', as he passed by. He must have stopped at every cohort to shake the hand of its commander, doing the same at the companies of horse archers and cataphracts. It took all morning but no one minded. Kewab was a true son of Dura and every legionary, horse archer and cataphract recognised that Carmania's gain was Dura's loss.

I stayed at Assur with Gallia for a day longer than Claudia, to ensure Dura's army could still transit through Hatran territory to get home, King Pacorus being in a volatile mood since he had been denied his chance to burn Vanadzor, and to pen a letter to Hatra's new ruler imploring him not to raid Gordyene. It was probably a futile plea, knowing full well the fine lords of my city of birth would be calling for vengeance against Gordyene even as I wrote the words. In any case, Pacorus had spent years quelling the hill tribes of Elymais and was an accomplished warlord. And now he could raise one hundred thousand of his own troops to punish Castus if he so wished. He was too good a commander to launch a full-scale war but raiding and plunder would keep his lords amused and satisfy their desire for vengeance, and the result would be years of bloodshed and an end to the alliance between Gordyene and Hatra that had served the empire so well.

Knowing this, it was with a heavy heart that I departed Assur for Ctesiphon in the company of my wife and the Amazons, plus Talib who was happy to be riding alongside his wife. But I had done my best and took a grim pleasure in knowing that at least I would not be responsible for the deaths of Castus and Yesim. The latter I had no feelings for either way, but Castus was the grandson of the man who had been one of my dearest friends, as I was reminded in the Pambak Valley, and I could not be the man responsible for his death, even if he had killed his own brother. Castus would answer for his crimes, either in this life or the next, but my conscience was clear regarding his ultimate fate.

Phraates had his faults, no one could deny that. He had a very malleable view of the truth, and often lied on occasion when it suited him. He could be cruel, manipulative and pusillanimous. But he knew how to put on a spectacle. When we arrived at Ctesiphon, the jewel in the Parthian crown, whose walls faced with white stone were kept pristine by an army of slaves washing each stone on a daily basis, we found it bedecked with peacock standards. Ctesiphon was in reality a mini-city, a sprawling complex housing thousands, the only difference between it and the nearby city of Seleucia was that at Ctesiphon every resident was hand-picked.

Phraates was a direct descendent of the kings of Persia, his mother having been Babylonian, as was her father and his father before him. And just as the Persians had displayed their power and prestige by undertaking grand building projects to honour the gods, so had Phraates lavished much wealth on the restoration of Ctesiphon to create a second Babylon. And so, its huge gatehouse had become a replica of Babylon's famed Ishtar Gate, comprising a huge double gate decorated with over five hundred figures of bulls and dragons. This led to Ctesiphon's version of the Processional Way, a road eighty feet wide paved with white limestone and red breccia slabs. Babylon's Processional Way was flanked by high walls, punctuated by buttresses and towers, but at Ctesiphon the walls were lower to allow bystanders to gather behind them and cheer and wave at the high king as he left and entered his great palace. But no expense had been spared when it came to decorating the walls with glazed bricks depicting rows of striding lions, the animals being the symbol of the Goddess Ishtar, who had her own temple in the palace complex.

Sentries on the gatehouse's battlements alerted the commander of the guard that a party of riders leading camels was approaching, which led to a unit of Babylonian lancers riding to intercept us. Or rather welcome us when the commander of the party, a devilishly handsome young man in dragon-skin armour with purple plumes in his gleaming helmet, recognised my griffin banner and the scarred, haggard face of the King of Dura. He sent back one of his men to alert the palace of our approach, falling in beside me after removing his helmet and bowing his head to Gallia. In the distance, I saw tents pitched to the south, perhaps a couple of miles away, near the river.

'Who are they?' I enquired.

'The horsemen of Satrap Kewab, majesty,' he replied.

'Why are they not inside the walls?'

'There is not enough room for them, majesty.'

I smiled and looked at him. He was the epitome of what Ctesiphon represented: nobility, youth, attractiveness and wealth. Their commander may have been feted by the high king, but there was no place for Kewab's rough-hewn, squat and ugly horsemen among the beauty and opulence of Ctesiphon. What a contrast between their scruffy, dour appearance and the officer riding next to me, whose horse was decorated with a large purple saddlecloth edge with gold, with golden bulls stitched in every corner, and whose bridle was studied with small gold bulls.

Above the gatehouse flew the banners of the two kingdoms Phraates ruled directly – the horned bull of Babylon and the eagle clutching a snake of Susiana – but when we rode through the entrance on to the road leading to the royal palace we saw the route was lined with a different standard. The iron-shod hooves clattered on white paving stones as we passed the specially built walls on each side of the road decorated with glazed bricks depicting standing lions, the symbol of Ishtar, the Goddess of Love. Either side of the road flew large red banners emblazoned with a golden peacock – the standard of Carmania and a salute to its new king.

Carmania got its new king a week later, in a grand coronation held in Ctesiphon's magnificent throne room. The ceremony that was a mixture of religion, theatre and superstition was conducted by the Temple of Marduk's high priest, a stolid individual with a thick beard, bulging eyes and powerful voice. I thanked Shamash seating had been arranged in the white marbled hall, because it seemed to go on forever and my leg would have given way long before the golden crown was placed on Kewab's head. As it was, the seating made the ceremony almost bearable.

Hundreds were packed into the chamber, all seated according to their social standing. As such, Gallia and I were in the front row, along with kings Ali, Scylax, Silani, Prince Khosrou and Satrap Otanes. Menwi, to her obvious delight, was also seated in the front row. The day was the culmination of all she could have hoped for and she wore a permanent smile that must have made her facial muscles ache by the end of it.

Ali still had his arm in a sling, the result of the wound that had incapacitated him at Lake Urmia.

'Sneaky bastards attacked us at night,' he complained.

'You should surround your camp with a ditch and rampart when on campaign,' I told him.

'Horsemen don't like to dig trenches, Pacorus,' he complained. 'Besides, you sent the Sarmatians on their way and put us all to shame.'

'I had some assistance.'

'The locusts? I heard. What are the odds?'

I looked at Claudia sitting next to Phraates on his throne, on his other side Adapa, commander of his bodyguard and the holder of the prestigious title 'master of a thousand'.

'I got lucky,' I said.

Everyone stood when Kewab entered the chamber, dressed in a white robe upon which diamonds had been stitched, dozens of them. He was escorted by white-robed priests chanting prayers, one holding a white cushion, upon which rested the gold crown that Phraates would place on Kewab's head. One of the priests began reading from a papyrus scroll, informing the congregation in a loud voice of Kewab's noble descent, his innate worth, wisdom and sense of justice, thus announcing to the world his qualifications for kingship.

Everything was pre-planned down to the smallest detail. Kewab's ludicrous costume was designed to awe the guests and to suggest he was possessed of magical powers. That he was sacred and capable of dispensing justice and prosperity, just as a god can dispense life and death. Tears of pride ran down Menwi's face when, after a seemingly never-ending recital of prayers, Phraates stood and placed the crown on the head of a kneeling Kewab, afterwards giving him the kiss of brotherly love.

The hall fell silent when Kewab turned and pledged to all present he would act responsibly and piously as King of Carmania, would defend the high king and Parthian people, as well as his own, and would dispense justice equally to lords and commoners alike. Thus was Kewab, formerly lord high general in the east, satrap and Lord Melitene, made King of Carmania. His wife was now a queen and his two sons, barred from being present on account of their youth, were princes of the empire. Claudia's prophecy had come true.

In the three days of feasting, hunting and general revelry that followed the coronation, I barely saw the new king or his queen. Protocol demanded they stay until the end of every evening feast, but I was able to slip away before the hour was too late. I did manage to see him when Phraates, who had insisted Kewab attend him every day, cosseting him in his office and taking him on trips to the Hall of Victory and his private gardens to see his collection of peacocks, tigers, lions and other exotic animals, had to retire to his quarters due to a headache. We walked through the corridors of the palace, courtiers and officials fawning and bowing to us both, which Kewab found embarrassing.

'You will get used to it,' I told him. 'When do you leave for Carmania?'

'Tomorrow, lord,' he said.

'You must call me Pacorus now,' I told him.

'That would feel strange, lord.'

'I just wanted to thank you, Kewab, for all that you have done for Dura, and Parthia.'

'It has been an honour, lord, and I will try to prove a good and honest king.'

'One more thing. If I had a son, I would want him to be like you, Kewab. Stay true to yourself and always trust the instincts that have served you so well to date.'

I extended my arm. 'The gods bless you, Kewab.'

He grasped my forearm. 'And you, lord.'

After Phraates and everyone else had formally said farewell to him and Menwi the next day atop the palace steps, I rode down to the gatehouse and climbed the steps to the battlements to observe the King of Carmania lead his army east. In addition to his own horsemen, Phraates had commanded that Otanes, his old subordinate, should ride east once more to support Kewab in quelling any insurrection in his kingdom. Accompanying him were a thousand cataphracts and five thousand horse archers from Susiana, plus a thousand camels carrying their supplies. Kewab would travel south through Susiana and Persis, where King Silani had pledged another two thousand horsemen to his army, and on to Carmania. I watched the column of horsemen and camels slowly fade into the distance, reflecting that I might never see Kewab again. But I took comfort he would still be in Parthia as opposed to Roman-controlled Egypt.

'King Pacorus.'

I turned and was surprised to see Phraates himself on the battlements. I bowed.

'Highness.'

'Watching Parthia's new hero embark on his quest?'

'Yes, highness.'

He was dressed in a flowing purple silk robe with a gold belt around his waist. A slave held a large parasol over his head to shield him from the sun. I wondered how he had ridden to the gatehouse in such garb, for he surely did not walk.

'I want to show you something.'

He walked to the edge of the battlements giving views of the interior of the palace complex, pointing down.

'What do you think?'

I peered down to see a chariot pulled by four black horses, a slave standing in the box holding their reins. I wanted to laugh.

'It is very convenient for getting around the grounds,' he said. 'I don't know why they went out of fashion.'

'In Rome, they are still in fashion.'

He scowled at the slave holding the parasol, who had not been paying attention. Phraates pointed up at the sun.

'The sun's over there, idiot.'

The slave moved the parasol so he was once again in the shade.

'What of Castus, highness?'

His brow creased. 'What of him?'

'You said you wanted him dead, if I recall, and I was wondering if you were still intent on removing him from power.'

'King Castus has been unwise in his decisions of late,' said Phraates, 'but now Kewab has a kingdom to rule, I do not desire Gordyene to be thrown into chaos. In any case, you had a chance to remove Castus but faltered, did you not?'

Phraates could always be relied upon to point out an individual's failings.

'It was the will of the gods that I did so, highness,' I smiled, having no wish to be drawn into an argument. 'But I assume you will be summoning Castus to Ctesiphon to answer for his crimes?'

He looked past me, totally disinterested.

'I do not think such a drastic course of action would solve anything, King Pacorus, especially as King Castus has pledged reparations to atone for his misdemeanours.'

I raised an eyebrow. 'Reparations, highness?'

'A significant sum of gold,' he informed me guardedly, 'which I feel brings the subject of King Castus' transgressions to a satisfactory conclusion.'

I felt otherwise.

'May I remind you, highness, that King Castus is responsible for the empire facing a crisis of monumental proportions, resulting in significant loss of life, damage to property and the wrecking of Media's economy.'

He did not take my mini-lecture well, his nostrils flaring as he raised his voice.

'And may I remind *you*, King Pacorus, that I am king of kings of the empire. I grow tired of hearing of King Castus. And you should be more grateful. You wanted me to find a position for Kewab and I have done so, eager to appease your prickly sense of honour.'

He lies like the rest of us breathe.

'But, highness…'

He stopped me dead. 'But nothing, King Pacorus, the matter is closed for discussion.'

So that was that. Castus had effectively bribed Phraates and the high king was more than happy to swell his already bulging treasury with more gold. I was going to suggest he donate the reparations being paid by Gordyene to alleviate Media's woes, but though better of it.

A smile replaced the high king's frown. 'Now, to other matters. Now, where was I? Oh, yes, the Romans. Negotiations with them are entering a critical stage, King Pacorus. I hope to have my son back beside me in a matter of months.'

'I pray for that, highness.'

'Which is why I want you to handle the negotiations from now on.'

'Me?'

'You are a logical choice, considering your vast experience of dealing with the Romans. And Dura is next to

Syria where the final details concerning the exchange of the eagles for my son will be thrashed out.'

'But surely, you have emissaries and legal experts to do that?' I pleaded.

He dismissed the notion with a flick of his hand.

'I want someone who can impress the Romans, someone they will respect. And that someone is you, King Pacorus.'

'But…'

He showed me a palm of his hand. 'It is not a request; it is a plea from one father to another.'

What could I say? He was the consummate manipulator, and in truth I did feel sorry for him. No father, not even the devious master of an empire, should be denied the company of his only child.

'It would be an honour, highness.'

'Excellent. Now, I am going for a ride in my chariot. You should get yourself one, King Pacorus, they are most gratifying to one's sense of worth.'

He walked briskly to the steps from the battlements, leaving me alone with my thoughts. I looked to the east and no longer saw the army heading for Carmania, only a vast expanse of yellow-ochre desert.

'This is the culmination of your career, Pacorus,' I said to myself. 'You are to be the high king's errand boy.'

Epilogue

To my dear friend Marcus Vipsanius Agrippa

The current peace that exists between Parthia and Rome has come about after years of bloodshed, destruction and mutual distrust between our two great empires. I know that you are as desirous to establish a new age of peace and cooperation between our two peoples as am I, and to nourish and encourage trade, cooperation and diplomatic resolutions to disputes, rather than recourse to war.

This being the case, I write this letter begging a favour of you, one that will benefit both Rome and Parthia. Following the defeat and ejection from Media of the Roxolani tribe of the Sarmatian race, which invaded Parthia at the invitation of King Castus of Gordyene and his wife Yesim, whom I believe your friend and ally, King Polemon of Pontus, is well acquainted with, my husband is leading an army with the intention to chastise the rulers of Gordyene.

As you will know, the Aorsi tribe of the Sarmatian race has long occupied the northern lands of Gordyene, having been invited into the kingdom by the late King Surena. The Aorsi have proved an irritant not only to other Parthian kingdoms but also to Armenia, having conducted cross-border raids into the lands of King Artaxias for many years.

Your own ambassador to Pontus, Gaius Arrianus, having suffered at the hands of King Castus in the same base manner as my husband, I believe a punitive expedition against the Aorsi would go some way to satisfying Rome's desire for vengeance. Such a campaign would be largely free of resistance, as most Aorsi warriors will be in the south of Gordyene, preparing to face my husband's own invasion of that kingdom.

With the caveat that any Roman expedition into Gordyene must not result in the territorial integrity of that kingdom being adversely affected, I can assure you that Dura, and indeed Parthia, would raise no objection to retribution being visited upon the Aorsi.

I remain your friend and ally
Gallia, Queen of Dura

Titus Tullus rolled up the letter after finishing reading it, handed it back to Gaius Arrianus and shook his head.

'I told you she was a hateful, spiteful bitch, ambassador. I trust Agrippa treated her idea with the contempt it deserves?'

Gaius Arrianus tapped the rolled papyrus on the table between them. Tullus' villa was a most pleasing residence, with splendid views of the Black Sea, well ventilated and richly decorated.

'On the contrary, Agrippa has fully embraced Queen Gallia's notion. He has requested that you command the army that is forming at Melitene even as we sit here in your well-appointed home.'

Tullus eyes narrowed. 'What army?'

'Four legions and a thousand Gallic horsemen. Agrippa thought their addition would add a touch of irony to the expedition, seeing as Queen Gallia is a Gaul.'

'What does King Polemon say about this, seeing he is the one who pays me?'

'He fully supports what Rome desires, and Rome desires someone answers for the gross insult against its ambassador, to say nothing of the wrongs committed against the commander of King Polemon's palace guard. It is quite simple, Titus. You will lead the army from Melitene, take as many slaves as you can from northern Gordyene, leave behind as much devastation as possible, and return before the leaves on the trees have turned brown. The sale of the slaves should pay for the campaign, and your bonus.'

Tullus' ears pricked up. 'Bonus?'

Gaius feigned ignorance. 'Apologies, I clean forgot. Agrippa is prepared to pay you ten talents of gold from his own purse to command the expedition.'

Tullus felt a tingle go down his spine. Over a quarter of a ton of gold was a tidy sum, and almost made up for the weeks he spent as a prisoner of the bitch Yesim and then her bastard husband Castus.

'I agree, ambassador,' said Tullus, 'though I insist on keeping a few slaves for myself, to sell here in Sinope when I return. I'm not getting any younger and I have to start thinking about my retirement.'

Gaius raised an eyebrow and looked around the luxurious, expansive office.

'It must be hard for you, Titus, what with penury constantly breathing down your neck.'

Tullus rubbed his hands together. 'Shall we say I can keep a thousand slaves?'

'We will say you may retain a hundred slaves for you own uses, general. The rest will be going to Rome, or wherever

Agrippa deems fit. All slaves will first be transported to Melitene where I will be personally overseeing their quartering and onward shipment.'

'I would like my bonus paid up front,' insisted Tullus. 'Just in case friend Agrippa buggers off back to Rome before I get back.'

Gaius was aghast. 'Are you casting aspersions on the honour of a friend of Augustus himself, a man who has held the posts of consul, governor of Gaul and *aedile*?'

'If he pays me what he promised, then I will respect him. Everything else is just piss and wind.'

Titus Tullus might have been a grasping murderer, a man who relished war and the carnage and butchery associated with it, but he was also a professional. He trusted only his own instincts and they told him to be wary of venturing into Gordyene. He assembled his band of former legionaries and rode with them to Melitene where he found four legions and an *ala* of horsemen. The legions were composed of *evocati* – soldiers who had retired but who had voluntarily re-enlisted again at the invitation of Agrippa – but they were all well-armed, equipped and supplied with enough food for three months' campaigning.

To ensure the campaign would proceed as smoothly as possible, Tullus hired scouts with an intimate knowledge of northern Gordyene to accompany the army, which marched two weeks before the army commanded by Pacorus of Dura crossed into southern Gordyene.

It was a pleasant campaign. The weather was mild and there was no shortage of water and fodder for the horses in northern Gordyene. But most pleasing of all was the lack of opposition. The hateful Gallia had spoken the truth: the able-bodied men were all away in the south fighting King Pacorus. That left the old, the women and the children, plus a smattering of warriors to watch over the inhabitants of the villages littering the valleys of the lands immediately south of the River Araxes. Rich lands, fertile lands, full of game, flocks of sheep, crops and civilians, and in that glorious summer also full of Roman soldiers.

The campaign was methodical and the tactics old and well tested. Scouts would detect the location of a village, which would be surrounded by detachments of horsemen as dawn was breaking. Cordoned off, the settlement was then assaulted by legionaries, the horsemen remaining outside the buildings to prevent any escapees from fleeing and warning nearby villages. The legionaries would then quickly storm the huts and barns, kill any who offered resistance and capture the rest.

To the Romans, and indeed everyone else in the civilised world, slaves were most valuable as adults, when they were at their physical and mental peaks. However, as the majority of adult males were away in the south, Tullus had to make do with women, girls, boys and infants. Not that these groupings were not valuable, far from it. Rather, they did not command the highest prices in the slave markets. Price was determined by age, sex, physical strength, general health, attractiveness, skills, intelligence and education. Then again, boys and girls were easy to transport after capture, and would grow into men and women and the latter would bear future slaves.

After a month of rapid marches, Titus Tullus had captured several thousand Aorsi slaves. He then ordered an about-face and marched back to Melitene, hugging the southern bank of the Araxes as his swollen army headed west. The army marched slowly so as not to fatigue the slaves trudging along in shackles on foot. He even allowed mothers with infants to travel on the carts. He had only penetrated a relatively short distance into Gordyene, but he was satisfied he had achieved enough. He had avoided a battle with King Castus, he had captured thousands of slaves, and he had left behind a land littered with destroyed villages and crucified Aorsi, albeit mainly the old, who were valueless as slaves.

Tullus selected the hundred slaves he would personally profit from carefully. He had attended enough slave markets to know the categories that commanded the highest price. They were slaves of great beauty and deformed men and women, specifically dwarfs, Rome's rulers having a predilection for surrounding themselves with human novelties. With the pick of the slaves, ten talents of gold as a bonus and King Polemon paying him a handsome salary, his life was certainly better than a few months previously when he had been detained in an animal pen while a 'guest' of the Pontic hill people. He had subsequently been dragged to Vanadzor where he had unexpectedly encountered King Pacorus, an enemy he liked and respected more than many men he called allies, which had led to the King of Dura's wife making this lucrative campaign possible. It was certainly a strange world and the fate that entwined the lives of men was even stranger. But Queen Gallia was still a hate-filled bitch.

The slaves were transported to Melitene without difficulty, notwithstanding a few perishing on the way, either from fatigue or being crucified to provide an example to the rest to keep in line. They were duly handed over to the safekeeping of Gaius Arrianus, who arranged for their onward shipment to Rome. Tullus' selected hundred captives were sold in Melitene's slave market where they fetched a handsome sum. In a magnanimous gesture, he distributed the profits between his colleagues, the men who made up his close-knit band of former legionaries who had marched hundreds of miles with him when in Roman service, before trading their hob-nailed sandals for leather riding boots as Tullus rose in rank and they shared in his good fortune.

Once back in Cappadocia, the *evocati* legions were sent back to Syria where they were disbanded. Tullus and his colleagues journeyed back to Sinope via Kayseri and Corum in Galatia, now a Roman province. The more direct route north from Melitene to Trabzon on the coast of Pontus was avoided – Tullus having no wish to be the guest of the kingdom's hill tribes a second time.

He was glad to see Sinope, the city he was pleased to call home, and one he never thought he would see again following his capture by Yesim, another hateful bitch who had become the Queen of Gordyene. He said farewell to his colleagues at the city gates and rode to his mansion alone. His walled, gated residence was located on the western side of the peninsula on which Sinope had been built, overlooking the shimmering turquoise Black Sea below. As the commander of Polemon's Palace Guard, half a dozen of its soldiers were permanently billeted in the small barracks in the mansion's grounds, two being on sentry at the gates at all times. The pair snapped to attention when he appeared on his horse, one of them opening the gates to allow their commander to enter.

He trotted into the courtyard where a stable hand rushed forward to take his mount. He dismounted and strode towards the entrance to his home, the head slave of the household appearing between the two marble columns framing the mansion's entrance.

'Welcome home, master,' he smiled.

Acacius was an old Greek who had been a slave for most of his life. Educated by his first master when he had been a boy, he had always been a house slave, tutoring the children of his subsequent masters and earning himself a reputation for being loyal and trustworthy. He ran Tullus' household in the general's absence, being responsible for the day-to-day affairs of the general's businesses, which included vineyards outside the city and a stake in a silver mine near Trabzon.

Acacius ushered forward a boy carrying a tray holding a cup, in which was wine. Tullus took it, emptied it, placed it back on the tray and washed his hands in a silver bowl filled with water held by another slave. He wiped his hands on a towel draped over the slave's arm.

'Anything to report?' he said to Acacius.

'Nothing of note, master. I have left a report of the accounts of the household and your business interests on your desk.'

'I will read it later. Please arrange a bath and massage.'

After washing away his aches and pains and being gently massaged into a blissful slumber by a young Greek slave with firm hands, he retired to his bedchamber for the afternoon. Normally, he would take a female slave with him, but today he was too tired. After a couple of hours' sleep, a gentle breeze ruffling the lace curtains at the open shutters to the bedroom to keep the temperature pleasant, he woke and walked to his office. Slaves cleaning the mosaic floor stood and bowed their heads as he passed them. He was now a wealthy man with commercial interests that were flourishing, thanks to the patronage of the king. On the way back from Melitene he had been mulling over an idea, and on seeing his mansion again he had made up his mind. He would retire. He was done with war and killing. He liked both, but on the battlefield there was always a chance an arrow, spear or slingshot would strike him down, and then who would spend all the money he had accumulated?

He entered his office, walked around the desk and pulled out his chair. And froze. There, on the upholstered leather seat, was a gold brooch. He stared at it for a few seconds, two thoughts running through his mind. Was it poisoned and who put it there? He saw the design and a chill ran down his spine. It was a griffin, the symbol of Dura, and he knew it was a warning. That he could be reached at any time, and anywhere. He had long suspected Queen Gallia had assassins, even though it had never been proved. But here *was* the evidence, though he would never be able to prove it. He would get a kitchen slave to remove it. That way he would see if it was laced with poison. His mind was made up: he definitely would retire, sooner rather than later. He took comfort from the fact that if Queen Gallia wanted him dead, he would already be so. Still…

'Hateful bitch.'

Printed in Great Britain
by Amazon